Vicious Circle

An Isabel Sinclair Mystery

Lila Richards

Millwheel Press

Published by:
Millwheel Press Ltd, Eyrewell Forest, New Zealand
www.millwheelpress.co.nz

ISBN: 978-0-473-50199-0 – softcover
978-0-473-50200-3 - Epub
978-0-473-50201-0 - mobi

When a listener to `The Psychic Connection' radio programme is emotionally blackmailed by self-styled spiritual teacher Bob Ferris, resident panellists Joss Cherry and Isabel Sinclair decide to investigate. Meanwhile, the remains of a woman's body are found in a creek-bed in Queensland, Australia. Detective Sergeant Declan Kelly's search for Richard Forster, the last person to see her alive, leads him to communes in Queensland and New Zealand and the flesh-pots of Auckland's infamous Karangahape Road, until his trail meets that of the `Psychic Connection' panel. Their investigations culminate in a dramatic confrontation at the disused church where Ferris attempts to implement his bizarre plans to give birth to the New Aeon.

DEDICATION

To Jenner, without whose input, this novel might never have been born.

CHAPTER ONE

Luke Marriot looked at the others over the control panel. He pushed back a disobedient strand of fair hair and lit yet another cigarette. Ignoring the glare Joss Cherry sent him, he leaned into the microphone. "And now it's time for another caller. Good evening, you're on The Psychic Connection, and you're talking to our panel of experts. How can we help you?"

"Well, yes," said a hesitant female voice. "It's Anne here. I was wondering if the panel would know if someone can really watch you in the shower."

Luke pushed his hair back again, arranged his face with calculated precision, and drew deeply on his cigarette. Avoiding eye contact with the others, he chose his words with care. "Panellists, over to you," was all he managed to get out before collapsing in silent hysterics over the control desk.

There was an obvious patch of dead air as the other four tried to regain control. James Myerson was the first to break the silence. He coughed slightly, straightening his tie and his professional manner.

"Now, Anne—it is Anne, isn't it?" he asked in his smooth New England accent.

"Yes, that's right."

"You believe someone's been watching you in the shower, do you?"

"Well, yes."

"And how do you think we can help you?"

Isabel Sinclair signalled to Luke to cut in her microphone. Her precise English accent overrode James's query.

"Do you think this has a psychic side to it?"

"Well, it must do," Anne replied. "He says he knows what I'm doing, even when I'm at home, and now he says he can see me in the shower."

"Is his room beside the bathroom?" Isabel asked, puzzled.

"Oh no. He lives on the other side of town to me."

The panel sent each other knowing looks. Luke, with great deliberation, lit another cigarette. As he drew on it, a haze of smoke rose in front of a face rescued from blandness by eyes of smokey blue and a mouth that expressed to perfection his particular meld of youthful exuberance and world-weary cynicism.

James stopped bouncing on the edge of his chair, threw Isabel his best miffed expression, and took back the microphone. Oozing bland, couchside manner, he asked, "How long has this been going on?"

"It all started last June. My mother had died suddenly in May, and I was feeling very upset and confused. My friend suggested I go for a tarot reading. I really didn't believe in all that stuff, but she made me an appointment, so I went along anyway."

"Yes?" James interjected with a sage nod.

Isabel rolled her eyes, and Joss and Luke exchanged cynical glances. In the world of paranormal investigation, there were all too many charlatans playing on people's vulnerability.

"The tarot reader was a middle-aged man. His name's Bob. His house smelled of incense and—and something else, and I just didn't feel comfortable. But his reading was spot on. He told me things he couldn't possibly have known about, so when he said I had untapped powers, I was—well—intrigued I suppose you'd call it. He invited me along to a group he ran, and I did go for a few weeks. Then he said I was progressing faster than the rest of the group, and he suggested private lessons."

By this time Luke's gestures with his cigarette had become positively obscene.

"Yes," said James again, running his fingers around the collar of his shirt as though it had become too tight.

"The lessons were at his house while my children were at school. He wanted to make it two or three times a week, but I thought once was enough. Besides, it was costing me quite a lot of money. He charged the same for each lesson as he did for a tarot reading. My husband's dead set against that sort of thing, so I couldn't spend too much money or he'd hit the roof."

"So when did the business about the shower begin?" Joss prompted.

"Oh, not for a while. During the lessons, he often mentioned his training, and sort of suggested he had magical powers, including the ability to travel out of his body and watch people. At first I didn't believe him, but he just seemed to know so much. I started getting frightened, and my husband told me I shouldn't go back. So I rang Bob and told him. He got very cold, and told me I had to continue—it was too late to back out. That really scared me."

By now the panellists were really taking notice. Luke leaned over the control desk, and James had even stopped fiddling with his collar. The fourth panellist, Geraldine Bird, looked up from the astrology chart she had been drawing. She mouthed silently to the others, "I know Bob."

Luke gestured at her microphone in an unspoken query, but she waved him away.

"But I didn't go back," Anne continued. "I still didn't believe anyone could do what he said he could, so I thought that would be the end of it. Then a few days later the phone calls started. He'd ring me and tell me what my children were wearing, or where I'd been. After a while, the calls got really weird. He said he watched me in the shower, and he even told me where my birthmark is. Last week he said he'd watched my husband and me in bed, and this morning he rang again with something really horrible. He can't really do that to me, can he?" She broke off, her voice trembling.

James's bland features now bore a look of serious concern. "Do you want to tell us the story?" he asked.

"It's awfully embarrassing," Anne replied.

Luke stepped in. "Would you prefer to talk about it off air?"

"Yes, I would, actually, if that's all right."

"Of course it is, Anne. Just hold the line and we'll be right back to you." His hands busy working panel buttons, he switched into his professional DJ mode. "And that's all the calls we have time for on The Psychic Connection Hotline this week. But, remember, you can call us any Wednesday night here on The Psychic Connection, and we guarantee your confidentiality."

He faded his microphone, and raised the slider on some music, then cued up the pre-recorded final segment of the show.

Now they were off air, the panellists returned to Anne.

4

"Are you still there, Anne?" Luke asked.

"Yes."

"Now," he continued reassuringly, "let me assure you before we start that you don't have to tell us anything you don't want to."

"No, I want to talk about it, but I'm afraid he can hear me here. I couldn't come and meet you somewhere, could I?"

"Of course you can," said Luke. "Why don't you come round to my place for morning tea tomorrow? I'll bake some scones."

"Will the other panel members be there?"

"If Luke is baking scones, you bet we will," Joss said.

Luke gave Anne his address and cellphone number, then put the phone down and said, "Come on, you lot. I think we need a coffee."

"And, Geraldine," said Joss, "we want an explanation." She placed her arm around Geraldine's shoulder and steered her firmly towards the lounge.

The three women took possession of the opulent brown leather lounge suite, leaving James to perch on the antique piano stool in front of Luke's precious baby grand. Luke reappeared with a tray of steaming coffee mugs, which he placed on the coffee table. He nudged Isabel aside to sit next to her on the couch.

Joss eyed the tray. "What, Luke—no biscuits?"

Luke smiled and replied with a polite, "Fuck you."

Joss favoured him with an acid-drop smile, and turned to Geraldine. "So you know this Bob character? Tell us about him."

"I don't actually know the man *per se*," said Geraldine, "but I know of him. His name's Bob Ferris. One of my

5

regular astrology clients said she'd had a similar problem with him, but he backed off."

Isabel leaned forward and asked, "Now why would he do that?"

"I don't know," said Geraldine. "She didn't tell me."

"So Anne's not his only victim," mused Joss.

"Barely the tip of the iceberg, I would think," replied James, fingering the piano keys as if he knew how to play. "His type doesn't usually stop at just one or two victims."

"He really shouldn't be allowed to get away with that sort of thing," Isabel said indignantly.

"So let's do something about it," responded Joss.

"It'll make a great programme," said Luke.

* * * *

Judging by the number of cigarette butts in the onyx ashtray, Luke had already been up for some time. The aroma of freshly baked scones verified this. Anne had arrived early, and Luke had kept her chatting amiably until the others had all arrived. However, in spite of his reassuring smile, she still perched nervously on the edge of her chair, a slim, sandy-haired woman in her early forties, dressed in a pink tracksuit and grey sneakers, twisting together fingers laden with expensive-looking rings. James, as usual, was the last to arrive. Luke left him to introduce himself, and soon returned with coffee, tea, and scones.

"Now," James began smoothly, "you said yesterday the problem had become embarrassing."

Anne put down her coffee mug. "Well, you know I told you he said he watched my husband and me in bed... Look, I really think I'm wasting your time. You'll think this is really silly."

"No, no, not at all," James soothed. "Just tell us in your own time."

Anne took a deep breath, steeling herself for the ordeal. "Astral sex. He says we have astral sex. He says he takes me out of my body, and he says we have sex."

Joss interrupted, "He's telling you all this, so presumably you're not aware of its happening?"

"Well, no. I asked him about that, and he said he makes me forget."

"And you believe this?"

"I didn't at first, but now I'm just so confused I don't know what to think."

Joss turned to Geraldine. "Geraldine, you told us yesterday he tried this on a friend of yours. Did he go this far?"

"I suspect he did. I don't know for sure, but I'll ask."

"You do that," Joss said. "Isabel and I will tackle our friend Bob."

"Don't stress yourself about this, Anne," James reassured her. "It's a hoax. A very nasty hoax, but still only a hoax. Astral sex is an absurd impossibility. To put it bluntly, no body, no sex."

Anne laughed, albeit a trifle nervously. "That's what my husband says, too. But I can't help thinking, if he isn't doing what he says he's doing, why would he be telling me all this?"

"That," said Joss, "is what we intend to find out."

CHAPTER TWO

"Hang on a minute, Joss." Isabel's voice on the phone sounded distracted. "I have a cat on the stove; I'll have to go and take it off." Her receding footsteps were followed by a dull thud and the sound of a door being closed. Seconds later, Isabel's voice announced, "That was Madame George, and that was nearly the end of our dinner."

"Poor, starving creature," said Joss, picturing the Amazonian proportions of the eldest of Isabel's feline menagerie. "Perhaps we should set her on our friend Bob."

"Huh! She's so lazy I doubt if she could be bothered; we'll just have to do it ourselves."

"Right. So what are we going to do?"

"I suppose the first step is to make an appointment for one of his much-vaunted readings," Isabel suggested.

"Both of us, one of us, singly, or together?"

"It would make sense for both of us to go, as a backup for each other, though I think we should go separately. It might be helpful if he doesn't realise we know each other."

"What if he listens to the programme?"

"He won't have seen us, so how about we use false names?"

"Good idea. And we should leave a few days between making our appointments, so he doesn't connect us in any way."

"Right. I'll ring him immediately; no sense in wasting

time. You give him a couple of days and then let me know when your appointment is, and we'll decide when to meet again."

* * * *

Isabel eased her red Corolla station wagon into the kerb in front of the overgrown macrocarpa hedge that loomed over a dilapidated wrought-iron gate. The gate clung to its post with touching, if misguided, faith, and through its bars Isabel caught a glimpse of peeling white paint topped by a rusting corrugated-iron roof. Feeling unexpectedly nervous, she peered into the rear-view mirror to make sure her unruly red curls were behaving themselves. She had decided on a nondescript look, so she had tied her hair back as severely as it would allow her to, and was wearing a borrowed grey track suit, a far cry from her usual dramatic style.

She pushed her way through the rickety gate, to be confronted by a veritable jungle of overgrown shrubs and vines. Cottage-garden flowers and herbs battled for space with convolvulus and honeysuckle. A ferociously abundant wisteria all but obliterated the front of the veranda, threatening an ancient armchair cowering at one end. More herbs loitered on the veranda, reaching out spindly, tentative stalks from a row of terracotta pots. Picking her way through the foliage, Isabel knocked on the once-green panelled wood door. The sound reverberated through the interior of the house, but attracted no immediate response.

As she waited, her nervousness returned and she felt compelled to remind herself why she was there. Just as she was about to knock again, the door opened to reveal a dimly-lit hallway, and the most unlikely-looking tarot reader Isabel could have imagined. Bob Ferris had definitely seen better days, although, Isabel reflected, that probably wasn't saying much. He probably still had a maroon crimplene suit with flared trousers lurking somewhere in his wardrobe, and perhaps even a pair of matching platform shoes. His fawn canvas trousers and pastel green designer sweatshirt proclaimed the New Age, but his dark, greying, slicked-back hair, thinning and worn longer than was fashionable, whispered of the sixties.

"Georgina?" His voice extended a welcome that fell just short of sounding sleazy as he used Isabel's chosen pseudonym.

"That's right," Isabel ignored his dramatic little gesture of welcome as she stepped past him into the gloom of the hallway. He led her into a small sitting room that seemed crammed from floor to ceiling and wall to wall with every conceivable variety of bric-a-brac, along with untidy heaps of books and papers and old-fashioned LPs.

"Through here," said Bob, indicating what proved to be a sunroom that had been built onto the house at a later date. By contrast with the sitting room, it was simple to the point of being stark, painted entirely in white, and furnished only with two elderly fireside chairs and a small coffee table on which sat a deck of tarot cards—one of the numerous New Age decks, by the look of it, one Isabel had not seen before. The windows, which ran the entire length of one wall, were covered by sagging bamboo blinds.

"Do have a seat," Bob said, with a vague gesture towards the chairs. "Shall I make us some tea?"

"That would be lovely."

"Would you prefer herbal tea or Earl Grey?"

Isabel was not a fan of herbal teas, and asked for Earl Grey. Bob strode off to get it, leaving her to gaze around the room in open curiosity. The plainness of the walls was broken by a gaudy poster depicting the signs of the zodiac, and a large, laminated photograph of a Japanese temple that she thought she remembered having seen before in a magazine. A Kelim rug in earthy tones covered the bare wooden floor, and above it all hung a white paper Chinese lampshade. All in all, thought Isabel, the effect was not unpleasant, especially compared with the claustrophobia she had seen elsewhere.

The smell of incense wafted into the room, followed closely by Bob, carrying a cane tray containing two smoked-glass mugs, a brown pottery teapot and a bottle of milk. Placing the tray on the table, he handed the tarot cards to Isabel saying, "Give these a shuffle while I pour the tea."

Isabel decided to play dumb. "How long should I shuffle them for?" she asked, echoing the question often posed by her own clients.

"Oh, until you feel you've shuffled them enough," said Bob, unwittingly echoing her reply to her own clients. "You'll know." He placed a mug of tea beside her on the table, then removed the tray to the floor.

Isabel shuffled the large cards, hoping she would not betray her expertise, born of more years than she cared to remember as what she liked to refer to as a 'semi-professional' tarot-card reader, meaning she charged a small fee, but the income was too erratic to rely on. After a few moments, she placed the cards back on the table. Bob leaned across and proceeded to cut the deck three times with an exaggerated air of significance. From the top of the resultant deck, he dealt out a number of cards and arranged them in the Celtic Cross layout Isabel herself generally used for her clients.

"Hmm," he mused, then sat back, rolling a cigarette with slow and meticulous care. Isabel waited. Finally he leaned forward to within an inch of her face. "You are a woman of great power," he intoned, before subsiding back into his chair. Isabel said nothing. She was not about to give Bob any leads. Not that he seemed to need any. He lit his cigarette, drew deeply on it, then commenced to tell her various things about her life and activities, which she had to concede were substantially correct. A good twenty minutes later, he at last returned to his original theme, saying, "You really are a powerful woman—aren't you?"

"Am I?" Isabel was enigmatic.

"I think you know you are. I can feel your psychic energies welling up from within, filling the entire room." With considerable effort, Isabel managed not to laugh. Sounding even more as though he had been scripted by Jackie Stallone, Bob continued, "The Empress here at the centre signifies the outpouring of forces that have been latent within you for years, awaiting the chance to develop and grow. The time has come for you to bring these to fruition, to share them with those around you."

"Oh," Isabel feigned innocence, "how do I do that?"

"Well," Bob replied, reverting to a business-like tone, "I think I can help you there."

"Oh, could you?" gushed Isabel, "that would be so helpful. I've always felt I had more to, um, share, but somehow I've just never found the opportunity."

"When the student is ready, the teacher will come," Bob said with a portentous air. "The Hermit, here, above the Empress, shows that your time is now. As a matter of fact, I run a weekly class here, just an informal little gathering. We meet on Tuesday evenings. You'd be most welcome to join us."

"I'd love to come," said Isabel, playing along with the prevailing imagery. Bob wrote the time of the meeting on the back of a shiny mauve business card and handed it to her with a slight bow. Isabel took the card, exchanging it for Bob's fee, and stood up to take her leave. "Thank you so much," she said. "You've been very helpful."

"You're most welcome." Bob's pale brown eyes gleamed with barely disguised anticipation, though of what Isabel was uncertain. "We'll see you next week then, shall we?"

Isabel smiled noncommittally and allowed him to lead her to the front door. Only when she had driven a safe distance from the house did she allow herself to give vent to uncontrolled laughter.

* * * *

"I know what you mean," Joss said, "but I found him quite different." The two women were sitting in Isabel's kitchen, sharing the chaotic space with three cats and a laptop computer, discussing their respective encounters with Bob.

"Don't tell me you actually liked the man!" Isabel's face was incredulous.

"Good God, no! And I suspect he knew it. I may not have helped matters, either—I questioned his accuracy. I'll admit he was right on some facts, and I suppose I should have just

13

kept quiet when he was blatantly wrong. I suppose you could say we just didn't hit it off."

"So you didn't get an invitation to his meetings?"

"No, but I gather you did."

Without a word, Isabel produced the mauve business card. Joss turned it over distastefully. "Gold on mauve! That is sublimely tacky!"

"If you think that's bad," said Isabel, "you should have heard his sales pitch."

"Oh, yes?" Joss raised fair eyebrows, her blue eyes sparkling.

"Great upwellings and outpourings of womanly power. Barbara Cartland would have been proud of him. In fact, she might well have been the teacher to his student."

"Eh?"

"When the student is ready, the teacher will come," quoted Isabel, imitating Bob's pompous tone.

"I see. And has he convinced you to come?"

"Not likely! But he entreated me to go, and so I shall—next Tuesday evening," said Isabel.

"Perhaps," suggested Joss, "you should go via Luke's place and collect one of his pocket digital recorders. Then we can all receive the benefit of Bob's cosmic wisdom."

"Good idea," said Isabel, "and just the sort of thing that would occur to a sneaky journalist like you."

"Why, thank you. How perspicacious of you."

Isabel chuckled. "That's just what Bob said—in his own inimitable way."

CHAPTER THREE

Isabel squatted on a large tapestry cushion, surveying the room with caution and wishing she had worn something more in keeping with its ambience. Somehow, her grey calf-length skirt and high boots did not seem appropriate. Though judging by the gleam in Bob's eye as he had greeted her at the door, they met with his approval, which she supposed was the object after all.

The room appeared to have begun its life as a master bedroom, and a rather grand one at that. But under Bob's idiosyncratic influence, it had transmogrified into a surprisingly pleasant cross between an Eastern temple and a massage parlour. The original Victorian frieze, resplendent with over-ripe fruit, still showed above the picture-rail, while the walls beneath were entirely covered with a mixture of batik wall-hangings and red velvet curtains. In one corner, two mattresses were stacked one on top of the other and covered with a cream folk-weave bedspread. They might, she thought, have any number of uses, but just now they served to support the semi-recumbent form of a huge, middle-aged man with an abundance of ginger hair covering both head and face. To his left, under the window, two women had made themselves comfortable on several of the cushions that formed the room's only other seating. Somewhat apart, and spurning the use of a cushion, a dark, intense young man sat in a position suggestive of possible yogic training.

Isabel had just turned her appreciative gaze on the carved woodwork of the fire surround, when Bob entered, wearing a white kaftan whose simple, uncluttered lines were broken only by an over-sized citrine hung around his neck on a plaited golden cord. He bore aloft a gilt candelabra containing five white candles, and processed around the room in a majestic ritual of purification before moving to the centre of the room and placing the candlestick on the low marble-topped table there. From each candle in turn he lit a stick of incense, which he placed at each of the room's four compass points in wall containers obviously designed for the purpose. Returning to the centre table, he lit the fifth stick and placed it in the folded hands of a small brass oriental deity squatting on the marble top.

With a broad gesture intended to encompass the whole group, he intoned, "The circle of light is now complete." He had scarcely completed this complicated exercise when a matronly figure burst into the room, gabbling an apology and carrying a straight-backed dining chair. Bob fixed her with a petulant glare that failed to stem the flow.

"So sorry, Bob, I know I'm late again, and I do apologise, but I've had *such* a busy day, and then I mislaid the car keys, and..."

"Yes Nancy, we all know what a *busy* life you lead." Bob's polite interjection was underscored with a hint of sarcasm of which Nancy appeared oblivious. She placed her chair near the door and settled her tweed-clad form onto it, while Bob, with a faint sigh, prepared to repeat his ritual from the beginning.

Isabel watched Bob's action replay, working hard to suppress her amusement. The first time round his routine had seemed merely pompous. On repetition, it seemed ridiculous. A line from John Lennon's *Ballad of John and Yoko* slipped into her mind, almost destroying her, by now, precarious composure. Bob really did look like a guru in drag. However, a surreptitious glance round the room revealed that the others were enthralled—either that, or just plain gullible. Having repeated the ritual without further interruption, Bob asked the group to stand and link hands in a circle.

In a rather obvious strategic play, Bob placed himself between Nancy and Isabel. On her other side loomed the red-haired giant, whose touch, Isabel noticed as they linked hands, was surprisingly soft. Opposite Bob stood the two women and, beside them, across from Isabel, the dark young man unravelled himself to take up a pose which she supposed was intended to look mysterious.

Clutching Isabel's hand with enthusiasm, Bob said, "Let us begin by focussing our energies. Let's close our eyes and be aware of our breath. Feel it as it enters our bodies, hold it in our lungs, feel it revitalise our bodies, then feel it as it leaves our bodies to mingle once more with the universal energy."

Just as well, thought Isabel, I didn't have that garlic bread with dinner .

The group's choreographed intakes of breath showed they were following his instructions like new recruits at a boot camp. Isabel concentrated on synchronising her breathing with the others. Bob's light, sing-song voice continued, "Visualise your base chakra. Visualise it as flaming, crimson red, pulsing with the fiery energy of the life-force." At this point, Isabel felt a slight, but meaningful pressure from

Bob's hand. She resisted the urge to recoil.

Fat chance of his lighting any fire in *her* base chakra. But Bob was already moving on. Intoning the properties of each chakra in the same reedy sing-song, he worked his way up the astral body, arriving at length at the deep purple vibration of the crown chakra.

"Visualise," said Bob, "the seven chakric energies melding their colours into a beam of pure white light. Send it forth to spread its healing rays to the four corners of the earth and then beyond, to fill the entire universe. Now breathe that empowering energy back in. Let it fill our bodies with its life-giving vibrations." The group breathed as one.

Gradually, the group members opened their eyes and moved back to their sitting positions. As he released Isabel's hand, Bob allowed his fingers to trail enigmatically along her palm. It was all she could do to keep from shuddering. Her instinct was to leave straight away, but the role of Georgina demanded that she stay, so she swallowed her revulsion and sat down again, rubbing her hands on her skirt in an involuntary motion and putting them in her jacket pockets. What was next on the agenda? she wondered.

It turned out to be an unexpectedly knowledgeable exposition of the Empress tarot card.

How apt, thought Isabel, as Bob expounded on the theme of fertility and abundance with some discreet sexual imagery. At the end of his discourse, he moved to stand behind Nancy's chair and placed his hands on her shoulders. Turning an unfocused gaze on the rest of the group, Bob said, "I'd like you all to send loving thoughts out to Nancy while she tells us what she's feeling at this time."

I know what I feel, thought Isabel, but I doubt if you want

to hear it.

Nancy stammered through a few halting sentences, the salient features seeming to consist of the words 'love' and 'vibration'. With some difficulty, Isabel kept herself in check. Using the same technique, Bob moved to the young man, whom he addressed as Jeremy. Jeremy's statement was fluent and intellectual, with dark undertones of a possibly unhealthy introspection. Isabel sensed danger, but it was hard to tell if it was for Jeremy or from him. He'd be a fascinating subject for a tarot reading—either that, or completely impossible to read for.

As she sat listening to the older of the other two women, a fortyish, plump woman in glasses, with short, dark hair and a pleasant, maternal face, telling the group she felt a positive, healing vibration surrounding the group with golden light, Isabel realised that before long it would be her turn for the 'laying on of hands'. With a vague sense of foreboding, she racked her brains to compose something that wouldn't sound too much like a send-up. While she couldn't imagine the rest of the group recognising a send-up if it rose up and hit them, she rather felt Bob would all too readily smell a fellow rat.

Right now, however, Bob's sensitive nostrils were probably fully occupied with the scent of patchouli wafting from the young woman to whom he next turned his attention. An op-shop junkie, but one with definite style, she wore the almost mandatory student attire of black tights and Doc Martin boots, but the leopard-skin mini-skirt was an unexpected touch of genius, teamed as it was with a forties-style black jersey and a string of chunky amber beads. The entire ensemble was topped off by the master stroke of an elderly purple felt hat set at a rakish angle atop her close-cropped, reddish hair. An ornate gilt hat-pin perched among its folds like some exotic insect.

The young woman was gazing up at Bob with an expression of bliss, her head tilted back at an angle that made Isabel fear for her hat. "I saw the power surging from you in waves of golden light. It started from your citrine, which began to pulse. And then the light just got brighter and brighter, and it filled the room and made everything glow."

"And could you feel it, Anita?" asked Bob encouragingly.

"Oh, yes," breathed Anita. "I could feel the power pulsing through me and opening up my energy centres. It was incredible!"

I can imagine, thought Isabel, rather wishing she couldn't. And I'll bet I know just which energy centre you'd like Bob's power to pulse through. She shuddered involuntarily. Bob patted Anita's shoulder, thanked her, and moved across to the man mountain, whose name proved to be Doug.

"And what did you feel, friend?" he enquired with an attempt at heartiness.

Isabel noted the change in his manner from ingratiating to brisk. Doug's reply took her aback, though.

"Sorry, Bob." Doug's rich, laconic voice suggested a rural background. "Didn't feel a thing."

"You haven't been doing your homework," Bob chided gently.

"Well, yeah, I have got a bit behind with it," Doug replied without a hint of remorse. "I only got back this morning. Took a load of furniture up to Auckland and brought a bunch of office desks and chairs back down. Not much room for meditation in the cab of a truck." A swiftly suppressed snigger came from Jeremy's direction.

Bob ignored it. "Keep up the good work, Doug. These things take time."

Now it was Isabel's turn, she realised with a stab of panic. Still, she reassured herself, if Doug could feel nothing, then so could she. Nevertheless, it was hard not to cringe when Bob placed his hands on her shoulders and she heard his voice saying, "Georgina, how did you find your first experience with our little group?" His tone was reminiscent of some sleaze-bag enquiring of a conquest whether the earth had moved for her. The effect was not reassuring.

Experience, thought Isabel, does not do it justice. But she said, "Well, it's all a bit confusing at this stage, but I found it very interesting."

Doug grinned sympathetically. "Takes a bit of getting used to," he said. Anita and the motherly woman smiled encouragement, while Jeremy's inscrutable gaze left her in no doubt that behind the expressionless mask, his brain was in overdrive. He reminded her unnervingly of her son Dominic.

Bob's voice cut through her reflections. "Thank you, Georgina. I realise you're new to all this, but I know you have strong powers lying dormant within you. I can feel them now." As if to prove his point, Isabel felt the subtle pressure of his plump fingers on her shoulders. "We, as a group, will all help you to bring them into outward manifestation—won't we?" Nods and smiles from Doug and the women, while Jeremy consented to a minute inclination of his head.

"Oh, thank you!" gushed Isabel, enfolding the group in an ingenuous smile. A sense of relief washed over her as Bob relinquished her shoulders and moved back to his place in the circle. She realised she had been holding her breath.

"Before I close the circle for tonight, let us send out healing rays to those in specific need." Turning to Isabel, he explained, "At this stage in our meetings, we each give out the name of a loved one who is in need of help or healing. Then we visualise that person in the centre of the circle, and we shower them with pink light."

There's really no answer to that, thought Isabel.

Bob himself began the proceedings, and the others followed him in contributing various names. Thinking rapidly, Isabel threw in the name Bartholomew, wondering how the others would envisage her rather frail black and white cat, who had, as it happened, just returned from yet another visit to the vet. When Bob seemed content that sufficient pink light had been generated, he began to close the circle. With a solemn air, he picked up the candelabra and blew out the central candle with exaggerated care. Then he walked round the circle in the opposite direction to that of the opening ritual, blowing out each candle in turn as he reached the appropriate compass point, at length announcing, "The circle is now released. Love and light be with you."

The group members all murmured, "Love and light," in response. Bob picked up the candelabra and left the room, faint wisps of acrid smoke trailing behind him, closely followed by Nancy. Minutes later, both returned with tea and biscuits. Chocolate biscuits, too, Isabel noted with approval, not just the wines and arrowroots usually served at meetings.

Nancy placed her tray of mugs on the central table and, beside it, Bob deposited a large brown enamel teapot on a woven mat. The group converged on them, chatting amiably.

Isabel found herself standing next to Doug, who told her, "I found all this a bit confusing too, at first. Don't let it put you off, though."

Isabel smiled at him. "I don't intend to."

"That's the story."

Isabel sipped her tea, thinking what an unlikely candidate Doug seemed for Bob's version of enlightenment. "How did you first get involved?" she asked.

"Well." Doug licked the last vestige of chocolate from a sturdy finger and put down his cup. "I've always known things were going to happen. You know, like knowing who it was when the phone rang, or someone knocked on the door." Isabel nodded. "When I was ten, and my grandad got ill, I knew it was cancer and he was going to die. I even knew when he was going to die—exactly—about two months before it happened. It really freaked me out. And I could always tell people where to find things they'd lost."

"I bet that came in handy," Isabel said.

Doug grinned. "Yeah, but some of the other stuff was real scary."

"Like what?"

"Well, when I started driving trucks, I was spending a lot of time on the road, and I started getting so I'd know when accidents were going to happen. Only thing was, I usually couldn't do anything about them. If I said anything, I'd get laughed at, so in the end I just kept my mouth shut. Then after something had happened, and I knew about it, I'd feel like it was sort of my fault—like I'd caused it or something." Doug paused and pushed his thick hair off his forehead. "Then, last October, I had three dreams in a row about lights coming round a hill, and I just knew something real bad was going to happen. And in every dream I could see the number plate of this particular truck. So the morning they gave me that truck to drive, I just freaked out. I told the boss I had the 'flu and I went home. So my best mate, Rastus—his real name's Stuart—got the job. Heading south out of Timaru it happened, just like in my dreams. He hit a sheep truck head-on. He's damn lucky to be alive, and I thought it should have been me."

"That must have been awful," said Isabel, and she meant it. Doug was obviously still upset. He poured himself another cup of tea, downed it in one gulp, and continued.

"Yeah. I felt damned guilty about it. So when my sister came up from Dunedin for a week, I talked to her about it. She's pretty down to earth, so it blew me away when she said I was probably psychic and I should learn how to use it properly."

"So what brought you to this particular group?"

"Well, I got some books out of the library to read. One of them was quite good, so I thought I'd buy myself a copy. While I was in the bookshop, I saw this group advertised on a poster. I thought, well, why not? And here I am."

"And have you found it helpful?"

"Well, they're a nice group, and Bob seems to know his stuff..."

Isabel sensed the doubt in Doug's unfinished sentence, but before she could explore it further, Bob was at her shoulder saying, "Georgina, I'm glad to see Doug is looking after you. Let me introduce you to some of the others."

Bob steered her towards the motherly woman and Anita, the op-shop queen. She had the distinct impression Bob's motive was not so much to introduce her to them as to prevent her questioning Doug any further. The older woman smiled cheerfully, while Anita greeted Bob with obvious admiration and Isabel with a smile that concealed a warning. Isabel noticed Bob's lack of response to this as he placed one hand on her shoulder and one on that of the older woman and said, "Georgina, meet Pat. She looks after us all."

"Hello." Isabel smiled.

Pat smiled back, her kindly grey eyes twinkling behind gold-rimmed glasses. Her pleasant, open face with its soft pink skin, and her quiet, slightly clipped voice, reminded Isabel of her English mother, as she said, "Hello, Georgina, I do hope you've enjoyed this evening."

"Oh, yes, it's been most interesting."

"Interesting enough to lure you back again, I hope. New friends are always welcome—aren't they, Anita?" Pat turned to include her companion.

"Oh, yes," Anita said brightly, though Isabel sensed her welcome might not be all-inclusive.

Isabel thanked Pat, assuring her that she would, indeed, be back again.

"Glad to hear it," Doug broke in cheerfully. "I'm off now, so I'll say goodnight to you ladies till next week. And, Pat, I'll be round on Saturday to do that pruning, I promise."

"Lovely," replied Pat. "I'll make a casserole, and one of my chocolate cakes."

"You beauty." Doug grinned, rubbing his hands in anticipation.

Following Doug's cue, the others began to drift out. Anita, however, remained, lingering unobtrusively over the task of gathering up the cups. Bob shepherded them to the front door and called goodnight as they made their way down the overgrown path, Isabel speculating on Anita's probable reason for staying behind. She was unlocking the door of her station wagon when Pat called out to her, "By the way, Georgina, I do hope your cat gets better soon."

CHAPTER FOUR

"That bit about the cat really did throw me." Isabel pressed the stop button on the digital recorder and reached for another of Luke's cheese scones. Suitably fortified, she continued, "Just when I'd made up my mind most of them were gullible but not much else, Pat comes up with something genuinely psychic. And, of all of them, she's the one of whom I'd least have expected it."

Luke stubbed out his cigarette, leaned back in his chair, then changed his mind and lit another. For a full minute he smoked it with deliberation, then leaned forward and said, "Even if Bob is a charlatan, I don't suppose it means everyone in his group is." He turned to Isabel. "But, do you think this Bob character is as dangerous as Anne thinks he is?"

"It's hard to tell at this stage, but I wouldn't dismiss the possibility. It would be all too easy to write him off as just another sleazy little con man, but he definitely knows his stuff about the tarot, and the way he conducted that ritual, he's either a damned good actor, or he's studied ritual magic."

"Or both," said Joss.

"Quite."

"Does anybody want the last scone?" Geraldine broke in. She uncurled herself from the corner of the couch and shook out her long muslin skirt. Interpreting the lack of response as a negative, she appropriated the scone and began to munch in a ruminative fashion. "What made you write the others off as gullible?" she queried at last.

Isabel thought for a moment. "On reflection, I'd have to say it wasn't so much the people themselves as Bob. I found him so incredibly cringeworthy I couldn't imagine anyone who wasn't gullible going back there week after week. But when I think about them individually, some of them at least I'd have to give some sort of credence to."

"Tell us about them," prompted Joss.

"Well, Pat, who asked about Bartholomew, seems like a really nice, genuine person. She appears to be a sort of den-mother to the group and, until that last remark, I had her picked as just a sweet, middle-aged woman trying to give a bit of meaning to an otherwise dull life. But since I was clearly mistaken, I'll have to reserve judgement about her for now. There's obviously more to her than meets the eye." Isabel placed her coffee mug on one of Luke's lacquered coasters with care and continued, "Nancy, on the other hand, appears to be your classic silly old duffer. I'd be surprised if she has a psychic bone in her body. I rather think she's useful to Bob in some other way—and I don't just mean as tea-lady, though she does seem to fancy herself in that role."

"And what about the men?" Luke finished placing crockery back on a black lacquered tray. He picked up his cigarette lighter and ran a hand through his hair. It immediately flopped forward again, and he leaned back, puffing resignedly on his cigarette.

"Doug's a truck driver. He's huge and hairy, and a real sweetie—a sort of psychic teddy bear." Luke laughed, and blew an almost perfect smoke ring. "But Jeremy—" Isabel looked thoughtful "—I really don't know what to make of him. He reminded me a lot of Dominic—you know how he stares at you with that basilisk stare and sort of dares you to guess what he's thinking." The others nodded, having all, at one time or another, been exposed to Dominic's disconcerting manner. "He patently wants to be seen as inscrutable, but there was something about him that felt— dangerous. I really don't think that's too strong a word, but so far I can't make out whether the danger is to himself or to other people. I'd love to get him for a tarot reading. At least I think I would," she added after a thoughtful pause.

"You haven't told us about the young girl—the one who stayed behind," Luke said.

"Not your type," Isabel said with a grin. Luke made a face at her.

"I think the wind just changed," Joss informed him helpfully. Luke reached for a cushion to throw, but she beat him to it, and held it just out of his reach, a grin of triumph on her face.

Luke turned from her with beautifully simulated disdain and said to Isabel, "What makes you say that?"

"Behave yourselves, you two," Isabel laughed. "Anita is probably what used to be called a 'free spirit'. Which means she dresses like a cross between a gipsy and a tart, and most likely lives that way, too. If you ask me, she's a guru groupie, and right now she has her eye on Bob. Well, rather more than her eye, I suspect. She wasn't exactly subtle the other night, and Bob strikes me as the type who picks up hints that aren't even there." She shuddered, recalling the touch of his hands on her shoulders.

"Do I detect just the teeniest hint of distaste there?" Luke queried.

Isabel's answering gesture was unequivocal. "He's a creep!" she exclaimed. "I could hardly bear to have him touch me, let alone what Anita seemed to be hoping for. Yuk!"

Geraldine uncurled herself once more. "It's not at all uncommon," she said, "for young girls—or older women, for that matter—to become attracted to these men who set themselves up as gurus of one sort or another. It's not the men themselves they're attracted to, but the fact that they have—or appear to have—wisdom or power. I think some women who, for whatever reason, feel weak or powerless are drawn to that sort of man."

"That's true," said Joss. "Look at Aleister Crowley. Judging from the photos that have been published, he was quite repulsive, especially when he was older. But he doesn't seem to have had any trouble attracting women."

"Or men, for that matter," Geraldine agreed. "Men who are perceived as powerful in some way do seem to have that effect on susceptible people. And, of course, there are always some who take advantage of it. It sounds as though Bob might be one of those. And I wouldn't mind betting Anita is extremely vulnerable beneath her facade."

Isabel nodded thoughtfully. "That would account for the way her manner towards me changed. At least, it wasn't exactly her manner, but something I sensed behind it." The others waited expectantly, Luke still leaning back in his chair, now on his fourth cigarette. Since no-one else was using them, he had moved his cigarette packet, lighter and ashtray to the broad arm of his chair for easier access. Geraldine was still leaning forward, engrossed, her long brown hair falling like a curtain at one side of her thin face, while Joss, at the other end of the couch, sat like Rodin's Thinker, listening intently, both physically and psychically.

Isabel continued, "At first, she was all sweetness and light—or do I mean love and light? But after Bob had done his little number on me, I noticed a district souring and dimming. Not on her face, or even in her voice. It was more of a feeling, really, an intuition. She was saying, as it were, 'Welcome to the circle', but at the same time the feeling was, 'Leave Bob alone, he's mine'. As if I'd want him!" She grimaced.

"So," said Joss, "to summarise, we have Pat, genuine and nice and definitely psychic; Doug, ditto; Nancy, a psychic brick, and most likely harmless; Jeremy could be anything, and probably worth watching; Anita, also worth watching, if only because she seems vulnerable to Bob's dubious charms; and finally Bob himself, a sleaze of the first order, but with some definite psychic knowledge, if not ability, and certainly worth further investigation. Talking of which—" she turned to Geraldine, who was once again curled up with her skirt wrapped around her long legs "—did you manage to find out anything from your astrology client?"

Before Geraldine could reply, a tall, athletic-looking man in his thirties strode into the room, coming to an abrupt halt as he realised Luke had company. "Oops, sorry," he said, an apologetic smile on his dark, handsome face. "I didn't realise you were in conference."

"That's okay," said Luke, "I think we need another coffee." His enquiring glance was met by nods all round. "Tell you what, give me a hand with the coffee and I'll fill you in on what we're discussing. You might be able to add something to the mix." He turned in the doorway. "You lot talk among yourselves."

Joss just missed him with the cushion.

"Who was *that!*" Geraldine exclaimed, a look of admiration lighting her brown eyes.

"Mmm! Tasty little number, isn't he?" Joss grinned. "That's Philip, Luke's new flatmate. When he isn't striding around looking like a Mills and Boon hero, he sells sports gear. He's also a champion squash player. I didn't realise you hadn't met him."

"No, I haven't yet had the pleasure. But I certainly hope to!"

"Hope to what?" asked Luke, as he and Philip re-entered the room.

"Never you mind," said Geraldine, hoping her face didn't look as red as it felt.

Philip retrieved the cushion Joss had thrown at Luke and made himself comfortable on the floor. "Sounds like an interesting case you've got yourselves into," he said.

"You obviously haven't met Bob," Isabel said. "Speaking of which—" She turned to Geraldine, "You were going to tell us what you found out from that client of yours."

"I invited Liz over for dinner the other night, so I now have all the gory details," Geraldine said with a laugh. "Her initial contact with Bob seems to have been fairly much like yours, Isabel. She went for a tarot reading and was invited to his meetings. Actually, she enjoyed them, so she kept going. After a month or so, he started hinting about 'further possibilities' and he invited her for private tuition. She was a bit dubious, but at the same time, Bob seemed to have a wealth of what you might call arcane knowledge, and that was what she was interested in. Besides, she felt sure she could handle him if she needed to. So she went along."

"So what did this teaching entail?" Joss asked, refilling her empty mug from the hand-crafted blue coffee pot. Beneath her smooth, blonde fringe, her eyes almost matched its subtle glaze.

"It began innocuously enough. Just visualisation and meditation techniques with a strong Buddhist influence. Then he began showing her books, particularly ones with erotic eastern artwork. And I believe he has a collection of *very* interesting statuettes." Ignoring the expression on Luke's face, and not daring even to look at Philip, Geraldine went on, "He started talking about how the pictures and statuettes could be used by two people meditating together to produce a much more powerful effect. Liz was not impressed. She put up with it for a couple of weeks, then just stopped going."

By now Luke had lost all control, and was rolling around helpless with laughter. Joss turned to Philip and said, "Do you think perhaps it's time for his medication?"

"There's no cure yet for what ails him," Philip said, chuckling. He turned to Geraldine. "Don't mind him. The fits don't last long. Do carry on, I'm intrigued."

"Well, then the phone calls began, just as they did with Anne. However, unlike Anne, Liz just didn't believe them. When it got to the astral sex bit, she just laughed in his face, so to speak. I believe her exact words were, 'Out of your body would be an improvement, but it would still be pathetic.' He never contacted her again."

Luke, now completely serious, asked, "Would Liz be willing to say that on air?"

"I can ask her," Geraldine said, "though it's not the sort of thing *I'd* like to talk about in public."

Luke, apparently ignoring her caveat, said, "Please do ask her. I think we have the makings of a fantastic programme."

Isabel added, "Not to mention stopping that creep Bob in his tracks."

"And, with any luck, teaching him and others like him a lesson they won't forget," said Joss.

Luke nodded. "Actually," he said, "you ladies aren't the only ones who've been working on this. I haven't just been standing round making scones, you know."

"Are we to take it you've been up to something devious again, Luke?" asked Joss.

"Indeed I have. I've invited Bob onto the programme!" Luke beamed at their stunned faces. "Well, not quite. What I've done is arrange to interview Bob, purely as a tarot reader and teacher, of course. Obviously, I don't intend to let on that we're investigating him—just a bit of background material."

"Well, watch yourself," said Isabel. "He might offer to show you his etchings."

Geraldine smiled, her face turning pink under her tan, and said, "I quite agree, Luke. I believe some of his statuettes *are* man-to-man." Philip giggled appreciatively, and Geraldine blushed again.

"Speaking of man-to-man," Philip said, "would it help if I went to Bob for a reading? I'm sure Luke can jack me up with a pocket recorder. Bob won't know me from a bar of soap, and a different perspective might be helpful. And, before you ask, Luke, yes, I'll be more than happy to go on air if I turn up anything useful."

CHAPTER FIVE

"Hey, Dekko." Police Constable Carol Anderson looked up in vague exasperation from her computer.

Declan Kelly closed the door behind him and raised an inquiring eyebrow as he made his way to the coffee machine. Even this early in the day, the temperature was above his comfort level, but he needed caffeine. Still, he reflected, it was practically his only vice these days—practically.

"Chief wants to see you." Carol's voice jerked him back to the present.

Sighing heavily, he downed the coffee and made his way along the sickly pallor of the green corridor. A summons from Voodoo usually meant trouble. Specifically, trouble of the kind that involved excessive heat and other varieties of physical discomfort. Declan was not into discomfort, and after two years working in Brisbane, he still wasn't used to the heat. Several times he'd tried for a transfer back to Tasmania, or Adelaide—or even Melbourne, though he didn't much like Melbourne. Full of bloody yuppies and opera-lovers. So far, though, he seemed to be stuck here in bloody redneck territory, feeling like he was living permanently in a sauna.

He ran a hand through his thick, dark curls, but it didn't help. Sighing again, he knocked on the painted glass pane of the Chief Inspector's door.

"Come in." The deep voice held the slightest hint of a

European accent. Pushing open the door, Declan saw the dapper figure of Chief Inspector Stefan Vodanovich framed in the large window behind him, his swarthy, sardonic face flanked on either side by two distant skyscrapers that gleamed like obelisks against the cobalt sky. The effect was surreal. Like a Magritte painting, mused Declan, thinking longingly of green fields, and orchards, and cool streams...

"Ah, Sergeant Kelly." Declan jumped. Inspector Vodanovich neatened the pile of papers he had been leafing through, and placed them meticulously in the centre of his desk. He waved Declan to a chair and regarded him gravely out of sad, dark eyes that drooped a little at the outer corners. "How would you like a nice little trip?" Declan tried not to look too sceptical.

"What's up, Chief?" he asked, keeping his voice bland.

"A body." The Chief Inspector consulted his sheaf of papers. "A female body," he corrected himself, "has been discovered up near Cairns. Or rather, the remains of a female body. It's been there for some considerable time. The local boys have come to a bit of a dead end in their enquiries." He appeared to ignore Declan's stifled snort, but eyed him sternly nevertheless. "So they've asked me to provide them with a couple of—experts."

"Who's the other lucky fellow?" Declan had never thought of himself as an expert—not in police work, at any rate. However, he judged it wise not to contradict the Chief.

A tiny plane flew lazily from obelisk to obelisk above Vodanovich's head. He leaned forward across his desk as though avoiding its flight path. "Inspector Marks, from Forensics."

"Ah," said Declan, inwardly heaving a sigh of relief.

Inspector Derek Marks, known affectionately as Harpo, was one of the good guys. Good at his job, too. Things could have been a great deal worse. Apart from the heat of course, and the flies, and the...

"Meeting at ten," the Chief said briskly.

Taking his cue, Declan stood up. "Right, sir."

* * * *

"Mum, make her give the sauce back." Rachel Cherry made another futile attempt to wrest the bottle from her twin sister Kate.

"Cut it out, you two," their father demanded. "Can't we have even one meal a week without you two squabbling? If you can't eat quietly, you'll have to eat in the kitchen. The news is about to start."

Without a word, Joss took the sauce bottle, poured out two scrupulously equal measures of tomato sauce, and took the bottle out to the kitchen. She filled the kettle and switched it on, then, from habit, began to wipe down the bench, which had acquired its usual spotty veneer of coffee stains and spilt sugar.

Martin's voice called from the lounge, "Joss, come and watch this. It'll interest you."

Joss wiped her hands hurriedly and went through. The newsreader was saying, "The remains of a woman's body have been found in a dry creek-bed a hundred and twenty kilometres west of Cairns. Queensland Police believe the body may be that of a woman who went missing from a commune in the area ten years ago. The commune is reputed to have been involved in drug use and to have practised a bizarre form of sexual magic."

As the newsreader faded into an advertisement for a reality show involving celebrities on a desert island, Martin pressed the mute button. "I wonder if Luke saw that," he said. "It'll make an ideal talking point for your panel."

"You're right." Joss nodded. "It's got everything Luke likes in a story—sex, drugs, *and* ritual magic."

"I didn't know Luke was into drugs."

Joss grinned. "Seriously, though, you're right. I'll print out a copy of the story and take it along on Wednesday night."

"Aren't you pre-recording stuff this week, then?"

"Not this week. No-one's had time. We're betting against Murphy's Law yet again, and going straight to air."

"You people have an awful lot of faith in Luke's speed on the cut-out button, haven't you?"

"Fastest finger in the West, that's all."

"You obviously like to live dangerously,"

"One has to get one's adrenalin rush somewhere." Joss delivered him a saccharine smile and fluttered her eyelashes.

"Oh," replied Martin in mock mortification, "don't I provide you with enough excitement?"

"Excitement is not the word I'd use to describe life with you, Martin dear. Mild stimulation, perhaps—when you're awake. Speaking of which, I'll make the coffee."

* * * *

"Well, what do you reckon, sir?"

Inspector Marks settled his hat, which he had been using as a fan, back onto his straw-coloured curls. Even though they were now sprinkled with grey, and severely curtailed by the dictates of the job, it was not difficult to see why he had received his nickname. From shrewd eyes the colour of stone-washed denim set in a crumpled brown face beneath sun-bleached brows, he regarded Declan. "Forget the sir. Harpo'll do. This is hardly the place to stand on ceremony."

Too bloody true, thought Declan, casting a jaundiced eye over the expanse of red, dusty earth broken here and there by clumps of curiously stunted, wind-blown trees cowering beneath the sun's relentless glare. Declan wanted to do the same. He and Marks were standing under a group of dilapidated gum trees beside what might charitably be described as a creek, its banks overrun with dowdy-looking scrub. What a godforsaken bloody place.

"Yeah, right." He grinned. "And you'd better call me Dekko. Everyone else does. So what do you reckon, then?"

"I tell you one thing, Dekko, if she died here, she was a long way from home," Derek said.

"I reckon. Where was home, anyway?"

"Some kind of commune, about twenty kilometres from here, run by this old bloke called Reuben. According to Sergeant O'Keefe back in Cairns, he reckoned he was some kind of magician, and he ran this sort of training programme on a farm he bought there. By the sound of it, there were all sorts of dodgy goings on, including communal sex."

"Bet that frightened the natives," Declan said drily, brushing a fly off his nose.

"We don't talk about the Abbos that way nowadays," Derek reminded him.

"Nah. I mean the local rednecks. I understand they're a pretty narrow-minded bunch, Bible-bashers of one sort or another."

"Ah," said Derek. "I wonder if one of them might have killed her? I mean to say, they can't exactly have approved of her lifestyle. Maybe she had a fling with one of their sons—lured him off the straight and narrow."

"Anything's possible, I suppose. Look, what say we head back into Cairns? The lab should have some info for us by now. If you've finished here, that is," Declan added, in hasty deference to his superior officer.

"Yeah, sure. I don't think there's anything more we can achieve here. Besides—" Derek licked dry lips "—I'd just about kill for a beer."

They headed back to the four-wheel-drive. A beer would be great, thought Declan, but what he really wanted was a long, cold shower—that and a posting back to Tasmania. Wearily, he flicked away another fly.

* * * *

Mercifully, Cairns Police Station was air-conditioned. Declan breathed in the cool air, and tried to concentrate on Sergeant O'Keefe's flat, drawling voice. "According to the preliminary lab reports, the woman was in her twenties when she died, and there was heroin in her system."

Declan and Derek exchanged meaningful looks.

"Oh, and she was pregnant, too—about seven or eight months."

"Jesus!" exclaimed Derek. "She definitely won't have died out where she was found then."

"Who found her?" asked Declan.

"Bloke called Jim Tollerton," O'Keefe said. "Stockman. He

40

was out looking for a bunch of cattle that had gone walkabout. Reckons he'd never have seen the body only there's been a drought around here for the last nine months."

I never would have guessed, thought Declan as he made a note of the stockman's name.

"Normally," O'Keefe continued, "that stretch of the creek's deep enough to cover a body."

"Yeah, with water in it, there'd be plenty of mud at the bottom," said Derek thoughtfully. "How long did they say she'd been there?"

O'Keefe said, "About ten years, as near as they can tell. They're still running tests. Luckily the teeth are still pretty much intact, and there's plenty of dental work, so hopefully we'll know who she was before too long."

Derek rose purposefully to his feet. "Meanwhile, Sergeant Kelly and I should maybe go and take a look at this commune outfit."

Declan, who recognised an order from a superior when he heard one, began to haul himself out of his chair.

Sergeant O'Keefe looked up. "The Tree of Life Community? That closed down years ago." Declan sat down again. "Not long after this woman's death, I reckon. The old guy, Reuben, died about six years back. He would have been well into his eighties."

"Shit," said Derek in amiable tones.

O'Keefe thought for a moment. "You could go and talk to Miriam," he drawled. Derek raised an enquiring eyebrow. "Miriam Golden. She used to be Reuben's High Priestess."

"His *what*?"

"It means she slept with him," Declan translated, with a short, cynical laugh.

"Yeah, well," O'Keefe looked embarrassed, "that and a few other things. She lives at the farmhouse where the Community used to be." He sketched a map on a sheet of paper and handed it to Derek. "It's about a hundred kilometres from here—take you about an hour and a half to get there, depending."

"On what?" Declan asked, knowing as he did so he'd regret it. He was right.

"The road," came the laconic reply.

CHAPTER SIX

"Luke, where did you say you put that recorder?" Philip was shuffling through the cluttered drawer in Luke's desk.

Luke's voice wafted distractedly through from the study, where he was searching for some obscure piece of information for the next edition of The Psychic Connection. "In the big drawer in the studio."

"Well, it's not there, and I'm due at Bob's in twenty minutes."

Philip heard Luke's footsteps heading in his direction. He didn't have to be psychic to realise Luke was annoyed. He tended to become engrossed in his work, and was convinced any interruption would completely ruin his concentration. Doubtless he'd need a cigarette and a coffee at the very least, before he could get back into it.

"Sorry, Luke," he said contritely, as Luke's blond head appeared around the studio door. "Sorry to interrupt you, only if I don't take the recorder it'll defeat the whole purpose of going."

Luke ran his fingers through his already tousled hair. A cynical smile played about his lips as he replied, "Well, I do realise you wouldn't be going just for the benefit of Bob's wisdom and insight. Now, where did I put the damned thing?" He paused as though expecting a reply, but no answer was forthcoming. "Never mind," he said at last, with a shrug of his shoulders. "There's another one in the study. It doesn't record quite so clearly, but beggars can't be choosers."

Philip gave him a quizzical look.

"Oh, don't mind me," Luke said. "You know I'm always bad-tempered until the programme's in the can for the week. Just as well you're going out, really. I'm sure Bob will be much better company."

"That would not be difficult," Philip agreed with a grin. "Now, where's that recorder? I don't want to be late for my first private-eye assignment."

Luke found the tiny recorder, made sure it was working, and that Philip knew how to switch it on with his hand in his pocket. Philip took it from him. "Here's lookin' at you, kid," he drawled with a hideous wink.

With a look of exaggerated disgust, Luke pushed him towards the door.

* * * *

Bob's house was exactly as Isabel had described it. It must have been a real beauty in its day, Philip thought. Even in its present run-down state it had an undeniable charm. What the real-estate blokes would refer to as a 'character cottage in need of TLC'. Definitely a 'handyman's dream', though, reflected Philip, as Bob, dressed in cream canvas trousers and a brown, gold and black batik tunic, led him through to the white room.

While Bob was preparing tea—his caffeine intake must be astronomical if business was any good—Philip gazed around the sparse room. It was definitely to his taste, unlike the clutter of the sitting room—not that there looked to be much

44

of that, what with the piles of books and papers, and the hoards of assorted ornaments. He was tempted to take a look at the tarot deck sitting neatly on the low table. He had, until recently, paid scant attention to things esoteric, but since flatting with Luke he had been unable to avoid developing at least a nodding acquaintance, and he had to admit he was now in danger of becoming as fascinated as Luke and the others.

He was saved from temptation in this instance, however, by Bob's return with the tea tray, on which he had also placed a stick of incense in a small brass holder. This he removed to the window sill before pouring the tea as though performing some ancient rite. "In the east," he explained, "I learned the importance of these simple, everyday ceremonies. Every act should be a meditation."

Philip thought of his sports training, and said, "Can't argue with that." He sipped his tea, which was very good indeed. No tea-bags here, and no stinting on the quality of the tea, either.

Bob smiled and handed Philip the cards. "Now," he said briskly, "I'd like you to shuffle these. Any way you like is okay. Just shuffle them until you feel you've finished, then place them back on the table." Philip shuffled, Bob watching him with a calm but alert expression through a haze of exotic-smelling tobacco smoke.

As soon as Philip placed the deck back on the table, Bob stubbed out his cigarette and leaned forward, seeming suddenly to activate some invisible switch as he cut the deck in three, then picked it up and began to lay out the cards. Philip reached unobtrusively, he hoped, into his pocket and activated his own invisible switch as Bob began to speak.

"I feel," Bob's voice sounded as though he had been practising voice projection, "that you have considerable talent." Oh, sure, thought Philip, I bet you say that to all the girls. "However," Bob continued, "you seem at the moment to be unsure where to focus your energies." He indicated the card at the centre of the layout, which showed seven cups, each with a different symbol emerging from it. Across it lay a card with a large full moon between two towers, and what looked like two dogs by a pool of water, baying at the moon. Some sort of crustacean was emerging from the pool. Pointing at this, Bob looked at Philip and said, "Mystery. Something is emerging which will change the way you use your energies. This man—" He pointed to the card beneath the central cross, which showed a rather fierce-looking man in armour, wearing a crown and wielding a massive sword. Storm-clouds scudded across the sky behind him, lending a bleak air to the picture. "This man," Bob went on, "is the cause of the mystery. Or at least he has something to do with its origin. Do you know a dark man, possibly older, very energetic and resourceful, possibly involved with legal or spiritual matters?"

"Well," Philip tried to sound non-committal, "it could be one of a couple of people."

Bob nodded. "He could be dangerous, and not just to you. The King of Swords is a man with power over life and death. It's as well to have him on your side."

"And is he?" Philip prompted. The reading was beginning to intrigue him.

Bob focussed his gaze on the layout once more, and again Philip had the impression of an invisible switch being turned on. After a few moments, Bob looked up and said, "He has no connection with your past, which is one of action in the world. This card here, the Knight of Wands—I feel this is you as you have been, a man of action, but also a man of highly developed intuition, a good communicator."

Leaving Philip somewhat taken aback by the accuracy of this thumbnail sketch, Bob moved on, pointing to the card at the top of the reading, which contained a highly dramatic picture of a tower with a bolt of lightning striking its crowned top, and two tiny human figures falling from its heights into a sea whose waves lashed the rocks beneath. This didn't look very promising, but Bob surprised him by saying that, although it signified the possibility of changes that would be difficult to work through, it also meant the mystery was likely to be solved, though in a very dramatic manner.

"This card," Bob went on, "shows what will happen." The card in question showed a woman in a long gown, a gold crown on her golden hair, in one hand a long, straight branch with leaves sprouting from it in several places, and in the other hand a sunflower. Bob threw Philip a conspiratorial smile. "The future," he confided, "shows a woman. She may or may not be someone you have met, but she looks certain to be part of your future."

"What's she like?" Philip's curiosity was well and truly piqued. He didn't have a woman in his life at the moment, and Bob's revelations so far had shown hints of genuine insight.

Bob picked the card up and stared at it for a long moment, his eyes half closed, then began to speak. "Long hair, but not as fair as in the card. I see horses, and..." he paused, with a puzzled expression on his face, "...numbers." He opened his eyes, like someone waking with difficulty from a dream, and looked at Philip. "Perhaps she's a mathematician."

"Or an accountant." Philip grinned. "That could be handy."

Bob laughed in sympathy and returned his attention to the cards. "Now, let's see. This card, the Eight of Cups, shows you treading a new pathway. It could be a new job, or perhaps a relationship." He indicated the Queen of Wands again to emphasise the possible connection. "At any rate," he continued, "it will involve something of a change of heart. You will be leaving old emotions behind, and moving in a different direction."

Apparently sensing Philip's unspoken query, he moved to the next card, which rather alarmingly showed a blindfolded woman making her precarious way between a number of swords sticking out of the ground. "Now this," Bob said, "is the Eight of Swords, in the position representing your close environment. Someone is in danger—or will be. Either you are in danger from someone close to you, or someone close to you is in danger."

"What sort of danger?"

"I can't see that," Bob replied slowly after looking hard at the card. Philip felt a prickling sensation at the back of his neck. He must be getting caught up in Bob's obvious talent for the dramatic, he told himself, but Bob confirmed his sense of foreboding by continuing, "I can't tell you exactly what it is, but I'd advise you to be very careful in all your dealings over the next few months."

Philip nodded, feeling by now more than a little odd about the whole experience. In spite of himself, he had to admit some parts of the reading were accurate, especially Bob's assessment of him and, in view of the last few cards, he found himself wondering what was coming next. The next card in the layout showed a young man in a chariot, driving hell for leather across a stormy landscape, waving a sword above his head.

"What does this one mean?" he asked, wondering if he really wanted to know.

"Ah," Bob replied, "this shows your hopes or fears. They seem to be connected in some way with the Knight of Swords, a younger man—or at least unmarried—dark-haired and strong-willed. A very strong intellect and a quick wit. A good friend, but a bad enemy perhaps. He does not forget things easily. I feel he may be connected with the law." Bob looked up at Philip suddenly. "I don't think you've met him yet—but you will before long." He pointed to the final card. "Now, this indicates the outcome of the entire train of events. This card is Justice. She represents balance and harmony, or the search for these. Also learning, but always in the pursuit of balance and equality—and, of course, justice. Coming as she does next to the Knight of Swords, there may well be some legal aspect to the outcome."

"Is it a good outcome?" Philip was by now feeling more than a little confused.

"Well," Bob said, "it's an appropriate outcome, I feel. All in all, I feel it will be satisfactory, though it may surprise you as well."

Sensing the reading was at an end, Philip reached into his pocket to turn off the recorder and to extract Bob's fee. As he did so, Bob suddenly said, "Oh, yes, Justice also represents the sign of Libra. You may find it relevant."

"Thank you," said Philip. "I'll bear that in mind. It's been most interesting."

Bob gathered the cards together and replaced them neatly on the table, then smiled at Philip as though acknowledging a compliment. He picked up the tea tray, and started towards the door. Philip moved to open it for him.

"Thank you," said Bob, adding over his shoulder as he moved off down the hall, "if you'd like to learn more about these matters, I run a weekly group."

"That sounds interesting."

Bob put the tray down on a cluttered sideboard and took a card out of his pocket and offered it to Philip. "We're quite a small group," he said. "We meet here each Tuesday to explore together the vast hidden possibilities within this wonderful universe of ours. You'd be most welcome to join us. I feel sure you have talents as yet undeveloped."

"Thanks." Philip took the card and slipped it into his pocket. "You may well be right. I have a pretty busy schedule right now, but I'll see what I can do."

Philip made his way with care down the dark pathway and pulled open the creaking gate. As he closed it behind him Bob called out from the doorway, "I'll see you again before long."

A slight shiver ran along Philip's spine. He stopped under the street lamp and pulled out the shiny mauve card. At the top was written in gold italic script, ' *CIRCLE OF LIGHT,*' and beneath this, 'Exploring the Inner Realms to Release the Power Within.' Bob's telephone number was next, and in small print at the bottom, 'Tarot Readings by Appointment.' That seems to cover most eventualities, he thought as he slipped the card back into his pocket.

He drove home deep in thought. The reading was

certainly intriguing, with just enough accuracy to make him wonder about the rest of it. And about Bob. He was a strange character all right. Ordinary enough on the face of it, apart, obviously, from what he did for a living, but there was something about him Philip could not quite put his finger on, something distinctly odd, and perhaps a little scary. He mulled it over as he drove, and eventually came to the tentative conclusion that it was something to do with the whole not quite amounting to the sum of its parts. Not more or less, necessarily, just not the same.

Luke was still up when Philip arrived home. He was watching something loud and lurid on television, a cigarette in one hand and a mug of coffee in the other. A bottle of brandy stood on the coffee table beside a tray holding a coffee plunger and a milk bottle.

"I take it you've finished the programme," Philip said, reflecting that Bob was not the only one composed of bits that didn't quite fit.

Luke looked up, silencing the television a trifle guiltily. "Yes, thank God," he grimaced.

"I've just made some coffee if you want one. How was the reading?"

"Interesting." Philip got himself a mug from the kitchen and sat down on the couch. Pulling the recorder from his pocket, he placed it on the table. "Very interesting indeed."

Luke pushed the brandy bottle towards Philip. "Right," he said, settling himself back comfortably. "Pour a shot of that in your coffee, and let's hear all the gory details."

CHAPTER SEVEN

Declan swung the steering wheel of the Subaru to avoid yet another pothole in the parched ground. The vehicle lurched somewhat, but continued manfully to negotiate the alleged road. In reality, it was little more than a track, and a virtually unused one at that, by the look of it. It was, however, partitioned off from the rest of the arid terrain by a wire fence with a decrepit wooden gate sagging between two posts. A straggling row of trees meandered in a dejected way along either side of it like refugees from some distant war zone. Rounding a bend in the road, he was forced to halt so suddenly that the vehicle's motor stalled, and Derek was thrown forward, almost dislodging his hat.

"Sorry, sir—Harpo," Declan said, surveying with dismay the massive gum tree that lay across the roadway. A crude sign whose ornate writing looked distinctly out of place imparted the somewhat superfluous information that no vehicles were permitted beyond this point. Through the now thicker and greener trees they could just glimpse a long, low, white house with a wooden verandah, glimmering like a mirage in the heat.

"Looks like we'll have to walk the rest of the way," Derek said, watching with some satisfaction as Declan turned off the motor and pocketed the keys. Derek, brought up on a Queensland cattle station, was in familiar surroundings. It was evident, even from brief acquaintance, that Declan was not. Ah well, he wasn't too keen on city life either, but cops couldn't always choose their place of work.

The pitted track proved easier to walk than to drive, though by the time they reached the unlikely green lawn that fronted the old bungalow, both men were coated with a fine film of reddish dust. Declan resisted an overwhelming urge to roll in the lush grass, instead commenting to Derek that someone must still be putting a lot of work in around the place.

"I reckon," Derek agreed. He was about to say more, when a figure appeared at the front door. A tall, slim young man wearing white cotton jeans and a loose-fitting white muslin shirt stood there, shading his eyes with an elegant hand gesture that suggested he might be a dancer.

"Hello," he called. "Do you have an appointment?" His accent was almost, but not quite, British public school. His hand fell to his side revealing a startlingly handsome face with pale olive skin and almost impossibly regular features dominated by huge brown eyes under a fringe of dark lashes. His thick, straight hair was an unexpected dark ash blond, making it impossible to guess at his ancestry. He looked to be around twenty-five. Declan wondered if he might be Miriam's son.

Fishing his ID out of his shirt pocket, Derek spoke laconically. "Didn't know we needed one. Detective Inspector Marks, Brisbane Police. This is Detective Sergeant Kelly. We'd like to speak to Miriam Golden. Is she here?"

The young man appeared to give considerable thought to the matter before saying, "I see. I'm Gerald Fernando, Miriam's—companion. Please wait here and I'll see if she'll speak to you."

"She hasn't got a lot of choice," Derek muttered at his gracefully retreating back, trying without success to brush the dust from his trousers with his hat. Declan was about to pass comment on the likely nature of Gerald's true relationship with Miriam, when he returned and beckoned them inside. He led them down a broad hallway to a long, pale, elegant room cooled by two ceiling fans. Its wide windows looked out over the lawn and the trees skirting it, which hid the dirt track from sight, creating an effect like a lush oasis. Along the inner wall of the room were two colonial couches, their pale pink Thai silk squabs scattered with a quantity of cream, fringed cushions. A huge painting hung above the couches, and Declan eyed it with interest. It was of a desert scene at dusk, beautifully executed in a rather idiosyncratic modern-realist style, though he didn't recognise the artist.

"Magnificent, isn't it?" Gerald's admiring voice invaded his reverie, and he nodded his appreciation. "It's one of Miriam's more recent works. She'll be along to speak with you soon." He indicated the settees. "Do sit down. Would you care for some tea?"

Derek nodded gratefully, "Thanks." Declan didn't quite like to ask for coffee. In this setting, it didn't seem right, somehow, so he nodded as well. Gerald gave a slight bow, and made an elegant exit. Declan looked at the couch, then somewhat dubiously at his dusty clothing.

Derek grinned at him. "If they don't mind," he said, "why should we? Anyway, I'm knackered. Must be your driving, Dekko." He lowered his solid frame onto the pink silk. Declan shrugged and followed suit, leaning back and savouring the cool, fresh air as the fans whirred softly above.

He had to admit he wasn't exactly feeling a box of birds himself after all that lurching about.

It was at least twenty minutes before Miriam arrived, closely followed by Gerald, carrying a large woven-cane tray which he placed on the low, carved table in front of the settees. Declan noted with approval the lovely, and doubtless expensive, china tea set. His knowledge of antiques, unlike his knowledge of art, was not great, but it looked like an antique to him, probably Chinese or Japanese. He was still pondering the unlikelihood of finding such luxurious items in such a remote setting, when he glanced up and saw Miriam properly for the first time. Mother of God! She was easily as beautiful as one of her antiques and, if anything, a damned sight better preserved. She was most likely in her mid forties, he thought, so she must have been considerably younger than Reuben. Of no more than medium height, she was dressed in a very simple straight white cotton dress that reached just below knee length, and brown sandals soft with age and wear. Her hair, thick and black with traces of grey, cascaded to her waist framing a fine-boned, high-cheeked face with olive skin so delicate it seemed translucent, despite the fine lines wrought by age and the desert climate. Her dress gave few hints of what the rest of her was like and, given their reason for being there, Declan didn't dare allow himself to speculate. Her amber eyes, when she looked at him, had a strange, almost electric glow, and Declan had the bizarre and unnerving impression of a spotlight being trained on his soul.

Miriam lifted a long brown hand in a gesture of greeting, and smiled serenely at them. Declan gulped, wishing she wouldn't do that. Fortunately, Derek, who seemed to be either immune or unbelievably professional, broke the spell by introducing himself and Declan once more, otherwise Declan doubted he would have been able to hold the thin porcelain tea cup without spilling its contents—or worse, dropping the thing.

"Nice place you have here, Mrs Golden," Derek said. "Quite a surprise finding something so—luxurious, in a place as isolated as this. You must find the upkeep a real burden, with only yourself and Gerald here."

Miriam regarded them over the rim of her cup for a moment as though to focus her thoughts, then lowered it to her lap. "Well, when Reuben, my late husband, passed on, I hadn't the heart to continue the work without him, but this is my home, the only one I have, and so I decided to stay here. He left me quite well provided for, so I was able to retain a small staff, originally a group of Reuben's students who wanted to stay on here. Most of them have gone on elsewhere now, but I have had the good fortune to be able to find suitably skilled people who are only too happy to leave behind the chaos of so-called civilisation for a while." Her eyes lighted briefly on Gerald as she spoke. "We bought a helicopter years ago for the Community, and we still have that. We find it very useful for transporting supplies and equipment. Gerald is a qualified pilot, you know—one of the benefits of a private education." She laughed, her eyes sparkling with ironic amusement. "And, of course, we have the farm." Declan felt that spotlight turned on him once more. "Have you heard of Findhorn?" He nodded, noting Derek's surprise and bafflement from the corner of his eye. Doubtless he'd be in for a grilling later on. Miriam resumed, "Well, Reuben and I, with the help of a couple who had spent some years there, created a farm here, which made our community almost self-sufficient at the height of its production. Of course, it's now neither possible nor necessary to run it at the same level, but we manage quite well. Gerald can show you afterwards, if you like." Including, Declan supposed, the fairies at the bottom of the garden. Feeling a trifle overwhelmed by now, he didn't trust himself to respond. Derek, taking in his predicament, demurred on behalf of both of them.

Miriam continued, "And I have earned a little from my paintings from time to time—" Her gesture took in the wall behind them "—enough to acquire a few small luxuries to make my life here more comfortable."

Presumably, thought Declan, Gerald came into that category.

"But tell me, Inspector, what is it that brings you here? We don't have many visitors these days, do we Gerald?"

Miriam's voice was deep and calm, an intriguing mixture of well-educated Australian and something indefinable that reminded Declan a little of Chief Inspector Vodanovich's accent. Gerald, revelling in the radiance of her smile, offered her another cup of tea. His action seemed almost to amount to a votive offering. Young Gerald was clearly besotted—and who wouldn't be? Well, Derek, for one, he realised, as the Inspector put down his tea cup and spoke briskly.

"Mrs Golden, I'm sorry to bother you, but I need to ask you some questions about a young woman we believe was formerly a member of the Tree of Life Community."

Miriam's face registered mild surprise. "But that closed down six years ago, soon after Reuben died."

"Yes, we know that. But this woman would have been here

57

about ten years ago. At least she would have left here about then. Her body has just been found in a creek bed twenty kilometres from here, and we know she died around ten years ago. We're trying to find out who she was."

Miriam gave a graceful shrug. "There were so many young women here then—men, too. Reuben had very many students, and naturally a lot of them were young. The young are more open to new and different ideas." She bestowed a fond smile on Gerald, who busied himself suddenly with the tea things. Not totally open then, thought Declan.

"She was pregnant—about seven or eight months," Derek stated in his blunt way.

Miriam's lovely features registered recognition. "Ah, Claire!" she exclaimed. "It must be Claire you are speaking of."

"Claire?" Derek pulled out his note pad and began writing.

"Claire Lomax," Miriam said. "She was such an unhappy girl. I think she was afraid for her baby. Because of the drugs, you know." Derek and Declan exchanged glances, then looked enquiringly at Miriam. Gerald gathered up the tea tray and slipped discreetly out of the room. Miriam ran a pink tongue over her full lips and went on quickly, "Yes. I didn't know much about it, really. Reuben could have told you a great deal more. She confided in him—they all did. But I knew she was using something on a regular basis. It was quite obvious from her behaviour. Reuben tried to help her through meditation and massage, and I have some knowledge of herbs. And that friend of hers—what was his name? Richard? Yes, Richard—-Richard Forster. He was rather older than she was, a New Zealander who came to us

58

from Asia, where he had been travelling and studying meditation. I think, you know—" She smiled slightly "—that they first became friends because she was also from New Zealand. She became quite devoted to him, and he naturally enjoyed the attentions of a pretty young girl." Miriam paused, apparently struggling with something in her mind. At length she said, "No, that's not being fair to him. I believe he was genuinely fond of her, I really do."

"Was he the father of her baby?" Derek asked, grateful for a pause in the flow of her monologue. He flexed his cramped fingers, wincing slightly as the blood recirculated.

Miriam rubbed the edge of her mouth with a smooth brown finger, then responded, her husky voice playing havoc with Declan's self composure, "No, I don't think so. In fact, I'm sure he can't have been, because if she was eight months pregnant when she left here, she must already have been pregnant when Richard arrived. He came here about two months after she did."

Declan began to speak, finding, to his chagrin, that he had to clear his throat before beginning again.

"Do you know why she came here?"

Miriam shook her head, her hair rearranging itself on her shoulders as she did so. Declan tried again. "Do you know why she left, then?"

Miriam shook her head again. "Well, you know, that was rather strange. I think she had been trying to give up the drugs. Sometimes she would go for a while, and one could tell from her behaviour that she had not had her usual dose. She would become very agitated, and unable to sleep, and Richard would stay up with her, talking to her or taking her for walks. Reuben and I wanted to isolate her so we could give her calming herbs, and Reuben could give her counselling—he was a trained therapist, you know."

I'll just bet he was, thought Declan, and found himself hoping Miriam could not sense his cynicism. Derek was busy scribbling notes.

Miriam's faced looked sad as she continued, "That poor girl. All she wanted was Richard. She was convinced only he could help her. But you know, there was something about him I could never quite like." Derek looked interested. Miriam shook her head again. "I don't know what it was, but I was not sorry when he left."

Declan took it on himself to steer her back on course. "You were telling us why Claire left the community."

Miriam threw him a heart-stopping smile. "I'm not at all sure I know, really. As I said, she seemed to be trying to give up the drugs. I thought she was beginning to succeed, but then one day she became very distressed. She refused to leave her room, but we could hear her weeping and raging for hours at a time, pleading with Richard to help her. Eventually he left her. We assumed he had finally given up on her."

"What time of day was that?" Derek looked up from his notes.

"Late afternoon, I think. Claire went on crying for a while, but later on she seemed to have calmed down. Her room was quiet, so we assumed she had gone to sleep. Reuben and I prayed for her, and performed a ritual to help bring her peace."

"Did it work?" Declan asked. He was finding it harder now to conceal his cynicism.

Miriam gave him a sharp look, the spotlight of her eyes

almost painfully piercing. "We didn't have time to find out," she said, her soft voice reproving him. "Next morning Richard told us she had left the community."

"Weren't you suspicious?" Derek flexed his writing hand again.

Miriam pushed her hair back from her face, and thought for a moment. "I was at first," she said, "but Richard told us he had arranged for her to go to a place in Cairns—some sort of drug rehabilitation place I think it was."

"In the middle of the night?" Derek sounded scornful.

A slight note of annoyance crept into Miriam's voice. "Look, Inspector—Marks? You have to understand, the community was rather large then, and we were dealing with the problems of many people, as well as our teaching and the ritual work. Also, when people came here it was on the understanding that each was responsible for him or herself. Ultimately, you know, that's the only way true spiritual development is possible. We are all responsible for working out our own karma, I still believe that."

Derek looked nonplussed. It was Declan's turn to feel smug. He might not believe in karma, but at least he knew what it was. "So," he said to Miriam, "Claire left here, and you never saw her again?" Miriam nodded. "And you don't know the name of this rehabilitation place in Cairns?"

"No, Richard didn't tell us that. The Community respected the privacy of its students, so we didn't ask."

"What about this Richard Forster," Declan went on. "What happened to him?"

"He left, too, almost immediately afterwards. I think he went back to New Zealand. As I said, I was not sorry that he left."

"He made you feel uncomfortable?"

Miriam thought about this, finally concluding, "No, not that, exactly. It was just—something about him that didn't quite fit."

"You mean he didn't fit into the community?"

"No—it was himself. He—didn't fit himself. It was as though the aspects of his personality were not properly integrated." Miriam's eyes widened in surprise at this sudden realisation.

Derek closed his notepad and stood up. "Thank you very much, Mrs Golden," he said. "You've been most helpful."

Miriam inclined her head with a slight smile. "I do hope so," she said softly. "I hope dear Claire's soul is at peace now, and I want you to know that whatever happened to her, however she may have died—if she did—the law of karma will take care of it all, sooner or later."

Derek was clearly well out of his depth now, and Declan, for very different reasons, didn't trust himself to handle the situation either. Fortunately for both of them, Gerald chose this moment to reappear—either that, or he had been lurking in the wings, awaiting his cue—and began, politely but firmly, to steer them towards the door. Appearing all at once to regain some of his professional aplomb, Derek turned in the doorway and said to Miriam, "Oh, Mrs Golden, one thing we may need is a description of Richard Forster—and Claire Lomax if possible." He took out his notepad again, flipped it open, and stood there stolidly, pen poised.

Miriam stood up, smoothing her dress with elegant hands, her brow creased with concentration, or perhaps impatience. "Ten years is a long time," she said at last, "and, of course, he may look very different now."

"Anything at all could be helpful," Derek said, his stance and manner making it clear he would not be leaving until some sort of description was forthcoming.

"Well," said Miriam, her eyes closing with the effort to remember, "as I recall, he had dark hair, dark and straight, and long, I think, down to his shoulders. He was not very tall, and quite thin. Oh, wait a minute!" She broke off abruptly, her eyes snapping open, and turned to Gerald. "Could you get that box from the bedroom, Gerald—the green leather one? Thank you so much."

Her eyes also thanked him as he hastened to do her bidding. In answer to Derek's questioning look, she said, "I've just remembered I have some photographs, and I'm sure there's one of Richard and Claire amongst them."

As Gerald vanished down the hallway, Derek said, "Er, Mrs Golden, would Gerald be able to add anything further—I mean, would he remember Richard or Claire?"

Miriam laughed. "Good heavens, no! He's been here less than a year."

"Ah." Derek's voice held a 'thought as much' tone as he scribbled in his notepad.

A few moments later Gerald returned and handed Miriam a flat box a little larger than a cigar box, covered in green tooled leather, darkened and shiny with age and use. Placing it on the low table, she undid its delicate silver clasp to reveal a number of old photographs, some in tarnished black and white, but most in colour with the yellow-brown patina that comes with age. One by one she glanced at them, placing them on the table afterwards. At last, near the bottom of the box, Miriam found what she was looking for. She held it out to them.

With an inscrutable glance at Declan, Derek took the small, square print, obviously taken with an old-fashioned Polaroid camera. It showed a man in his late thirties, thinnish, but somehow rounded looking, his shoulder-length dark hair bound, Native American style, with a plaited leather thong above bland features with thin eyebrows and a nondescript nose. The colour of his eyes was impossible to discern, being almost entirely hidden in a broad smile that was focussed on the young woman who sat next to him. She looked to be in her early twenties, and was thin almost to the point of emaciation. Her smile, perched hopefully on a face that would most likely have been freckled, showed her vulnerability, even in the casual snapshot. Pale reddish hair, very long and fine, hung limply around her shoulders. Both of them wore loose shirts of some light fabric over jeans. Claire's was pale blue with darker embroidery, while Richard's was white, unadorned except for a large golden-yellow stone nestled in the folds of its open neck.

Derek turned to Miriam, who seemed to read his thoughts as she smiled. "Please take it if you think it will help you."

"Thank you. It should be a great deal of help. We'll make a copy and return the original as soon as we can."

Miriam shook her head. "Keep it, please." She smiled briefly at Gerald—obviously a signal, as he moved towards them, polite as ever, but inexorable. They took the hint.

From a safe distance, Declan glanced back to see Miriam standing in the hallway, smiling up into Gerald's handsome face as he placed his arm about her waist and kissed her lightly on the mouth. He quickly looked away again. Derek glanced across at him and seemed about to say something, then apparently thought better of it. Declan kept walking.

CHAPTER EIGHT

As she got out of the car, the telephone was ringing. Isabel put the heavy bags of groceries down on the doorstep and tried to unlock the door while using her foot to fend off Bartholomew, a handsome black and white cat with a rakish air, who was intent on helping her to unpack the cat food. By the time she got inside, the phone had stopped, but the red light on the answering machine was winking at her. Bartholomew continued his assault on the groceries, joined now by the ever hungry Madame George and a small, slightly scruffy black and white cat who went by the name of Dali, on account of his black moustache and at times bizarre behaviour. Ignoring the feline claims of starvation, Isabel stowed the groceries away in safety, then went impatiently to the telephone.

She listened to the message, then dialled Joss's number. "Hi, Joss, it's Isabel. I just got your message. What's all this about Bob and the Circle of Light? Have you been doing some research?"

"You could say that. I've had a vision."

Isabel laughed. "Well don't expect beatification until you're well and truly dead."

"Twit! You know what I mean." Joss was known to have clairvoyant visions of often remarkable accuracy. "I was doing the washing up, actually—have you ever noticed what an inordinate amount of time one spends doing washing up?

No, I don't suppose you have, have you?"

"Are you implying I'm a bad housekeeper? I do my dishes regularly—once a week, whether they need it or not," Isabel stated cheerfully.

Joss laughed. "I meant you don't have a husband and two kids to clean for. Anyway, I was gazing idly out the window, and I suddenly saw Bob out on the lawn, so to speak. Only, of course, he wasn't on the lawn, he was in his house, in the hallway if memory serves. He seemed very agitated. Then he wasn't there any more, and there were all these other people. Actually, I think it was Bob's group, because they looked like some of the people you described—the big red-headed guy, Doug, wasn't it?"

"Yes, that's right."

"And Jeremy was there, and the girl with the purple hat, Anita, and a little, thin woman with a sharp face and odd, jerky mannerisms. She reminded me of a bird, probably a sparrow."

"That certainly sounds like Bob's lot," said Isabel, "though I've never seen the last one. There was no-one like that there last week. What were they all doing, anyway?"

"They were at Bob's house, I think, but it was completely empty, and they seemed like they didn't know what to make of it. Anita was crying, and Jeremy seemed angry. The thin woman seemed to be in charge, and was trying to get them all organised. Then some wretched salesman knocked at the door and the whole thing went away."

Isabel was sympathetic. She hated being interrupted in the middle of a tarot reading. It was disorienting, like being woken from a vivid dream. "What do you think it meant?" she asked.

"I'm not sure. I had the distinct feeling they were all at sixes and sevens over something. I think it was to do with Bob."

"Yes," said Isabel. "He was there at first, wasn't he, and apparently in a state of panic. Then he wasn't there, and the others were all upset. And that little thin woman intrigues me. I wonder who she is?"

"Search me. Perhaps it was about something that hasn't happened yet?"

"Yes." Isabel absentmindedly stroked Bartholomew, who had jumped up onto her lap. He certainly seemed a lot better, she reflected, remembering Bob's healing exercise. "That seems likely. Well, it's Tuesday, so I'll be going to Bob's again tonight. I'll ring you if anything interesting happens."

"Yes, do, but not after one a.m., okay? I may work nights but, unlike you, I do actually need regular sleep. I have a husband and two daughters, none of whom seem able to get up and about successfully in the morning without my help," Joss said.

"I do wish you'd stop flaunting your wretched nuclear family at me. Can I help it if I'm a poor solo mother with a son who's never home and leaves me languishing here with only my cats for company?"

"Please, you'll have me in tears." Joss laughed, going over in her mind the extraordinary variety of activities with which Isabel filled her life. Dominic's admittedly rare appearances at home didn't exactly leave her bereft. They had developed a complex but effective communication system involving an answerphone, a whiteboard and numerous notepads. "But do call me if anything comes up."

* * * *

Isabel sipped her tea, watching with interest as Jeremy talked, with considerable animation for him, to the small, intense young woman who was a newcomer to the Circle of Light. Her name was Jessica, and she was a university student doing her Masters thesis, she had informed the group, on 'Feminist Elements in Ancient Greek Religion.' Jeremy was questioning her avidly on some obscure point or other. She seemed unfazed by his onslaught, and was explaining her ideas with evident enthusiasm. Looking at Jessica's long, straight black hair worn in a thick plait that lay like a cable between her thin shoulders, and her pale, pinched, intelligent face with its hint of long-buried pain, it occurred to Isabel that she and Jeremy would make ideal bookends, being virtually mirror-images of one another in both looks and style.

Doug was away this week, apparently hauling someone's worldly possessions down to Invercargill. Unexpectedly, she had missed his down-to-earth good humour. It would have been pleasant to have something to relieve the relentless stream of 'love and light' and 'higher vibrations' that emanated from most of the others. Thank God, though, Bob had been less assiduous in his attentions. He seemed, in fact, somewhat distracted, and Isabel wondered if it had something to do with Anita, who had outdone herself sartorially this evening in a stunning high-waisted burgundy velvet dress, its tiny covered buttons left partially undone to reveal something black and lacy beneath. Around her slim waist she had tied a black, fringed scarf embroidered with red roses, completing the effect with a pair of intricate gold earrings and a gold-embroidered black cap atop her cropped hair. She also seemed distracted, alternating between wandering from group to group of the others, and perching on Nancy's vacated chair, plaiting the fringes of her scarf with nervous fingers.

Her speculations were interrupted, however, by Pat's enquiry about Bartholomew's health, and she was glad of the diversion. She had the distinct impression something was afoot—something involving Bob and Anita. Though her normally insatiable curiosity was piqued, she couldn't rid herself of a sick feeling in the pit of her stomach, which she had learned to recognise as a warning sign, and she was pleased when the others started leaving, giving her a cue to do likewise.

Assuring Pat that Bartholomew definitely seemed to be on the mend, she went to say goodnight to Bob. On a whim, she offered to help clear away the supper things, but suddenly Anita was there. She said nothing, but managed to make it clear Isabel's help was not required, thank you very much. Isabel contented herself with thanking Bob for what had, in its way, been an enjoyable evening, and left knowing some deep suspicion of hers had just been confirmed, but having no clear idea yet of what that suspicion might be. She wondered if it was worth phoning Joss when she got home.

* * * *

Bob was out in the hall, saying goodbye to Jeremy and Jessica, inviting her back to next week's meeting. Anita could hear Jessica's low, dramatic voice thanking him, then asking Jeremy if he'd like a lift home, but Bob shut the front door before she could hear Jeremy's reply. Picking up the laden tray, Anita made her way through to the tiny kitchen. She filled the kettle and plugged it in, in case Bob might like another cup of tea. He certainly seemed to drink an awful lot of the stuff. She preferred herbal drinks herself. According to her training at the health shop where she worked during the summer break, too much tea at night kept you awake. She giggled a trifle nervously to herself as she rinsed out the teapot. Well, after all, Bob always seemed to know what he was doing.

Closing the front door, Bob walked back up the hallway past the meeting room, and opened the next door along. The room it led into was somewhat smaller, though decorated in a similar style. Switching on a brass bedside lamp, he made his way past the double bed, pulled shut the dark-green velvet curtains, and bent to light a stick of incense, which he took from a yellow packet on the table beneath the window and placed carefully in a small ivory holder. Next to the holder a massive piece of golden quartz blinked gently in the soft lamplight.

A once sumptuous brocade bedspread, the colour of oak leaves in summer, covered the bed, and Bob turned this back to reveal two pale gold pillows. Briefly checking to ensure the electric blanket was switched on, he opened a drawer in the bedside table and took out a small green leather box and an ornate silver cigarette lighter inlaid with a piece of particularly dark lapis lazuli. Finally, he got out a deck of large cards, mellow with age, placed them beside the box, shut the drawer, and returned to the doorway, surveying the room with satisfaction before leaving.

When he entered the kitchen Anita was standing with her

back to the door holding the teapot. The steaming kettle was beside her on the bench. He stood surveying her slim form, enjoying the way the carefully casual scarf emphasised the curve of her hips, until she sensed his presence. She turned to face him, her slightly pouting lips parted in a smile that somehow managed to be both shy and provocative. The thought flickered across his mind that maybe the latter was due to the former.

With a slight gesture of the teapot, her expressive face silently offered him tea. Bob went to the refrigerator and took out a bottle of white wine. He smiled, holding it up with the same gesture, and she nodded, so he put it down on the bench and reached up to the cupboard for two glasses. When he turned, she was standing very close to him, and he could smell the heady fragrance of her patchouli perfume. "I'll take the glasses, shall I?" she asked, her voice soft and breathy.

To his surprise and disquiet, Bob found his thoughts travelling old and disturbing pathways. That perfume held memories for him, not all of them pleasant. With an effort of will, he banished them to the furthermost reaches of his mind, and returned his attention to the here and now. He gave the glasses to Anita, brushing her cheek lightly with his fingers. She shivered excitingly in response. "I think," he murmured, "it's time for that tarot reading I promised you. Would you like that?"

"Oh, yes, please," breathed Anita, and followed him out of the kitchen.

CHAPTER NINE

Luke placed the recording equipment on the coffee table, made himself as comfortable as he could in the ancient armchair, then looked around him with interest. Yes, there was the astrological poster, and the garish picture of the temple, as reported by Isabel and Philip. Philip was right, though, he mused, the room was quite agreeably pleasant after the clutter and cramp of the rest of the house. It must have been built on later. There were no tarot cards in evidence, so presumably he only brought them out when he was expecting a client. No ashtray either, he thought wistfully, wondering whether leaving him waiting like this was a deliberate ploy to put him at a disadvantage with the interview. He licked his lips and pushed his fingers impatiently through his hair. If it was a ploy, it was working.

"Sorry to keep you waiting." Bob pushed the door shut with his heel and crossed to the table with a cane tray containing a teapot, two mugs, a bottle of milk and, thank goodness, a brass ashtray. "I couldn't find the tea. Someone had put it away in a different place. You don't mind if I smoke, do you?"

Luke moved the recording gear aside to make way for the tray. "Not if I'm allowed to as well," he grinned.

With a conspiratorial smile, Bob placed the ashtray in front of Luke with a flourish, then busied himself pouring the tea. Gratefully lighting a cigarette, Luke studied Bob, trying to gauge his feelings towards him in the light of Isabel's and Philip's somewhat differing assessments. To all intents and purposes, he was a fairly ordinary looking middle-aged man, his dark hair just beginning to show a little grey—though, granted, his dress sense left something to be desired. He was attired today in pale grey canvas trousers and a pink, short-sleeved shirt with embroidery on the collar and pocket, of the type sold to tourists in places like Singapore. On his slightly chubby feet were a pair of black velvet scuffs embroidered with pink roses. He should have looked effeminate, but for some reason he didn't. Perhaps, Luke reflected, that was what Philip meant by the whole not quite amounting to the sum of its parts.

"Milk?" Bob's voice cut through his reflections.

"Oh, yes, please."

Bob placed a mug of tea before him. "Now," he said, blowing a thin stream of smoke towards the ceiling, "would you like to start now, or shall we wait till we've finished our tea?"

Luke pushed his hair out of his eyes and gave the matter some thought. For some reason, he always felt nervous when he was about to begin an interview, and Bob was by no means an exception. He sipped the admittedly excellent tea, but found no solace there, and so resorted to nicotine. Through a blue-tinged haze he addressed Bob.

"It would probably be easiest if I simply turn on the recorder and we talk. I have some questions to start with, and we can go on from there. When we've finished, I'd appreciate it if you'd show me where you hold your meetings—I'd like to describe where you work as well as what you do. Then I can edit it all and voice an intro—er, record an introduction—and we should end up with something nice and natural and conversational. How does that sound?"

Luke shook the accumulated ash from his cigarette into the ornate ashtray and breathed in another lungful of smoke, watching Bob closely but, he hoped, casually. Behind Bob's deceptively bland gaze, Luke was very well aware that his mind was in top gear. He was somehow put in mind of a lizard—or a snake, perhaps, if Anne and Geraldine were right. He suppressed the laugh, part cynicism, part nerves, that threatened to emerge and instead sipped his tea and waited. Impatient by nature, Luke's years in radio had taught him the value of silent waiting—though not without cost, he thought, stubbing out his cigarette with a wry inner shrug and reaching once more for the teapot.

He could almost sense the cogs in Bob's mind clicking into place as he straightened himself in his chair and nodded briskly. "That sounds fine to me. Let's start, shall we?"

Luke smiled assent and switched on the recorder along with his professional manner. "Bob," he began, "could you start by telling me exactly what it is that you do?"

"I regard myself," said Bob, "as a teacher of spiritual wisdom."

Clearly, thought Luke, Bob also had his professional manner. His voice seemed richer, fuller than before, and, in some indefinable sense, he seemed to have gained in stature. Luke was intrigued.

Bob continued, "I have been a seeker for many years, and still am, of course. The search, once undertaken, has no end, and in that sense I am, and always will be, but a pilgrim on the path. But I have come to see that the next step for me is to pass on what fragments I have learned to others, to try to expand the circle of love and light that ultimately enfolds us all." He paused, sipping tea that by now must be cold.

Suppressing a shudder at the thought, Luke judged it time to clarify Bob's focus a little. "And you do this through your tarot readings?" he asked with apparent innocence.

"They can, indeed, provide some insight on an individual level," Bob opined with what Luke hoped was unconscious pomposity. "But my main work is with groups and individuals, teaching meditation and other tools for spiritual development." Luke awaited enlightenment. He did not have to wait for long, as Bob now appeared to be getting into his stride. "My aim is to provide an environment where my students can expand their knowledge and experience of the spiritual realms, not just by teaching them from my own store of knowledge, but by encouraging—by allowing—their own insights." He looked at Luke with a serious expression that stopped just short of self-parody. "You see, the world at large neither values nor encourages the true spiritual life. And since I have been lucky enough to have been aware of life's spiritual dimension for most of my life, I feel that I, in my turn, must pass this on to others. That is why I have begun my little group."

Luke took advantage of his brief pause for breath to encourage Bob to return to his spiritual roots, so to speak. "How did you first start out on this path?" Bob lit another cigarette. Good idea, thought Luke, and followed suit. The cigarette was a great interview aid. It induced a sense of sharing as useful as it was spurious. Always provided, of course, that the interviewee was not a non-smoker. In that case, it had entirely the opposite effect. Bob leaned forward a little and tapped his cigarette against the side of the ashtray with short, plump fingers. Wafting a cloying mix of cigarette smoke and sandalwood in Luke's direction, he began his response.

"Oh, when I was very young. My grandmother was psychic. She taught me to read the cards—not the tarot, that came much later. My grandmother read playing cards, and I used to beg her to show me how to do it. I suppose I thought I'd be able to show off to the boys at school, though at the same time I was genuinely fascinated. Well, when she started teaching me—I was about eleven, I think—she made me promise not to tell anyone about it at all until she said I could. I was so disappointed I nearly gave up the whole idea." He chuckled, remembering.

"And you never considered breaking the promise?"

Bob snorted, "You didn't know my grandmother! Looking back, I think she was a genuine Wise Woman in the Celtic mystical tradition. She came from Scotland and had what they call 'the sight'. So while she was teaching me to read the cards, she was also helping me to develop my own inner sight—my ESP if you like." Luke nodded encouragement while Bob paused and extinguished his cigarette. He appeared to have all but forgotten his self-created persona in remembering a past that obviously still fascinated him. "I suppose I was about sixteen when she finally gave me permission to practise what I'd learnt on people outside the immediate family. Just as well, too, because she died soon after that, and I left home."

Luke nodded again, wondering if the recorder he'd brought with him had enough memory left. Unusually for him, he hadn't thought to check. Bob's next statement made him wonder if the man wasn't truly a mind reader.

"Well," he said, "to cut a long story short, since then I've travelled the world, seeking further wisdom wherever I went."

"Tell me about the places you've been," Luke prompted.

"Oh, well, let me see... I went to India, and studied there for some years under a Maharishi. He taught me yoga and meditation, then finally sent me on my way to learn more. So I travelled north to Nepal and studied Buddhism under a Tibetan monk there." Luke must have been showing his scepticism, as Bob paused to reprove him, "He had left Tibet after the Chinese invasion. Many of them did, you know, including the Dalai Lama himself." Luke looked suitably chastened, and Bob continued, "After two years there, I felt the need to study other aspects of Buddhism, so I went to Japan. After some months spent living on my wits in Tokyo, I heard of a Zen master who was willing to take western students, so I took the first train out of town, and finally reached the place where he lived, near a small monastery. I think he was quite impressed that I had made the effort to find him. At any rate, he took me on as a student and, for the best part of a year, I lived at the monastery, walking out to his home twice a week for instruction. The rest of the time I practised meditation alone in my room, or helped with the housework."

He forestalled Luke's query. "Zen is a very down-to-earth practice." He grinned, his eyes almost vanishing as his sallow, puffy cheeks rose up to meet them. His entire body had the look of a plant which, never particularly vigorous, had gone to seed early as the result of inadequate growing conditions. It would be fascinating to see a photo of him as a young man. Luke stored the thought away for future consideration.

"What happened next?" he asked. To his surprise, he was finding Bob's story rather entertaining, though he suspected a fair amount of embellishment.

This seemed even more likely as Bob continued, "One day when I went to visit my teacher, he began questioning me about what I had learned. Some kind of examination, I suppose. Well, at the end of it he smiled at me and said he couldn't teach me any more. When I protested I still had much to learn, he told me I must look elsewhere, as he had taught me all he could. He suggested I look to the west for further enlightenment."

"And did you?"

"Yes. Well, I hung around for another week or so, but it was obvious he wouldn't see me any more, so in the end I packed up and went back to Tokyo. I felt very disoriented there, as you can imagine. However, I had to get some money if I was to go anywhere else, so I forced myself to stay there and find work." He smiled. "All that meditation training came in very handy, I can tell you."

By now Luke was dying to know. "What sort of work would a westerner find in Tokyo? Did you teach English?" Bob seemed suddenly cagey. Instead of replying, he lit another cigarette, taking his time about lighting it and drawing on it deeply. Too deeply, it seemed. He coughed slightly, covering his mouth with his hand, then gazing with apparent fascination at the golden topaz in the massive ring he wore on it. It was the first time Luke had seen him look even slightly disconcerted. He waited to see how Bob would deal with the raw nerve he appeared to have touched. Given an adequate supply of cigarettes, he was capable of waiting almost indefinitely in the interests of a good story.

When Bob continued, it seemed he had anaesthetised the nerve with nicotine. He skirted round Luke's question saying, "For a westerner with a good knowledge of Japanese, as I had by then, of course, it wasn't too difficult to make a living. Then I was able to work my passage on a ship going to the United States, and I ended up in Los Angeles."

But, of course. Luke's thought was heavy with irony, but aloud he merely asked, "And you were able to continue your—studies there?"

Bob's reply was unexpected. "Well, of course, Los Angeles is full of people claiming to be spiritual teachers, as I'm sure you realise only too well. But real teachers are, as always, difficult to find. My quest eventually led me to Arizona, where I lived among the Hopi Indians for some time, studying their inner teachings. They are, of course, far more spiritually advanced than is recognised in the west. Did you realise their very name means peaceful?" The sudden question took Luke by surprise and, to his chagrin, he realised he was beginning to feel a little out of his depth. So far, Bob had told him nothing that was not available in any New Age bookshop or halfway decent library, but something about the way he told his story prevented Luke from dismissing it out of hand. He shook his head, not only in response to Bob, but also to clear it as Bob resumed his autobiography.

"Of course, there's a limit to what I can tell you of what I learnt there. There are things I *may* not tell. However, I can say that one of my discoveries there was that I was, myself, a Hopi shaman in a past life." Luke hoped his scepticism was not showing. Personally, he had no beliefs on the subject of reincarnation, one way or the other. He was quite prepared to live and let live. It was just that Bob's story was passing well beyond trite. It was like a soap opera in that, while no single incident was beyond belief, it was unlikely in the extreme that all of them should happen to the same small group of people within one lifetime. Or in this case, more than one, according to Bob.

He arranged his features into an expression of polite fascination, to which Bob responded, "Yes, that was an experience unlike any other in my life. I think it was a turning point for me, the point at which I first realised it was my sacred duty to give out knowledge as well as receiving it."

"Was that when you began to run your group?" Bob had fallen into a retrospective reverie, and Luke's question skilfully returned him to the subject.

"Oh, no," he replied, "that was much later. While I was with the Hopi, I met a young woman who had come out from Northern California. She was a student of the Rosicrucian teachings, and she offered to introduce me to her teacher, so when she returned to San Francisco, I went with her. With the blessing of my Hopi teachers, of course."

She must have been some woman, mused Luke, observing the expression on Bob's face. Not for one moment did he suppose it was the Hopi teachers or their blessings that lit Bob's eyes in that particular way, and he was vaguely aware that here was a key which might fruitfully be turned at some later date.

Bob continued, "In San Francisco I met Susan's teacher. He was from Germany originally, though he had lived in the States for at least twenty years. When I met him he was in his sixties. I think by now he is no longer with us."

"What was his name?"

"Max Muller," said Bob. "Dr Max Muller. He was quite a recluse, I don't expect you've heard of him."

He was right. It was unlikely they'd be able to check out this one of Bob's purported teachers, either. A pity, but par for the course it seemed. Luke pushed his hair off his face and reached once more for his cigarette packet. Well, at least he'd end up with some decent material for The Psychic Connection.

"Max was a fascinating character, well over six feet tall, with long, white hair, a flowing beard, and a wicked sense of humour. Apart from his teaching, he seemed to have been working for many years on the Great Work, as he called it. He considered it to be of enormous importance, but none of us were ever told anything about it. Except, presumably, Clara, his wife. I'm sure they were partners in the magical sense as well." Bob glanced at Luke as though to discern whether he understood this last statement. Luke deliberately remained neutral, but Bob did not elaborate. "I learned a great deal from him about mind control and self-discipline, but nothing at all about his Great Work, unfortunately. It wasn't too long before I realised my path still lay elsewhere." Surprise, surprise, thought Luke, noting ironically the look of sincerity on Bob's face. It was obvious he meant every bit of it. The first requirement for a good con man was to believe his own story, though it also proved the undoing of most of them, sooner or later. Luke thought of Anne, and hoped for Bob it would be sooner.

Bob went on, "Susan and a group of her friends were planning to go up to Mount Shasta to stay with the community there, so I went with them". He sat back and lit another cigarette.

"Mmm, I've heard of Mount Shasta," said Luke. "It's in Northern California, isn't it? So, what did you learn at Mount Shasta?"

"Mount Shasta," Bob declared, exhaling contentedly, "is where I discovered my purpose in life."

Luke leaned forward. Perhaps they were getting somewhere at last. "How did that happen?" he asked.

"The feeling there was wonderful, wonderful," Bob enthused. "Such a sense of community, so many people all working together in love and harmony to bring light to a darkening world. It was truly inspiring. I think it was the atmosphere there, the majesty of the place, and the wonderful people, that made me see how I could put together what I had learned over my years as a student of the inner self, and pass it on to others." His eyes closed in minor ecstasy at the memory.

"So Mount Shasta was a catalyst for you?" prompted Luke.

The eyes snapped open beneath their narrow brows. "Yes, that's it exactly. I saw what I had to do, and also how I could do it. I did a lot of past life work there you know, and it put a lot of things in perspective for me. I realised that what I wanted to do, what I had to do, in fact, was to pass on my knowledge to others, to help raise people's awareness to a higher vibration. And here I am!" He was almost beaming at Luke as he spoke. It seemed incongruous, somehow, and once more Luke was reminded of Philip's words.

"So you came back here to Christchurch?" he queried, wishing he could pin Bob down to a definite time-frame. But,

82

no such luck, it seemed.

"Well, I went to Auckland, initially," Bob offered, "but it wasn't the right place for my work. I tried several other places, but so far this seems the best. It has the right atmosphere and, I think, the right students."

Luke forced back a laugh that hovered uncomfortably between sarcasm and hysteria. "Thank you, Bob, that was very interesting indeed," he said with studied calm, and switched off the recorder. "Now, perhaps I could have a look at your meeting room?"

He stood up, giving Bob no real choice in the matter, and Bob dutifully led the way out of the white room and back through the cramped sitting room into the hallway. Through an open door just past the over-large hall stand, Luke caught a brief glimpse of green curtains and bedspread, and a magnificent kauri dressing table above which hung a painting of what looked like an Australian outback scene done in a dramatic modern style. What he wouldn't give for the opportunity to have a good look round in there. He suspected that room held quite a few secrets that would help Joss and Isabel in their current 'search for enlightenment'. But Bob was holding open the door to the next room along and beckoning him through.

"This is it," he was saying, "the room where we hold our little meetings."

Luke's gaze took in the high, ornate ceiling and Victorian frieze, then down at the curtains and batik cloths Bob had hung around the walls. The effect was, as Isabel had said, surprisingly attractive. The kauri fireplace, however, with its lovely carving and its soft, honeyed lustre, was definitely the *pièce de résistance* of the room. Not even the massive bay windows that ran almost from floor to ceiling could match it. As a lifelong connoisseur of beautiful things, Luke was impressed. He told Bob as much.

"Yes," said Bob, with obvious pleasure, "it is beautiful, isn't it?" I consider myself blessed indeed to have this house. It has its bad points, old as it is, but this room is perfect for my group work."

"You do other kinds of work, too, then?"

But Bob was not to be drawn along that trail. "Well," he admitted, "I do tarot readings. You may have seen my advertisements in the paper." Luke played him at his own game and remained noncommittal. But this time the waiting game gave no results. Bob was not about to tell him more. So, after a further look round the room to fix its details in his memory, he made to leave.

"Thank you again, Bob," he said with professional politeness. "It really has been quite fascinating." He patted the digital recorder in his pocket. "I should have this edited in time for next week's programme. Would you like me to let you know for certain when it will go to air?" Bob nodded assent, then held out his hand for an old-fashioned handshake. He really was an odd mixture of styles. Perhaps it came from having lived in so many different cultures— always assuming he really had, of course. All of a sudden, Luke realised he was exhausted, and desperately in need of a coffee. For some reason, tea just didn't do it for him. Odd, that, Isabel always swore the same about coffee. Realising his mind was rambling again, Luke pulled himself severely together. He shook the proffered hand and took his leave, promising to let Bob know when he would be on air.

CHAPTER TEN

"Feeling a bit calmer are we, Dekko?" As he looked up from behind the borrowed desk, there was a gleam in Derek's pale eyes that told Declan he was in for a hard time. Derek had insisted on driving back to Cairns, which had left Declan far too much time in which to think, and worse, to feel—time he could seriously have done without. A few hours, a shower, and several cups of coffee later, he was just starting to feel more or less normal again, and the last thing he needed was Derek exercising his heavy-handed humour on him.

Since the Inspector was obviously expecting a reply, Declan put on his blandest 'Who, me?' expression and said, "I certainly feel a lot better for a shower and a cup of coffee. I never was much into rally driving."

An infuriating smirk still hovering about his mouth, Derek said, "Made quite an impression on you, didn't she?" Noting with satisfaction Declan's ill-disguised embarrassment, he added, "Well, I must say she's certainly a looker—for her age."

"Didn't think you'd noticed." Declan sat down, vaguely disappointed by his inability to come up with anything better, but Derek, it was clear, was just getting into his stride.

"Ah, well," he said, tapping the side of his head with his forefinger, "it's the trained police mind, you see, sharp as a well-honed knife, and totally unaffected by emotion. That's the theory, anyway."

Declan grinned. "Yeah, well, you know what they say about theories."

"What's that then?"

"They're all right in theory."

Derek laughed.

Declan took a deep breath and said, "Look, I know I made a bloody fool of myself. There was just something about that woman, something in her eyes—hypnotism, maybe, or something like it. I don't know if she does it to everyone, or only to selected victims, but..." He ground to a halt, embarrassed by his inability to analyse what had happened to him.

"You've been on your own too long!" Derek observed. "Don't worry about it. I can see why she got to you and, if you ask me, she *was* doing it on purpose. I notice she didn't turn those big cat's eyes on *me*." His short bark of laughter was without mirth. "If old Reuben had half her charisma, it must have been some outfit they had there." He glanced at his notebook, which lay on the desk beside an elderly looking file. "Which brings me to the reason we're here. Sergeant O'Keefe will be here in a minute—they've got the results of the lab tests."

Before Declan could reply, O'Keefe's bulky form appeared in the doorway, carrying another file, and several forms and papers.

"Ah, Sergeant, those must be the reports. Come in and grab a chair."

"Thank you, sir. Sorry it's taken so long, but we had to get her dental records emailed over from New Zealand, and it took the blokes over there a while to track them all down. She seems to have moved around a fair bit." O'Keefe placed the papers on the desk, pulled up an empty chair, then sat down heavily on it and crossed his arms.

Derek ran his eyes over the material. When he looked up at Declan, his eyes bore a steely sheen, all trace of humour gone. "It was Claire Lomax," he said, "and I think we may have a murder on our hands. According to this, she was almost certainly already dead when she went into the stream, possibly for several hours."

"I thought it might come to that," said Declan with a sigh. "But it's not going to be easy proving anything after all this time."

"Mmm." Derek scratched his head thoughtfully, looking down at the papers again. "There's a bit more forensic work here that might prove helpful, and I wouldn't mind having a chat to the bloke who found the body..." He consulted the file. "That's right, Jim Tollerton. I guess we should check any rehabilitation centres of the time in Cairns, too, though I don't believe for one minute that she ever went to one. Which brings us to Richard Forster. As far as we know, he was the last person to see her alive, and it seems he went back to New Zealand—right after the girl died, too."

"Bit suspicious, wouldn't you say?" asked Declan.

"Could be." Derek was noncommittal. "At any rate, we'll have to see if we can track him down now the case has been opened up again." "He'll most likely have flown out from Brisbane, sir," said O'Keefe, "but we'd better check Sydney as well."

"Yeah." Derek nodded. "Looks like it's back to Brisbane for us, then, Sergeant Kelly. I expect you'll be pleased."

To Declan's surprise, he was. In his mind he pictured himself relaxing over dinner at Como's, enjoying the air conditioning and looking out at the high-rise buildings, their lights blinking contentedly in the warm night air. Compared with where he'd spent the last few days, city streets, even in Brisbane's heat, seemed like heaven—relatively speaking, of course.

"Yes, sir," he said.

* * * *

Isabel arrived at Luke's just as Joss was alighting from the yellow Fiat Bambina she used to ferry herself to and from work and her various professional assignments. Joss called out to her,

"I see you've been summoned into the presence, too."

"If you mean Luke's reached an impasse and he's panicking again, yes."

Joss laughed. "Well, he did seem to be having a bit of trouble deciding whether his interview with Bob amounts to something or nothing."

"Probably both," Isabel sighed, "if it's like the rest of our dealings with him. Is it just me, or are you beginning to feel that for every step we take forward, we're slipping two back?"

"Yes, we do seem to be getting nowhere fast."

"Well, let's go and put Luke out of his misery, shall we?"

Joss fixed her with a sardonic eye. "I suppose there's a first time for everything," she said.

As soon as Luke saw them he stopped pacing and crossed to the coffee table to stub out the remains of his cigarette. Coffee pot and recorder stood there at the ready. "Thanks for coming over," he said, pouring coffee for each of them. "I've been trying to edit that wretched interview, but it's like trying to nail jelly to the wall."

Joss seated herself in her usual corner of the sofa and reached for a mug of coffee. "Apt analogy," she said. "Isabel and I were just saying we seem to be walking fast and getting nowhere. Every avenue we try seems to come to a dead end."

Isabel sipped her coffee thoughtfully. "What say we listen to the interview, and see if we can find a pattern? Or something, at any rate, that might give us some clue to what he's up to."

"Right," said Luke. "Though frankly, I wouldn't hold your breath." He switched on the recorder, and they all settled back.

* * * *

Luke emerged from the kitchen with a fresh pot of coffee and a plate of homemade biscuits.

"Well," he said, "tell me what you make of it."

"As I said, apt analogy." Joss took a biscuit and bit into it.

Isabel had been leaning back with her eyes closed, apparently lost in thought. She opened them now, and said, "Some of it has got to be true—you can tell from his voice." The others looked at her with interest. "I mean, that Dr Muller, the way he describes him, I doubt if he made that up. And the woman he went to San Francisco with—Susan. It's obvious from the way he talks about her that she was a very real person indeed. I'd say he really fancied her, too."

"You're right," Joss replied. "Come to think of it, it seems to me there's a feeling running through the whole interview of...well, I'm not sure what, really, but whatever it is, it makes me think there's a part of him that really does believe in what he's doing."

"Yes," said Isabel slowly. "Much as I hate to admit it, I think so, too. Yet at the same time, there's a hell of a lot of what he says that could be straight out of one of those tacky New Age books—you know, the ultimate secrets of life in seventy-five easy lessons channelled by Martian adepts through Wanda Crystalgazer during her pilgrimage through the mystic Andes—or what I did on my holidays."

"Isabel, you really should know better," said Joss. "Now look what you've done." She indicated the other end of the couch where Luke was helpless with laughter. Leaning over and patting him on the head, she murmured, "There, there, would you like a biscuit?" Luke composed himself with an effort and accepted her offer. "You're right, though," Joss continued, "and that's the nub of our whole problem with friend Bob, I think. Just about everything you can say about him, you can also say its opposite, and they're both likely to be true."

"And," said Luke, now returned to some semblance of normality, "we don't seem to be any closer to finding out what it is he's up to. It's damned frustrating. Tell you what, though, for what it's worth, although he had plenty to say in general, there was no way I could pin him down on when anything happened. And somehow, without my realising it at the time, he managed to manoeuvre me so I didn't even try. I can see it now, in retrospect, but at the time I just went along with him."

"Yes," Joss agreed, "I did think you weren't quite your usual pushy self." She ignored Luke's pained expression and went on, "He certainly does seem to be able to exert some sort of mesmeric influence."

Isabel had been absentmindedly tapping her teeth with her thumbnail, frowning in concentration. Now she unwrinkled her brow, rubbing it with her fingers as if to smooth it, and said, "You know what I think? I think Bob has some sort of fatal flaw to do with women, and I wouldn't mind betting it originally had something to do with his Scottish grandmother. Of course, we're not ever likely to find that out for sure, but I do think we could do a lot worse than concentrate on that angle."

"*Cherchez la femme*," murmured Luke with a knowing look.

"Oh, God, he's speaking in tongues again," said Joss with a theatrical sigh. "I suppose we'll have to do another exorcism now, and I haven't even got a book with me, let alone a bell or a candle. I wonder if we could make do with just strapping him down till he gets over it."

Isabel chuckled appreciatively, while Luke endeavoured to suppress his giggles enough to threaten Joss with a cushion. Joss merely regarded him with a look of exaggerated pity, then turned to Isabel and said, "Seriously though, I think you may be onto something there. I wonder what we can do about it?"

"Damned if I know right now. Something's starting to brew in my subconscious, though. I can feel it. I think what I need to do is let it simmer for a while until it rises to the surface."

Joss and Luke nodded. They were both by now familiar with the way Isabel's mind worked. Luke said, "In the meantime, we can get some feedback from the others after next week's programme."

"Are you sure you'll have the interview edited by then?"

Joss asked.

"Well, after talking with you two, I think it's futile to go looking for a specific angle, which is what I was trying to do. I'll just play it straight, so to speak. There's plenty in there to interest our listeners. After all, they aren't trying to work out what he's up to—at least, not the way we are."

Isabel said, "Don't you think we should say something to Anne about the interview before it goes to air?"

Luke nodded. "You're right. Given her experiences with Bob, she could find it pretty upsetting if she hears it cold. It could sound like we're ignoring her request for help. It's time I gave her a progress report, anyway. I'll give her a call tomorrow and let her know where we're up to."

"Meanwhile," said Isabel, getting to her feet, "I'm going home to do some subconscious simmering."

CHAPTER ELEVEN

"That's all from The Psychic Connection for this week. Tune in again next week at the same time for the second part of our interview with spiritual teacher and tarot reader, Bob Ferris, and more news and views from the world of the paranormal. Till then, goodnight from all of us here on The Psychic Connection." Luke pushed his hair out of his eyes, and several buttons on the control panel, and permitted himself a 'Thank God that's over' sigh. Reaching for his cigarette packet, he announced to the other panel members, "I don't know about you lot, but I need a coffee."

"Predictable as ever, Luke," said Joss, "but I have to agree with you. It's been a difficult week."

"More frustrating, wouldn't you say?" Isabel stood up and stretched her arms above her head to release tension.

James uncrossed his legs and straightened his tie. He turned to Isabel and said, "How did your visit to Bob's group go?"

"That's right, you haven't heard the recording, have you?"

Luke turned to them from the studio door and said, "If you lot would like to stop cluttering up my studio, we can listen to it in comfort."

They all trooped after him down the hallway.

As the recording came to an end, James straightened his tie once more. It was an unusually flamboyant one for him, and the fact seemed to bother him. From his accustomed perch on the piano stool it was clear he had been itching to say something for some time. "I know that girl's voice," he announced. "Anita. She's one of my second year psych students." All attention now focussed on him, James expanded almost visibly, a born lecturer in his element in front of a captive audience.

"Needless to say, I wouldn't normally give out background information on one of my students, but from what you've told me, the girl may be in danger, and I guess I can count on strict confidentiality from you all." They nodded. "Well, Anita Thorne has been in my psychology class for two years now. I guess I wouldn't know anything about her background myself if her personal problems hadn't affected her work. Last year she applied for an aegrotat pass, as she'd missed a whole bunch of lectures, and hadn't been able to complete half her essays. I think she'd missed a couple of tests, too, which were twenty percent of her total marks—that's on top of the forty percent for the essays."

Sensing impending waffle, Joss asked, "So what did you find out?"

James's smooth features assumed an air of mild affront. "Okay, I'll get to the point. The thing is, she's had a very difficult life—sexual abuse by her father as a child, followed some years later by his death in a car accident. I suspect he was an alcoholic, though she hasn't ever said so in as many words."

"Maybe she wasn't aware of it," said Isabel, her grey eyes full of compassion.

James nodded. "Maybe so. At any rate, she seems to have followed the classic pattern for abused children, demonstrating low self-esteem, periodic bouts of depression, and a marked tendency to fall for any man who showed an interest in her, bordering, I suspect, on promiscuity. She didn't say too much about any previous relationships, and naturally we didn't ask her to, but early last year she had an affair with one of her lecturers. Of course, it ended in disaster for Anita, and she had a breakdown. She spent much of the year in therapy and, not surprisingly, that affected her work. She's bright, though, very bright indeed, but extremely vulnerable. Especially, I would say, to the influence of older men."

"Like Bob?" Geraldine suggested.

"Exactly." James abandoned his attempts to subdue his tie and addressed himself to the remains of his coffee.

"Hah!" exclaimed Isabel, her eyes lighting up. "I knew it!" The others turned expectant faces towards her. She pushed a straying red curl off her forehead. "The other night at Bob's, I had a feeling Anita and Bob were up to something. Anita was nervous, and Bob seemed uncharacteristically distracted. No suggestive innuendo or anything—I felt quite insulted! But I'd lay odds that Anita is involved with Bob, or about to be. It was pretty obvious at the first meeting I went to that she was just dying for some 'personal tuition' from her adored guru. Remember I said as much when we listened to the recording?"

"Yes," said James gloomily, "I'm afraid that's all too likely. But unless she asks for help, there's very little anyone can do."

"Well," said Joss, "it's not much consolation, I know, but at least we seem to have another piece for the puzzle. Thank you, James." James inclined his head in a formal gesture of acknowledgement.

"You're welcome. But please remember, this is all in strictest confidence."

"Don't worry, James." Joss smiled. "We won't do anything to compromise your professional status."

* * * *

"The thing is—" Isabel played in an absentminded way with one of her curls, twisting it round her fingers in a habit formed in infancy and never abandoned "—we really don't seem to be much further ahead than when we started."

"I know." Joss's tone was glum. "We've gathered up quite a bit of information, one way and another, but it doesn't seem to be leading us anywhere."

They were sitting in the miniature conservatory Martin had built the previous summer onto the back of his and Joss's house. Usable space in their back yard was severely limited, what with the fern garden and the oak trees, and the miniature scale model of Stonehenge, but Joss had for years hankered after a conservatory, so Martin had finally given in and built her one for Christmas. On days like today it was a pleasure to gaze out on the garden without having to suffer the cold northeast wind blustering in from the sea and venting its spleen on the greenery.

"If only we could think of a way to find out what he's really up to."

"I'll tell you one thing," said Isabel, "I really don't fancy many more weekly doses of love and light from the likes of Nancy and co., much less Bob's grubby little mitts and his equally grubby innuendo—not unless it's going to turn up some information we can use."

Joss stared thoughtfully out of the window, her eyes following the cobbled path to where it vanished through a gap in the bushy hedge that partially hid 'Stonehenge' from view. There was something blue lying on the cobbles, and she couldn't quite make out what it was. In the same instant she realised the blue object was a ball left there either by one of the twins, or by the boxer cross, Spock, (so-called because of his lugubrious face and large, pointed ears), Isabel also seemed to come to a conclusion of her own. She straightened herself up in the cane armchair and relinquished her curl, which sprang instantly back to join its companions. "I was planning to wait until next year before applying for my martyr's halo," she announced cheerfully, "but I think I've just thought of a shortcut."

Joss laughed. "I hope it won't come to that. Besides, don't you have to be a saint to qualify for a halo? That can take centuries—look at poor Saint Joan. Still, we certainly need to find a way to speed things up. Bob seems to be so damned good at psychic invisibility that it could take us months to get anywhere, otherwise. So what's your idea?"

"You know how Geraldine's friend, and Anne, became private students. Well, why don't I become one, too?"

"Are you sure that's wise?"

"Frankly, no, I'm not. Though I'm sure I can handle Bob if I need to."

"Oh, I don't doubt that for a minute," Joss averred. During a period of boredom some years ago, she and Isabel had both taken up karate, and Isabel, with her inbuilt sense of co-ordination and timing, had proved to be a natural. She still practised it on a sporadic basis as a form of exercise, though she no longer attended classes. "However, I can't help wondering what it's going to achieve. I mean, first-hand evidence of his dubious activities is all very well, but I suspect you'd have to push him pretty far before we'd turn up anything we can take to the police and, if it gets to that stage, it could get pretty nasty for you."

Chewing thoughtfully on a strand of hair, Isabel considered this. Spock's rangy, brindled form appeared from the general direction of Stonehenge, peering moodily round a shrub. Noticing his ball, he pounced on it in an enthusiastic, if awkward, fashion and carried it off behind the garage, his ludicrous ears held high. The pantomime being now over, Isabel returned her attention to Joss. "It might not achieve anything," she said, "but unless someone can come up with a better idea, I think it's worth a try. I don't honestly think I'm in any physical danger from Bob, and I'm sure I can handle the rest."

Joss nodded. "I suppose so. I must say physical violence doesn't strike me as his style. How do you propose to persuade Bob to admit you to the inner circle?"

Isabel grinned. "I'll just have to dazzle him with my inner potential."

"I'm not sure I like the sound of that. And what about Anita?"

"Mmm, she could be a bit of a problem, though not from Bob's point of view, I suspect. Assuming that Anne, and Geraldine's client, may be only the tip of the iceberg, so to speak, it would seem Bob isn't precisely a one-woman man. Actually, I suspect he sees sex as a sort of teaching aid."

Joss's laugh was not entirely humorous. "Well, he would, wouldn't he, since he seems to be into tantric magic. The trouble is, he seems to have got his wires crossed somewhere along the way. I'd be careful if I were you. When do you plan to begin your campaign?"

"No time like the present," said Isabel, getting to her feet. "Tonight, as fate would have it, is Tuesday, and Tuesday is Circle night. Besides, I don't want to give myself time to lose my nerve."

CHAPTER TWELVE

When the telephone rang, Isabel was in the middle of dishing out cat food, attempting simultaneously to divide it into three even portions and to fend off Madame George and Bartholomew who, if his appetite was anything to go by, was now fully recovered. The strains of a tenor saxophone, snaking through the house like aural incense, stopped in mid-note, then Dominic's voice could be heard murmuring out in the hall. Isabel just had time to take the cat food out to the washhouse before his voice boomed, "Mother! It's for you," and the saxophone resumed. Hurriedly, she wiped her hands and went through to the hall.

"Georgina," said the voice at the other end of the line. Isabel took a deep breath.

"Oh, hello, Bob," she said. All last night at the Circle of Light meeting, she had dropped hints about wanting a way to gain further spiritual insight, and wondering how she might do this. Books, she had implied, were all very well, but how was she to know if she was on the right track without someone to guide her? And she did so want to go further! But, as the end of the evening arrived without Bob rising to her lure, she became convinced that he did not. Perhaps, however, she was wrong.

"I wanted to let you know, Georgina, that I've been most impressed with your progress so far."

"Why, thank you." Isabel tried to sound flattered. She

didn't need clairvoyance to know what was coming, and her heart sped up. Despite her recent bravado with Joss, she was only too aware that she could be letting herself in for a very unpleasant time. She didn't exactly anticipate danger, but the thought of having to fend off an over-enthusiastic Bob without the restraining influence of the rest of the group, and without jeopardising their enquiries, was not her idea of a fun evening. It wasn't so much a matter of whether she felt able to cope, as whether she wanted to.

"I feel you may now be ready," Bob went on, using his pompous guru voice, "to fulfil the potential I saw when I read the tarot for you." Isabel was momentarily stunned. She had not expected him to remember what he had told her several weeks ago. She barely remembered most of it herself.

"Oh," she remembered to gush, "do you really? That's wonderful!" She forced a wistful tone into her voice. "I just wish I knew how to go about it."

"Well, Georgina, I believe I can help you. You see, as well as my group, I also offer private tuition. I trained with several masters, you know, in Asia and North America, and I have been empowered to pass on what I have learned. Indeed, I believe it is my duty—my sacred duty—to do so; to play my part in completing the circle of light."

"That sounds wonderful!" Isabel repeated, swallowing involuntarily, as though to suppress her true feelings. "When can I start?"

"How would next Thursday evening suit you? I have a vacancy then at, say, eight o'clock?" Isabel made a pretence of pondering his offer. Now that 'private tuition' was becoming a reality, she was beginning to have qualms. Just think of England, she told herself, and made her reply, "That sounds fine." Her immediate realisation of the implications of the advice she had just given herself was hardly reassuring.

"Wonderful. I'll look forward to seeing you then, Georgina." Isabel cringed at the silken tone in Bob's voice. Still, she couldn't back out now. It might be their only chance to find out what was going on, and without that there was little chance of stopping him.

"Thank you so much, Bob. I'll see you on Thursday."

As she turned from the telephone, Dominic's head appeared in the doorway. "Who was that?" he asked, his long eyelashes fluttering in mock innocence. Isabel realised she had not heard his saxophone for some minutes.

"You've been listening!" she accused.

Dominic shrugged thin, elegant shoulders. "Well, I don't see how else I'm supposed to find out what's going on."

Isabel gave vent to a hollow laugh. "Point one," she parried, "you could try coming home more than once a week. And point two, what makes you think you're supposed to find out anything, anyway?"

A smile hovered fleetingly about Dominic's lips, then apparently he thought better of it. Large eyes the colour of treacle regarded her warily beneath brows whose depth of colour made the auburn of his long, thick hair seem artificial by comparison. It was not. However hard Dominic might work at his expression of post-Wildean cynicism, the pre-Raphaelite colouring was entirely his own.

"I'm always interested in your welfare, Mother dear," he ventured, almost managing to pull off a look of angelic innocence.

"A likely tale! Still," Isabel said, rubbing the side of her head thoughtfully, "it might be as well for you to know." She steered him into the kitchen and began to fill the kettle.

"The tea ceremony!" exclaimed Dominic. "It *must* be serious." He took two mugs from the dish-rack.

* * * *

The creak of the gate as it swung warily inwards sounded like a warning. Isabel felt the knot in her stomach tighten as she negotiated the overgrown path. Smelling lavender in the cool night air, she paused to pick a sprig, crushing it in her hands and holding it to her nose as she took several slow, deep breaths. Feeling calmer, she marched up to the front door and knocked before she had time to change her mind.

Speaking to Joss about her appointment, she had countered Joss's doubts by quoting from A Tale of Two Cities: "'Tis a far, far better thing I do...", and Joss had replied that she wasn't so sure that it was, actually. And, anyway, look what happened to Sidney Carton. To which Isabel could only say, if Joss could think of a better way to find out what they needed to know, would she please divulge it forthwith, because a date with Bob was not her idea of a good time. But in the meantime, at least she was doing something practical, and she was sure she could handle Bob if she needed to.

Now, standing on his doorstep, she was no longer quite so certain. However, before she had time to think of changing her mind, the door opened, and there stood Bob in a waft of incense and a white tunic with matching trousers, his massive citrine glinting at what Isabel imagined to be his heart chakra. The effect was reassuringly ludicrous. With a smile that attempted serenity, but produced instead a shark-like combination of self-satisfaction and voracity, he ushered her inside and led her through to the white sunroom.

With a gesture of his hand, Bob invited her to sit down, then left the room. The chairs had been removed from the room, but two fat cushions had been brought in from the front room and placed on the floor. Isabel sat down on one, then gazed about her, taking in the little room's altered ambience. On the coffee table under the window stood a brass candlestick in which two fat pink candles drenched the room in subtle, flickering light. In front of her stood another small, low table on which two sticks of incense poured forth a cloying fragrance that reminded Isabel of burning roses.

Bob soon returned, carrying the inevitable tea tray, which he set down on the floor, lowering his plump body onto the other cushion with surprising grace. Or amazing grace, Isabel caught herself thinking with what she recognised as impending hysteria. She took a deep breath, held it for a moment, then slowly released it.

"I thought we would begin with tea," Bob spoke for the first time, "so that I can explain what we'll be doing. And if you have any questions, I can answer them." He handed her a mug from which a delicious scent of cinnamon arose. Whatever else he might lack, he certainly made an excellent cup of tea. Isabel smiled and nodded.

Bob sipped his tea in silence. He seemed lost in thought. Then, suddenly, he leaned towards her, his shadow looming over her in the dim light. For a moment, Isabel thought he was going to grasp her hand or her shoulder, and she felt herself stiffen. Instead, he said, "There's no need to be nervous, you know. There really is nothing difficult about

any of this. It just takes practise, and a degree of dedication."
He smiled benignly at her, his eyes disappearing into his
chubby face. In the candle-glow his face reminded her of a
laughing Buddha, but the effect was not amusing.

Trying to sound more confident than she felt, Isabel
asked, "What exactly are we going to be doing?"

Bob placed his empty mug back on the tray. Isabel
expected him to light a cigarette, but he did not. "We'll
begin," he said, "with breathing. Yogic breathing. Self-
mastery begins with self-control. The first step to self-control
is control of the breath and, to control our breathing, we
must begin by being aware of the breath. Aware of each
breath as it enters the body, aware of it as it moves through
the body, and aware of it as it leaves the body." His voice had
taken on a slightly hypnotic quality. "And you must strive to
be aware of the quality of the breath, its feel, its texture—
everything about it. When you have achieved that, you can
gradually extend that awareness to all things, to encompass
both inner and outer space. The benefits of this are
enormous, as you can imagine."

"Oh, I can," Isabel lied. It all sounded pretty innocuous so
far, though she supposed that must be part of the plan.

"Well," said Bob, "if you've finished your tea, shall we
begin?" Isabel handed him her mug. Placing it back on the
tray, Bob activated a small CD player she had not noticed
before, and the strains of some soft, pleasantly vague
instrumental music seeped out.

Then, for what seemed like forever, Bob guided her
through breathing exercises she vaguely recognised as being
yogic in origin. As her crossed legs became more and more
uncomfortable, then began to go numb, she remembered the

two reasons she had resisted all attempts by Stephen, Dominic's father (a hippy of near-legendary status in his day, though he had gone on—or retrogressed, depending on one's viewpoint—to become a marketing consultant), to persuade her to become a regular practitioner of meditation. These were boredom, and physical discomfort, and both were evident now.

Just as boredom was beginning to give way to extreme irritation, Bob changed tack and introduced a visualisation exercise. "Now, focus your awareness on your heart chakra," he instructed as the background music faded slightly.

Aha, thought Isabel, a designer meditation CD. Focussing on anything aside from her numb legs and aching back was all but impossible, but Isabel did her best, reasoning that if she was going to carry off this little charade with any degree of credibility, she would have to try to follow Bob's programme, at least until he showed his true colours. With any luck, this would occur before she died of either boredom or gangrene.

"Imagine at your heart chakra," Bob intoned, to the gentle undulations of massed violins, "a ball of soft, rose pink light. See it pulsing, like a living thing." A pause to allow her to do this. "This ball of light is pure love. See it radiating out in all directions, growing and growing, sending love to all parts of the universe." Another pause. Years of reading tarot cards, allied with a strong visual sense to begin with, made this an easy, if somewhat pointless exercise for Isabel. She used the time trying to think of some appropriate response for the feedback Bob would no doubt require afterwards. "Now, slowly bring the light back into your heart, bringing with it the love of the universe."

As the CD came to an end, Isabel was surprised to find she actually did feel quite peaceful and relaxed. This came to an abrupt end, however, soon after she opened her eyes, as she attempted to move her legs. The pain was excruciating, as blood once more forced entry into her veins. She began to rub her calves, making the manoeuvre as obvious as possible in case Bob should feel inclined to offer to do it himself. Fortunately, he was busy with the CD player and, by the time he turned to her again, she was able to face him without a grimace of anguish.

"Perhaps we should stand for a few moments," Bob said, gliding to his feet with practised ease and reaching out a helping hand. "Subduing the body is almost always the most difficult part of meditation."

Fat chance of your subduing mine, mate, thought Isabel, as she dragged herself to her feet and began to walk about. One of the candles spluttered, sending golden waves dancing up the walls and across Bob's face. For a brief moment his face seemed to dissolve into something primitive, fashioned out of bronze, or old gold. A shiver ran up Isabel's spine and ruffled the hairs on the back of her neck before making its eerie way across her scalp. She pushed her hand through her hair as though to halt its progress, then blinked hard. She opened her eyes again, and Bob's face wore its usual expression, but somehow she could not quite rid herself of a lingering feeling of something not bland at all, but implacable.

"Now," Bob's practised smooth tone did little to dispel her misgivings, but Isabel forced herself to pay attention, and gradually the feeling subsided. "Now, Georgina, tell me about your meditation experience. Were you able to visualise the light?"

Have you seen the light? Isabel paraphrased to herself, suppressing a sub-hysterical desire to laugh. Aloud she replied, "Oh yes. I was able to visualise it quite clearly."

"Good. Good. Clearly, visualisation is one of your spiritual gifts."

Isabel nodded. She was not about to let Bob know that that particular ability had been well-honed by 20 years of studying and reading the tarot.

Having completed his tour of the room, Bob reseated himself and invited Isabel to do likewise by patting her cushion. She would have preferred to keep her distance by remaining standing but, since her role as Georgina, the avid acolyte, required it, she sat down again and waited, as though for her teacher's next pearl of wisdom. Bob smiled. "Is there anything you'd like to ask me?" Apparently it was question time.

Isabel thought for a moment. "The exercise was very interesting, but wasn't it just like what we've been doing at the group meetings?"

Bob placed one forefinger against his cheek, resting his chin on the remainder of his hand. Isabel found herself imagining him practising such gestures in front of a mirror. "Well," Bob's voice broke through the image, "yes and no. I do use the same basic technique with the group, for our absent healing. But here it was used in a much more controlled and focussed way, as I dare say you were aware." Isabel nodded, noticing yet again his way of appearing to assume she understood what he was doing. It lent a conspiratorial air to the proceedings, which must be hard for an innocent and devoted follower such as Anita, for example, to resist. "The aim is to develop awareness and control of the energies of the universe. And ultimately, of course, everything in the universe is composed of energy. Most of us fail to control it because we believe the energies within us are different from the energies around us. This exercise is designed, partially at least, to rid us of this delusion."

"Fascinating!" said Isabel. And it was, though perhaps not for quite the reasons Bob might imagine. She opened her eyes wide, and gazed at him. "But why are we supposed to try and control the universal energies?"

Bob smiled the smile of a fisherman who has just hooked a fish. "Well, of course no-one *has* to," he said, "but imagine what riches lie in store for the man—or woman—who can control and use the energies that gave rise to the magnificent abundance of this little planet we live on, let alone the greater universe. Oh, I don't mean just material wealth—" He dismissed such mere fripperies with a wave of his hand, his heavy rings flashing in the candlelight. "I'm talking about *real* wealth—the power to control one's life, to have all that one truly deserves, despite the best efforts of those who *think* they control the world." His eyes, pools of darkness with something alarming lurking in their depths, were turned on Isabel, but he was not seeing her. They were completely unfocussed. "This is the dawn of the New Aeon," he went on, his voice a harsh, fierce monotone. "The time has come for men of true wisdom and insight to take control..."

Bloody hell, this is real, Isabel realised, he's in trance! Determined not to panic, and knowing better than to touch him, or alarm him in any way, she silently got to her feet and blew out one of the candles. The change in light seemed to do the trick. Bob blinked several times, and his eyes became animated once more. He flicked his hands across his forehead as though to banish something, then, in his normal voice, continued as if nothing had happened. "So, Georgina, if you wish to attain these fruits of the path, practice the breathing and the visualisation as I showed you—say, fifteen minutes a day to start with—and next week I can show you the next step on the way." Apparently reading her thoughts, he continued, "I know it doesn't seem like much, but remember, the longest journey in the world begins with just one step."

Isabel smiled. "Thank you. I'd like to continue the journey."

"Wonderful!" Bob was beaming as he opened the door and led her out. "I'll see you next Thursday then, at the same time?"

"And on Tuesday night, of course," Isabel said, trying hard to keep the wariness out of her voice. By now they had reached the front door, and Bob stood in the doorway so that she had to brush past him to get outside.

"Of course," he oozed, grasping her hand as she edged past. He gripped it in both hands as though administering healing, his face unpleasantly close to hers as he assured her, "Of course, you realise that these *private* classes are *completely* confidential. No-one else knows about them, and nothing that is said or done will be passed on to anyone else."

That's what you think, Isabel thought as she smiled politely to mask a feeling in which she thought she recognised elements of distaste and misgiving. She started at a sudden loud creak from the gate. Bob hurriedly released her hand as a tiny, birdlike woman emerged from the

110

darkness and picked her way along the path making faint clucking noises in the back of her throat. She stopped when she saw Isabel, bobbing her head and peering at her myopically as though she were an intruder to be chased from the farmyard.

"Ah, Rhoda," Bob said with determined bonhomie. "How was your holiday? You haven't met Georgina, have you? She's just recently joined our group."

Rhoda gave her a polite, if frozen, smile.

Bob turned to Isabel and said, "Rhoda is one of the mainstays of the group. She handles our correspondence and publicity. I really couldn't manage without her at all." These calculated words and the microwave rays of his smile had the desired effect, and Rhoda thawed visibly.

Smiling politely once more, Isabel left them to it. As she closed the gate behind her, she felt like an escapee.

CHAPTER THIRTEEN

Joss was pouring coffee into three large mugs. In the Cherry household, everyone drank coffee from large mugs—almost constantly, it seemed to Isabel. The twins, by way of variation, drank milk or fruit juice out of large glasses. From the lounge came faint sounds from the television, broken at intervals by guffaws from Martin that were anything but faint. Spock lay half under Joss's kitchen table, snoring. Isabel found these tokens of everyday domesticity pleasantly reassuring. She stroked Spock's pointy ears and he sighed in his sleep. Then the chink of the coffee mug as Joss placed it beside her on the table made her jump. Coffee slopped over the side of the mug and onto the table.

"Sorry!" She leapt to her feet. "I'll get a cloth."

"Don't worry about it. It'll keep." Joss eyed Isabel with concern as she subsided into her chair and began once more to stroke Spock. "Are you all right?"

"Mmm, I think so. I'm not sure."

"Okay, I'll just take Martin's coffee through, then we can talk."

When Joss returned, she had a bottle of rum in her hand. "Kindly donated by Martin," she said as she sloshed a liberal amount into Isabel's coffee. "Well, I'm sure he would have, if I'd bothered to ask him."

"Thanks." With a weak smile, Isabel took a grateful swig and closed her eyes as the rum burned its way down to her stomach and spread its warmth through her.

"Now," said Joss, "do you want to tell me what's wrong?"

Isabel released a long, pent-up breath. "To tell you the truth, I'm not entirely sure. I've just come from my private session with Bob."

"He didn't try anything on, did he?"

"No, he didn't do anything, really," Isabel assured Joss, taken aback by her fierce tone, "except for holding my hand a bit too long when we said goodbye. God, it sounds like some old film, doesn't it?"

"Brief Encounter?"

"If only! It seemed more like From Here to Eternity." Isabel sipped her coffee. "You know, that's peculiarly apt," she said thoughtfully.

Joss picked up the bottle of rum. "Are you going to let me know what you're on about," she asked, "or do I have to pour the rest of this down your throat to loosen your tongue? Either that or thump you over the head with the bottle out of sheer exasperation!"

Isabel laughed. "Okay," she said, "I'll tell you what happened."

As she finished her account, Joss got up to refill the kettle. "I see what you mean about From Here to Eternity," she said. "It is appropriate, in a bizarre sort of way. And I can see why it made you feel peculiar."

"Yes," Isabel mused. "It was weird, as though he'd let some mask he's been wearing slip for a moment, and I got a glimpse of something quite different from the face he usually shows. Something I can't quite put my finger on but...well, let's just say I didn't much like the look of it."

"You don't suppose he arrived here in a pod?" enquired

Joss, straight-faced.

Isabel giggled. "It would explain a lot," she said. "But seriously, it does make me feel there's something quite strange going on in that convoluted little mind of his. You know what flashed through my mind at the time?" Joss shook her head. "Hitler. No, no, not literally," she hastened to add, seeing the look on Joss's face. "It's just that when he went into trance, or whatever it was, there was a quality to his voice quite different from the way he usually sounds. Something almost verging on the fanatical, and completely impersonal. That's why it was frightening, I think."

Joss said nothing for a few moments, but busied herself making more coffee. She took a packet of biscuits from a shelf and placed them on the table. When they were both sipping their coffee and munching on gingernuts, she spoke. "I was thinking more Aleister Crowley."

"Funny how he keeps cropping up," Isabel commented. "But you don't really think Bob belongs in such exalted company, do you? If exalted is the word."

"I doubt it. But then, who knows whether Crowley belonged there either. I mean, he thought he was a poet, too. Who knows if there ever really was any such 'company', come to that. Still, it's not inconceivable that Bob sees himself as some a sort of latter-day Crowley. That mention of the New Aeon was a bit of a giveaway, don't you think? Crowley was always going on about that."

Isabel took another gingernut and dunked it in her coffee. "It seems obvious he's got *some* sort of hidden agenda."

"Mmm. And it may well be hidden, even from himself."

"True, because when he 'came to' again, he just sort of flicked his hands across his face as though he'd dozed off for a minute, and seemed quite unaware of what had been happening."

"Either that, or he was acting rather well," said Joss. "Funny how that keeps cropping up, too. Though, in fact, I suspect it's a bit of both. From what you've found out, and from what the man himself told Luke, I think we can assume he has an active interest in ritual magic, and that in itself suggests some sort of dramatic flair. What I'd like to know is why? What's it all in aid of—apart from generating a source of female admirers?"

Isabel looked up, with a cynical laugh, from contemplating the depths of her coffee mug.

"You mean like Rhoda, the bird-woman?" she said. "No, he may fancy himself as God's gift to the female of the species, but I don't believe that's all there is to it. As I said before, I think he has some sort of hidden agenda, and if we can find out what that is, we'll be starting to get somewhere."

"And I suppose," said Joss severely, "that involves you going to more of these 'private classes'?"

Isabel shrugged. "Can you think of a better way?"

"Unfortunately, no. But honestly, Isabel, dealing with some New Age con man is one thing, but it sounds as though what happened tonight is in a different league entirely. We need to find out what he's really up to, but there *must* be something else we can do." She pushed her hands through her thick, blonde fringe, and screwed up her eyes in frustration.

"Well," said Isabel slowly, "we could always try using our psychic abilities."

Joss raised her head and regarded Isabel with the air of one attaining sudden enlightenment. "Of course!" she exclaimed. "After all, that's what this is all about, isn't it? Why don't we try a combined tarot and clairvoyance reading, like we did for Luke when that religious nutter was sending him threatening letters?"

"Yes, okay. It worked then," Isabel replied. "We managed to find out what it was he was really after, and to persuade him to get help. Not," she added, "that I expect dear Bob to admit needing help."

"No." Joss's laugh was without humour. "Unless it's the sort supplied by some 'tantric' partner. Still, if we can just get a decent lead to follow up... When do you want to try it?"

"Not tomorrow," said Isabel. I've got three clients in a row, and I reckon I'll be completely taroted-out by the time I've finished with them. Then I've got Bob's group in the evening. Wednesday afternoon we're recording at Luke's, and I intend to spend Wednesday evening doing something totally mindless, like watching a Doris Day film on the DVD player. I've got a bottle of semi-decent scotch stashed away for that very purpose, in a place even Dominic wouldn't think of looking."

Joss laughed. "That's okay. The only night this week I'm not working is Thursday, and Martin and I are going to the girls' school music performance. They're part of an all-girl rock band—The Tall Poppies. They're most of the rhythm section: Rachel on bass, and Kate on rhythm guitar and backing vocals. To tell you the truth, I'm rather looking forward to it."

"So it looks like Saturday might be our best bet then," said Isabel.

"Yes, that sounds good. Kate and Rachel are apparently having a post-performance debriefing—or bitch session—at

Poppy's place. She's their namesake and lead singer. And Martin, weather permitting, will be outside pruning the roses, so we should have a clear run."

"Phew! And you say *I* lead a full life! What time shall I come over?"

"Come for lunch if you like, say, around one?"

"Right. One o'clock it is, then."

* * * *

"See you later, Mum."

Without waiting for a response, Kate and Rachel dashed down the path and out the gate, slinging their instruments over their shoulders as they went. Martin appeared at the back door, pulling on a pair of strong gardening gloves. "I've cleared the table," he announced, "and put the kettle on for you. So I'll leave you to it."

Joss smiled warmly at him. "Thanks, dear." She turned to Isabel. "I think we could use another coffee to fortify ourselves before we begin, don't you?" Isabel nodded, and they returned to the dining room, which lay basking in the early afternoon sun, as did Spock, stretched out on the gold tiles of the patio on the other side of the french doors.

Isabel pulled her deck of cards out of her bag, sat down at the dining table, and spread the large cards out face down in front of her, moving them about with her hands to mix them thoroughly. Then she began to pick them up again one by one at random, until they were all in one stack again. As Joss brought the coffee over, she placed the deck back on the table, ready to be shuffled when they began the reading. They drank their coffee slowly and in silence, both trying to

117

tune in to one another for their joint effort, as well as focussing on their pre-arranged aim, to discover the true purpose of Bob's teaching.

Joss quietly moved the coffee mugs aside as Isabel picked up the cards. She sifted through them for a few moments, finally picking out a card and laying it face upwards in front of her. "I thought this would best represent Bob, under the circumstances," she said. It was the Magician. She shuffled the cards and began to lay them out.

With a glance at Joss, who was gazing at the cards through half-closed eyes, intent, yet calm, Isabel began. "This must be the group," she said. "See, here's the Seven of Wands covering him, that's teaching and learning, or opposition that leads to learning. And the card crossing it is the Moon—things hidden, or deception. Oh, that's odd. Underlying everything is the Three of Swords, sorrow and loss. And there's a woman in the past—the Queen of Cups. That's someone loving and sensual, possibly psychic. I wonder if it's his grandmother?"

"Someone younger, I think," Joss murmured. "No, it could be an older woman—or both? It's a bit confusing."

"Well, in the realm of possibilities there's the High Priestess, then in the future, the Devil. Looks like he's going to have something heavy to deal with. What do you make of it, Joss?"

Joss shook her head slowly. "Nothing," she said. "No, really, after the Queen of Cups, it's all gone blank, like a door being suddenly slammed shut."

"Okay. Well, in the realm of the self, there's the Hierophant, so it seems he sees himself as a spiritual leader, and perpetuator of some spiritual tradition. I suppose we already knew that. So what about influences from his environment? Ah, the King of Swords. Could be legal problems, illness, or worries of some sort."

"With any luck," said Joss.

Isabel grinned. "Well, it's not what he's hoping for, at any rate. Look at that, the World. He doesn't want much, does he? And the outcome is the Fool, a new pathway, or a beginning. You know, I can't make a hell of a lot out of it either. For some reason, it's extraordinarily difficult to read. I know there are things there, but I can't make out what they are."

"Me too," admitted Joss.

"Let's try another layout, shall we?" Isabel suggested, gathering the cards together. "Sometimes a reading just seems to go haywire, and you have to start again."

They were about to begin their third layout when Martin's bearded head appeared round the dining room door. "How's it going?" he asked.

"Don't ask," Joss responded gloomily. "It isn't. There are things there, but neither of us can make any sense of them."

Martin came into the room, pulling off his gardening gloves and stuffing them into the pocket of his elderly parka. He ran a hand through his already tousled hair. "Maybe you're both too personally involved."

"Mmm, perhaps you're right. But what else can we do?"

"Have you thought of trying Tarot?"

Joss picked up her coffee mug and regarded it speculatively. She looked at Isabel. "Shall I throw this at him, or would you like first shot?"

Martin raised his hands as though to defend himself. "No, I mean Tarot." Joss looked blank. "You know, Terry Ryder-

White."

"Oh, *that* Tarot!" Now Isabel looked blank. Joss explained, "Terry Ryder-White, known as Tarot, is an old university friend of Martin's. In fact, it was due to him that Martin and I met. He was living in this sort of horse-drawn housetruck, and one night when he was staying at Martin's place after a party, it got stolen."

"Stolen?" Isabel looked incredulous. "How could someone steal a horse-drawn housetruck for God's sake?"

"Hitched it up to the back of a Bedford truck and just drove it away," Martin laughed.

"So how did you get involved?" Isabel asked Joss.

"I was a cub reporter on the *Star*," said Joss. "It was my first big story. Well, a step up from covering school drama productions and Women's Institute meetings, anyway. And who should I meet but this tall, dark and handsome English graduate, complete with beard, shoulder-length hair and embroidered waistcoat. Yummy!"

"And did Tarot get his housetruck back? Why's he called Tarot, anyway?"

"Yes to your first question," said Joss. "He had a pretty fair idea who did it, anyway—this crazy character he'd met in the pub who fancied having it for himself."

"Yes," said Martin, "that's where the Bedford came in. He towed it out to this bit of land his friend had, out near West Melton, and he was going to remodel it to fit on the back of his truck, then take off to the West Coast to live in some drug-crazed commune. Tarot and I and a couple of other friends took off out there to get it back. And, of course, Joss came along to cover the story for her paper."

"Nothing to do with 'tall, dark and handsome,' of course,"

teased Isabel.

"Actually," grinned Martin, putting his arm round Joss's shoulder and giving her a squeeze, "it was more to do with 'five foot two, eyes of blue'. I figured the best way to get to know her was to give her the chance of a good human-interest story for her paper."

"Not to mention an hour or so in the back seat of a car with her," said Isabel. "Plenty of 'human interest' there, I imagine."

"Who told you about that?" asked Joss in mock indignation.

"I must be psychic. Anyway, what about Tarot?"

"Oh, well," said Joss, "like every second tarot reader, it seems, he learned to read playing cards first—from an aunt, I think. Then when tarot cards became all the go, and everyone who was anyone was buying a deck 'for meditation purposes'..."

"Like drinking brandy 'for medicinal purposes'," grinned Martin, "or reading Playboy 'for the articles'."

Joss laughed. "Anyway, Tarot thought it was about time he graduated from playing cards. So he bought a tarot deck, and of course it was the Rider-Waite deck, as it invariably was, back then, and it wasn't long before all his friends had made the connection, and he's been Tarot ever since." She turned to Martin. "What's he up to these days, anyway? Not still living in the housetruck, surely?"

"No. He still has it, actually, though the Clydesdale had to be sold when he moved back to his mother's place. Poor old dear has Alzheimer's, and he looks after her. He also runs a printing business from a couple of spare rooms."

"Does he still do tarot readings?"

"Yes. I ran into him in town the other day, fortuitously enough. He was saying he listens to The Psychic Connection from time to time, and he's heard you doing your thing, Joss. He was quite impressed."

"Well," said Joss, brushing aside the compliment, "if he's as good as he used to be, he's certainly well worth a try. Martin could be right. Perhaps we are too emotionally involved to get a clear reading."

"Well, something's certainly blocking us," Isabel said. "Would he be at home now, do you think?"

"He's home most of the time these days," Martin replied. "I'll give him a call, and see if we can go over there tomorrow." He flashed Joss a smile from the doorway. "Put the kettle on, will you, me old dear. That there rose pruning be thirsty work."

CHAPTER FOURTEEN

"My God! Is this a home or a prison?" Isabel gazed up at eight-foot sagging brick walls topped with wrought-iron, rust-encrusted spikes. These and the heavy, oppressive embrace of ivy seemed to be all that kept the walls from collapsing, yet the effect was dramatic, if a trifle jaded.

"Wait till you see the house," said Martin, and dragged open the heavy hurricane netting that was not too convincingly pretending to be a gate. As he pulled it to again and fastened it behind them, Isabel and Joss stared through the shaggy screen of vastly overgrown oak, elm and chestnut trees which flanked a weed-infested gravel driveway. The house, like some vast, shabby-genteel matron, stared back in defiance. Its brick frontage was dominated by an improbable Romanesque portico whose chipped concrete pillars guarded an entrance-way as large as a room, atop a dozen wide, curving steps held together by a low stone wall on either side. These ended in two square concrete tubs in which a duo of stunted cypress trees languished. Taciturn brick towers slouched, glowering, at each end of the house, their conical grey tile roofs topped by wrought-iron dragons which might once have been painted green. The one on the right was missing most of its head. A row of iron spikes, miniatures of those on the fence, stood guard across the top of the main roof. The effect of the whole was decidedly less than the sum of its parts, like someone who can afford expensive, stylish clothes, but has a complete lack of dress sense.

"I see what you mean," breathed Joss at last. "It's a bit of a change from a housetruck!"

"Yeah," said Martin. "I believe it's been in the family since last century. Tarot's great-grandfather built it as a combination home and consulting rooms. He was a wealthy specialist of some kind."

"Is there any other kind?" muttered Joss.

"I fear you're becoming cynical in your old age," Martin responded.

"Smile when you say that, stranger," Joss drawled with mock menace, but Martin had already dodged the arm she swung playfully at him.

They crunched their way up the drive, arriving at last at the double front doors. These had fairly recently been painted black, but the original dull green showed through in places where the paint had begun to peel. In the centre of the door was a great brass knocker shaped like the head of a dragon. As Martin reached out to lift it, the door slid open to reveal a tall, thin, angular man of around forty, with wiry, greying hair, once ginger, a shaggy beard, and a great beak of a nose. Pale, sea-green eyes looked out at them from under unruly eyebrows, and a lopsided grin added further creases to a long, lived-in face whose wide brow tapering to a pointed chin suggested Celtic ancestry. Long, thin fingers stained with ink curled like talons around the edge of the door.

"Martin! Great to see you, man! And you, Joss." He hugged Martin and Joss warmly and held out his hand to Isabel. "Terence Ryder-White—Terry," he declared in a mellow, educated voice that seemed at odds with his weather-worn face and aged corduroy trousers. Though his checked shirt was viyella, and would once have been expensive, Isabel noticed as she shook his hand and introduced herself. So would the brown tweed sports jacket, its elbows bearing shiny suede patches, and its lapels a quantity of badges, the largest of which proclaimed, 'Religion is Man's Attempt to Communicate With the Weather'.

"Lovely to meet you." His grin spread to embrace them all. "Come on in. The kettle's on the hob. Or, if you prefer it, I've a brew of cider just dying to be sampled."

Joss smiled. "From what I remember of your cider, Terry, that sounds like an offer I can't refuse."

Within minutes, they had passed through the vast, dark, panelled hallway with its worn Persian rugs, and were seated around a heavy refectory table in the large but cosy kitchen. An earthenware flagon stood before them, surrounded by a clutch of pottery beakers. Terry, as he explained he now preferred to be called, opened the door of the enamel coal range behind them and a warm, delicious smell filled the room.

"Pumpkin scones," Terry declared, swiftly transferring them to a large blue platter.

"Remember this?" he asked Martin as he placed it next to the cider flagon, together with a dish of butter and a knife.

"The plate? How could I forget?" Martin turned to Joss and Isabel. "Eleanor Ross," he explained, "witch and potter extraordinaire. Took young Terry home from a party one night and stayed for the best part of two years. Not that I ever heard him complain, mind you. Built her a couple of kilns, and she was in business. That plate was part of her first successful firing." He turned to Terry, who was busy pouring cider into four beakers. "What happened to Eleanor?"

"She moved on," said Terry, a wistful expression softening his features. "You know her. Free spirit and all that. I did see her once, at an art show. She was about to leave for Britain, to study Celtic magic and have a look at the sacred sites there, she said. That must be about ten years ago now. I suppose she must have stayed over there. I haven't seen any of her work exhibited here since. Probably met some English bloke."

He placed brimming beakers in front of them. "Right, see what you think of this and I'll go and find my cards."

He returned carrying a rectangular package wrapped in dark blue silk. As he unwrapped the cards and spread the silk on the table, the others saw it was embroidered round the edges in silver with the signs of the zodiac and symbols of the planets. Noticing Isabel's interest, Terry said, with the merest hint of sadness, "Lovely, isn't it? Another of Eleanor's works of art."

"Yes, it is lovely," Isabel agreed. "Oh, I see you use the Golden Dawn deck."

"Mmm, I like the Celtic style of the art work. Mind you, if I had enough artistic talent I would have designed my own." He was shuffling the deck, his big, bony hands easily managing the large cards.

"This cider's even better than I remember it," Joss said. "Did Martin mention what our visit is all about?"

"No, apart from your needing some insight from an unbiased source. But I'd prefer not to know, at least until I've done an initial layout. Do you want to take notes?"

Joss fished in her bag and brought out a small voice

recorder. "Borrowed it from work," she said, placing it on the table.

"Right," said Terry. He put the deck of cards on the centre of the blue cloth, took a long draught of cider and beamed at them. "Are you all sitting comfortably? Then I'll begin."

He picked up the deck with a flourish, and rapidly laid out eight cards, one upright at the centre, another crossing it, then three in a row beneath and three above. "This is just to get an idea of the basic situation," he explained, surveying the cards with his pale eyes half-closed. He sat there immobile for what seemed an age. Isabel, resisting with difficulty the temptation to try and interpret the layout, noticed that the centre card was Justice, and the card crossing it, the Magician. Underneath these two lay, from left to right, the Queen of Cups, the Nine of Swords and the Eight of Cups. Above them were the King of Swords, the Devil and the Tower. Fortunately for Isabel's battle with temptation, Terry began to speak.

"Okay, Justice here is you lot, now. You're trying to right a wrong, or put things in their proper perspective. Something like that. No." He waved his hand at Joss, who was about to speak. "Don't say anything yet. It might interfere with the vibes. Now, the Magician is someone who's getting in your way, or somehow interfering with the workings of Justice. Hmm." He closed his eyes and fell into silence for another apparent eternity.

Joss nearly choked on her cider when Terry suddenly sat bolt upright, his eyes still closed, and said, "This man lived in the desert. Now he lives in a desert of the soul. He wants to get back to Eden, but Eve is gone. No-one else can take her place, and he has forfeited his place in the garden." His eyes

127

opened. "I don't know if that means anything to you." He grinned.

"I don't suppose you can see what he looks like?" asked Joss. "I'll just consult the old inner vision," said Terry, downing a hefty swig of cider, as if that might help. "I can't get anything very clear at this stage, but I'd say he's pretty nondescript for a magician. Or maybe he's one of those people who just sort of blend in with the scenery, like a camouflage. One of the manifestations of the Magician is the Trickster—he's ruled by Mercury, you know. Anyway, on with the story. These three underneath are sort of the background to the situation, or things which have influenced it. The Queen of Cups is, or was, a woman—a young woman. A beautiful spirit, but not strong. I get the feeling of a short life, far too short, and filled with sadness. She never had any control, poor soul." He shuddered, and shook himself slightly as though to banish what he was feeling. "Now, the Nine of Swords here—that's often depression or illness."

"Or death," murmured Isabel.

Terry nodded. "Or all of the above," he said with a sigh. "At the risk of sounding morbid, I'd say that's about the size of it. Then, as a result of all that, we have the Eight of Cups, leaving behind emotional attachments and starting down a new pathway."

"Does that refer to the Queen of Cups?" asked Isabel.

Her suspicions were confirmed when Terry replied, "I don't think so. In fact, I'd practically swear she never survived to go anywhere. So I guess that leaves the Magician."

"Whoever he is," muttered Martin. He looked about to say more, but Joss nudged him with her elbow, and shook her head in warning when he seemed about to remonstrate with her.

Terry continued, "Now, these three above show what may come of the present situation. Oh, look." He pointed at the King of Swords. "There's Mr Plod."

Martin stifled a snort of laughter, and Joss flashed another warning look. Isabel said, "It could be a doctor or a lawyer, though, couldn't it?"

"Could be, but it isn't! That gentleman is definitely a member of the constabulary, though he's not entirely what you might think." Joss opened her mouth to speak, but Terry forestalled her with a shrug. "It's no use asking me what I mean," he grinned. "I haven't the remotest idea what I'm talking about. But I do know there'll be a copper on the case in the not too distant future."

"So, what about the Devil?" Martin ventured.

"Oh, he's a very complex fellow, and he's rarely, if ever, what you think. In this case, I'd say he represents Nemesis, Kismet; someone's karma running over his dogma—I saw that written on a wall in Manchester, of all places—and the result—" He pointed at the Tower "—is that the whole house of cards comes tumbling down, along with anyone who's in it at the time." He pushed his beaker across the table and turned to Martin. "More cider, please, Squire."

While Martin refilled all their beakers, Isabel asked, "Can you tell us more about the Devil? What exactly did you mean by 'Nemesis'?"

Terry rubbed his beard thoughtfully, replying at last, "What it feels like is that it all has to do with the Magician. He's the one this reading is really about, I think. It seems a lot of past actions are about to come home to roost for him, and it'll end with some kind of showdown, possibly both literally and figuratively."

"Hmm." Isabel sipped the cider Martin had passed her, and reached for another scone. "So what we need to find out, if we can, is some more about the Magician."

"No problem!" Terry gathered up the cards. Placing the Magician card at the centre of the silk cloth, he shuffled the rest and laid out twelve this time, in a circle around the Magician. "Each of these," he explained, "represents a year in his life, starting now, and going back twelve years. They can also be the months of the past year. I can read them both ways if you like."

The others nodded, and Terry downed the last of his cider and began to read.

* * * *

The setting sun clutched with dazzling fingers at the kitchen windowsill in a last-ditch effort to delay the inevitable. Terry glanced at the clock. "Christ!" he exclaimed, jumping up. "Is that the time? Mother will be wanting her dinner soon. We eat quite early, you see, then I usually watch television with her or play cards or scrabble till she goes to sleep. We're playing euchre tonight." He lifted a large pot onto the electric stove that stood beside the coal range, and turned on the element, then refilled the kettle and put that on to boil. As if to verify his earlier statement, a bell rang from somewhere above them.

"Ah," said Terry with an apologetic smile, "I was going to offer you a cup of tea, but that's Mother. I'll have to go. She gets upset if she thinks I'm not here."

"That's okay." Joss smiled. "Martin and I have to go, too. The twins will no doubt be dying of hunger by now. They'll be down on the kitchen like a plague of locusts if we don't go and stop them."

Terry turned to them from washing out the teapot in the great enamel sink. "Well, look, now that we've caught up with each other, come and visit again, soon. And leave me your phone number and address. I do manage to get out sometimes. Lovely to have met you, Isabel. I'd love to talk tarot with you properly sometime."

Isabel nodded, smiling. "So would I."

"And I meant it, too," she said to Joss as they scrunched back down the driveway. "Quite apart from being a dynamite tarot reader, he seems like a real sweetie."

"He is. Even in his wilder days, he was one of nature's gentlemen—in both senses of the term. Got a real Irish taste for booze, too."

"What did you make of the reading, then?" Martin asked, opening the car door.

"There's far too much of it to tell, at this stage." Joss reached back to unlock the back door for Isabel. She patted her pocket where the recorder lay. "We've got an hour and a half of tarot reading here and, for what it's worth, my thumbs were pricking all the way through it. There's no doubt in my mind that the Magician is our man Bob."

"I agree," said Isabel, "though I'd like more time to let it all sink in before we go over it in detail. We'll have to tell Luke and the others, so how about we play it to them after we record the show on Wednesday? Look, can I borrow it until then? I've got another session with Bob on Thursday night and, who knows, something else may click into place there."

Joss's face wrinkled with distaste as she handed the recorder to Isabel. "Just you make sure it isn't Bob," she said.

CHAPTER FIFTEEN

Isabel pressed the digital recorder's Off switch. There was a moment's silence while they all reflected on what they had just heard. Luke was the first to speak. "Reading between the lines," he said, stubbing out his cigarette and pouring himself more coffee, "and allowing for a fair amount of symbolism, I'd say it pretty much ties in with what Bob himself told me when I interviewed him."

Geraldine leaned forward and took another afghan biscuit. "So we can assume we're dealing with a man who, following strong, early influence by an older woman—presumably his grandmother—and after travel, and study of religion and the occult, and a disastrous involvement of some kind with a younger woman, now sees himself as some sort of magician and teacher heralding a new spiritual era. These biscuits are divine, by the way, Luke." Luke bowed as gracefully as he could from the depths of his armchair, and leaned forward to pick up the plate and pass it round.

James declined a biscuit, instead sipping his coffee with an air of ponderous deliberation. "What interests me," he said, "is the Devil."

"And to think," Joss said with a sigh, "they allow you to influence young minds."

James glared while pretending to ignore her. "The Devil," he continued, "seems to represent some sort of inevitable outcome of his past actions—the working out of karma, if you

133

like. And, if I remember rightly, this is still to come."

"Yes," said Luke. "In the near future. That seems to be where the policeman comes in. Your friend was quite insistent on that, wasn't he?"

"Yes," Joss replied, "then comes the Tower, with the Ten of Pentacles right next to it. Didn't you say that's to do with building a house or something, Isabel?"

"It can be, yes. But it can also be setting up a home, founding a family, anything like that. Mind you, I seem to remember the Knight of Wands was lurking there too, and, unless he represents a person, he almost invariably means moving house."

Joss refilled her coffee mug then sat back on the couch, her fair hair swinging. "Terry seemed to relate that to the Tower. He said it was metaphorical, as well as being an actual place, and that in the end it would all come tumbling down."

James stood up, smoothing his navy blue suit. It seemed he had abandoned his brief flirtation with flamboyance. Today he was wearing a maroon tie bearing what was presumably the heraldic device of his *alma mater*. "I'm afraid I have to go now," he said, "I have a lecture in less than an hour. You'll keep me in touch, won't you?"

Luke nodded. "I think, though" he said, "I'll have to turf you all out soon. I have to go and talk to a psychic artist who's just hit town."

"Going to show you his etchings, is he?" said Joss with an exaggerated leer.

Luke smoothed his hair back with one hand in a preening gesture and donned a wounded look. "Actually," he replied, "*she's* a woman, so I wouldn't be at all surprised if she does."

"I trust you enjoyed your little holiday, gentlemen." The Chief Inspector's solemn eyes refused to collaborate with the smile that played about his thin lips.

"Some of the scenery was pretty spectacular," Derek said, dead-pan. "Isn't that right, Sergeant Kelly?"

"You could say that, sir," Declan answered, looking Derek straight in the eye. Derek's expression was, thankfully, reassuring.

"Good," Vodanovich's tone was now business-like. His dark head nodded briskly between the two office towers framed in the 'Magritte' window, reminding Declan of one of those articulated Victorian dolls sometimes still seen in antique shops. The Chief Inspector looked down at the papers on his desk for a moment, then up at Derek. "You're right," he said, "we are going to have to check the drug rehabilitation centres. We can get someone up in Cairns to do the preliminary work, then you can contact people as necessary. Though, frankly, I agree with you it's highly unlikely the girl was ever taken to Cairns. Still, we'll have to go through the motions." He smiled a thin, arid smile.

"Yes, sir," Derek said, "and I'd like to spend some time going through the forensic reports more thoroughly. There might be something there that will help us."

Vodanovich nodded again. "And someone," he stated, "will have to go over to New Zealand and follow up the movements of this Richard Forster. It seems he flew out from Brisbane two days after the girl disappeared, on a flight to Auckland. Apparently he worked for a time at a nightclub there—the, um, Big Apple." The Chief Inspector's voice cringed in distaste. "He appears to have left there rather suddenly a year or two later. The last record we can find of him is a couple of years later on the Coromandel Peninsula, not far from Coromandel town itself. It seems he was involved in some kind of commune there."

Surprise, surprise, thought Declan.

"I take it the New Zealand Police will be in on the act?" Derek asked.

"Oh, yes, we've already contacted them through Interpol. But we're going to need to send someone over there who's familiar with the background of the case from our perspective." He turned to Declan, his smile taking on an ominous aspect. "Sergeant Kelly, you're a lucky man. Not one holiday, but two, and it isn't even Christmas yet. You'll be leaving first thing on Monday, so you'll have the weekend to do your homework. We don't want the New Zealand C.I.B. thinking we're a bunch of incompetents, do we?"

"No, sir."

"You don't sound very enthusiastic, Sergeant Kelly," Vodanovich observed.

"Just tired, sir."

"Well, you'll have to have an early night tonight then, won't you?" Vodanovich beamed at him with jovial malice. "Meanwhile, you'd better have a good look at these." He handed Declan the files with one hand, pushing the forensic reports in Derek's general direction with the other.

As they made their way back down the corridor, Derek turned to Declan, his pale eyes glinting. "What's the matter, Dekko, don't you fancy a trip to New Zealand? Rather go and have another chat with Miriam Golden, would you?" The expression on Declan's face was gratifying, and he laughed, though not without good humour.

Declan, suddenly resigned to his fate, grinned back at him. "Well, at least I might get some decent weather for a change," he said.

* * * *

"Care for a sherry before dinner, ma'am?" Martin held the bottle up to the light, savouring its pale amber glow.

"Luxury! No twins, a night off, *and* sherry! All on a Monday night, too!" Joss exclaimed, curling up beside him on the couch as Martin poured two glasses of Amontillado.

"Well, it's a luxury not having the twins here, that's for sure, and, as fate would have it, I don't have to be at school tomorrow until third period, either. My lot are being taken on some sort of supposed cultural outing—though I can't imagine it having much of an impact on most of them." Martin handed Joss a glass. "How many of these do you think we can get through before that Chinese chicken dinner arrives?"

Joss smiled and kissed him on the cheek. "At least three I hope," she murmured. "I need *something* after the week I've had! Oh, can you turn the television on, love, we're missing the news."

"...and finally, Australian police have released further information about the body found recently in Queensland. It has been identified as that of Claire Lomax, a New Zealander who disappeared ten years ago, while living at a cult commune inland from Cairns. Police would like to speak to her former companion, Richard Forster, also from New

Zealand, who is believed to have been the last person to see her alive. He was last known living on the Coromandel Peninsula near Amodeo Bay, where he ran a cult group similar to the Australian commune. Police expect to be able to release a description soon, after a Queensland Police officer arrives in the country. And now, here's Jenny with the latest weather update..."

Martin muted the television and turned to Joss. "That's interesting. Have you come across anything about it at work?"

"They don't seem to have thought it worth running so far. Still, I expect that'll change now it's come a bit closer to home. I wonder what became of Richard Forster?"

"Not still running his little cult, anyway, presumably. There's a lot of it about, isn't there? I mean, look at your friend Bob, for example."

"Whatever Bob may be," Joss poured a second sherry for herself and Martin, "he is *not* my friend. In fact, I'd be surprised if he's anybody's."

"Oh, I don't know. What about that bird woman you and Isabel were on about?"

"You mean Rhoda? No, if she's in love with anything, it's the idea of the guru, not with Bob himself—if you can call that love. Same with Anita, poor kid. If you'd ever actually met Bob, you'd realise how extremely unlikely it is that anyone could love him for himself."

"Unlike you." Martin smiled, sliding his left arm round Joss and pulling her close. Putting his own glass down, he removed Joss's from her hand and placed it beside his. With his right hand he began to caress her neck beneath her hair, smoothing away the tensions of the week. Joss could feel herself relaxing, melting like wax under Martin's warm hands.

The doorbell shrilled. "Damn! That'll be our meal." Martin kissed her, and reluctantly levered himself off the couch.

Joss could not resist saying, "Saved by the bell!" as he headed for the door.

Martin turned as the doorbell rang once more. "That's what you think!"

* * * *

The remains of the chicken dinner lay unheeded on the coffee table beside the sherry glasses. On the television screen, a British police officer and an unkempt youth mouthed silent antagonism at each other across a table in an interview room that appeared to have been modelled out of plywood and plastic. Martin, one hand buried in the blonde silk of Joss's hair, the other stroking her thigh, lifted his mouth slightly from hers.

Taking advantage of the pause in proceedings, Joss murmured, "I propose we slip into something more comfortable—like bed," and to emphasise her point, she moved her one free leg and pushed her bare foot under his jersey, moving it slowly down his back. Martin pressed closer to her and kissed her again. "I second that," he replied, his voice suddenly throaty.

The sound of the doorbell thrust them apart. "I'm going to rip that damned thing out one of these days!" Martin growled, straightening his trousers and hurriedly tucking his shirt back inside them.

Joss glanced down at him as she tidied her own clothes. "I think I'd better answer the door," she said. "You look as if you need time to—um—settle down."

Martin grinned. "Saved by the bell, huh?"

"That's what you think," Joss replied, her eyes sparkling, running her hands through her hair as she hurried to the front door.

"Oh, hello, Isabel, I thought you were at Bob's tonight."

"I was, supposedly," Isabel began. Then, taking in Joss's uncharacteristically tousled hair and rumpled clothes, added, "Sorry, am I interrupting something?"

Martin's voice called out from the lounge, "It's all right, she had to get up anyway to answer the door."

"Oh dear." Isabel grinned. "I only came round because I thought it might be important."

"That's okay. Martin and I were just taking advantage of the extremely rare conjunction of an absence of twins and my night off." She turned her head and raised her voice for Martin's benefit, "I'm sure we'll manage to take up where we left off—later! Meanwhile, perhaps a coffee to keep our energy levels up!" Then, turning back to Isabel, "Anyway, what's up?"

"Bob's gone."

"*What!*"

Isabel shrugged, turning her hands outwards. "He's gone. Scarpered. Done a runner. He wasn't there when I turned up for my session. The whole place was in darkness, and the doors were locked. I had a look in the windows, and there was no sign of life. The wardrobe door in the bedroom was slightly open, and there was nothing at all on the dressing table. There were a couple of other small tables, and two bedside tables, and nothing on them either, except the bedside lamps."

"Hmm, it does rather suggest he's packed up his personal effects and decamped. Odd that he didn't contact you, though."

"Perhaps he was in too much of a hurry. But why, I wonder?"

Joss shrugged. "God knows! Look, let's take our coffee into the lounge, and see what we can come up with."

Martin was now sitting on the couch, pretending to leaf through a magazine. Joss handed him his coffee. "Feeling more comfortable now, dear?" she enquired innocently, batting her eyelids at him.

Martin mouthed a kiss at her and murmured, "I'll see you later."

"Ooh, promises, promises!" Joss returned his kiss lightly, then sat beside him on the couch, cupping her coffee mug in her hands.

"Now," said Martin, "what's all this about the lovely Bob?"

"It seems he's left," Joss told him, "and in a hurry, by the look of things."

Isabel nodded. "What I'd like to know, though, is why."

"Not to mention where," said Martin.

Joss put down her coffee mug and looked at the others. "I wonder..."

"What?"

"I've just remembered a dream I had the other night. I had meant to mention it to you, Isabel."

"Go on." Isabel tried not to sound impatient.

"It was about Bob. He was in church, of all places. At least, he was in *a* church. It looked like an old stone church,

141

but the pews had been taken out, and there were cushions all over the floor. The altar was still there though, and Bob was standing in front of it. He seemed to be busy doing something, but I couldn't see what. I had the feeling he was about to turn round, and that when he did, something very important would be revealed, and I felt sort of excited and terrified at the same time."

"Was there anyone else there?" Isabel asked.

"Mmm, quite a few, but they had their backs to me, and for some reason, even though I could see them quite clearly, I wasn't specifically aware of who they were." She shrugged. "Dreams can be like that."

"So really," Martin put in, "the important aspect of the dream seems to have been the altar, and what Bob was doing there, what was about to be revealed."

"Thank you, teacher." Joss smiled. "You've summed it up nicely."

"And the church," Isabel pointed out. "That might be important, too."

"I wonder if it's a clue to Bob's whereabouts?" Martin suggested.

"That's a point," said Joss. "Come to think of it, the whole dream seemed to tie in somehow, or be connected with that vision I had recently." She clapped her hand to her head as realisation hit her, and turned to Isabel. "Of course! Remember I told you Rhoda and the others were at Bob's place, and they all seemed to be upset and confused?" Isabel nodded. "I'll bet he hasn't told *them* he's gone, either!"

Isabel nodded again. "So, if we assume he left suddenly, that brings us back to why. What on earth would make him take off without telling anyone, or even bothering to cancel his classes?"

"Lack of professionalism?" suggested Joss drily.

"No." Isabel shook her head. "I don't think it's that. For what it's worth, there was an odd feel about the place. I think he had to get out in a hurry."

"Maybe you should keep an eye on the place," Martin suggested. "He might come back to get the rest of his things. I doubt if he owns the property, so he's not likely to just leave them there."

"Good point," Joss said. "She turned to Isabel. "Do you know how to contact any of the others in the group? One of them might know something."

"I expect Rhoda would," Isabel said, "but I've only ever seen her once, and I wouldn't have a clue how to contact her. I don't even know her surname. She turned her coffee mug, watching moodily as the cold remains of the coffee swirled round, leaving a tide-mark where the milk had begun to congeal. "Some investigation this is turning out to be. We've spent over a month already—not to mention more money than I can afford—and we're no further ahead than when we started." She looked across at Joss, but Joss was distracted by the picture on the television, which had been silently playing in the background during their discussion. She motioned to Martin to turn up the sound.

Turning to Isabel, she said, "Sorry, but the late news has just started, and there was something on earlier that I think will interest you. I was going to tell you, but they might repeat it on this bulletin as well."

They sat through politics national and international, war, crime and an item about an elderly widow holding two burglars prisoner in her laundry until the police arrived.

Then, just when they had decided that television programmers had no idea what really interests the viewing public, the earlier item came on.

As the cameras crossed to the weather report, Martin turned the television off. "The result of yet another misguided guru, I suppose," he said. "I don't suppose your little absconder friend, Bob, had anything to do with that lot? From what I've heard, he seems to have been involved at one time or another with everyone who was anyone in the realm of spiritual enlightenment."

"Come to think of it," said Isabel, "didn't Terry say something about police involvement?"

"It's a tempting theory," Joss countered, "but of all the places he claimed to have visited when Luke interviewed him, Australia was not one."

"Good Lord!" Martin's voice was sarcastic. "Don't tell me there's actually some small corner of a foreign land that *isn't* forever Bob."

"So it would seem." Joss began to gather up the remains of their meal.

Isabel stood up. "All right, I can take a hint. I know when I'm not wanted. I'll just go on back to my cold, lonely flat and leave you two to finish whatever it was you were doing before you were so rudely interrupted."

"There you are," Martin said to Joss, "I told you—works every time." But he got to his feet and went to give Isabel a hug. As he walked with her to the door, he assured her, "You feel free to come over any time you like. You've put so much into investigating this Bob character, it must be a real pain to have it fizzle out like this."

"Thanks. It really helps to have friends like you and Joss.

I'll let you know if anything further develops."

Martin went back to Joss in the lounge. He took her hands, kissed each one in turn and placed them round his waist, then wrapped his arms around her and pulled her close. "Now, where were we?"

* * * *

Rhoda's message was brief and to the point. Isabel found it a week later on her return from the library. She had decided some in-depth research into the nature of cults might not go amiss, given she could no longer research Bob directly. Her hopes of finding some mention of the Queensland commune were in vain, but she had found a book that mentioned Max Muller, albeit briefly, as part of a wider discussion of modern-day Rosicrucians. Dumping her pile of books on the floor beside the hall table, Isabel pressed 'message' and waited with pen poised.

"This is Rhoda Hewitt, Bob Ferris's secretary," said a voice like a bird's claw scraping grit-paper. "I'm phoning to let you know that all classes have been suspended until further notice. You will be advised when they are to start again. We apologise for any inconvenience. Thank you."

Isabel waited for the answerphone to complete its cycle of clicks and whirrs and flashing lights, then dialled Joss's number.

There was a moment's silence while Joss digested the news. Then, "Oh, great! I hate investigations that come to a dead end."

"Especially when it's dictated by outside circumstances," Isabel agreed. "We'll have to let the others know. Luke wanted to do another interview, I think. And he'll have to tell Anne our investigations have failed. He won't like that."

"I don't suppose Anne will be too thrilled, either. Still, there's not a lot we can do about it. In the meantime, I suppose Luke will just have to fall back on his psychic artist. I gather he's booked her as a guest on next week's programme, so she'll be there in person."

"You don't happen to know if Luke has any etchings?" Isabel queried in demure tones.

"Well, I don't imagine he'd waste them on me if he has," Joss said, adding, "or on the psychic artist, come to that. It turns out she's not only well over fifty, but very happily married to a large husband, with dog to match."

"Ah," said Isabel, "not Luke's type, then."

Joss laughed. "Definitely not. So I guess it's back to the drawing board for all of us, in more ways than one.

CHAPTER SIXTEEN

The water gurgling down the plug hole in the shower sounded like some demented Peruvian playing the Andean pipes—badly. But after the last few days, no insane Inca was going to spoil his enjoyment of life's simpler pleasures. Declan stretched, and flexed his shoulders as the warm water washed over them, easing away the tension. Then he lowered his head and allowed it to massage his aching neck. He'd be tempted to say this was better than sex, only he wasn't sure he could remember with any certainty what sex was like. Still, at least this wouldn't end in divorce. He silenced the mad piper in mid-gurgle and reached for the towel.

The sliding doors of his motel room opened onto a small courtyard and, beyond that, the sea, deep blue under the setting sun, gave new meaning to the colour ultra-marine. It glowed invitingly between the trees clinging to the rocks of the shoreline. Their dark green leaves, and the tatters of crimson and scarlet flowers, reminded him of the Christmas card some friend of Carol's had sent her last year. She'd showed it round the station proudly, as proof of her cosmopolitan contacts. He searched his memory for the name of those flowers. They looked a bit like bottlebrushes or gum flowers. Oh, well...it had been a long day. Christ, it had been a long week!

He'd been met in Auckland by one of the local constables and, after a briefing with Chief Inspector McLaren and a nondescript young man from Immigration, she'd deposited him at his hotel along with various maps, files, and papers, informing him a car would be round for him first thing next morning. The constable had been very young, and very pretty, even with most of her fair hair tucked away under her cap. But her only effect on him had been to make him aware of his years. And that had made him feel even older. He'd sent down for a bottle of red and resigned himself to the company of his maps, files and papers.

The next few days he had spent visiting what was known of the former haunts of Richard Forster. This had been made easier by the fact that most of them were confined to Auckland's infamous Karangahape Road (known to the locals, quite sensibly in Declan's opinion, as 'K Road'), and the area immediately surrounding it. A comprehensive survey of some of Auckland's more colourful businesses had turned up little more than a few interesting propositions which, under different circumstances, he imagined might interest McLaren more than him. In fact, he had come across only one person who even remembered Richard Forster—a rather worn-looking middle-aged woman ('Madame Mimi, dear') with mauve hair and a matching dress, who supervised the almost certainly dubious operations of a place called The French Connection. Though the only possible connection he could see with the homeland of champagne and the Impressionists was a lurid neon Eiffel Tower which crowned the narrow doorway. It was being fondled in a suggestive manner by a naked neon blonde with a bad case of sunburn.

Madame Mimi's memories of Richard Forster were hardly extensive. He was a rather quiet young man, she had recalled, who had worked at The Big Apple for a year or two, around eight or ten years ago, initially as a barman, then later as Assistant Manager. He had left all of a sudden just before Christmas—she didn't know why. Des, the manager, a *close* personal friend of hers, had refused even to talk about it. The Big Apple, it seemed, had closed down shortly after that. 'Financial difficulties,' Madame Mimi had said, with a conspiratorial lowering of her voice. And no, she really couldn't tell him where the owner was now, or any of his employees. Des had died not long afterwards of a heart attack. It was all the stress, if you asked her. She went on to observe that he looked a trifle tense himself. She knew, only too well, how stressful it could be finding one's way round in a strange city, but she was sure one of her delightful girls would be only too happy to help him relax. Declan hastily declined her offer before she could ring the pseudo-antique bell on the pink marble counter, and made good his escape. How would she have reacted, he wondered, had she known his true identity? He suspected an iron fist beneath the mauve silk glove.

Still, K Road had not been a complete loss. He had discovered a wonderful little coffee shop presided over by a motherly Hungarian woman who had given him a blow by blow account of her escape to freedom in 1956, as he drank her excellent coffee and sampled her mouth-watering strudel. Declan wondered how many other customers had been treated to the same saga. Then he had come across an inconspicuous little art gallery run by a dynamic young man with a ponytail and his wispy girlfriend, where he had bought a delightfully bizarre little abstract which he looked forward to appraising further back in Brisbane.

Three days later, however, no further information had come to light, and the frequent rain had ceased to be a novelty. So he had filed a report, such as it was, at Auckland Central, hired a car, and driven to Thames, enjoying lush scenery that was gratifyingly unlike his usual surroundings. It had put him in mind of Grandad Kelly's hand-me-down tales of the Ireland his father had left as a small boy. To Declan, four generations later, these had acquired an almost mythical quality and, driving through the rich green grassland, broken here and there by rocky outcrops, he had expected at any moment to see a cavalcade of the Little People riding by, beckoning him to the Land of Youth and certain doom. When he had found himself speculating whether this might be an omen, he had turned up the car radio in disgust.

In the event, all that had happened was lunch at Thames, followed by a leisurely drive up the coast to Coromandel township itself, dominated by a massive kauri tree, by all accounts of historic significance. It had not been difficult to find a motel overlooking the water. In Coromandel just about everything seemed to overlook the water, and that suited Declan just fine.

He lowered himself onto the settee in his room, leaned back, and gazed out through the open sliding doors until a chill breeze drifting in off the darkening water reminded him he was still wearing nothing but a towel. Yawning and stretching, he wandered across to the somewhat irrelevant double bed with its regulation candlewick bedspread, and snapped open his suitcase. The first thing to meet his eye was the files and papers McLaren had given him. They could wait. Nothing was going to detract from his enjoyment of this magical place—not tonight. He pulled on a pair of jeans, a t-shirt, and the navy blue ribbed jersey he had brought instead of the bomber jacket that was supposed to stop him from looking like a cop, but in his opinion didn't. Then he shut the papers back in the suitcase, turned his back on them and went off in search of Coromandel's nightlife.

This turned out to be largely of the small, winged variety, though the local pub boasted a fascinating mix of farmers, fishermen, tourists, and hippies—nowadays known as 'alternative lifestylers'. Declan was musing over a long, cold lager as to why it was that every time human beings managed to simplify something, they would immediately proceed to complicate it again, only to repeat the entire process ad infinitum. He was about halfway through the history of his chosen example, rock music, when he became aware that someone had sat down beside him.

"Been a great day, man, eh," drawled a laconic voice in what might equally have been a question or a statement of fact.

Declan looked up at a short, wiry man in his forties, wearing a faded floral shirt and a long, weather-beaten face with sky-blue eyes under hair like a bundle of straw bound together with a pink silk scarf. His smile revealed crooked teeth stained with nicotine—or possibly less legal substances. One of the sergeants at Auckland Central, hearing he was heading for the Coromandel, had regaled him with the story ('It's true, I swear it! A mate of mine told me his mate was there when it happened.') of the police helicopter flying out a massive haul of marijuana, which had lost its load when the strap holding it had broken. ('The whole load got caught in the rotors, and scattered over half the bloody peninsula. Talk

151

about the shit hitting the fan, eh!')

Declan smiled, savouring the irony of the situation. The floral shirt interpreted this as an invitation, and extended a bony hand. "Gidday, mate. Name's Alister."

"Nice to meet you, Alister." Declan shook the proffered hand. It felt hard and calloused, used to manual labour.

"What part of Australia you from, mate?"

"Brisbane, currently."

"Ah, Breesbane eh? Nice place—really laid back."

"You can't have been there for a while. I'm Declan, by the way. But call me Dekko; everyone else does."

Alister grinned. "Cool. Can I get you a drink?"

"Thanks. Mine's a lager." Declan watched as Alister made his way to the bar. He had the rolling gait of someone who spent a lot of time on boats. Declan guessed he worked as a fisherman, and this was confirmed when he returned.

An idea was forming in Declan's mind. "Have you lived here long, Alister?"

Alister scratched his sun-bleached thatch. "Must be going on ten years now, I reckon. Yeah, that'd be right. I came down from Auckland with Britt and Micah in their bus. We had plans to live off the land—you know, a bit of fishing, a few chickens, a vege garden, maybe a bit of the old New Zealand green among the tomato plants." He winked at Declan over the top of his glass. Pulling a battered tin out of his pocket, he proceeded to roll a cigarette with an expertise clearly born of long practice. Declan shook his head when Alister offered him the tin, but observed the age-old ritual with interest. It didn't seem to have changed since he had watched Grandad Kelly in fascination as a young boy. Alister attached the finished cigarette to his bottom lip, delved once more into the depths of his trouser pocket and brought out a box of matches. No fancy modern appliances for him.

"So what happened?" prompted Declan as Alister lit his cigarette and stowed his matches and tin away.

Alister drew deeply, then coughed and picked a few shreds of tobacco from his tongue. "Oh, Britt and Micah only lasted here a few months. Britt got pregnant, and they moved back to Auckland. They left me the bus, and I got a job on the boats over on the East coast—fishing, right?—and I sent them the money for it later. Still got it, actually, though I've bought some land and built myself a house. Well, more of a shack, really." He puffed some more on his cigarette. "Still, it's home, eh. But I lived in the bus for a fair while. Still use it sometimes—music festivals and the like."

Declan went across to the bar and refilled their glasses. Then, casually, "I was hoping to meet up again with an old mate of mine who used to live round here. Richard Forster. You wouldn't happen to know him, would you?"

Alister blew a cloud of smoke to join the thick layer hovering above them. "Can't say the name rings a bell. How long's he been here?"

"I think he moved here around eight or so years ago from Auckland. I'm not sure how long he was here, but the last I heard, he was running a sort of religious commune somewhere near here. I thought he might still be here."

Enlightenment dawned in Alister's eyes. "Oh, that place! That closed down years ago, mate. I didn't have anything to do with it. I'm not into gurus myself. I like to do my own thing, eh. Tell you what, though," he stubbed out the browned butt of his cigarette and took a long swig of beer. Declan drank his beer and waited. It wouldn't do to appear too keen. "I know a joker who might be able to help you."

"Yeah?"

"Yeah, his name's Keith. He used to live at the commune, up near Amodeo Bay, about thirty k's north of here," Alister explained. Then, as though it had just crossed his mind, "You don't look like the sort of joker who'd be into all that esoteric stuff."

Declan shrugged. "Well, most of us end up joining the real world, sooner or later. I'm an art dealer these days." This was his standard line. Art was his hobby, and he had enough knowledge to back it up convincingly if need be and, since art dealers can end up following some pretty strange trails in pursuit of the forgotten masterpiece that was their particular Holy Grail, he could justify being in some very unlikely places. Like this pub, for instance.

Alister laughed, and scratched his head. "Know what you mean, eh."

Feeling some sort of explanation might be in order, Declan extemporised, "Richard seems to have got into it pretty heavily. I don't suppose we'd have a lot in common, now, but I promised his sister I'd look him up while I was in the area. She hasn't heard from him for years. Does this mate of yours live near here?"

"Keith? I wouldn't call him a mate exactly. Like you said, we haven't got a lot in common. I used to know him fairly well in the old days, though. He doesn't live far from here – about five k's. We could go over there now, if you like."

Clearly, thought Declan, he was proving better entertainment than the pub. "Are you sure he'll be there, on a Friday night?"

"This isn't Brisbane, Dekko." Alister's laugh was scornful,

but good-humoured. "Besides, he doesn't go out much at night because of young Enoch—his kid," he added by way of explanation.

Declan wondered whether a dozen beers might be appropriate. Alister reckoned they'd just about hit the spot.

A brief, but bumpy ride later, they drew up before an old house with a verandah along the front. Somewhere behind the house a dog began to bark. A voice yelled at the dog, and the row ceased abruptly. As Declan and Alister reached the verandah, the door opened revealing an aura of warmth and light in which stood a tall, well-built figure in patched jeans, an Indian cotton tunic of faded purple, and a brown leather waistcoat decorated with painted stars and moons.

Alister called out, "Keith, hi, man. This is Dekko. He's over from Aussie, looking for an old mate of his who used to be at the commune, and I thought you might be able to help him."

"Come on in, then, and I'll see what I can do." Keith's voice was rich and deep, with the hint of an English accent— London, Declan thought. His skin was smooth and golden, making it difficult to pinpoint his age, and his long brown hair would probably be curly if released from the leather thong that bound it back. There was something vaguely exotic about the set of his striking, high-cheekboned face, and his off-centre nose somehow added to the effect. He certainly didn't look English, despite the accent.

Keith's living room resembled an Eastern bazaar. The walls were draped with a multitude of what looked like faded cotton bedspreads. Some were garish batiks, some striped, others, plain. Still more of them were thrown over three sagging settees which gathered for warmth about the fireplace. A couple of guitars, one acoustic, one electric, leaned in a corner beside a cardboard box of children's toys, and a built-in bookcase covered the whole of one wall. It was crammed with messy piles of books and papers. At one end of the wooden mantelpiece stood a large pentagram, hand-painted in gold on a black ground, and at the other, a golden cross with a rose at its centre, also painted on black. Declan's eyes, however, were drawn to a brass statuette that sat—or rather, squatted—between them, flanked by incense sticks in two small soapstone containers. He recognised the statue as a cheap reproduction of one of many tantric depictions of male and female deities in sexual union. Oh, well, no accounting for tastes, but give him a nice, challenging abstract any day.

Declan produced his pack of cans.

"Hey, neat! Thanks, man," said Keith. "Have a seat." He waited until they were all seated on the lumpy sofas with a beer each, then, "You say this friend of yours used to be at the Rose and Star Community?"

Sounds like a pub, Declan thought, but he said, "I never knew its name, but that must be it. His name was Richard Forster."

Keith's leonine hazel eyes opened wide. Declan thought he detected a hint of fear, or at least wariness. "Richard was our teacher. He founded the community. He was a very powerful man, you know." Again that glimmer of fear—or was it just awe? Declan said nothing, creating a vacuum for Keith to fill. "The community closed down," Keith said, "about seven years ago, I think."

"What about Richard? Is he still in the area?"

"Oh, no." Keith shook his head. "He left about a year

before that, just before we had all the trouble."

"Oh?" Even Alister was showing interest now. Declan tried not to register more than a normal curiosity at a potentially juicy bit of scandal.

Keith looked uncertain about whether to continue. Eventually, however, he shrugged his shoulders and went on. "One of the girls there, Julie, got pregnant. Her parents must have found out, and they came to take her away. She refused to go—she had a thing going with Richard. All the girls wanted him, I suppose because he was the teacher." Declan got the impression from Keith's tone that he couldn't imagine it being for any other reason. "But Julie was really in love with him, and I think he was with her. He used to tell us she was carrying the Child of the New Aeon—something like that." He paused, and poured beer down his throat.

Declan said nothing. Keith's story was becoming pretty weird, and he wanted to let him tell it at his own pace. No sense in frightening him off now, when he might, finally, be getting somewhere.

Keith wiped his mouth with the back of his hand and went on, "Anyway, Julie's parents went away, and we thought that was that. It was about then that Richard left. Then, a few days later, the fuzz turned up. Apparently, Julie's parents had told them she was under age, and they wanted her home. She said she wasn't, and refused point blank to leave. Julie told us she was going to join Richard in a few days' time. She said they had an agreement."

"And did she? Join him I mean."

"Well, no. A couple of days later the cops turned up again, along with her parents. And they had her birth certificate with them. So Julie went with them—I guess back to

Hamilton, where they lived." Keith reached for another beer. "The funny thing was, after all the fuss she made before, she didn't seem to mind going with them at all, this time. Odd, that."

Declan nodded. Julie's agreement with Forster had most likely been a lie, told to preserve her dignity after Forster had deserted her. Just as well her parents had turned up again. By the sound of it, she would have been too proud to contact them. Thoughtfully, he crushed his empty beer can. "Seems I didn't know old Richard as well as I thought I did. I never would have picked him as the hippy commune type."

Keith looked at him oddly. "It wasn't that sort of community. Some of us were hippies, I guess, but it was much more than that."

"Oh?"

"It was based on Kabbalistic magical teachings, and Rosicrucianism and so on. The whole point of the exercise was to create a community in tune with the New Aeon which is coming into being, so that when it arrives, we'll know how to live in it, and to deal with its enemies."

"Ah," said Declan, trying hard to suppress his cynicism. It sounded as though Keith still half-believed all this New Aeon rubbish. "I don't suppose Julie ever said where she was supposed to be meeting Richard?"

Keith shook his head.

"Pity. Sounds like he became a bit of a ratbag. Still, I expect his sister would have liked to hear from him."

"Sorry I can't help you, man." Keith unfolded himself from his cross-legged position on the settee and padded across to a battered old stereo to change a CD that had been softly playing rock music with an Indian influence.

Declan looked at his watch, then at Alister, who had once more sunk into the reverie of the terminally bored. "Well," he said to Keith as he got to his feet, "we won't take up any more of your time. It looks like Richard's sister won't be hearing from him after all, but thanks, anyway."

Keith went to open the door for them. Alister was stretching his arms above his head, cracking his knuckles loudly and yawning. Suddenly Keith went to the bookcase and began to scrabble through a cardboard box that seemed full of random scraps of paper. "Ah, here we are. I knew I had it somewhere." He handed Declan the frayed flap from a packet of cigarette papers. "This might be some use to you."

On it was scrawled, 'Julie Hazelwood, c/o 26 Arthur St, Hmltn.'

"Julie's parents' address in Hamilton," Keith explained.

"Thanks, I was heading that way soon, anyway," Declan lied, genuinely grateful for the further lead, though he doubted Julie would still be living at home. He hoped she had found someone better than Forster—not that that could provide much difficulty, he imagined. Still, it was amazing how often women seemed to go for the bastards. Then he remembered Lynn's parting speech to him, and told himself not to be so smug. Nothing was ever that simple in practice.

Back at the hotel, Declan felt that, under the circumstances, it would be churlish to decline Alister's suggestion of another beer or three, though what he really wanted was a good, strong coffee. He realised with dismay that he hadn't had a coffee since lunchtime. No wonder his head was aching.

As he sipped his beer, a thought occurred to him. "I wonder what happened to the commune? I meant to ask

Keith. I mean, the land must have belonged to somebody."

Alister shrugged. "I wouldn't know about that. As far as I know, it finally folded about four years ago. I guess the buildings are still there, though. It was a farm, originally, I think—a small-holding."

As soon as he could, Declan excused himself. "Thanks for all your help, Alister," he said.

"Hey, don't mention it, man. Maybe you'll have better luck in Hamilton, eh."

"Maybe I will. Thanks again."

As he made his way back to the motel, the moon slid in and out of dark clouds, and the soft lap of the water was soothing. Or it would have been, only he couldn't clear his throbbing head of the image of Julie, waiting in vain for Richard Forster to contact her. And Claire, totally dependant on both drugs and Forster, and let down by both. He was beginning to seriously dislike this Forster character.

* * * *

Declan drove past the surreal, giant soft-drink bottle, kitsch roadside symbol of the main industry of the town of Paeroa, and swung the car onto the road to Hamilton. The drive up to Amodeo Bay, picturesque as it was in the early morning sun, had revealed nothing of any use. Even the few locals seemed utterly bored by the former status of the dejected cluster of buildings behind the unkempt hedge. No-one had lived there for at least four years, it seemed, and no-one would admit to any knowledge of its present owner. To Declan, this seemed unlikely. Even someone as urbanised as he was knew how country people loved to gossip. They

160

probably just didn't want to divulge their affairs to an outsider—and a foreign one at that. Still, it was probably of no real significance, and, if necessary, there were other ways of finding out.

A little over three hours later, he was cruising down Hamilton's broad main street. His early start had left him feeling hungry, so he pulled up at a restaurant with a steaming plate of some unguessable foodstuff painted on its window, and had lunch while consulting his map.

Due to the city's conducive street layout, and the river running through its centre, it didn't take long to find Arthur Street. Number 26 was a typical suburban house, neat and plain in red brick with a green roof, net curtains at the windows, lawn and gardens trimmed into submission. Despite local variations in style, they all looked unnervingly similar.

From well-mown lawns and herbaceous borders and suburban architecture, good Lord protect us, Declan thought. He rang the doorbell. Moments later, the glass-paned, net-clad door opened to reveal a neat, slim woman with greying, salon-coiffed hair, dressed in a navy skirt and pale blue blouse. She had the stub of an orange pencil stuck incongruously behind one ear.

Declan smiled. "Mrs Hazelwood?"

"Yes." Her voice had a tentative quality. She probably hadn't expected to be confronted by a strange Australian so soon after lunch.

"I'm sorry to bother you, but I'm trying to trace an old acquaintance of mine, and I was told your daughter Julie might be able to help. I believe she used to know him. I wonder if you'd tell me where I might contact her?"

Mrs Hazelwood, as if suddenly realising she had a pencil behind her ear, removed it self-consciously and began to fiddle with it. She seemed rather suspicious of him, as well she might. "Who are you?" she asked at last.

"My name's Kelly—Declan Kelly. But it won't mean anything to Julie. It was this—acquaintance she knew."

"And who was that?"

Declan had been hoping to obtain Julie's address or telephone number without mentioning Forster's name. It now seemed, however, that full disclosure might yield better results. He fished in his pocket and brought out his police badge. "Actually, Mrs Hazelwood, it's Detective Sergeant Kelly, Queensland Police. I'm trying to find the current whereabouts of Richard Forster, whom I believe knew your daughter." He ignored the sudden, sharp intake of breath. "I was hoping she might be able to help me."

Mrs Hazelwood had pressed her lips together in a thin line. "If you'd like to come in for a moment," she said, her polite voice reeking of panic, "I'll call Julie and see if she's prepared to talk to you. But I won't have her upset. That man has done enough damage."

Declan nodded. "So we believe, ma'am. That's why we want to find him."

Mrs Hazelwood led him to the neat lounge, from where he could hear her on the telephone, though to his chagrin he was unable to make out what she was saying. A moment later she returned, still tense, but perhaps a trifle relieved. "Julie will be round in a few minutes," she announced. "Would you like something to drink while you're waiting?"

"Coffee would be great, thanks." Declan smiled. "Milk, no sugar."

Julie Hazelwood turned out to be a slim, rather tense young woman in her twenties, with long, lacklustre hair of a light sandy colour. Her pale, elfin face was redeemed by huge, bright-blue eyes which at the moment wore a haunted look. Declan had the feeling she had not relaxed properly for a long time.

He smiled at her in what he hoped was a reassuring way. "I'm sorry to bother you, Julie, but I'm trying to trace the whereabouts of Richard Forster. I was hoping you might be able to tell me where he went when he left the, um, Rose and Star Community."

Julie shook her head. Her mother thrust a coffee mug into her hand, and she smiled a wan little smile.

"He didn't say anything to you about where he planned to go?"

"It was a long time ago." Julie's voice was as faded as her face.

"Please try and remember." Declan felt sorry for the kid. She was only a year or so older than his own daughter, Dana. He tried to make his voice as gentle as possible. "Anything at all that might help me find him."

Julie shook her head again. "He didn't say anything to me about where he was going." She glanced up at her mother, who gave a faint nod. "I told the others we'd agreed to meet somewhere. But we hadn't, really." Her voice sank to a sigh. "I was hoping he'd come back for me, because we were—we were—I was pregnant. But he never did, and then..." she faded out altogether.

"It's okay," Declan told her. It was clear she had nothing of value to add to what little he already knew. "You don't have to tell me any more. Thank you for coming to talk to me. You've been very helpful."

Julie looked doubtful, but she raised her head and smiled at him. "What do you want to find him for, anyway?"

Declan took a moment to think. He had no wish to frighten her. She seemed scared enough already. But there seemed no way round it. "It's to do with a girl who died in Australia ten years ago," he said.

Julie's eyes grew wide, and she drew in her breath.

"Did Richard kill her?" Mrs Hazelwood's expression made it clear she wouldn't be at all surprised.

"We don't know," Declan told her. "But it seems he was the last person to see her alive, and we want to talk to him if we can, so we can close the file. Thank you very much for talking to me." He included Mrs Hazelwood in his smile. "And thank you for the coffee. I appreciate it."

Back in the car he heaved a frustrated sigh. Yet another bloody dead end. This Richard Forster was beginning to be a major pain in the bum. Not only was he not turning up any information on the man, he wasn't even getting to enjoy the scenery properly. Which was a pity, because it beat all hell out of what he usually got to look at. Almost as good as Tasmania. With a grimace, he turned the key in the ignition, shoved the car into gear, and headed back to Auckland.

CHAPTER SEVENTEEN

"Rhodo calved, massage on machine." Isabel waved a disgusted arm at the whiteboard in the hall and turned to Joss. "I do wish Dominic would learn to write. What on earth do you suppose *that* means?"

Joss chuckled. "I don't know about the rhododendron, but your answering machine's flashing."

"Ah!" Isabel's brow cleared. "Of course! Message, not massage."

"I'll go and put the kettle on, shall I?" Joss disappeared into the kitchen as Isabel, pen at the ready, activated the answering machine.

The rasping voice was familiar. "This is Rhoda Hewitt, phoning to let you know that the new Circle of Light Centre is opening on the thirty-first of October. The new centre is at the former All Saints Anglican church near Oxford. Drive through Oxford, then take the road to Cooper's Creek. The old church is on the right, just past Gammans Creek—a small stone church back off the road behind some poplar trees, with a wooden hall and another more modern building nearby. There will be a dedication ceremony at eleven o'clock, followed by a pot-luck lunch. Please bring some food to share. We will be providing hot and cold drinks. We look forward to seeing you there. Thank you."

Triumphantly, Isabel rushed to the kitchen, waving the message pad. "Joss, look at this! Bob's back in business again! In new, improved premises—a church, no less, near Oxford. The opening is next Sunday, see."

"I see he's chosen an appropriate date for it—All Saints Day." Joss set a mug of coffee in front of Isabel.

"Doubly appropriate then," Isabel said. "The church is All Saints, too—at least it used to be. As of next Sunday, it's the Circle of Light Centre."

"Of course, it's Hallowe'en too. Well, Beltaine, I suppose, seeing as we're in the Southern Hemisphere. So, one way or another, anything could happen."

"Oh dear. Perhaps I shouldn't go, after all." Isabel's expression was one of comical anxiety.

Joss said, "I take it you are planning to go, then?"

"Good Lord, yes!" exclaimed Isabel. "I wouldn't miss it for anything!"

* * * *

Isabel pulled the Corolla off the gravel road, swung it round and parked on the wide grass verge in front of the row of tall poplars. Pat's car was parked in front of hers, and a number of others, as well as two motorcycles, lined the road. She looked at her watch. Eighteen minutes to eleven—good, not too early, not too late. Getting out of the car, she picked up a cardboard box from the passenger seat, and locked the door. The box contained a batch of cheese scones she had made for the pot-luck lunch (not up to Luke's standard, of course), and some basic crockery and cutlery, in case they were needed.

Behind the poplars, her eyes took in one of the prettiest little churches she had seen. It was built of grey stone in the

166

classic English style, with a slate roof and matching steeple. Above its wooden doors was a circular, stained-glass rose window. In its other windows, with pointed arches in mock-Gothic style, were diamond-paned leadlights. Beside it was a large wooden hall, in need of a good coat of paint, and behind both church and hall, largely obscured, stood a solid-looking concrete-block building of more recent vintage. The mountains she had been following all down the long, straight, main road, gleamed palely in the background.

Isabel heard someone call her name (or rather, her pseudonym), and saw Pat walking towards her, a smile of welcome on her face. "Lovely to see you. I'm so glad you could make it. Come along, and I'll show you where to put your things." She took the box from Isabel and peered into it. "Ooh, lovely—scones!" Pat led the way to the hall, where trestle tables had been set up in two rows, and down to a room at the far end from where sounds of cheerful industry floated out through a large open hatch. "This is the kitchen," said Pat. "We'll leave your things here, and I'll show you the rest of the Centre."

In the kitchen, Rhoda, Nancy, and another middle-aged woman were busy washing cups, and boiling water in the jumbo-sized Zip. Nancy waved to her cheerfully, and Rhoda gave her a thin smile. Isabel put her box down on a table with the other votive offerings, and followed Pat towards the church.

As soon as they walked through the door, her eyes were drawn to the stained-glass window at the far end, above where the altar had been before it was moved to the front of the chancel. Whoever had donated it had had exquisite taste—as well as plenty of money. In beautifully executed

Renaissance style, it showed Jesus as The Good Shepherd tending a flock of plump sheep in a lush meadow flanked on the left by a sparkling blue stream, and on the right by a curiously cultivated-looking garden of red roses and white lilies. Snow-capped mountains in the distance were crowned by a rising sun whose rays reached out to a blue sky studded with fluffy clouds. Isabel was wondering where she had seen a sun like that before, when she noticed the Good Shepherd's crook. It appeared to be sprouting clumps of leaves in several places, just like....

Bloody hell! It was the wand from the tarot, near as damn it. And the roses and lilies—they were tarot symbols, too. Even the stream and the snowy-peaked mountains were symbols used often in the tarot. And wasn't that strange blue belt girding the Good Shepherd's white robe the ouroboros—the snake biting its own tail, symbol of eternity—as worn by the Magician? Come to think of it, she knew where she had seen that sun before, too. It was on several of the Major Trumps—Death, for example—but it was also a Masonic symbol. No wonder Bob had chosen this place, but who, she wondered, had donated the window to an unsuspecting church congregation?

"As you can see, we've moved the pews back against the walls, so we'll have room for our circle."

With difficulty, Isabel dragged her eyes away from the window and forced herself to concentrate on Pat's words.

"As soon as we can, we plan to put more rugs down on the floor. That should make it more cosy," Pat went on.

Isabel nodded. At the moment, apart from the long runner that still marked where the aisle had been, the floor was bare. Scattered in front of the pews, she recognised the fat cushions from Bob's house.

The altar, in its new position at the front of the chancel, was covered with a dark green heavy cloth, and what looked like, and probably was, a white lace table-cloth. The effect was not incongruous, however, especially with Bob's big brass candlestick taking pride of place, surrounded by a glass bowl of water, one of salt, a brass incense holder, a fat red candle, and a wicked-looking knife with an ornate silver hilt inlaid with one of Bob's favourite citrines.

A brief burst of music came from behind a heavy door to the right of the chancel—the vestry, Isabel guessed. A peal of female laughter was followed by a soft murmur in a deeper tone.

Pat's voice interrupted her suppositions. "This is where we'll be holding circle activities. Would you like to see the dormitories?"

"Dormitories?"

Pat nodded. "There's a more modern building behind the church. I think it was used for camps by the local scout troop, but it will be ideal for when we start holding retreats and seminars."

In some surprise, Isabel followed Pat out of the church and over to the concrete block building she had glimpsed earlier. It was considerably larger than she had thought, consisting of two large rooms, each with fifteen or twenty bunk beds, separated by a central covered corridor. At the end of this, one on each side, were two toilet and ablution blocks, each with two showers and several washbasins. The entire block was severely functional, but it looked clean and dry.

A shout went up from behind the dormitory block. "Come

and have a look," said Pat, hurrying out.

A small crowd had gathered on an area of flat ground, where Jeremy seemed to be supervising the erection of a large bonfire, watched by Jessica. Doug was throwing an armful of small branches onto the pile, but Isabel did not recognise any of the other dozen or so there. Two tough-looking young women in jeans and heavy jackets stood together slightly apart from the rest, deep in conversation. One had pale blonde hair cut short, and thick, pale eyebrows that glinted in the sun. The other wore a spectacularly sculpted close crop, dyed in two shades of purple. Several others looked as though they might have been university friends of Jeremy or Jessica. Neither Bob nor Anita was anywhere to be seen. Isabel thought of the laughter from the vestry and gave an inward shudder.

Doug caught sight of them and came striding over. "Gidday. Good to see you again. What do you think of our bonfire?"

"Great," said Isabel. "What's it for?"

Doug rubbed his shaggy head and grinned. "It's for the dedication ceremony at eleven."

"Which is mid-day under real time," explained Pat.

"Ah," said Isabel, "a baptism of fire." Neither Doug nor Pat appeared to recognise her reference. She tried again. "This is an interesting place," she suggested, "but a bit isolated. I wonder why Bob has moved out here?" She decided not to mention his failure to inform her before the event. No sense in upsetting people unnecessarily—or arousing their suspicions.

It was Pat who answered her. "Bob wants to set up a true community," she said. "A centre where like-minded people

170

can come and prepare for the advent of the New Aeon."

"Is that like the New Age?" asked Isabel. "I thought it was already here."

Pat smiled. "Most people don't understand what the New Age really is. It's been coming for some time, and will be for some time to come. We are still on the cusp of the Aquarian Age. It takes decades for the Precession of the Equinoxes to complete the journey from one Great Age to the next." Isabel nodded, making a mental note to ask Geraldine for more information. Pat continued, "The cusp period is always a time of confusion, and it is up to those of us who want the best for mankind to prepare ourselves to work with the energies of the incoming era."

Before Isabel could pursue the matter further, a gong sounded loudly from the direction of the church.

"Come on," said Pat, "the dedication is about to start."

As people hurried from the bonfire area and the hall towards the front of the church, Isabel scanned the area, but there was still no sign of either Bob or Anita. The heavy church doors now stood wide open. Standing in front of the altar, Isabel could see a slim figure clad in a loose white dress, a gold-embroidered white cap on her close-cropped head. Anita. She seemed not to notice as the rest of them filed through the doors and made their way to the cushions placed in a wide semi-circle before the altar. Her eyes were fixed on the altar, where she was lighting the sticks of incense in their brass holder. But as she turned and moved to sit on a cushion to the right of the altar, Isabel had the feeling her attention was elsewhere.

They waited. Soft music began to drift through the church from an unseen source, though it was definitely not church music. There was a slight creak, and the vestry door opened. On a swelling wave of violins, Bob stepped through the door. His citrine on its gold cord gleamed against his white kaftan as he moved slowly to the altar. In his hands, for all the world like a middle-aged Christmas tree angel, he clasped a white candle, which he used to light the candles in the candelabra.

While the rest of them waited in silence, Bob took up a small spoon and carefully measured salt into the glass bowl of water, stirring it to dissolve it. The music died obligingly away as he raised the heavy candlestick above his head and turned to face his followers. This appeared to be the signal Anita had been waiting for. She scurried to the altar and picked up the bowl of salt water. Followed by Anita, sprinkling salt water in his footsteps and onto the group members, Bob moved off to pace a slow circle around the church, finishing up behind the altar. He stood with the candlestick held high, while Anita replaced the bowl and resumed her seat, then lowered it slowly as he spoke for the first time.

"The Circle of Light is complete. In Love and Light we welcome you."

As the others murmured the 'Love and Light' response, Isabel wondered who 'we' was supposed to be. Perhaps Bob was using the royal 'we', or maybe he had acquired a spirit guide. Somehow it seemed unlikely that he was including Anita, although the expression on her face showed she had no doubts on that score.

Bob gave a brief speech of welcome, explaining he had been 'shown' the church, and led to it as being the ideal place for the flowering of the spiritual teaching he felt under obligation to bring to the world. Here, in a purer, freer environment, they would be able to run courses, study meditation, learn and practice healing techniques—it would be a veritable university of the spirit.

Isabel glanced around at the upturned faces. Anita looked to be in the preliminary stages of rapture, gazing at Bob in open adoration. Pat's face wore an almost wistful expression, although Nancy, seated next to her, looked uncomfortable without her chair. Rhoda was as tight-lipped as ever, though her mouth was curled up slightly at its lined corners. Presumably, this was a smile, though it bore closer resemblance to a sneer. Jeremy and Jessica, surreptitiously holding hands, emanated an air of intense concentration, their faces serious, their eyes closed. Again, Isabel had the impression Jeremy was pursuing his own agenda, this time supported by Jessica, both of them working in unison. She wondered whether Bob was aware of this double act, and, if so, whether it worried him. She had a feeling it should.

A general shuffling as everyone stood up made her aware Bob's speech had ended. She hurriedly got to her feet as Bob picked up several sticks of incense and, with Anita at his heels like a devoted puppy, processed down the remains of the aisle and out through the double doors, the others straggling after them. With the fragrant smoke of the incense drifting after him, he led his little flock in another circle which encompassed all of the buildings and ended at the bonfire pile.

"Love and Light be with us all!" proclaimed Bob, as he threw the incense into the pile of branches. At that moment, it burst suddenly into flame.

Startled, Isabel looked at Bob, wondering what he had

done. Then she saw Jeremy crouched on the other side of the fire, a large taper in his hand and a pyromaniac gleam in his eye. Still, it had been highly effective. As the flames took hold and leaped higher, Bob led them in a stately circle dance around the fire, first counterclockwise in silence, then clockwise, chanting "Love and Light," the chant building to a climax, then slowly subsiding, skilfully controlled by Bob.

Out of the corner of her eye Isabel noticed Nancy and Rhoda slip away, and before long the sound of the gong summoned them to the hall, where the lunch offerings were set out on the trestle tables, along with tea, coffee, and fruit juice. Like most of the others, Isabel took her paper plate and mug of tea outside to sit and watch the bonfire. Bob seemed to have vanished once more, though Anita was standing on the far side of the fire, talking to the purple-headed woman and her friend.

A few minutes later, Pat and Doug came to join Isabel. "We couldn't have had a better day for our dedication," Pat observed, balancing her mug of tea beside her on a large, flat stone.

Isabel nodded. "And Bob has certainly managed to find a lovely spot here," she added, "secluded, without being too far from town."

"Yeah," put in Doug. "It's a bit on the primitive side at the moment, but I reckon we'll soon get it licked into shape." He indicated the hall. "Spot of paint here and there wouldn't hurt."

"Mmm." Something had been nagging at the back of Isabel's mind since she arrived. She decided to approach it in an oblique way. "It's going to be a lot of work."

Doug said, "We're going to hold work parties once the

weather's a bit warmer."

"Won't it all cost a lot, though?" queried Isabel, now pursuing her main point. "I mean, you'll need gallons of paint for the hall, and the church roof looks as though it could do with some repairs. And what about heating? Or is Bob not planning to keep the Centre running during winter?"

"Oh, yes," said Pat. "We'll be running public courses and seminars, and a fee will be charged for those. And those of us who are members of the Circle of Light have agreed to pay a regular sum—dependent on our circumstances, of course—towards the running costs. Really, it's the least we can do."

Isabel nodded once more. That still left the question of where Bob had got the money to buy the church in the first place. But she had no wish to be seen as asking too many awkward questions. On the pretext of getting another mug of tea, she excused herself and wandered off towards the hall. As she was entering the hall, she was startled by the gong clanging close behind her. It turned out to be Rhoda, looking like a stern little schoolmarm summoning her recalcitrant pupils back to class. Slowly, people stopped what they were doing and made their way over to the hall.

"You're all welcome to stay as long as you like," she announced, "but in case any of you need to leave early, I need to tell you that our first weekend retreat here at the Circle of Light Centre will begin on the fifth of November, at six p.m. The theme will be Development of the Group Mind. We'll begin with dinner, then Bob will outline the programme for the weekend, and we'll end the evening with circle dancing, to help us get to know one another better. The programme itself will begin on Saturday morning, and we'll finish at around four-thirty on Sunday afternoon.

"Anyone who wants to attend, please contact me by Wednesday, as we need to know how many to cater for. My telephone number will be on the noticeboard in the hall, or you can write your own name and phone number on the notice I'll put up, and I'll contact you during the week. Now, I think that's all." She consulted her notepad. "Ah, yes, the fee for the weekend will be sixty-five dollars, which will cover all expenses for the weekend, including food. Now, as I said, you're welcome to stay for the afternoon if you wish. Thank you all for coming, and thank you for your food contributions. There's plenty left, by the way." She attempted a smile, achieving a near miss.

The group members drifted back into the hall, chatting excitedly about the course. Isabel drifted with them, turning the situation over in her mind. The price was a bit steep, just for a couple of days. Still, a whole weekend at the Centre constituted a not-to-be-missed opportunity to spy on Bob. Judging by the activity around the notice when Rhoda pinned up her notice, most of the others had no misgivings. A cup of tea later, Isabel had made up her mind. She wrote down her name and telephone number, then left quickly before she had time to change her mind. Bob was still nowhere in sight.

* * * *

Isabel tried surreptitiously to flex the muscles of her legs as she sat cross-legged on her cushion. It was to no avail. She would just have to let them go numb. The old church was lit by candles in metal sconces around the walls, and the brass candlestick that stood on the altar. In the subtle, golden glow, lights and shadows danced across the faces of the others forming the rest of the circle, lending the scene a somewhat sinister air. She could imagine them all in hooded robes, their faces hard and inscrutable as Bob did unspeakable things to a black cat or a rooster, or celebrated the Black Mass on Anita's naked body.

In practice, the circle dance had been the liveliest event of the weekend so far. Today's activities (if you could call them that) had consisted of two rather esoteric lectures by Bob, interspersed with breathing exercises and meditation, which was what they were supposed to be doing now. Though how impeded circulation was supposed to help one to meditate, was something Isabel had yet to fathom. Presumably it had something to do with 'subduing the body', which appeared to be one of Bob's major themes at the moment. She hated to think whose body (or bodies) he was referring to.

Her reverie was interrupted by the tinkle of the bell which Bob used to indicate the end of each period of meditation. After a few moments, someone—she thought it was Jeremy— got up silently and went to turn the lights on. They all sat blinking in the light, and rubbing their eyes.

"Now," said Bob, his round face suffused with an expression that might have been either benevolence or self-satisfaction. It reminded her of the man on the Nine of Cups in the tarot—the so-called 'wish card'. She was not, it seemed, to get hers, as Bob went on, "Now, take a moment to return to full consciousness, and we'll share our meditation experiences. As I explained earlier, our aim is to develop the group mind, so it will be particularly interesting if two or more of you had the same, or similar, experiences. However, nothing is ever irrelevant, so please feel free to express yourselves fully. Jeremy, would you like to start?"

Jeremy, who had returned to his seat on the floor, paused for a moment for dramatic impact, then said in his peculiarly intense way, "First I experienced a deep calm, then I felt myself drifting upwards towards a huge ball of light. I entered the light, and felt a meeting of minds—or maybe souls. I found this... unsettling. Not very pleasant at all." He broke off, shaking his head with an air of slight bewilderment.

Bob, however, was able to dispense reassurance. "Excellent, Jeremy. You were aware of the beginnings of a group mind. But it's a new experience for most of you, so of course you found it unsettling. This is quite natural, and will disappear in time."

He turned to Jessica, who seemed to have had a similar experience to Jeremy's. Each of the others, in turn, spoke of their experiences, and Bob commented on each one. When Isabel's turn came, she kept her true thoughts to herself, and went along with the ball of light which seemed to be the prevalent image, adding in the sunflowers and the white horse from the Sun tarot card for good measure. Bob seemed impressed.

"Your images are ones of *great power*," he told her, dwelling almost lovingly on the last two words, and looking at her in a way that made her feel distinctly uncomfortable. Out of the corner of her eye, she was aware of Anita shuffling on her cushion. "They are both *powerful* symbols of *masculine energy*."

They would be, thought Isabel, and no prizes for guessing whose masculine energy, either!

The evening session concluded with the ritual opening of

the circle, followed by supper in the hall. Isabel dawdled as much as she could without actually staying behind in the church, and waited in the dark porch, where she could see the church through the partially open heavy curtains. Bob stood with his back to her, doing something at the altar, apparently alone. Then Isabel noticed Anita's slim form, moving around the walls of the church extinguishing the candles with a brass candle-snuffer. Presumably it had been found on the premises.

Anita went across to stand behind Bob at the altar. She placed the candle-snuffer on the floor beside it. Bob seemed oblivious to her, and continued whatever it was he was doing. Moving up close to him, Anita slipped her arms around his waist. Bob turned so suddenly he almost knocked her off-balance, and instinctively reached out to steady her. Anita gave a little laugh, keeping hold of his outstretched hand.

Isabel could not hear what he said to her as he withdrew his hand from hers, but Anita did not look pleased. Bob spoke to her again, keeping his voice infuriatingly low.

Anita's voice, being pitched higher, carried better. Isabel heard her say, "Well, all right, if that's what you want, but—" Bob spoke again, interrupting her, and she smiled briefly at him, then turned and walked towards the church porch. Isabel had just time to see the look of despair and anger on her face before slipping outside and hurrying towards the hall.

* * * *

Next morning, Isabel noticed Anita seemed angry and

withdrawn, barely participating in the day's activities. Since it was a mild and sunny late spring day, these took place outside. First there was more circle dancing (to free body blocks, and facilitate the flow of energy between them all), followed by what Bob called a 'trust exercise'.

This consisted of each of them in turn standing in the middle of a circle of the others, falling backwards with eyes closed, and being caught by the rest of the circle. Some of the group, Nancy and Doug in particular, obviously did not enjoy this at all. Bob told them they needed to learn to trust more, to allow the group mind to develop, though Doug insisted, to much good-natured laughter, that it was just that he was a bit worried he would prove too heavy for them to hold.

Anita said nothing, but her manner made it clear she was only going through the motions, and would much rather be off somewhere by herself, sulking. Bob maintained his usual affable manner, but Isabel could see it was taking some effort.

Stage two of the trust exercise called for each of them in turn to fall into Bob's arms, since trust in the teacher was also of major importance. Isabel observed that Bob must have taken Doug's words to heart as, when his turn came, he made sure the rest of the group were behind him as a backstop. So much for trust, Isabel thought. It was interesting to see how some group members seemed more willing to trust Bob alone, and some less. For herself, she regarded it as an ordeal to be endured for the sake of her investigations. Nevertheless, it was hard not to flinch at the feel of Bob's arms clasping her. Even with her eyes closed, she had the impression he was enjoying every moment of the experience. When she opened her eyes again, she noticed

Anita had disappeared.

She was nowhere to be seen for the rest of the day, though she re-emerged later in the afternoon, in time for the closing ceremony. This took place in the church, where candles had been lit, though sunlight was still streaming in through the leadlight windows.

Under Bob's instruction, they all stood in a circle with their eyes closed, holding hands to feel the energy flowing between them. At first, Bob stood in the circle with them, but after a few minutes, he began to move round the circle, placing his hands on the shoulders of each of them in turn, bestowing his 'love and light' blessing. Isabel had deliberately placed herself as far away from him as possible, but somehow he contrived to reach her last, murmuring "May love and light be with you," in her unwilling ear, and squeezing her shoulders slightly before returning to his place in front of the altar.

"I think," he announced, "that what we all need now is to earth ourselves. One of the best ways to do this is with food, so we'll adjourn to the hall for a cup of tea and something to eat, as our final act of sharing."

They all trooped across to the hall, where tea and coffee with sandwiches and biscuits awaited them. Pat and Nancy must have slipped away before the closing circle, as they now emerged from the kitchen, Nancy carrying a plate of biscuits, and Pat wiping her hands on her apron. The others must have been as hungry as she was, Isabel thought, since they all obeyed Pat's advice to 'tuck in' with alacrity. Jeremy and Jessica moved immediately to one side to continue what appeared to be an ongoing secret conversation. Nancy joined her two friends in an animated conversation, while Pat and

Doug stood by the table, eating and chatting. Anita seemed to have disappeared again.

Bob, who had been talking to Rhoda, clapped his hands for attention, then announced, "Thank you all so much for coming along and making this weekend such a success. And since I'm sure you'll all want to continue to build on what we've achieved so far, in two weeks' time there will be another retreat, this time for a long weekend, Friday, Saturday and Sunday." He paused to allow gasps of pleasure, which everyone duly emitted, then continued, "We'll begin on Thursday evening with an opening ritual at eight o'clock, and finish on Sunday afternoon, and the theme I want us all to explore is 'Spiritual Preparation for the New Aeon'. The fee will be one hundred dollars, and, as with this weekend, that will cover all expenses, including food. I hope to see you all back again in two weeks, and if you know anyone else who would be interested, please feel free to invite them. Rhoda will organise bookings. Thank you all once again. Enjoy your food."

Isabel was running complicated calculations in her head, wondering how on earth she was going to be able to afford the fee, when she felt a hand on her shoulder. It was Bob. He seemed to have perfected the art of silent movement. "Ah, Georgina, I do hope you enjoyed the weekend." Isabel nodded with what she hoped resembled an enthusiastic smile. "Good, good. Then we'll be seeing you again on the next retreat? I'll be scheduling plenty of time for individual tuition, so I'll be able to make it up to you for having to cancel your last lesson." His hand moved down her arm and came to rest above her elbow.

Isabel gulped. "Well, of course I'd *love* to come, but I

really don't see how I'll be able to afford it." She leaned forward to put her cup down, forcing Bob to let go of her arm, and took a deep breath, suppressing the urge to rush outside.

Bob appeared not to notice her discomfiture. "Look," he said, leaning forward and speaking very quietly, "you have a great deal of potential. I'd hate to think of you losing a chance to develop that. I'll talk to Rhoda. I'm sure we can arrange something. You just come along, and pay what you feel you can afford at the time." Before he could say more, Nancy caught his eye and waved to him across the table. He patted her arm again, and drifted off. Isabel had the feeling he was not as much in control as he seemed, but perhaps it was just taking time for him to get used to his new setting.

Pat was beginning to clear plates and cups off the tables. Isabel went across to her. "Can I help?"

"Oh, thank you," Pat smiled. "There's a big tray in the kitchen."

As they washed and dried crockery, Isabel asked, "Is Anita all right? She seemed a bit upset earlier."

Pat's face showed concern. "She has been a bit moody recently. I think she takes things to heart too much."

"She hasn't said anything, then?"

Pat shook her head. She ran her fingers through her short hair, then resettled her glasses. "Anita doesn't talk much about her problems. But I'll have a chat with her. I don't like to see people upset."

So much for that avenue of enquiry, Isabel thought gloomily. She folded her tea towel and hung it back on the rail on the kitchen door. All of a sudden she felt exhausted. Rubbing her eyes, she said to Pat, "I think I'll be going now.

It's been a really interesting weekend. Perhaps I'll see you again in a couple of weeks."

"I'll be here," smiled Pat.

Isabel gathered her sleeping bag and overnight bag from the dormitory. As she made her way to the Corolla, she could feel Bob's eyes following her as he stood in the church porch. A shiver of apprehension ran through her.

CHAPTER EIGHTEEN

"Isabel! Thank goodness you're back." Joss's voice on the telephone sounded relieved.

Isabel laughed. "Why, what did you think would happen to me?"

"It's not that. But there's something I thought you ought to see. Can I come round now?"

"Okay. I'll put the kettle on." Isabel replaced the receiver.

Fifteen minutes later, as Joss slotted the DVD she had brought with her into Isabel's DVD player, she explained, "This was on the news on Friday night. Unfortunately, I wasn't fast enough to record all of it, but anyway, tell me what you make of it."

The female newsreader was saying, "...but little further information has come to light concerning Richard Forster, the New Zealander believed to have been the last person to see her alive. News Tonight has been asked to broadcast the following photograph of both Forster and Claire Lomax. It was taken about ten years ago at the Tree of Life Community in Queensland, the cult commune near where Ms Lomax's body was found recently."

The screen was filled by a faded looking photograph of a golden-haired girl in a blue top and jeans. She looked to be about twenty, and would have been very pretty had she not been so underweight. She was smiling up at a man who might have been in his late thirties. He had long, straight, dark brown hair hanging lankly under a band of woven leather tied round his brow. His face looked smooth and bland, its features curiously undeveloped. He wore a white top similar to the girl's blue one, and a pendant on a cord around his neck—a large, round, golden pendant...

"Hang on, Joss! Take it back a bit. I want to see that pendant again!"

Joss wound the DVD back and froze it.

Isabel stared at the golden stone nestled in the folds of the white shirt. She looked at Joss. "Would you say that could be a large citrine?" she asked slowly.

Joss smiled a grim smile. "Like the one Bob wears, you mean?"

Isabel nodded.

"It certainly looks like it," Joss said. "But the name is different."

"Mmm. Is there any more?" asked Isabel, indicating the screen.

Joss wound the DVD on again, and the newsreader reappeared. "The police would like to hear from anyone who recognises either Claire Lomax or Richard Forster, particularly anyone who knows Richard Forster's current whereabouts, or any of his movements since he left the Coromandel Peninsula around six years ago. Anyone with information should contact their local police station. From information already to hand, it appears Richard Forster, who would now be in middle age, may have put on weight since the photograph was taken."

"You can say that again." Joss chuckled as she ejected the DVD.

"If it really is him," said Isabel. "What about the name?"

Joss pressed a button on the remote, and the DVD slid out of the DVD player with a soft click. "Maybe he changed it."

Isabel tapped her tooth with a fingernail and looked thoughtful. "You could be right," she said at length. "And if he did, it seems he kept the same initials. Forster to Ferris. And Bob is short for Robert, which has the same initial as Richard."

"QED," said Joss. "We'd better tell the police then."

Isabel looked doubtful. "It's not much to go on, though, is it?"

"True, but I suppose every little helps. Besides, I've been getting more and more worried about this whole business for a while now. I'd feel much happier if the police were involved."

"Oh, all right. I'd like to see a better copy of the photo, anyway. But not tonight, please. I've had an exhausting weekend."

Joss glanced at her watch. "Oh, God! I have to go. I've got work tonight, and no-one's been fed yet. I'll pick you up tomorrow at ten and, after we've seen the police, you can come over for lunch, and tell me all about your weekend."

* * * *

"Well, no, I'm not a hundred percent certain." Isabel looked at the duty constable as he bent over his notepad. He looked ridiculously young, his pale, close-cropped hair curling defiantly over the tops of his pink ears. He raised his head, his blue eyes showing mild disappointment. His must be a frustrating job at times. She felt sorry for him. "But he has the same straight, dark hair, and the same sort of features," she said, "or lack of them."

"And there can't be too many men around who wear a large citrine on a gold cord," added Joss.

"Especially," said Isabel, "ones who run a group similar to the one Richard Forster was involved in."

"Okay," said the constable. "I think it's worth following up, but I'll have to check with Sergeant Williams."

Detective Sergeant Williams was a massively built man in his thirties, well over six feet tall, with crew-cut hair and a face like a friendly bull terrier. "Good of you to come in," he said. His voice was a surprising light tenor. "I think Detective Sergeant Kelly from the Queensland Police should see your statement. We'll email it up to him in Auckland immediately, and we'll get back to you as soon as we hear something. We've got your phone numbers, have we? Good. Thank you again for your help." He escorted them down a stark, neon-lit corridor to the glass door that opened onto the entrance foyer.

As they negotiated the wide concrete ramp leading down to the street, Joss turned to Isabel. "Well, that was pretty painless, wasn't it?"

"They weren't exactly jumping up and down with excitement," Isabel replied. "We probably won't ever hear from them again."

* * * *

Isabel popped the last morsel of wholemeal bread into her mouth and surveyed her empty soup bowl with satisfaction. "That was great," she said to Joss. "Just what I needed.

Thanks."

Joss placed a mug of coffee on the table in front of her. "Now I intend to exact payment," she said. "I want to hear *all* about your weekend."

The telephone rang and, with a grimace of exasperation, Joss went out to the hall to answer it. She returned a moment later, her eyes sparkling. "Who do you think *that* was?" she asked smugly, then sat down and began to drink her coffee.

"Well, come on, the suspense is killing me."

Joss drank some more coffee. "Someone," she said, "whom *you* said we'd never hear from again."

"Not Sergeant Williams, already?"

"The very same. By all accounts, Detective Sergeant Kelly of the Queensland Police is extremely interested in finding out more about Bob Ferris, and will be flying down from Auckland tomorrow morning. I said we'd talk to him here tomorrow after lunch. Is that okay with you?"

"Aren't we recording at Luke's then?"

"Damn. So we are. I'd better let Sergeant Williams know." At the door she turned. "Hang on! We should be finished recording by around half past three. If this Sergeant Kelly meets us at Luke's place then, he can talk to all of us. Luke has met Bob, and so has Philip, if he's there. What do you think?"

"Brilliant! Why don't you go and run it by Sergeant Williams now?"

* * * *

Luke was in the kitchen making coffee, while Isabel, Joss,

and Geraldine waited in their habitual places in his lounge. James had already left, as he had a departmental meeting to attend. Philip, to Geraldine's disappointment, was absent. It would have been nice to see him again, but she hadn't quite liked to say anything to Luke, especially in front of the others.

The doorbell chimed, and Luke appeared from the kitchen. "Well, I'll say one thing for Sergeant Kelly—he's got good timing. Could someone go and get the coffee while I play the good host?"

Isabel, who happened to be sitting nearest the kitchen, went to attend to it.

Declan had been wondering what to expect, but whatever it had been, it certainly wasn't this rambling, gracious, cream wooden house with leadlight windows, half hidden from the street by massive rhododendrons and camellias, a graceful birch tree weeping over them. The garden had clearly been magnificent once, though it was now looking rather shaggy, as though it could do with a good haircut. He pressed the button that constituted the centre of a brass art nouveau camellia, its form echoed in the stained glass of the top panel of the door. A chime sounded somewhere in the depths of the house.

"Hi. You must be Sergeant Kelly. I'm Luke Marriot." The man who stood at the door was not at all Declan's idea of someone who dabbled in the paranormal. Of average height, good looking in an unprepossessing, boyish sort of way, with large hazel eyes and a quirky mouth, he looked far too—well—normal.

Declan pulled his badge out of his pocket and offered it to Luke's gaze. "Detective Sergeant Declan Kelly, Queensland

Police," he announced, with an air of 'thank God we've got that over and done with'. Then, with a lop-sided grin, "You can forget the title if you like. I usually save that for the bad guys."

Luke grinned back. "Come on in," he said. "You're just in time for coffee."

Declan followed him along a panelled hallway hung with several pleasant landscapes done in oils. They were obviously all painted by the same hand and, since they were not top quality, he guessed they had been done by some family member and handed down through the generations—approximately three of them, judging by the style. The door at the end of the hallway opened onto an L-shaped room which appeared to be two rooms made into one. Filling the space in front of him was a baby grand piano, old, but beautifully cared for. Luke might not be much of a gardener, but he seemed meticulous about what he was interested in.

To the left of the piano, the larger part of the room looked out onto lawn and shrubbery through full-length french doors. In front of these, bathed in muted afternoon sunlight, was a large, carved wooden coffee table, flanked by a comfortable looking leather couch on one side, and two similar armchairs on the other. The couch was occupied by two women. One, who looked around thirty, was tall and tanned with long, straight brown hair, a small, straight brown nose, and rather serious looking brown eyes. She was wearing a dark green tailored shirt and a long, ethnic-patterned brown cotton skirt tucked around her curled up legs. The other woman was fortyish, small and blonde, a thick fringe falling over cornflower blue eyes that sparkled with good humour. Everything about her looked neat and efficient, including her jeans and navy jersey. The small pendant on a chain around her neck was a five-pointed star with a blue sapphire set at its centre.

Luke announced to the couch's occupants, "This is Detective Sergeant Declan Kelly. Declan—" he indicated the tall woman with a wave of his arm, "—this is Geraldine Bird, librarian and part-time astrologer and numerologist. And this is Joss Cherry, our resident clairvoyant, as well as being a journalist. She covers the night beat."

Before Declan could respond, a door opened and a striking red-haired woman came through, carrying a laden black lacquered tray from which wafted the aroma of freshly brewed coffee.

"Ah," said Luke, "I wondered where you'd got to. Declan, this is Isabel Sinclair, professional tarot reader and amateur sleuth."

The woman who smiled back at him was probably in her late thirties, of above average height. Although quite slim, she gave the impression of solidity. She was dressed in a spectacular scarlet skirt that would have done justice to Bizet's Carmen, black calf-length boots, and a black top smothered with strings of red and black wooden beads. Her hair reminded Declan of a pre-Raphaelite painting—not one by Rossetti—she lacked the overt sensuality. More like a Millais or a Waterhouse, though without the fey, mystical air. A mass of red-gold curls tumbled over her shoulders, framing a longish, triangular face, interesting and intelligent rather than pretty, with eyes the colour of pewter, and with the same subtly shaded look. Her nose—a classic Celtic nose, he thought, straight but slightly enlarged at the tip—was spattered with pale freckles.

"Hello, Declan. Nice to meet you." The voice was deep, with the clipped manner of an English accent, though the slightly flattened vowels told him she had lived at least most of her life in New Zealand. Dragging his eyes away, he sat down in the nearest armchair and gratefully accepted Luke's offer of coffee. He noticed Joss looking at him with a gleam of amusement in her eyes. Probably good at her job, he judged—those blue eyes wouldn't miss a thing.

Luke passed a plate of home-made biscuits his way. Declan declined with a shake of his head. "No, thanks, I had my fill on the plane. Great coffee, but." He nodded at Joss. "I understand you recognised the photograph of Richard Forster."

"Or Bob Ferris, as we know him," Joss replied. "To be precise, it wasn't so much Bob we recognised, as the pendant he was wearing."

"Yes," said Isabel. "A whacking great citrine. He still wears it—just about all the time I should think."

"And then," Joss added, "when we thought about the names, assuming Bob is short for Robert, the initials are the same. And it seems Bob is currently running the same sort of group Richard Forster was running up in the Coromandel. It all seems too much of a coincidence."

"It does, doesn't it?" Declan finished his coffee and put the mug back on the tray. "From what I can see, it's the same sort of organisation he was involved with in Queensland, where Claire Lomax died."

"The funny thing is," said Luke, "when I interviewed him, he seemed to have lived and studied on practically every major land-mass on the planet, but he never once mentioned Australia."

"Perhaps that's not so surprising, really," Geraldine suggested, "if he was responsible for this girl's—Claire's—death."

"Was he?" Luke's question was avid enough to make Joss smile.

"Well," said Declan, "it's difficult to be sure after ten years. She was pregnant, and she died of a heroin overdose. But *someone* had to have dumped her body out where it was found. It's a pretty remote place—" his nose wrinkled in distaste at the memory, "—and there's no way she got there by herself, not in her condition. Forster seems to have been the last person to see her alive, and he left the country in a big hurry straight afterwards, so I guess it looks pretty suspicious. And he seems to have repeated the pattern up on the Coromandel Peninsula."

"Not another death?" Geraldine looked shocked.

Declan shook his head, then ran his fingers through his hair. "Not this time, fortunately. But apparently he got a girl pregnant there, at a commune he was running, called the Rose and Star Community."

"Sounds like a pub," said Isabel, and wondered why Declan gave her a strange look.

Declan continued, "Seems the girl was underage, and her parents called the police in. About the same time as they appeared on the scene, Forster vanished, never to be seen again."

There was a silence as the others took in this new information.

Finally, Joss suggested softly, "Until now, perhaps?"

Declan shrugged. "Looks like it. What does he look like now?"

The others described Bob, each giving a slightly different perspective. When they had finished, Declan let out a long, whistling breath, rubbing his temple with one finger. "You don't happen to know where he is now?"

"Oh, yes. Indeed we do," Isabel said. "The Circle of Light Centre."

Declan laughed. "Where on earth do they get these names from? And what and where is the Circle of Light Centre?"

"Perhaps," sighed Joss, "we'd better start at the beginning."

"In that case, I think we need more coffee." Luke stood up and picked up the tray.

An hour later, Declan put down his coffee mug, stretched his arms and flexed his shoulders. He now knew as much as the rest of them about Bob's——or Richard's—— more recent activities.

"Well," he said, "it certainly looks as though Richard Forster and Bob Ferris are one and the same. I wonder how I can get to see the bloke without arousing his suspicions?"

"Ah, I think Isabel can help you there," Joss said, observing with amusement the expression that flickered in Declan's eyes before he suppressed it and looked across at Isabel.

Isabel looked up, unwrapping a strand of hair from her finger. "There's a retreat there next weekend. It's a long weekend, so we'll have three whole days—with *plenty* of time for *individual tuition*, or so Bob assured me."

"I take it you're going, then?" Declan asked with a wry smile.

"He's promised to make up for the lessons I missed when he moved out to the new centre, so I couldn't possibly not go, could I?"

"And what exactly do these—ah—lessons consist of?" asked Declan. He had not failed to notice the slight shudder that had accompanied Isabel's flippant words.

"Oh, just boring meditation and breathing exercises, mostly."

Geraldine looked at her. "So he hasn't got to the tantric stuff yet?"

"Tantric?" Declan's voice was sharp with recognition. "Is *that* what he's into?"

Isabel shrugged. "So it seems. But it's okay," she added, just a trifle defensively, "I'm sure I can handle him if I need to."

"I'm sure you can."

Joss picked up the note of amused admiration in Declan's voice. She wondered if Isabel had.

"The thing is," Declan went on, "I'm going to need to see Bob for myself. Would it look too obvious if I turned up next weekend—not with you," he hastened to add. "I don't want to cramp your style, especially if you're having *individual tuition*."

Isabel gave him an unfathomable look.

"Actually," said Geraldine, "I'm sure I saw a notice in the New Directions bookshop when I was in there yesterday, advertising Bob's weekend retreats. So, presumably he's hoping for some newcomers."

"Yes," Joss said sarcastically, "he'll need more disciples if he's going to be able to afford the upkeep on his new premises."

Declan laughed. "That reminds me," he said, "do you know if he's officially vacated his former premises? I'd like to have a look around there if I can."

The others shook their heads. "We could go and have a look now if you like," Luke suggested.

Joss looked at her watch. "I can't," she said. "Martin's cooking dinner tonight, and I promised I'd be home by six at the latest."

Luke thought for a moment. "Have you made any plans for dinner?" he asked Declan.

Declan shook his head. "I hadn't really thought about it yet."

"Right, come and have dinner here, then. And Isabel and Geraldine, you're both welcome, too." He gave Geraldine a bland look. "Philip will be home by then."

Geraldine nodded and smiled her assent.

Isabel said, "I'd love to have dinner with you, Luke, but I'll have to nip home first and feed the cats."

"Right." Luke was now in high gear. "Shall we go round to Bob's place now, and see what we can see—we can use my car. After that, we'll stop off at your place, Isabel, then come back here. Dinner may be a little late, but I'm quite happy to ply you all with strong drink until it's ready."

"Sounds good to me." Declan grinned.

Joss picked up her bag and slung it over her shoulder. "It will be well worth waiting for, I can assure you," she said, "and afterwards you can all listen to The Psychic Connection on the radio."

* * * *

Luke parked the car, and they sat for a moment surveying the straggly hedge. The rusted gate looked, if anything, even more dejected than before.

"There certainly doesn't appear to be any sign of life," said Luke.

"It feels empty," Isabel agreed.

"We'd better knock on the door first," Geraldine said. "If there's anyone there, I suppose we can concoct some sort of story."

"No worries." Declan grinned. "I've had years of practice."

They made their way past the jungle of foliage to the verandah. Declan knocked loudly on the peeling paint. The sound echoed through the house. He knocked again. They waited. The herbs reached out their spindly stalks from their terracotta pots, and the wisteria creaked, releasing its subtle perfume into the cooling breeze, but no-one appeared at the door.

After several minutes had passed, Luke said impatiently, "Come on, let's have a look around."

They peered through the bay window to the left of the front door, shading their eyes against the glare of sunlight on the glass.

"This is the room where he has—had—his group meetings," Isabel said to Declan. "It looks pretty much as it did, except all the cushions and the mattresses have gone. The cushions are in the church now—I saw them there."

"Mattresses?" Declan's voice held a quizzical tone.

Isabel grinned. "As far as I know, they were only used for people to sit on. Though it did occur to me they could have other uses."

Declan gave her a look tinged with irony. "What's this room?' He indicated the smaller window on the other side of the door. It was shrouded with dingy curtains of indeterminate hue.

Isabel shrugged. "I've never been in there. The sunroom where he did his tarot readings and held his private classes is at the back of the house. The kitchen is too, I think."

Pushing their way through the small thicket of bushes which grew between the verandah and the boundary fence, they came to another window, its frame almost denuded of paint by the weather, and showing signs of serious rot.

"This should have been replaced years ago," Geraldine said, picking at the softened wood. She gazed rather pointlessly at the heavily curtained glass. "I wonder what this is?"

Luke said, "I think it's his bedroom—or was. When I was here to interview him, I'm sure we went past it when he took me from the sunroom at the back of the house to have a look at his meeting room at the front. The door was slightly open, as I recall."

"And you just happened to glance through it, I suppose?" Isabel's query was tinged with sarcasm.

"Of course not. I did it on purpose," Luke responded, with an infuriating grin. "There was a double bed there with a green bedspread, and several tables with brass ornaments and incense and such—oh, and the big brother to that citrine he wears."

"Why don't we go round the back," Declan suggested, "and see what else we can see?"

They followed him along the narrow concrete pathway, green and slippery with moss.

This must be the damp side of the house, Luke decided. He had one or two window frames of his own that ought to be replaced before too long. At the back of the house was a small rectangle of shaggy grass that must once have been lawn, bordered on one side by a mass of overgrown vegetables, and on the other by several fragrant bushes bearing the shrivelled remains of a crop of blackcurrants. A long clothesline sagged across the edge of a square of pitted concrete beside the house. Its wooden prop lay almost hidden in the long grass. What had once been an outside toilet was connected to the house by a sort of corridor of green corrugated plastic leading to what was presumably the back door. To the right of this was a small window, set high in the wall.

Luke pointed this out to the others. "That must be another window to the bedroom."

He scouted around for something to stand on, while Declan squinted through a small window to the left of the 'ablution block'. It revealed a tiny, old-fashioned kitchen. He followed Isabel's red skirt round to the other side of the house, where she indicated the long window of the sunroom. Through a gap in the sagging blind a glimpse was possible of what was now a completely bare white room. Further along the wall was another bay window, smaller than the one at the front.

"That must be the sitting room," said Isabel. "The sunroom is off it." She made her way past a spindly, overgrown rose bush and looked in. "Yes, this is it. Someone's been doing some packing, by the look of it. A lot of the books and papers are gone."

She was aware of Declan's face close beside hers at the window. "Mother of God! What on earth was it like before?" he exclaimed, surveying the messy room.

Isabel's reply was forestalled by Luke's voice calling,

"Come and have a look at this."

He was perched on an old galvanised iron rubbish tin, looking through the high window of the bedroom. "All the furniture's still there, and some of the other bits and pieces, so either he owns this place, or someone's still paying rent."

Luke stepped down, and Declan took his place on the bin. In front of him, against the left-hand wall, he saw an old-fashioned double bed. Its bedclothes had been removed, except for a grey brushed-cotton underblanket. Two rather attractive art deco oak bedside tables stood either side of it, but they were empty. So was a low table beneath the other window. Then he saw the painting, just visible on the wall beside the larger window, above another low table. Declan gasped. It was one of Miriam's paintings!

* * * *

Philip poured himself another whisky. "So you're pretty sure now that Bob's the man you're looking for?" he queried, sliding the decanter across the coffee table towards Declan, slouched comfortably in the armchair opposite.

Declan refilled his glass then turned to Isabel in the armchair beside him. Isabel held out her glass for him to top up and he caught a whiff of her spicy perfume. He glanced across at Geraldine, curled up again on the couch, but she shook her head. She was drinking white wine, if you could call her miniscule sips drinking.

"I'd say Miriam's painting pretty well clinches it," Declan said. "She has a very distinctive and unusual style, and I've never seen one of her paintings for sale, even on what you might call her home turf. If I had, I'd have bought one," he admitted with a characteristic lop-sided grin.

He sipped his whisky, savouring its warmth on his tongue before swallowing. Luke's whisky was like his home, full of opulent good taste. "I want to find out who owns that house of his," he said at last. "Luke's right. If he was just renting it, you'd expect him to have moved all his things out when he left. Not that I envy him the task," he added, with a smile at Isabel.

"I imagine," she said, "he'd have plenty of willing helpers."

"Mmm." Declan ran his fingers thoughtfully round the rim of his glass. "I think I'll commandeer a couple of helpers myself, tomorrow. I want to have a good look through that place before Forster—or Ferris—comes back for the rest of his things."

"I don't envy them the task," Isabel murmured with a mischievous grin.

There was silence for a moment as they sipped their drinks and reflected on the latest turn of events. From the kitchen came faint sounds of culinary industry. Luke had sequestered himself in the kitchen with the remains of a bottle of red wine, flatly refusing to allow anyone to help him, claiming they'd only interfere with the creative process.

Geraldine freed her long legs from the folds of her skirt and leaned forward to pour herself another half glass of wine. "Have you spoken to Anne yet?" she asked Declan.

"Who's Anne?"

Geraldine explained, "Anne was the person who first told us about Bob," and she went on to give an account of Bob's phone calls and veiled threats.

Declan's lip curled as though he had a nasty taste in his

mouth. "Sounds like a real creep," he commented. "Yeah, I think I should talk to Anne, and get a proper statement from her. This Bob may or may not be a murderer but, either way, I reckon he's up to no good, and he needs stopping before he does any more harm."

The others nodded their agreement.

"What about that friend of yours, Geraldine?" Philip asked. He couldn't help noticing how her skin glowed warm and golden in the lamplight, like peaches in brandy. "Didn't Bob run the same trip on her?"

"You mean Liz?" Geraldine gave Philip a shy smile. "Yes— at least he tried to." She turned to Declan. "I'll give you her phone number if you like. I'm sure she'll be only too happy to talk to you."

"Thanks." Declan pulled a notepad and pen from his pocket and Geraldine furnished him with the details.

"I might as well get contact details for Anne while I'm about it," he said, with a hopeful look at the others.

"Luke will have those," Isabel told him. "The rest of us have only ever met her here."

Right on cue, the kitchen door opened and Luke materialised, a look of triumph on his face. "Dinner," he announced with a flourish, "is served!"

CHAPTER NINETEEN

Searching Bob's house was, as Isabel had predicted, no enviable task. Gaining entry was a simple enough matter, but sifting through the clutter in the sitting room was distinctly daunting.

"Well, I guess we'd better get stuck in," Declan said to the two young constables who had been detailed to help him. "Standing looking at it won't make it any easier." He sent them off to check out the rest of the house, and moved purposefully towards the bookshelves.

He began flicking through the dusty books and magazines, none of which seemed the sort of thing a man like Bob would own. From what he had discovered of Bob so far, he somehow didn't see him as an avid reader of The Woman's Weekly, of which piles of yellowed copies filled most of one shelf. Above it were dozens of old hard-backed copies of novels by the likes of Georgette Heyer, Mary Stewart, and Agatha Christie. Declan scratched his head, puzzled.

He was about to check through a pile of long-playing records lying on the floor, when Constable Johns stuck his pale, cropped head round the door. "The other rooms seem to have been pretty well cleaned out, sir," he said, "but we can't get into the room next to this one. There's a bolt and padlock on the door. Do you want us to break in?"

Declan nodded, and went back to the pile of records. Bing

Crosby, Perry Como, Hits From the Shows. Something was distinctly odd here. He moved across to the piano that stood in one corner. The pile of music on top of it proved to be mainly hymns and songs from light opera. His puzzled musing was broken by Constable Johns's voice calling from the other room, "Come and look at this, sir."

The dingy curtains had been pulled back to reveal a room of medium size whose peeling, rose-patterned wallpaper must once have been quite attractive, in a twee sort of way. The plaster ceiling rose also had the motif, appropriately enough, of roses. The floor was uncarpeted, covered only with a square of worn linoleum doing its feeble best to emulate a Persian carpet. Constable Johns was busy picking the lock of a relatively new-looking metal cabinet in one corner while, in the other, Constable MacIntosh, a stocky, dark-haired man with the physique of a body-builder and the personality of Father Christmas, stood over a pile of a dozen or so boxes.

Intuition sent a ripple of excitement through Declan. He strode across and pulled open the lid of one of them. It was full of paperbacks. Declan picked one up. Its black cover bore in silver lettering the title, The Book of Thoth, and the name of the author, The Master Therion. A glance inside revealed that the Master was, in fact, one Aleister Crowley.

"This is more like it," he muttered.

At that moment, Constable Johns succeeded in opening the cabinet. On its shelves were neatly stacked bundles of letters, and numerous boxes of photographs and slides. There was also a digital camera and a couple of memory sticks.

"Right—" Declan turned to Constable MacIntosh "—we

may as well do this in comfort. Let's get this lot down to the station."

MacIntosh stumped off to phone for a van, and Declan went to get Miriam's painting from the bedroom. He had no intention of leaving any evidence for Bob to reclaim.

* * * *

"Mother, it's for you."

"Who is it?"

As Isabel entered the hallway, Dominic's voice sank to a stage whisper. "It's a strange man!" he said, holding out the receiver.

As she held it to her ear, Declan's voice said, "I didn't think I was all *that* strange."

Isabel laughed. "Take no notice of Dominic. If anyone's strange, it's him."

"Dominic?"

"My son."

"Ah." There was a moment's enigmatic silence, then Declan said, "Look, I hope you don't mind me phoning you at home like this, but I've found out one or two things about Bob I thought you and your friends would be interested in. Also, I was hoping you could put me in the picture about this retreat of Bob's since I'm planning to go to it."

"Would you like me to arrange a meeting with the others?" Isabel asked, a little puzzled by the call.

"Well, yes, I think we'll need to get together again soon. But..." another slightly awkward pause, "look, I was wondering if you'd have dinner with me. I've spent all day buried in old papers and photographs, and I reckon I deserve a break, and I dare say you could do with one, too."

Isabel's immediate instinct was to ask, 'Why me?' More than a decade as a single parent had given her little time or money to seek or foster relationships with men. Over the years she had developed a busy social life, consisting entirely, she now realised, of group or business activities, either with people she had known for years and felt safe with, or with people she had nothing to do with at all outside of a specific mutual interest. Besides, five years with the charismatic but disturbed Stephen had left her extremely wary of men. Handling creeps like Bob was relatively easy. You knew exactly where you were with them. But men like Declan, who were pleasant and—well, to be honest, attractive...

"So, what do you think?" Declan's voice required an answer. Isabel told herself not to be so daft. It was only dinner. And anyway, in another week or two he'd be out of the country and she'd never see him again. No danger there, surely.

"Okay," she said. "I'd like that. Only please don't ask me to suggest a restaurant. It must be ten years at least since I've been anywhere more exciting than the local pizza parlour."

Declan chuckled. "In that case, you need a break even more than I do. Don't worry, I'm sure I can sort something out. Do you like Italian food?"

Isabel did.

"Great," Declan said. "I'll make a few enquiries then, and pick you up at seven-thirty. How does that sound?"

"That'll be fine." Isabel gave him her address, though she suspected he already knew it. Declan hung up, leaving her to panic about what she should wear.

To Isabel's relief, Declan had booked them into a modest bistro-style restaurant with a cosy, candlelit atmosphere and a live guitarist ensconced in a corner playing soft, Neapolitan melodies. Declan refilled her glass with the mellow red wine he had chosen to accompany the ravioli. "So you reckon I can just turn up on the Thursday evening and say I saw a notice in that bookshop—what was it called again?"

"New Directions."

"Right. And I suppose there's some sort of exorbitant fee involved?"

"Oh, yes. The New Age is very big on personal responsibility—which in practice means you pay through the nose for everything. It's a hundred dollars. Mind you," Isabel added with a sardonic smile, "that does cover everything, including food."

"It's going to look great on my expenses sheet. Voodoo's going to love it."

"*Who?*"

Declan grinned at her. "Chief Inspector Stefan Vodanovich, my boss."

With a chuckle, Isabel reached for her wine glass and took a sip, revelling in the sheer luxury of dining out. Declan's down-to-earth manner and wry sense of humour made him a pleasant, and distinctly non-threatening companion. "So, when am I going to hear your new information about Bob?"

"I'll tell you over dessert. Do you want dessert?" Declan signalled to a waiter hovering at a discreet distance.

Minutes later, Isabel was sampling a mouthful of the

zabaglione she had chosen principally on the strength of its intriguing name. It was delicious. "Mmm," she enthused, "I could definitely get used to this."

"It's not hard to make," said Declan. "I can give you the recipe if you like."

"Please," Isabel said. She had a suspicion she could get used to Declan, too, given half a chance. She liked the way his thick, dark hair rippled, and the way he ran his hand through it in moments of thought or uncertainty. She liked the way his eyes changed colour, reflecting inner changes of mood or emotion. And she liked the way he left room for her input in all his suggestions. Deliberately ignoring the possible ramifications of these thoughts, she went on, "So what else have you found out about Bob?"

Declan sipped his wine. He was enjoying watching Isabel enjoying herself. Come to that, he was enjoying watching Isabel. Tonight she was wearing a patchwork skirt of soft fabrics, predominantly in greens and blues, that flowed around her legs, swishing when she moved, and a deep blue top embroidered at the neck with gold. Long gold earrings set with triangular pieces of turquoise swung from her ears. With her colourful clothes, her red-gold curls flowing over her shoulders, and her frank, grey eyes, she put him in mind of some latter-day Boadicea.

Declan found himself wondering if she had the same warrior spirit as that famous queen, and beginning to speculate on how he might respond to it if she had. Best not to go down that road, though. Instead, he said, "Well, for a start, the house we saw the other evening belongs to a woman called Nancy Elizabeth Whittaker. Her brother left it to her when he died about five years ago, but she doesn't appear ever to have lived there, so presumably she's been renting it out."

"Nancy!" Isabel exclaimed, her eyes dancing. "I *knew* there had to be some reason why Bob was being so nice to her."

"Why? Who is she? And why shouldn't he be nice to her?"

"She's one of the 'older ladies' in Bob's group. She's very nice, really, but she's one of those silly, dithery people who can drive you up the wall in five minutes flat."

"Ah, doesn't like ditherers. I'll have to bear that in mind." Declan pretended to make a note on his hand.

Isabel strove with mixed success to ignore the effect his teasing eyes were having on her composure. "I always thought at the meetings that she acted as though she owned the place," she said. "Now I know why. How did you get on with the search of the house, anyway?"

"Now that," said Declan, pouring more wine, "is what I really wanted to tell you. You know you said it looked as if some of the things from the sitting room had been packed up and taken away?" Isabel nodded. "Well they had. They were all stacked up in the other front room, the one that had the curtains drawn."

"Aha!" Isabel felt a surge of excitement that had nothing whatsoever to do with Declan. "So what was in them?"

"Books—mostly stuff about magic and tarot, and various philosophical and religious teachings. A number of them had 'Richard Forster' written inside them, and an address in Blenheim, here in New Zealand. Pending further inquiries, we're assuming that's where he grew up."

"That's up near Nelson, near the top of the South Island," Isabel told him.

Declan nodded. "Then there was a box full of letters. We're still sorting through them, but so far we've discovered a *very* interesting exchange between Forster and a Max Muller in America." Declan paused to order coffee.

Isabel nodded. "Yes, he told Luke about Max Muller. I found a bit about him in a book I got from the library. He was a Rosicrucian adept who was part of the early New Age movement in the San Francisco area. What was Bob writing to him about?"

Their coffee arrived, and Isabel waited impatiently while Declan stirred his thoughtfully, although he added no sugar. At last he looked across at her. His eyes, which were neither grey nor blue nor green, exactly, but reminded her somehow of the sea on a cloudy day, bore a faintly cynical air as he said, "He didn't exactly come straight out with it, but he seemed to be trying to find out how to be a guru."

Isabel laughed. "Surprise, surprise! Did you find anything else interesting?"

"We certainly did! There was a metal cabinet there, locked of course. But the very useful Constable Johns picked the lock for me, and guess what we found inside?" Realising this was a rhetorical question, Isabel said nothing. Declan, grinning like a very worldly schoolboy, went on, "Your mate, Bob, has a file card for everyone in his group—possibly even everyone who's ever been to any of his groups—some of them go back years. You're in there. So is Anne."

"The bastard!" Isabel was shocked. "What sort of information does he keep?"

Declan tried to be reassuring. "Oh, mostly just names, telephone numbers, addresses. Some of them, including Anne's, have what look like symbols of some sort under the names. We're working on the theory that they're some kind of personal code to record information he wants to keep confidential."

"You mean secret!" exclaimed Isabel. Declan could hear the anger in her voice, and a tinge of fear as well. Instinctively, he reached out for her hand. It occurred to him, however, that she might misinterpret the move, so he picked up his coffee cup instead. It was empty.

"Well," he said, putting the cup down again, "we now have quite a decent list of potential informants, so long as we can trace their current whereabouts. Oh, and there was a box of photos, as well as a camera and a couple of memory sticks. We've only been through the photos so far, but some of them were extremely interesting."

"I'll just bet they were!" Isabel drank the last of her coffee.

"Yeah. There's no way now that Bob can deny he was in Australia, or at the Tree of Life Community. There are photos taken at the place in the Coromandel, too, including a couple of that poor kid he got pregnant—Julie Hazelwood. There are a lot more as well, but it's difficult to tell where most of them were taken. Though there were a couple of him with his mother and his grandmother. His mother was a very pretty red-head, maybe a bit weak-looking, but his grandmother looked a real hard case. The name Ferris was his grandmother's, by the way. It was written on the back of the photos—'Richard, Mother, Granny Ferris.'"

Isabel said, "Ah, so it wasn't just a matter of using the same initials. Would it be possible to show them to Luke and the others? We might be able to tie some of them in with Luke's recording of his interview with Bob."

"Yeah, that shouldn't be a problem." Declan looked at

Isabel, watching the way the candlelight played on her red curls, creating little gleams of red and gold. Red and gold. It reminded him of something his mind had vaguely registered while he was looking through the photographs. "Would you like another coffee, or shall we go now?"

Isabel declined a coffee. Declan called the waiter over and asked for the bill. It wasn't until they were leaving, and Isabel's hair caught the full glow of the light in the foyer, that it finally hit him. As far as he could tell, every significant woman in Bob's life, including his mother, had had red hair.

* * * *

"So—" Joss settled herself more comfortably on Luke's couch "—how was your dinner with Ned Kelly?" They were there at Declan's request to review the situation in the light of his enquiries over the last week. So far, however, only Isabel and Joss had arrived, and Joss took advantage of Luke's temporary absence from the room to satisfy her curiosity.

For a few seconds, Isabel contemplated feigning innocence, but she knew Joss well enough to realise this would get her nowhere. Instead, she grinned a trifle sheepishly, and said, "How did you know?"

"Aha!" Joss donned a melodramatic look, enjoying herself hugely. "Actually, Dominic told me. I phoned your place on Friday night, and he said you were out with some foreigner. From his description, it could only have been the wild colonial boy."

"What on earth was Dominic doing at home on a Friday night?" Isabel asked, momentarily side-tracked by this rare phenomenon.

Joss shrugged. "Judging by noises off, I should say it involved the stereo, and at least one young lady. I dare say he was taking advantage of the cat being away, if you'll pardon the expression. Anyway, you haven't answered my original question."

Attempting an air of nonchalance, Isabel said, "He just wanted to talk to me about the retreat next weekend."

"A likely tale!" said Joss. "I saw the way he was looking at you the other day. And you still haven't answered my question." Then, seeing Isabel's discomfiture, "Oh, look, I didn't mean to badger you. For what it's worth, I like Declan—and frankly, if anyone deserves a night out, it's you."

"The fact is, I'm well and truly out of practice at this sort of thing," Isabel admitted, "but I like him too. He's good company, and we had a lovely meal. I had zabaglione for dessert, and he's going to give me the recipe."

Joss raised her eyebrows. "A man with hidden talents, forsooth!"

Before she could say any more, the doorbell chimed, and Luke reappeared with Geraldine and James. James had asked for an evening meeting so he wouldn't have to rush off to any other meeting or lecture. He had also hinted, with an air of mystery, that he, too, had some interesting information to impart.

Instead of his usual seat on the piano stool, James went through to the dining room and brought back an easy chair, setting it down at the end of the couch, next to Joss. "So," he said, automatically reaching to straighten his tie before realising he wasn't wearing one, "where's our friend from the Queensland Police?"

"Detective Sergeant Kelly," said Geraldine.

"Declan," Luke added, bending to stub out his cigarette. "He should be here any time now."

As if to prove his assertion, the doorbell chimed once more. As Luke went to answer it, Joss slipped out to the kitchen to get the coffee—its aroma had been tantalising her for some time.

"Right," Luke said, once they were all settled. "Philip won't be back till after nine-thirty. He's got squash practice. But I can always fill him in later." He turned to Declan, who seemed to be contemplating a box file he had brought with him. "In the meantime, we're all dying to know what you've come up with."

"Except, possibly, Isabel," murmured Joss, ignoring the brief warning look from Isabel, and the sharp one from Declan. She noted with interest, however, his smile as he glanced at Isabel before placing the file on the coffee table and opening it.

"Okay," Declan said, "I don't want to bore you with a lot of detail, but basically, we now know Bob's real name is Richard Forster. For all I know or care, he got the name Bob out of a fortune cookie, but Ferris was his grandmother's name."

"The one who taught him to read the tarot?" Luke asked.

"I guess so. And the house he was living in, the one we looked at the other night, where we found all this fascinating material, belongs to a Nancy Whittaker, who's a member of his current group, the Circle of Light. So, one way or another, mainly through letters and photos, it's clear Forster was associated with the Tree of Life Community in Queensland and, more importantly, with Claire Lomax, who almost certainly died there. We also now have photographic evidence of his involvement with Julie Hazelwood at the Rose and Star Community near Amodeo Bay on the Coromandel Peninsula. He got her pregnant then left in a hurry," he explained to James, who was looking bewildered.

"He seems to make a habit of it," James responded with a sigh, rubbing his smooth forehead. "Anita's pregnant, too. She told me a couple of days ago. Anita is one of my psychology students, and a member of this Circle of Light group," he added for Declan's benefit. Acknowledging the astonished looks of the others, he went on gloomily, "Apparently, she hasn't bothered sitting any of her exams, and she said she's left university as of last week to go and live at the Circle of Light Centre. I did my best to dissuade her, but I'm afraid she wouldn't listen. Just muttered something about being a High Priestess and giving birth to the Child of the New Aeon."

"Oh, God, we all know what that means!" Joss exclaimed. Seeing how genuinely distressed James was, she leaned across to pat his arm. "James, you can't hold yourself responsible. I'm sure you did everything you possibly could."

James smiled at her gratefully, but he still looked worried.

Luke stood up. "I think," he said, pushing his hair back from his eyes, "we could all do with something a bit stronger than coffee."

Joss had been thinking, abstractedly twisting the tassels of her scarf around her fingers. "Have you been able to find out anything more about what he was up to in Auckland?" she said at last, accepting a brandy from Luke.

"Well," said Declan, "Madame Mimi, who I spoke to at The French Connection..." He broke off and waited for the hoots of laughter to subside. "...a massage parlour in

Karangahape Road," he explained, adding, "you should have seen what they'd done to the Eiffel Tower."

"I shudder to think," chuckled Joss. "Do go on."

"Well, according to Madame Mimi, Forster worked for a year or two at a nightclub called The Big Apple, then left suddenly. Not long after that, the place closed down. She claimed to be a 'close personal friend' of the owner, but it seems he didn't tell her why it closed down. Wouldn't even talk about it, according to her. Though she did say she thought it was some sort of financial trouble."

"Hmm." Joss had been deep in thought again. "After that, he surfaced in the Coromandel, running a commune. And now he's down here, running what amounts to another commune, and buying a church to run it in. You know, I can't help wondering where he got the money."

Geraldine said, "I suppose we can assume he's been doing tarot readings professionally for most of the time he's been here. That must bring him in a regular income."

"I'd hardly call it regular," Isabel said scornfully. "Granted, in a good week it can be quite substantial, but sometimes you can go for weeks with barely an appointment. Most of your clients only ever have one reading. People tend to 'do the rounds', going to any new reader to see what's on offer. So, unless Bob has cracked the secret of developing a large and regular clientele, I can't see how he can have made that much money in, what, five years at the most."

"Oh, I don't know," said Joss, "some people do seem to make a fortune from that sort of thing. Remember that woman who was done for tax evasion a few years ago? Mind you, if Bob had had that sort of following, I think we'd have heard of him a lot sooner. What about donations from the faithful, though? I wouldn't mind betting Nancy let him have that house for little or no rent."

"How many followers has he got?" Declan asked, looking at Isabel.

Isabel thought for a moment. "I doubt if there are more than a dozen at the moment, unless there are some I haven't met yet."

"So much for that theory, then," sighed Joss.

James stopped sipping his unsupplemented tonic water, and said, "I wonder if there might be a connection between Bob's—or Forster's—sudden departure from the nightclub, and its subsequent closure due to financial difficulties?"

"You mean he may have taken off with the proceeds?" Declan asked succinctly. James nodded. "That would solve a couple of outstanding queries, but unfortunately we're not likely to be able to prove anything, what with Des, the manager, having died, and the owner being God only knows where by now."

"What about his grandmother?" Luke suggested. "Or his mother, assuming the grandmother's not still alive? Might one of them have left him money?"

"That's a thought." Declan ruffled his hair with one hand. "It shouldn't be too difficult to check that out. We have an address in Blenheim to start from."

"It was in some of his books," Isabel put in, then stopped abruptly, blushing as the others looked at her. To her relief, Declan's expression remained neutral.

Joss obligingly deflected attention from Isabel by asking Declan, "Have you spoken to Anne yet?"

"Yeah, and Geraldine's friend, Liz. They've both corroborated aspects of what you people have already told me, though neither of them had anything new to add. I must say, though, that the more I hear about this Forster character, the less I like him, or trust him."

"Just as well Isabel won't be going to the Centre on her own this weekend, then," Joss commented, her face a study of innocence.

Declan put his hand to his face as though to rub his forehead, but Joss could see his grin through his fingers for a moment, before he composed his features. He was all right, she told herself. Her intuition was definitely right this time, she was sure of it.

CHAPTER TWENTY

Isabel parked her car beside the poplar hedge, and saw from the late-model fawn Holden Barina standing nearby that Declan had arrived already. So had a number of other newcomers, judging by the half dozen or so unfamiliar vehicles lining the roadside, along with Pat's blue Honda Civic, Jessica's ancient Volkswagen beetle repainted New Age mauve, and the red Mini she recognised as Rhoda's. The motorcycle parked in the lee of the hedge told her the girl with the purple hair was there too, probably with her blonde friend.

Hauling her rucksack out of the Corolla, she made her way up to the hall. Pat waved to her from the doorway. "Georgina, good to see you. Rhoda's taking registrations in the hall, and there's tea and coffee if you want it."

From Rhoda's lack of surprise at her reduced fee payment, Isabel deduced Bob had had a word with her already. Her only comment was that dinner would be served in the hall at six o'clock, and the opening ritual would take place at eight in the church. Isabel thanked her, took the name-tag offered, and made for the tea urn at the other end of the hall.

Among those she had not seen before were an exceptionally tall and thin man with an extravagant nose but a paucity of chin, accompanied by a little round ball of a woman wearing a tightly fitting pink-and-green tracksuit which served to make her hair and complexion look more drab than was strictly necessary. Her slightly bulging eyes gave her the look of an overfed Chihuahua. By comparison, her rangy companion had the look and build of an unhealthy Afghan hound.

Seated on one of the wooden benches lining the walls of the hall was Nancy, holding court amongst a bevy of what was clearly a group of her friends. They were all female, around her own age, and dressed like her in sensible, conservative clothes and shoes. Isabel did a brief head count. There were five altogether, including the one who had been at the previous retreat.

As she sat sipping her watery tea, she looked around the rest of the hall. There were two young men deep in earnest conversation, one rather handsome with dark hair and a beard, his friend a slightly built Asian with fine features and skin like wax. Isabel had the feeling they were a couple. Well, Aleister Crowley wouldn't have disapproved, so why should Bob? (She still found it hard to think of him as Richard Forster). Near the two young men stood the crew-cut blonde from the previous retreat, chatting with her companion, whose hair was now shorn into a matching crew-cut and died magenta. She had a matching scarf draped about her shoulders. Jessica was also with them, but Jeremy was nowhere to be seen.

Neither was Declan. Isabel wasn't sure whether she felt relief or disappointment. Glancing at her watch, she realised it was almost half past five. She picked up her rucksack and headed for the door. She wanted to have a bunk organised before it grew too dark. As she reached the doorway, she met Declan coming the other way, dressed in old jeans and a navy-blue jersey. He murmured a casual greeting, such as one might give to anyone in passing and, keeping his face in neutral, winked at her.

* * * *

Dinner—vegetarian, naturally, but no less enjoyable for that—gave Isabel the chance to further survey the newcomers to the Centre. At the far end of the long table, next to the Chihuahua and the Afghan, sat a tense-looking blonde woman of around fifty, looking incongruous in bright makeup and a red trouser-suit. Next to her, though apparently unconnected, was a tall, distinguished man of about the same age, wearing designer jeans and a grey sweatshirt that matched his expensively styled longish hair. He looked like a media man, Isabel thought—probably television.

Finally, seated almost opposite, was another couple. The woman was a voluptuous Willendorf Venus, her ample curves enveloped in a long, loose, handknitted jersey patterned with Aztec designs in greens, browns and a rich brick-red, doubtless all hand dyed. A quantity of thick brown hair fell over her shoulders and down her back, and her face, which was oval and curiously flat looking, was enlivened by a pair of vivid eyes of a startling golden brown. Her companion, a fair-haired man in his twenties, with the mobile face of an actor and the supple hands of a musician, was a good twenty years younger than she was, yet no-one could have mistaken him for her son. Isabel wondered if she would sacrifice him come autumn, like Cybele in the myths. Somehow, she imagined he would not be entirely unwilling.

By the time dinner was over and the last teas and coffees had been drunk, it was almost a quarter to eight. The night had grown chilly, with a slight mist, so Isabel went to the dormitory block to fetch her jacket. On the way, she passed Jeremy and Jessica, deep in conversation, their arms about each other's waists, walking slowly towards the church.

From the darkness of the night, the church seemed a haven of brightness. Its strange altar window, lit from within, glowed brightly like the one on the Five of Pentacles in the tarot. All it needed was a couple of poverty stricken cripples hovering outside. Instead, however, Rhoda hovered, ushering people in like a diminutive sheep dog—a Corgi, Isabel thought, imagining her running about yipping and nipping at the heels of Bob's flock, keeping them in line for him.

Inside, all the candles burned in their sconces, casting a warm, golden light. Several heaters were also glowing, taking the chill off the large area. All about the church, people sat on pews or cushions, waiting for the ritual to begin. Isabel noticed Declan, seated cross-legged on a cushion near the front, looking about him with apparent interest. He caught her eye briefly, but didn't wink at her again, thank goodness.

To the right of the altar, Anita's head was just visible, clad in a white-and-gold cap. In front of it, with his back to them and his head bowed, stood Bob in his white kaftan. He was lighting the candles in the big candlestick. The music died away. Bob turned to face them and raised his arms in a gesture of benediction. On his chest the citrine pendant caught the light of the candles and gleamed.

* * * *

The clanging of Rhoda's bell woke Isabel next morning at seven o'clock. From the look of the others yawning and stretching in the bunks around her, it was a rude awakening not only for her. Shivering, she pulled on her trousers and thick jersey, stuffed her feet into her boots (she had kept her socks on to ward off the night chill) and made her way to the ablution block at the end of the dormitory. To her surprise, Anita was just in front of her, heading in the same direction. She was swathed in a long, green garment—a sort of cross between a dressing gown and a woollen ballgown. So she was no longer sharing the vestry with Bob, then.

Catching up with her, Isabel spoke cheerily, "Hello, Anita. Let's hope it warms up a bit before long."

Anita turned. She managed a tight little smile, but her face looked drawn and tense. Without a word, she hurried on. When Isabel reached the wash-basins, there was no sign of her. With a shrug, Isabel splashed her face with cold water and rubbed it vigorously with her towel. Feeling slightly more awake, she stowed her toilet gear back in the dormitory and took herself off to the hall for breakfast.

Pat hailed her from her seat at the long trestle table, and Isabel went to join her and the Chihuahua, whose name, it transpired, was Vicky. Her partner, the Afghan, when he joined them, turned out to be Paul. They had been studying the Western Tradition, Vicky enthused, for—oh, it must be at least three years now—and were absolutely thrilled to have the opportunity to learn more about the ultimate purpose of it all. Isabel groaned inwardly. Another Nancy in training!

Fortunately, Vicky and Paul soon took their leave. Isabel poured milk on her second helping of weetbix. "Doug not here this time?" she asked.

Pat shook her head. "One of his friends was taken ill, so Doug had to take over for him at the last minute."

"Pity," said Isabel. "Doug's always good company. Talking of which, I saw Anita just now, and she didn't look very happy at all. Is she all right?"

"She hasn't said anything to me—or anyone else as far as I know. But you're right. She hasn't been herself at all lately. To be honest, I'm getting quite concerned about her. I'll see if I can take her aside sometime soon for a bit of a chat."

Isabel thought it best not to mention Anita's pregnancy, in case Pat wanted to know how she had found out. Jessica and Jeremy drifted past, arms linked, and headed for the tea urn.

Pat smiled fondly after them. "It's lovely to see those two getting on so well. I think they're made for each other, don't you?"

Isabel agreed. There was no denying they did, indeed, seem made for one another. Probably in the same factory.

Rhoda, who had been chatting with Nancy and her coterie, strode with her bell to the front of the hall, and sounded the call to prayer. The day's activities were about to begin.

* * * *

Unlike the previous retreat, this one seemed designed to cater to the mind, rather than the body. Apart from the lunch break, it had consisted of wall-to-wall lectures on aspects of the New Aeon which, according to Bob, was currently being brought to birth. From what her overworked brain could recall, it was a more esoteric version of the Age of Aquarius beloved of the hippies of her parents' generation, and latterly transmogrified through various incarnations, spinning money all the way. By comparison, Bob's version seemed almost quaintly old-fashioned, harking back to the likes of Society of the Golden Dawn, whose members boasted such strange bedfellows (one should pardon the phrase!) as Aleister Crowley and William Butler Yeats.

In the gospel according to Bob, the true teachings underlying the popular trappings of the New Age had lain dormant and misunderstood now for many years—since the death of Crowley himself, or so Bob had hinted—but now was the time for them to be brought out of hiding once more, so that a new generation of students might bring them to a world now not only ready for them, but in direst need. Somehow, without saying so in as many words, he had managed to include green issues and world politics in his expositions, as well as the more expected magic and mystery.

It was now mid-afternoon, and lectures were over for the day. They had all stopped for an afternoon snack before the circle dancing that would end the afternoon. Isabel was sitting on a tree stump behind the hall, soaking up the last of the late spring sunshine, eyes closed, not quite dozing. Wondering drowsily how Declan was handling his introduction to esoteric philosophy, she felt, rather than heard, soft footsteps behind her. She opened her eyes, half expecting it to be Declan. It was Bob.

"Georgina, I was hoping I'd get a chance to talk with you."

Isabel blinked at him, still feeling slightly dazed. He was wearing the white kaftan that now seemed to be his regular uniform, but Isabel noticed he wore trousers and a jersey under it, in deference to the cool weather.

Bob squatted on the ground beside her, a chubby gnome in a nightshirt. "I wanted to assure you I haven't forgotten my promise."

"Promise?"

"To make up for the private lessons you missed."

"Oh, yes. Thank you." Isabel gazed at the back of the hall where the pale green paint was peeling from the gnarled weatherboards. Sitting out here on her own, she was a perfect target for Bob's dubious intentions. She couldn't have done better if she'd planned it.

Bob went straight for the target. "As it happens, I have some time now, while Pat's taking the circle dancing. Come on over. It would be such a pity for you to miss the opportunity for further—development."

His final word was redolent of unspoken possibilities. Isabel was not at all sure she wanted to develop in any direction Bob might lead her. Still, it was, so to speak, an offer she couldn't refuse. As she got to her feet and followed him to the vestry, she was relieved to see Declan looking in their direction.

Bob (with Anita's help, perhaps?) had transformed the old vestry into compact but cosy living quarters. In the corner behind the heavy door were the mattresses from the meeting room at his former home, covered with the same cream cotton covers, and strewn with several of the fat cushions. A wooden trunk stood against the outer wall underneath a double diamond-paned window. Beside it was an oak cabinet whose top was littered with a number of ornaments—a large golden crystal, possibly another citrine, an incense holder with musky incense burning in it, several brass statuettes in interesting poses, and a small green box. Beside the far door, which opened into the main body of the church, a small table held an electric jug and tea-making equipment, including a selection of tea packets. Steam drifted up from the jug.

The floor was spread with several ethnic rugs, including the Kelim Isabel remembered from the tarot room. Taking two cushions from the bed, Bob placed them on the floor and gestured to Isabel to take a seat. As usual, he made tea for both of them. It smelt of citrus and cinnamon. He must have been pretty sure of finding her, Isabel reflected, unless he had just put on the jug on the off chance. Either way, there was something predatory about the manoeuvre that she found disturbing.

In the event, however, her lesson consisted of nothing more worrying than a meditation exercise (visualising a 'cone of energy' this time, culminating in a blue sphere—Bob told her the aim of this was to create a 'platform from which to explore the inner and outer realms,' whatever they might be), and a short discourse on the importance in the general scheme of things of male-female polarity, with some interesting illustrations from the tarot.

This was brought to a conclusion by the distant clamour of Rhoda's bell, summoning the faithful to dinner. Isabel fancied a look of annoyance flitted across Bob's face but, if so, it was gone immediately. Springing to his feet with the grace that always surprised her, he reached out a hand to help her up, holding her hand only slightly too long before going to open the door.

As she left, Bob placed his hands lightly on her shoulders. "Thank you, Georgina," he murmured. "I promise you I'll find some more time for you before the weekend is over.

And, as you know now, I do keep my promises. Besides, I couldn't let such a talented student slip through my fingers, could I?"

To Isabel, these words sounded more like a threat than a promise. With a smile she hoped looked suitably grateful, she stepped backwards and slipped from his grasp. As she made for the dormitory, she was aware of Anita heading in the opposite direction, but she didn't feel like pausing to exchange pleasantries. What she wanted most of all was a shower, to wash away the feeling of Bob's hands, but there wouldn't be time before dinner. She made do with an ice-cold wash.

During dinner, she made a point of asking whether Bob made a practice of giving private lessons, but neither Pat nor Rhoda professed to know anything about it. Isabel deduced that they were probably 'by invitation only'. Certainly Bob had never mentioned the matter to her while anyone else was around—a wise policy, since it wouldn't do to have witnesses if any of his private students 'misinterpreted' their introduction to tantric magic and made a formal complaint.

Isabel realised she was beginning to feel extremely uncomfortable about the trend of Bob's teachings. A worrying number of references to Crowley and his ideas was becoming apparent. She suspected few of his followers knew much about Crowley, caught up as they mostly appeared to be in the sillier and more harmless aspects of New Age love and light. However, she hadn't spent five years around Stephen and his bizarre circle of acquaintances without becoming all too familiar with the bombastic and frequently distasteful beliefs and practices of the self-styled 'Great Beast'. And she was becoming more and more convinced that something far less benign was afoot than showering absent friends with pink light.

This disturbing reverie was broken by a familiar voice at her elbow. "The evening class starts in a few minutes. Are you going?" It was Declan, pretending to be a friendly stranger. Looking up, Isabel realised the hall was almost empty, the last few drifting towards the open door. She stood up and shook herself, but could not quite banish a vague feeling of unease.

"You okay?" Declan murmured as they headed towards the door. He kept his voice and facial expressions to a tone of polite enquiry, so that anyone watching would imagine a simple exchange of pleasantries between two strangers.

Isabel maintained the same tone as she replied, "I think so. Brain's on overload, that's all."

"Yeah, I know what you mean. Never heard such a load of unmitigated garbage in my life. I enjoyed the tea-dance, but. Where were you, by the way? I was going to ask you for the last waltz."

Isabel suppressed a giggle. They were nearing the hall. "Private tuition," she hissed.

"Well, you look after yourself." With that, Declan vanished into the church porch ahead of her. Isabel was about to follow suit when she caught sight of a bulky-looking shadowy figure standing near the back of the church. Curious, she lingered in the shadows to watch. The figure moved and separated into two. The dim light from the vestry windows revealed that the shorter of the two was Anita. The other went behind the church, or possibly into the vestry. Anita began to move in her direction, so Isabel slipped quickly into the church.

As she took a seat next to the Venus of Willendorf and her consort, Bob emerged from the vestry and glided into position before the altar. A few seconds later, Anita came through the front door and positioned herself in a corner on the far side of the church. Her face looked pale, even in the golden glow of the candles, and her eyes showed both anger and fear.

* * * *

The brazen clamour of the bell next morning dragged Isabel from a dream in which she was being pursued by a vague, shadowy figure that kept changing shape each time she thought she knew who it was. Relieved, she opened her eyes and shook herself awake. The thin calico curtains drawn across the high dormitory windows glared with a red glow that reminded her alarmingly of blood. Then she became aware of a muted roar outside. Oh, great, a nor'wester! The strong, warm, dry wind that roared off the Southern Alps so often at this time of year invariably made her feel irritable and slightly nauseated.

All day the wind blew, as they sat through more lectures designed to pull together the varied strands of tarot, meditation, and the magic and philosophy of what Bob termed the Western Tradition, into something resembling a coherent whole. By the middle of the afternoon, Isabel had a raging headache. There was no way in hell she could cope with any circle dancing, she thought, through a fog of pain. Declan would just have to find someone else for the last waltz. Leaving the others to it, she pushed her way against the warm gale back to the dormitory block. She knew from experience that a cool shower and a lie down would at least help a little.

When she woke again it was dusk. Her headache was gone, though she felt drained. To her immense relief, the wind appeared to have died down. She looked at her watch. It was quarter past six. She must have slept through the dinner bell. She pulled on her boots and made her way to the hall. As she passed the vestry, a shape materialised in the dusk in front of her. For a moment, it reminded Isabel of her dream that morning, and she gave an involuntary start.

"Georgina! I didn't mean to startle you," Bob's voice spoke softly out of the gloom.

Just what I need, Isabel thought, another bloody headache. "Oh, hello, Bob. I'm just off to dinner," she said, hoping he would take the hint.

"I won't keep you long, then. I had hoped to see you earlier about finishing the lesson we began yesterday, but unfortunately there was something else I had to deal with. However, since there's no lecture after dinner tonight, I thought we could get together then, say about half past seven?"

It was like a dinner invitation from Lucrezia Borgia, thought Isabel, or a business offer from the Godfather. Oh, well, greater love hath no person, and all that... "Thank you," she replied, "that will be lovely."

"Wonderful!" Bob patted her arm. "You go and get some dinner now, and I'll see you soon."

He merged once more into the deepening murk, leaving Isabel to hurry towards the warmth and cheerful chatter wafting out from the hall. Much as the sessions with Bob were one of her main reasons for being at the Centre, she couldn't rid herself of the sick feeling in the pit of her stomach which had nothing whatsoever to do with the nor'wester. She barely tasted her meal, and found the tea almost undrinkable. Some feeling, or instinct, was pushing its way up from her gut, choking her and making it difficult to breathe.

With a shock, she realised the last time she had felt panic this strongly was when Dominic was barely three years old. She had returned early from a meeting and walked in on Stephen and that repulsive woman, Maxine, stark naked in front of an altar they had erected in the spare bedroom, draped with an altar cloth Maxine had stolen from St Anne's church down the road. Bloody hell! No wonder the churches had stopped leaving their doors unlocked.

She had managed to rescue the cat ("A *cat* for Christ's sake!" "Well, we couldn't find a black rooster, and we have to do it tonight, while the vibes are right." "Well you're not doing it in my house. You've got five minutes to get your clothes on and get the hell out of here—both of you!"), though she never did find out where they had got it from. She had named him Dashwood, after Sir Francis Dashwood, fifteenth Baron Le Despencer, the rakish leader of the eighteenth-century Hellfire Club in England. It had seemed appropriate under the circumstances, and he certainly looked the part, with his sleek black coat with a touch of white at the throat. He had become the first in a varied menagerie of mostly rescued cats.

Stephen and Maxine had dressed in record time, and that was the last she had seen of either of them, apart from one or two half-hearted efforts on Stephen's part concerning access rights to Dominic. The incident itself had left her feeling sick and disgusted. But the sensation she was feeling now had come as a prelude to it, washing over her like a wave before she had even reached the house. But that was then, she told herself sternly, and this is now. With an effort of will, she pushed it to the back of her mind.

As she knocked on the vestry door, she thought she caught sight of Anita hurrying from the hall towards the dormitory, but she pushed that to the back of her mind, too.

"Ah, Georgina! Do come in." Bob had obviously dressed for dinner, in a new kaftan of creamy white soft woollen material with cream silk embroidery around the neck. The citrine, as usual, gleamed on his chest, reflecting back the light of a pair of red candles. In their silver candlesticks they presided over a bottle of wine and two glasses set out on a tray on the floor. Soft music insinuated itself from some unseen source, and incense infused the room with a warm and heady fragrance. With a sinking feeling, Isabel realised this was not going to be any ordinary lesson.

"Wine?" Without waiting for a reply, Bob poured her one anyway, and patted the cushion that awaited her. The last thing she felt like right now was wine, but she accepted the glass on the principle that, after all, she didn't have to drink it.

They sat in silence for a few minutes, Bob sipping his wine, Isabel pretending to sip hers. To her surprise, she had the distinct impression that Bob was nervous, and using the silence to steel himself for something, wording and rewording it in his mind until it was composed to his satisfaction. She said nothing, partly to allow him scope for whatever it was he was grappling with, and partly because she could think of nothing to say. The music, some vague instrumental piece, wove itself through and around the incense to form a soft, sensual tapestry.

At length, Bob placed his empty wine glass back on the tray in an oddly deliberate act. "I consulted the tarot before you came," he said, "and I feel sure you are now ready for the next stage in your spiritual development. You remember I told you, you are a woman of considerable power?"

Isabel nodded, and swallowed some wine in an effort to get rid of the lump that had suddenly materialised in her throat. Bob smiled at her, the candlelight casting bizarre shadows on his face.

"Tonight," Bob went on, "I want to begin to show you how that power can be used. You'll understand, of course, from the lectures I've given this weekend, the importance of polarity and balance in the universe."

Isabel nodded again, not trusting herself to speak.

"As each aeon progresses, and true spirituality dwindles, the universal energies become unbalanced. When that happens, those of us who have the power—and the understanding—are charged with the task of restoring that balance. This is best done through sympathetic magic—that is, by imitating that which we want to bring about. Do you understand that?"

"I think so," said Isabel. In fact, she was beginning to think she understood only too well.

"Good, good." Bob's hand reached out to rest on her arm. By the pretence of drinking some more of her wine, Isabel managed to dislodge it. Bob breathed deeply, and went on. "Of course, in order to perform this essential magic, the magician needs a magical partner. As in the tarot, the High Priest needs the High Priestess, the Emperor needs the

Empress." He reached out again, in one smooth movement removing the wine glass from her hand to replace it on the tray, then grasping both of her hands in his. "Georgina," he breathed, "I want *you* to be my High Priestess. I want you to perform with me the holy magic that will bring this world safely into the New Aeon!"

Isabel was stunned. She had set out to discover what Bob was really up to, but somehow this wasn't quite what she had been expecting. Still, at least it explained the sick feeling in the pit of her stomach. Every cell in her body was urging her to put as much distance between her and Bob as was humanly possible, but somehow she had to induce him to state his purpose more directly. Otherwise all her efforts would have been for nothing.

She drew a deep, slow breath and thought very quickly. "I-I'm very flattered, of course," she stammered, "but I really don't think I'm ready for that yet." She tried to pull her hands away from his.

"Oh, but you are. I know you are." He began to stroke her hands in what he presumably imagined to be a soothing manner. "And you know it too, really, don't you, Georgina?" His voice was soft, but there was a disconcertingly hard edge to it, like a knife wrapped in silk. Keeping hold of her hands with one of his, he moved closer and began to brush her cheek with the other. His fingers, soft and smooth and slightly damp, felt like snakes crawling over her flesh. She shuddered involuntarily.

His hand crept down under her chin, and he moved closer still. "I need your help," he said, his voice smooth and hypnotic. Isabel moved back a fraction, and felt the edge of the bed against her back. Bob was leaning over her, forcing her to lean back over the bed. She wrenched her hands away from his grasp, and tried to roll out of his reach and get to her feet. Immediately, Bob's hands went to her shoulders, pushing her onto the bed and pinning her there.

"Please, Georgina, don't try to fight it." The sound of his voice was like being smothered with oiled silk. For one hysterical moment, Isabel expected him to say, "This thing is bigger than both of us." Instead, he said, "The Universe is calling us to complete the Circle of Love and Light. You can't ignore it!" which was more original, but amounted to much the same thing. Either way, it was hardly reassuring.

He began to stroke her forehead with one plump hand, smoothing her hair back with even, rhythmic movements, while his body held her down, and his voice went on talking in a soft monotone. Against her will, Isabel found herself beginning to breathe more slowly, in time with his strokes on her brow. It became harder and harder to keep her eyes open. She realised he was trying to hypnotise her.

Forcing herself through the soft, enveloping curtain of his voice, Isabel heard, "You can't back out now, Georgina. You and I both know it was destiny that brought us together. We chose it, both of us. You may not realise it consciously, but look inside yourself and you'll see it just as I can." Still stroking her brow with one hand, Bob pressed his body closer to hers. Clearly, he had mistaken her lack of reaction for acquiescence. Isabel felt panic rising like a hard lump in her throat. She knew she had to do something.

"What about Anita?" she threw at him, saying the first thing that came into her head. Anything to break the spell he was trying to weave.

It worked. Bob withdrew his hands and drew back, a look

of surprise on his face. "Anita! Why on earth would I want Anita? She's just a child!"

Isabel rolled swiftly away from him and scrambled to her feet. "You didn't think that when you got her pregnant!" she spat at him, and immediately regretted it. Bob was bound to wonder how she knew about Anita, and the last thing any of them needed was for him to turn the tables and start investigating them. Cursing herself, she made a dash for the door. Bob, with amazing agility, leapt up and literally threw himself at her, pinning her against the heavy planks before she could lift the iron latch, his arms holding her firmly on either side.

"Who told you she was pregnant?" he hissed in her face. "It's a lie! She's just saying that to try and trap me." Collecting himself, he made a visible effort to calm himself, and went on, "I don't want a mere child as my High Priestess. I need a woman, a woman with real power. I need *you*, Georgina!" He leaned forward and tried to kiss her. She could smell the wine on his breath, mingled with the musk of incense that permeated his clothing.

Suddenly Isabel was filled with fury. She couldn't remember ever being so angry before in her life. "You fucking bastard!" she yelled in his face and, as he pulled back slightly, she lifted her knee and jabbed it as hard as she could into his groin.

Bob staggered backwards, clutching at himself and groaning. Without so much as a glance in his direction, Isabel wrenched up the latch on the door, shoved it open, and ran, her breath rasping in her throat, to the dormitory. She grabbed her rucksack and slung her sleeping bag over her shoulder. As she fled towards the roadway, she was vaguely aware of someone calling out after her. It must be Bob. She took no notice, but kept moving.

The sleeping bag kept slipping and wrapping itself round her legs as she ran. After a few yards, she simply dropped it and went on without it, terrified that Bob would come after her. But although the vestry door had been open as she passed it, spilling golden light and the scent of incense into the night, there had been no sign of Bob. She did not notice Anita standing in the doorway of the dormitory, staring after her, a thoughtful expression on her pinched features.

After what seemed an eternity, Isabel reached her car. Panting, she fumbled in the rucksack pocket for her key, and felt for the lock. Two frantic minutes later, the car's engine roared into life. There was a CD in the player. Not caring what it was, Isabel turned the volume to full, and drove.

* * * *

The young man sitting next to him was listening avidly, elbows planted on the table, strong brown hands cupping his chin, as his companion, a massive middle-aged woman in a homespun tunic, discoursed intelligently in a soft, melodious voice about the psychological importance of colour. A pity, thought Declan, it wasn't her running the course, and not that—

Rhoda's voice broke through his thoughts like static interrupting a radio broadcast. "As you all know, Bob will not be giving a class tonight. Instead, we will be showing two short films here in the hall. One is a very interesting film about the chakras, and the other is a fascinating look at the work being done at Mount Shasta in California where, of course, Bob lived and studied some years ago. If we could have some help moving the furniture and setting up the DVD player, we should be ready in about half an hour."

Declan glanced at his watch. It was just after half past seven. He took his empty coffee mug back to the counter at the back of the hall, and went to help the large woman's companion stack the top sections of the trestle table against the wall. He had no intention of staying to watch the DVDs— they sounded bloody awful. He thought he might see if he could cadge some more coffee, and spend some time making notes for the report he would have to file later. He quite fancied the idea of going for a walk after that. What with all the sitting around listening to Bob, he was beginning to feel like he was seizing up.

He wondered if Isabel might like to go with him. Quite apart from enjoying her company, it seemed to Declan it might be a good idea for them to compare notes. There were certainly one or two things he'd like to have clarified. If everyone else had their eyes glued to the screen, it should be easy enough for them both to slip away unnoticed for an hour or so, and even if someone saw them, it would only look as though they had met and made friends on the course. It would only matter if Bob saw them, and he seemed to be incommunicado in his lair.

Declan looked around the hall. There was no sign of Isabel. He realised he hadn't actually seen her since they all sat down to dinner. Oh, well, maybe she was feeling tired, or had something else she wanted to do. He shrugged, and went to the kitchen to see about some hot water. As he left the hall, mug in hand, Rhoda and Pat were shepherding everyone into the chairs that had been set out in rows, and a tall, distinguished-looking man with longish grey hair was fiddling with the projector.

He was squatting on his bunk, his sleeping bag wrapped around him, coffee mug balanced carefully on a flat part of the mattress, chewing his pen hopefully, when he heard a muffled shout, followed by the sound of running feet heading towards the dormitory block. Declan threw off the sleeping bag. He gulped the last of the coffee, threw the mug back on the bed and made for the doorway.

There was no-one in sight. Whoever it was must have gone into the women's dormitory. Declan hesitated. His appearance there probably wouldn't be appreciated. Then he noticed the vestry door was wide open, though Bob was not in evidence. He had begun to move towards the bright patch of light when someone rushed past him out of the women's dormitory, trailing what looked at first glance like a thick cloak. As the form passed through the perimeter of the light from the vestry, Declan caught the glint of red-gold hair. "Mother of God!" he exclaimed under his breath. "That's Isabel!"

He called out after her, remembering just in time to use her pseudonym. She took no notice. As she ran, the article she had been trailing fell to the ground. She kept running, and was soon lost in the darkness. As he stood there, the vestry door swung shut with a dull thud, leaving nothing but the black velvet of the country night. The pinpoints of the stars glittered like sequins on a ballgown, but neither they nor the crescent moon made any impression on the darkness. As he waited for his eyes to acclimatise, Declan made a swift assessment of the situation. He reckoned he had already got as much out of the weekend as he was likely to. And now was neither the time nor the place to do to Bob what his whole being was itching to do.

He returned to the empty dormitory and gathered up his things. As he made his way to his car, there was no sound from the vestry, though a soft light still shone through the diamond-paned windows. The dark bulk of the church squatted inscrutably next to it. A few faint sounds drifted from the dimly-lit hall. As he passed by it, he almost tripped over something lying on the ground. It was the sleeping bag Isabel had dropped.

Declan bent and picked it up. As he straightened up, a slim form hurrying from behind the vestry caught the periphery of his vision. The form stopped for a moment, looking in his direction, then hurried on. He recognised immediately the long, dark hair and intense face caught briefly like an icon in the glow from the vestry window. It was Jessica, Jeremy's constant companion. What was she doing skulking around out here on her own? And, more to the point, what the hell was he going to say if she asked him the same thing? But Jessica merely hurried off past the dormitory block, to be swallowed up by the darkness. Breathing a sigh of relief, he threw the sleeping bag around his shoulders and continued on his way.

CHAPTER TWENTY ONE

The sudden blare of the car radio as the CD finished made Isabel aware she had reached the outskirts of the city. Turning the volume down, she took two left turns then a right. No longer hysterical, she was still in shock, functioning more or less on automatic. So it was with some surprise that she found herself outside Joss's house. She realised then that subconsciously she had wanted someone to help her talk things through.

But the house stood in darkness, washed by the pale, lonely light of a streetlamp. Isabel looked at her watch. Quarter to ten. It seemed unlikely that the entire Cherry family was in bed that early on a Saturday night. They must have gone out. If it was a family outing, they had probably gone to a movie. It would be at least an hour before they were likely to be home, assuming they didn't go somewhere for supper afterwards and, knowing them, they probably would.

A wave of depression swept over her, and she felt tears pricking behind her eyelids. Close on the heels of depression came anger—anger with Joss, with Bob, and above all with herself for giving way to it all. Suppressing the urge to scream, she slammed the car into gear and made for home.

Dominic, of course, was out, and a scrawled message on the whiteboard told her not to expect him home that night. The light on the answerphone was flashing, but Isabel ignored it. Instead, she went to the kitchen and filled the kettle. Feeling as though her head was embalmed in some viscous fluid, she collapsed onto a chair and waited, her head sunk on her arms, for it to boil.

She was still waiting half an hour later when the shrill buzz of the doorbell startled her into consciousness. And fear. Could Bob have come after her? Would he do that? And if it wasn't him, who was it? Dominic had his own key, and everyone else, as far as she knew, was expecting her to be away for the weekend. She had leapt to her feet when the doorbell rang, and stood there, curiosity, panic, and indecision chasing each other around inside her, wreaking havoc on both mind and body. As the bell rang again, a tiny voice somewhere inside her insisted, with an irresistible authority, that she answer it. Slowly, dragging her feet as though they were encased in concrete, she went out to the hall.

A dark, bulky shape was visible through the glass. It looked too big to be Bob. In fact, it didn't look recognisably human at all. Isabel felt a prickle of fear. Then a voice called out softly, "Isabel, it's okay. It's me, Declan."

With a cry of relief she flew to the door. As she opened it, Declan took her sleeping bag from around his shoulders and held it out to her with his lopsided grin. "Thought you might want this back," he said.

Isabel took the sleeping bag and clutched it to her like a child's comfort blanket. "I'm sorry I didn't answer before. I thought it might be..."

"I know. Can't say I blame you." Declan grinned lopsidedly again, then, looking shrewdly at Isabel's bleached-out face and tense body, "I was a bit worried when I saw you leaving in such a hurry—" He broke off as his glance along the hallway took in the flashing light on the answering machine and Dominic's message on the whiteboard. "Are you here on your own?"

Isabel nodded.

"Are you going to be all right?"

Isabel shrugged wearily. "I went to Joss's, but they're all out. Probably at a movie..." Her voice sounded abnormally slow in her ears, like a machine running down. It seemed almost too much of an effort to speak at all.

Declan saw her begin to sway, and moved swiftly to catch her before she fell. Throwing the sleeping bag to one side, he steered her firmly down the hallway. "Where's the lounge-room?" he asked. "You need to sit down."

Isabel waved her hand in the general direction of a door to the left at end of the hall, and Declan took her through and seated her on the couch, placing a cushion for her to lean her head on. He switched on the heater, then surveyed her with an air of authority which he was some way from feeling.

"Right, you just sit there, and I'll make us some coffee."

Isabel gave him a vague, puzzled look. "I put the kettle on when I got home," she said. "Why hasn't it boiled yet?" Then she sighed as if the whole matter was just too much for her, and closed her eyes.

When she opened them again Declan was standing in front of her with two mugs. "Do you have any brandy?" he asked, handing one to her. "I reckon you need something a bit stronger than caffeine."

Isabel shook her head. "Would whisky do? There's some in the linen cupboard in the bathroom—on the bottom shelf under the blankets." In response to the look Declan gave her, she added, "Don't worry, I'm not an alcoholic. I keep it there so Dominic won't find it." Declan grinned, and went to get the whisky.

He was gratified to see Isabel regain some of her colour as she sipped the liberally fortified brew.

For some time they sat in silence, then Isabel put her mug down and said, "Thanks. I feel much better now."

"Hey, no worries. I'm just glad I noticed you leaving. You're in no state to spend the night here alone. I mean—I didn't mean..." he faltered, red-faced, to a halt, mentally cursing his stupidity.

Isabel couldn't resist chuckling. "It's all right. I'm pleased you turned up. To tell you the truth, I'm surprised I made it back here, the way I was feeling."

Relieved she had chosen to ignore his Freudian slip, Declan smiled at her. "If you feel like talking about it..." he began. Then the phone rang.

Startled, Isabel jumped to her feet. "Who the hell can that be?"

"You don't have to answer it if you don't want to. They can always leave a message," Declan pointed out. But Isabel was already halfway to the door. He heard her say, "Hello," then a gasp of surprise. Something in the tone of it bothered him. In two seconds he was beside her in the hall.

She placed her hand over the mouthpiece and stared at him, wide-eyed. "It's Bob!" she whispered.

Declan spoke to her in the calm, reassuring tone he used professionally for people who had just been through an unpleasant experience. "You don't have to talk to him, you know."

"It's okay, I can handle it. Anyway, he might incriminate

himself or something. Come and listen in if you like." Declan moved closer and she held the receiver away from her face a little as she spoke, keeping her voice as calm as she could manage. "What do you want?"

"Georgina," Bob's voice oozed from the earpiece, "There was no need to run away like that."

"Wasn't there?"

"Look, on reflection, I realise I must have frightened you in some way. But surely you must have been expecting something of the sort."

"Must I? How do you work that out?"

"Well, you told me more than once that you wanted further spiritual training. You said you needed someone to guide you." Bob's voice sounded vexed, and slightly puzzled as well. It was difficult to tell which, if either, was genuine.

Isabel took a deep breath to quell her rising anger. "Perhaps," she said coldly, "you'd care to explain to me precisely what sort of 'guidance' you were giving me tonight."

There was silence at the other end of the line. When Bob spoke, it sounded as though he, too, was striving hard for control. "I've already explained to you," he said, "about the vital importance of polarity in recreating the balance and harmony needed to give birth to the New Aeon. I thought you understood that."

"Oh, yes, I understood."

Bob appeared to have missed the irony in her voice. "Then you *must* have known what I wanted. I've been attracted to you since I first met you, surely you realised that."

"I bet he says that to all the girls," Declan murmured in the background. Isabel shook her head at him with a warning frown. She was already perilously close to hysteria, and she

247

had to stay calm.

Bob's voice went on, "Georgina, you told me you *wanted* my teaching. You can't back out now, not when you've made a promise."

"Don't be ridiculous. What promise did I ever make to you?"

Bob's ears may have been deaf to irony, but they couldn't have missed the scorn. His voice, when he spoke, sounded hurt, but anger lurked, menacing, in the background. "When I first told you how special you were to me, you never backed away. You told me you wanted to go further. You can't back out now. There's so little time left, and it's just too important. Besides, I won't let you."

"Bob, you can't make me do anything."

"Is that what you think?" Bob's voice was still silky smooth, but it made Isabel think of the polished steel of a dagger. "You should realise, Georgina, that it's very unwise to trifle with the laws of the Universe. The power that works through me will not be mocked." Before her reeling brain could summon up a suitable reply, the phone line clicked and went dead.

Slowly, Isabel replaced the receiver and turned to Declan. "There's really no answer to that, is there?" she said, her voice trembling. She began to giggle, then to laugh uncontrollably. "I'm sorry," she gasped, then burst into tears.

For a moment, Declan felt panic. He very much wanted to hold her, yet he feared she might misunderstand his motives, especially after what she had just been through. In the end, training took over. "Come on," he said firmly, and led her back to the lounge.

He found some glasses in the kitchen and poured them

both whisky.

Isabel took a deep breath and let it out slowly. "I'm sorry," she said again.

"Don't be. It's a perfectly normal response to shock."

Isabel swallowed some whisky. "Mmm, that's better. Funny, isn't it, how something can still come as a shock, even when you're more or less expecting it?"

Declan thought of the day he had come home from work to find Lynn had finally moved out, taking Dana with her. He said nothing, but sipped his drink in reflective silence. This assignment was proving to be a learning experience in more ways than one. "You handled Forster well," he said at last.

"Thanks. I'm glad you think so. I don't suppose he said anything that helps you, though."

Declan shrugged. "No, but he made it pretty clear what he wants from you. He made threats, too, albeit veiled ones. And this time you had a witness."

"A police witness at that." The hint of a smile flitted from Isabel's grey eyes to her mouth.

Declan felt a sudden need to do something. He stood up and began to walk around the room. It was a large, high-ceilinged room, in a flat that was part of an old house, of more or less the same style and vintage as Forster's former headquarters. The decor, however, could not have been more different. Both walls and ceiling were painted in the same light golden yellow, which made the room look even bigger. The full-length curtains at the massive windows were in a geometric pattern of rich reds and blues that echoed the colours and patterns of the rugs that lay everywhere, presumably to hide the bilious green of the carpet. Not for the first time, Declan wondered if there were some unwritten law decreeing that all landlords should have appalling taste in decor and furnishings.

Isabel's furnishings, presumably, were all her own. They were an astonishing, but highly successful, amalgam of Art Deco and Victoriana, the piece-de-resistance being a black wrought-iron candlestick, as tall as he was, and formed to resemble arum lilies. In each of its three blooms sat a thick red candle.

"This is beautiful!" he said, aware, suddenly, that Isabel seemed to feel as awkward as he did.

"Thanks. A friend made it for me, years ago. It makes a nice change from a lamp." She sat up suddenly, as though reaching a painful decision. "Look, I think I'd better tell you what happened this evening."

Declan sat down again opposite her. "Only if you feel up to it. It can wait."

Isabel shook her head. "I need to tell someone, to get it out of my system. That's why I went to Joss's place. Besides, after that phone call, I think it's important for you to know. There is something you can do for me first, though." There was that smile again.

Declan breathed deeply to slow his heart. It failed, significantly, to work.

"Pour me another whisky, please. I think I may need it."

She swallowed a mouthful of the drink he handed her then told him, in her direct way, what had happened at the Centre that weekend. By the time she had finished, her hands were so tightly clasped around her glass she was in danger of cracking it. Declan reached across and gently pried it loose. With the inevitability of destiny, she left her hand in his, and he held it in both of his as he said softly, "Boadicea would have been proud of you."

"What?"

"Oh, it's just something I—look, just ignore me. I have these flights of fancy sometimes. It's nothing." He broke off in confusion.

Isabel smiled at him, and he had to look away, quickly. "It's Boudicca, anyway," he heard her say. He looked back again in surprise.

"Sorry?"

"Boadicea was a scribal error back in the Middle Ages. The Venerable Bede, probably, or someone like that. It's meant to be Boudicca," and she spelt it out.

"Ah. Okay then, let me put it another way. Ya done good, kid."

Isabel grinned. "Thanks. I knew the self-defence lessons would come in handy one of these days."

Declan could see the tension draining out of her as she spoke. Her hand in his felt warm. He could feel the veins on the back of it, and the thin bones through her slightly rough skin. It was the right sort of hand for a warrior queen, not large, but strong and resilient.

"What happens now?" Isabel asked. With a stab of disappointment, Declan realised she was referring to Forster. It was an effort, but he managed to haul himself back to the here and now, and released Isabel's hand.

"I'll need a proper statement from you," he said, "and, of course, I can corroborate what Forster said to you on the phone. But I still need to find out about the business back in Queensland. Somehow, I don't think a simple question and answer session is going to do the trick. So far, he seems to have managed to avoid admitting he's even been in

Australia, much less anywhere within cooee of the Tree of Life Community."

"Will I need to go to the Police Station to make a statement?" Isabel asked.

"Not necessarily. I just need it on the proper form, that's all."

"Oh, because I was going to say..." Isabel broke off, doing her best to stifle a yawn. As the tension slowly left her, extreme weariness was creeping in to take its place. "Sorry. I was going to say, would you like to come over for lunch tomorrow, and we can do it then." She yawned again.

Declan stood up. "Thanks. I'd like that. But what you need now is sleep. Will you be okay on your own?"

Isabel got to her feet, rubbing her eyes. "I'll be fine. I'll just go and set the answerphone so if Bob calls I won't have to listen—at least until tomorrow." She wandered out to the hall with Declan in her wake. The red light was still flashing on the answering machine.

"I suppose I'd better hear the worst," Isabel said with a grimace, and pressed the 'message' button. But it was not Bob's voice that spoke to her.

"Isabel, this is Joss. Can you call me as soon as you get back? I've had a feeling all day today that something's wrong, and I'm worried about you. I think I've had a premonition, and I'm sure it was about you. I didn't see any people, but I could smell incense, and I was looking through a window with little diamond-shaped panes. It looked like a church window. And there were snakes crawling all over the place—it was creepy, and I felt afraid. If I don't hear from you by eight o'clock Sunday evening, Martin and I will be paying Bob and his Centre a visit. Take care."

Declan gave a long, low whistle. "Any more of this," he said, "and you'll have a convert. But what's with the snakes?"

Isabel smiled. "It's hard to explain, but I think she was talking about Bob." She looked at her watch, surprised to find it was after one o'clock. No wonder she was so tired. "I'll call Joss in the morning, and see if we can arrange a meeting with the others in the afternoon if you like. They might come up with some useful ideas."

"That sounds good. I'll come over around mid-day, okay? Meanwhile, you get yourself some sleep." He waited in the car until he saw all the lights were off before driving back to his motel.

* * * *

Luke drew on his cigarette and leaned back in his chair. "Well," he said, blowing a lazy smoke ring towards the ceiling, "now we all know about Bob's latest little bit of nastiness, what are we going to do about it?"

Joss leaned forward, ostentatiously brushing away cigarette smoke. "I've been thinking about it since Isabel phoned me this morning, and I'm not sure we're in a position to do anything much yet."

"Right," Declan agreed, swallowing the last of his coffee. "I'm waiting for information from Blenheim, where Forster grew up. I've got someone checking up on his family and, depending on what they find out, I may have to go up there myself in the next day or so. Then I'll need to go over all the information I've got, and pull it together into something we can use when the time comes. In the meantime, though, I'd really like to be able to keep an eye on him at the Centre, if it can be done without rousing his suspicions."

In a characteristic gesture, Joss leaned her chin on one hand and looked thoughtful. "Since you left the course rather suddenly when Isabel did, I rather suspect Bob's suspicions will be well and truly aroused if you turn up there again. And we can hardly expect Isabel to go back into the lion's den."

"Don't you mean the snake pit?" said Declan, throwing her a wry look. "But you're right. It would be counterproductive for me to go back there, even if I had the time, and for Isabel it could be downright dangerous." He studiously avoided looking at Isabel as he said this, but Joss noticed the storm clouds that drifted across his sea-green eyes, and smiled to herself.

There was silence for a moment, as they all digested the ramifications of this. Geraldine curled herself more comfortably on the couch, and smoothed back her long hair. "He's still looking for recruits," she said. "There was another notice on the noticeboard at New Directions when I was in there on Thursday. He's now looking for people to go and stay there long-term—couples especially welcome, apparently." She looked thoughtful for a moment. "I've got a week's leave due, and I think the library would just as soon I took it now, before the school holidays start. I'll go out there if you like."

Declan regarded her with a worried frown. "Under the circumstances, I have to advise you against going on your own. As far as I can make out, he seems to have a distinct preference for red-heads, but still..."

Philip, who had looked up sharply at Geraldine's words, said in what he hoped was a casual manner, "Declan's right. It sounds as if Bob's beginning to crack under the strain of being the messiah of the New Aeon. If he's looking for couples, why don't I go with you? I'm sure I can wangle a week off, too. My boss owes me a favour or two." The grateful look Geraldine gave him was ample compensation for the difficulty he anticipated in persuading Jacko to dispense with his services for a week.

"If you'd been to one of Bob's classes," said Isabel with a grimace, "you wouldn't be talking so cheerfully about a week off."

"Yeah," Declan agreed, "a week on desk work would be a breeze compared to one of Bob's little talks. Still, if you're willing to do it, it would be a big help. Why don't you go ahead and arrange everything, and let me know when you'll be going out there. I'll get onto my bloke in Blenheim first thing tomorrow, and see what he's found out. Then, once I've got all my information together, perhaps we can meet again and have another look at the situation."

"Sounds good to me," said Luke. He stubbed out his cigarette and began to gather up the coffee mugs.

* * * *

The ringing of the telephone dragged Isabel from a deep, dreamless sleep. Declan had picked her up and taken her to the Sunday afternoon meeting, and driven her back to her flat afterwards. Although she had felt a twinge of disappointment when he had left straight away, saying he had paperwork to catch up on, she had realised that what she really needed was some time alone to catch up with her feelings. So she had spent a quiet evening on her own and gone to bed early, falling asleep straight away.

As the phone continued ringing, she realised the answerphone must be turned off. Cursing, she shook her head to clear the fog that was clouding her brain, and reached for her dressing gown.

"Georgina?" Isabel was wide awake immediately.

"What do you want?" She didn't even try to keep the hostility out of her voice.

Bob's voice flowed out of the receiver like treacle. "Georgina, I'm sorry if I upset you the other night. I certainly didn't mean to. But now you've had more time to get over the initial shock, I feel sure we can come to an agreement if we can just see each other and talk things through."

"I don't think so, Bob. I'm not upset, believe me. I just don't want any more to do with you or the Centre, so please don't contact me again."

"But, Georgina, you don't understand. I'm sure if you'd just let me explain more fully, you'd see how important it is for us to work together."

"Bob, it may be important to you, but I'm not interested. Please don't call me again." Isabel replaced the receiver. She went into the kitchen, put the kettle on to boil, then switched on the radio to shut out thoughts of Bob and his bizarre intentions. "...and it's almost half past seven," the announcer's voice told her cheerfully, "time for some more music before the news at eight." Bartholomew strolled into the kitchen, stretching and clawing at the rug on the floor. Two dull thuds on the lounge floor told her Dali and Madame George were also awake. Not much point in going back to bed then. She opened the fridge and got out the cat food. "But not," she told the three of them as they hovered hopefully by their food bowls, "until I've made the tea."

As she was about to pour her tea, the phone rang again.

"Georgina, please don't hang up on me again." It was an order, rather than a request. Isabel's immediate reaction was to disobey orders. However, she was also curious to see what Bob would come up with next, so she said nothing and waited. "Georgina," he went on, in a voice that oozed barely controlled anger, "you obviously don't realise what it is you're dealing with." Isabel said nothing. "Do you really think you can leave me?"

"I rather thought I had." The words slipped out before she could stop them.

"Oh, no," he said, "it isn't that easy. Surely you must have heard of astral travel?" Isabel remained silent, assuming this was a rhetorical question. She was right.

"I have the power," Bob informed her, "to leave my body and travel anywhere at will." The treacle of his voice had congealed into hard granules. "So, wherever you are, and whatever you do, remember I can be there whenever I want to. I'll say good bye now—your tea will be getting cold. I'll be in touch with you again soon—one way or another." There was a click as the line went dead. With a puzzled frown, Isabel returned to the kitchen.

CHAPTER TWENTY TWO

"I reckon it was just a lucky guess." Declan bit into a piece of cheese toast and chewed thoughtfully. "I mean, wouldn't *you* expect someone to make tea or coffee if they'd just woken up?"

Isabel had called him at the number he had given her as soon as she had tipped the tea in question down the sink. The thought of actually drinking it had been too much for her after Bob's comment. Declan had said, "Put the kettle on and I'll be round in fifteen minutes," and he had been as good as his word.

"Nice piece of deduction there, Holmes." She grinned. "And he would have known I drink tea from the meetings. I've suspected all along that much of his supposed clairvoyance is a combination of careful observation and clever guesswork. It's known in the trade as cold reading. Still, it can be quite disconcerting when you're not expecting it."

"But isn't that the whole point of the exercise? Having failed to seduce you with his physical charms, now he's trying to convince you he's a force to be reckoned with on some other level."

Isabel nodded. "Yes, that does seem to be his general *modus operandi.*"

"I must say, though," Declan commented, "I don't think he's much of a clairvoyant if he thinks *you'd* fall for all his astral nonsense."

"Thank you," Isabel acknowledged his compliment with a wry smile, "but I don't know that it is nonsense, entirely. If you read the literature, there's a fair amount of evidence that's quite convincing, even if it's not actual proof. Which is not to say that it's what Bob's doing, of course. Still, credit where it's due, he does seem to have some genuine abilities. His tarot readings can be quite impressive, and his general knowledge of esoteric matters even more so."

Declan pushed a hand through the crinkles of his hair. Conversation with Isabel could be a bit like trying to sail on an unknown sea without a proper chart. He hadn't figured out yet whether it was her or the subject they were dealing with. But, for the first time in years, he was beginning to feel it might be worth getting lost for as long as it took to learn to navigate by the stars.

Across the table, Isabel was toying with a teaspoon, her long fingers slowly curling and uncurling. He still remembered the feel of them from the other night. This morning she was wearing jeans and a big scarlet shirt of some velvety material, open at the neck. The skin of her throat was as pale and translucent as a petal in the garish morning light. 'With him is one sweet-throated like a bird.' He remembered the fragment from a poem in one of Grandad Kelly's books. Once or twice he had heard him recite it from memory, his rich Irish voice rising and falling like the sea...

A massive tabby cat jumped up onto his lap and began to purr ostentatiously.

"That's Madame George," Isabel told him. "I hope you realise you're greatly honoured."

"I've got every record Van Morrison has ever made—" Declan grinned, scratching the delighted Madame George behind the ears "—so she obviously recognises a kindred spirit when she sees one."

"Obviously," Isabel laughed. "Dominic named her when she decided to make her home here a couple of years ago. Astral Weeks was one of his favourite records at the time. He'd only just discovered its existence, though I've loved it for years. You must be about the only other person who's ever recognised the reference."

"It's still one of my favourites."

Isabel's eyes met Declan's, and for a timeless moment she was lost in a grey-green sea. Only it felt more like being found.

Disconcerted, Declan pulled his gaze from hers. "I have to go up to Blenheim today," he said into his coffee. "I shouldn't be more than a day or so. I'll—um—call you as soon as I get back." He took a deep breath and looked up again, both relieved and disappointed to find the spell was dissipated. "In the meantime, do you want me to get hold of a voice recorder for you? By a clever combination of observation and guesswork, I've deduced that this morning's call from Forster probably won't be the last. I think you ought to keep a record of them."

Isabel laughed. "It hasn't taken *you* long to master the art of cold reading, has it? I'll get a recorder from Luke. He uses them all the time, for interviews. If nothing else, it should keep us all amused while you're away. Haven't you forgotten something, though?"

"What's that?"

"A special camera to film him when he drops in on me

during his astral travels."

* * * *

"Sergeant Dukes should be back in about twenty minutes, sir. I expect you could do with a cuppa." Constable Pahi, a stocky, comfortable-looking man of around forty, beamed at him as though he were the prodigal son returning. Still, a 'nice cuppa' was probably the closest thing to a fatted calf the Blenheim Police Station was likely to produce.

"Thanks. Coffee would be good, if you've got it—strong, with milk and no sugar."

Pahi took him to a cramped, claustrophobic office and went away to get the coffee. The room was dominated by an oversized wooden desk, stoically bearing up under the weight of two piles of fat folders and a well-used computer.

It's the same the whole world over, he thought with a sigh.

The coffee, when it came, was accompanied by two biscuits on a small plate, and Constable Pahi, who had also made himself a drink. Leading his teabag on its string in careful circles round his mug, he perched himself on a corner of the desk, since the only other chair was piled high with box files, and stated, "Nice day for a drive, eh."

Declan acknowledged this with a nod. He had, indeed, thoroughly enjoyed the trip up the long coast road in the crisp spring sunshine. The bright sea leaping energetically over black, jutting clusters of rock was full of subtle energy and movement. In some strange way, it made him homesick, not just for Tasmania, but for some other, mystical, mythical homeland, though he suspected the two had long ago become inextricably entwined. It had something, he knew, to

261

do with Grandad Kelly's tales of an Ireland both remembered and imagined, which had figured large in his childhood. Mostly, he was able to believe what he told himself, that he was longing for a fantasy home that had never existed. But sometimes, and today had been one of them, he became convinced there existed a place so real that everything else he had known would pale in its presence. Isabel's fair, sunflecked skin and red-gold hair appeared before his mind's eye. She was standing on a black rock, with the sea crashing round her...

Reluctantly, Declan pulled himself back to the present as Constable Pahi repeated his statement, this time turning it into a question, "Yeah, nice day for a drive, eh?"

"Great. It's a beautiful country, what I've been able to see of it."

Pahi grinned, and proceeded to give him a verbal tour of the area. He had a gift for storytelling and, by all accounts, a large and highly amusing family to provide good material. Declan felt quite disappointed when Sergeant Dukes, a thin, desiccated man with a smoker's cough and a voice like car tyres skidding on gravel, finally arrived.

Disappointment, however, was soon eclipsed by the thrill of the chase as Dukes briefed him on what he had discovered so far. Old Mrs Ferris had, of course, died years ago, though she was still remembered by former neighbours as an eccentric, formidable old lady with a mind of her own, and a Scottish accent as thick as the tea she brewed for her tarot clients. Her daughter, Margaret Forster, had, it seemed, been a shy, pretty redhead, thoroughly dominated by Mrs Ferris, as was young Richard.

"What about the father?" Declan looked up from the file

262

for which he had managed to clear a space on the desk in front of him.

Sergeant Dukes carefully finished rolling his cigarette and stowed his tobacco tin in his desk. His stained fingers were skinny, like the rest of him, with spatulate tips and flat, yellowed nails, one of which was severely deformed. It looked like a piece of beeswax left too long in the sun. Declan's mind formed a momentary image of Sergeant Dukes strapped to a chair, with some jack-booted villain holding a cigarette lighter, a thin, cruel smile slicing his face, hissing, "Tell us vat you know, or it vill be the vorse for you." He had no doubt that Dukes had refused to talk.

Dukes struck a match and lit his cigarette, taking his time about drawing in the pungent smoke and breathing it out again, coughing fitfully as he did so. Then he shrugged. "General opinion seems to be George Forster took off when the kid—Richard—was about five. After that, old Mrs Ferris pretty much ruled the roost."

"Hmm." Declan ran his fingers through his hair and looked down again at the file. "This Jessie MacMillan, who's down here as a friend of Mrs Forster's, what did she have to say about him?"

"I haven't been able to talk to her yet—she's been out both times I called."

"I'll pay her a visit first thing tomorrow, then."

"Okay. There's a couple of others you might want to talk to as well." Dukes leaned across the desk, exuding a noxious aroma of stale cigarette smoke, and flipped the pages of the file back, pointing out names.

When Declan left his motel at eight o'clock the next morning, he had a small list of names and addresses in

Dukes's spidery handwriting tucked inside the notepad in his pocket.

* * * *

The Barina glided to a halt outside the high laurel hedge that fronted Isabel's flat. Just visible behind the mass of glossy leaves was the dark grey gable of the tall white wooden house, its finial sticking up aggressively, a reminder to any lurking demons of what was in store for them should they dare to alight on the roof. As Declan hurried up the path, the sound of someone practising scales on a saxophone floated out through the open front door to meet him. The first time he knocked, there was no response. The waves of sound continued to rise and fall. He knocked again, louder. A tall, slim youth dressed in black appeared in the hallway. He had very long dark-auburn hair tied back from a long, pale, triangular face that reminded him of Isabel's rather than actually looking like it. Everything about him seemed so meticulously planned and executed that Declan, in spite of stopping off at the motel for a shower and a change of clothing, felt positively scruffy in his jeans and navy shirt.

"Hi. Is Isabel home?"

Declan could almost hear the click and whirr as Dominic's brain rapidly put two and two together. "Ah, you must be Declan," he said, his voice deep and precise like Isabel's, but curiously devoid of expression.

"And you're Dominic, I guess. Nice to meet you." Declan held out his hand. As Dominic came forward and shook it, Declan had the impression he'd be more at home bowing, and doffing his hat with a flourish.

"Mother's out, but she'll be at Luke's this afternoon. They usually start recording at one-thirty."

Declan looked at his watch. It was just after mid-day. His intention had been to surprise Isabel with a lunch invitation. Oh, well, he wasn't really hungry yet, anyway. "Okay, thanks."

Dominic said nothing, but inclined his head in a gracious and graceful gesture, then turned and glided back up the hall. As Declan left, he heard the smoky tones of the saxophone again, playing, a slow, sensuous version of Waltzing Matilda. So Isabel's son did have a sense of humour, despite appearances to the contrary.

Back at the motel, he made a call to Luke, then pulled out his notepad and file and began making notes.

* * * *

"Thank you for calling, Malcolm. That's all we have time for on our phone-in this week. Next week we hope to be able to bring you another fascinating interview with tarot reader and spiritual teacher, Bob Ferris. So don't forget to listen in again at the same time for more news and views from the world of the paranormal, on The Psychic Connection." Luke switched off the control panel. "Bloody idiot!" he muttered in the general direction of the microphones, and reached for his cigarettes.

Joss eyed him primly. "Just be thankful it wasn't you he was gunning for," she told him.

"True," Luke conceded, "though I'm sure he thinks I'm guilty by association. Anyway, I need a shot of caffeine. Just listening to you two is exhausting. Come on, you lot."

Declan, who had been sitting behind her in a corner of the cramped studio doing his best to keep a straight face during her skirmish with Malcolm, asked, "Are all your callers like that? If they are, I'm surprised Luke gives out his private phone number."

"You mean Disgusted of Dingley Dell? No, thank God!" Joss said with a grimace. "Malcolm's an ex-drug addict who got religion. It seems he used to be into what he calls 'devil worship' as well, so he feels he has inside information on our wicked, wicked ways. He started calling a couple of months after we first went on air, and now he rings up about once a month on average, to have another go at saving us from ourselves. But Luke has an unlisted number, and he doesn't let it be known that his studio is at home so, as far as our listeners are concerned, they're calling the radio station we link in with. Anyway, come on, I want to hear all about the boyhood of Bob."

Philip had already made the coffee and was sprawled on the couch waiting for them. He and Geraldine had both arranged leave, and planned to drive out to the Circle of Light Centre next morning. As Geraldine made for her usual place at the end of the couch, Philip sat up and moved to sit on the arm of the couch next to her. It seemed, Joss observed, they had already been putting in some practice for their masquerade as a couple.

"Thanks." Declan took the coffee Luke offered him. "I take it you've already arranged the interview with Forster, then?"

"Only tentatively. Depending on how things pan out, I might need to set it up at short notice, so I thought it would help if I already had his basic agreement. When I spoke to Rhoda on Monday, I told her at this stage I'm planning it for next Wednesday, but I'd get back to her and let her know for sure. She called this morning to say Bob's happy to do the interview pretty much any time. He just needs a day's notice so he can arrange for transport into town and back."

"I'm surprised he doesn't have his own car," Philip commented. "I thought a Jag or a BMW, or both, was pretty well mandatory for these guru types."

"I think you're confusing him with the Maharishi—or am I thinking of the Reverend Moon?" Luke collapsed into a chair, flicking his hair off his face with an abstracted air. "Anyway, I don't think Bob's quite in their league. He needs a better publicity manager, for a start."

"I suppose you can't be too choosy if you're relying on voluntary labour," said Joss. "Still, that church set-up won't have been all that cheap. There's no way he can have financed it out of voluntary donations from the likes of Rhoda." She turned to Declan. "So we've got five days before we need to contact him and finalise things for next week. Is that going to be enough, do you think?"

Declan blinked and rubbed his eyes. He was beginning to feel tired, and more than a little hungry. He poured himself another coffee and gulped a large mouthful before replying, "As from tomorrow, we'll have Geraldine and Philip keeping an eye on things at the centre..."

"Speaking of that," Philip broke in, "I'll have my cell phone with me, so we can report back if there's anything you might need to know in a hurry."

Declan nodded. "Good idea. And Isabel is already organised to record any further calls from Forster."

"So they can be taken down and used in evidence against him," said Isabel. "Not that he's made any more so far, surprisingly enough."

Luke gestured with his cigarette in Declan's direction. "So really, it all depends on whether we have enough solid evidence by next Tuesday to pin Bob down."

"Did you manage to find out anything useful in Blenheim?" Joss said to Declan.

"You could say that." Declan's reply was laconic. "It's all background stuff, of course, but it does help explain a few things."

Five pairs of eyes fixed on him impatiently. Declan, who knew well the dramatic value of making people wait, smiled as he carefully set down his empty coffee mug and sat back.

"I'll start with his grandmother," he said at last. "Her name was Ellen Ferris and, by the sound of things, she was very much the head of the household, at least after Bob's—or rather Richard's—father left. That was just after young Richard turned five."

"Why did he leave?" asked Isabel.

"Well, according to Jessie MacMillan, who was a friend of Richard's mother's from their school days, George Forster was a ratbag anyway, and Margaret—that's Richard's mother—should never have married him in the first place. Seems he had some sort of hold over her. He could make her do anything he wanted. She was nineteen when he asked her to marry him though, according to Jessie, it was more like he just told her it was going to happen, and a month later it did. Her mother advised her against it, and so did Jessie." Declan gave a short laugh. "By all accounts, even George's friends told her not marry him. But she went ahead anyway, and a year later, Richard was born."

"Were there any other children?" Joss asked.

"No, and apparently that was when things started going seriously wrong for Margaret. Something happened when Richard was born so she couldn't have any more children. George took it as a personal insult, and from then on, he never let his wife forget it—or young Richard. Or anyone else who'd listen. He seemed to take pleasure in reducing Margaret to tears, then just walking out and leaving her to deal with it on her own. Well, to cut a long and sordid story short, about the time Richard started school, George took off with another woman."

"Leaving Margaret to deal with it on her own, as usual," Isabel said softly. "So what did she and Richard do then?"

"Good old George had left them with debts up to their eyeballs, so they sold up and moved back in with Mother." Declan pushed his hands across his forehead and back through his hair. "Seems Mrs Ferris doted on young Richard, so she looked after him while his mother worked. She found work in an old people's home in the area. One way and another, Mrs Ferris became the major influence in both their lives."

"That figures," Luke said. "What was she like, Mrs Ferris?"

"Oh, pretty formidable, by the sound of it. I had a talk to an old chap who used to be a neighbour of theirs. He was full of praise for her. She'd had a very tough upbringing in Glasgow—drunken father and semi-invalid mother—and came out to New Zealand in her teens after her mother's death, as part of some immigration scheme. She worked as a domestic servant until she married."

"No doubt she worked as one afterwards, too, one way or another," Geraldine commented.

"I imagine so. She and Robert Ferris had eight children. Margaret was the youngest, and quite a lot younger than the rest. They moved to Blenheim from somewhere in the North Island after Robert retired, and he died a couple of years later. That was when Mrs Ferris really got stuck into the tarot readings, to help support herself and Margaret. According to this neighbour, Arnold Pemberton, Mrs Ferris didn't like being beholden to anyone for anything. She'd always made her own way in life, and she was damned if she was going to let anything stop her—even her husband's death. At least, that was her story. Another former neighbour, an old dear called Connie, who kept forcing tea and cake on me..."

Pointedly ignoring the sarcastic murmurs of, "Poor thing!" from the others, Declan continued, "Connie said she reckoned it was Mrs Ferris's way of dealing with her grief. But whatever it was, she became something of a legend in the district. A tough old bird by all accounts, but everyone liked and respected her. Both Richard and his mother were devoted to her, and after Richard had left home, Margaret looked after the old lady till she died. She left the district after that, and no-one seems to know quite what happened to her."

"What did the neighbours think of young Richard?" Isabel's question was accompanied by a thoughtful expression.

"You know it's odd," Declan replied, "but although no-one actually came right out and said so, I got the distinct impression that they didn't really like him that much. There seemed to be a feeling of relief all round when he left home and moved out of the district."

"Except for his mother and grandmother, presumably," said Isabel.

"Presumably. His grandmother, at any rate, seems to have thought he was something pretty special."

Joss pursed her lips sardonically. "What a pity he was gullible enough to believe her."

"Oh, I don't know," said Luke. "Hopefully it means he'll be gullible enough to believe me when I invite him into the studio for an interview."

"I rather imagine his ego will take care of that." Joss got to her feet and began to put her jacket on. To Declan she said, "I take it we just let things take their course now until you and Luke are ready to act."

"Yep," Declan said with a grin, "don't call us, we'll call you."

CHAPTER TWENTY THREE

"So that's the married quarters. Just as well we brought the thermal underwear!" Philip exclaimed, surveying the dozen or so tents set out in three rows beside the concrete dormitory and ablution block.

"Which one's ours, I wonder?" Geraldine pushed a strand of hair back under her corduroy cap and rubbed her hands together briskly before thrusting them back into the pockets of her oilskin riding coat. The thin morning sunlight had finally retreated altogether. Now a cold, stinging wind whipped across the open grassy area, and the wispy tails of the grey clouds glowering at the edge of the sky threatened rain. "From the look of that sky, we ought to get our gear under cover as soon as possible."

At that moment, a dark-haired woman in a blue parka with the hood pulled up against the cold strode towards them, smiling cheerfully. "Hello. Welcome to the Circle of Light Centre. I'm Pat. You must be Geraldine and Philip. I'm sorry we've only got tents to offer you at this stage. We're planning to get something much more substantial before long." She waved a hand at the canvas village. "Come on, I'll show you which one is yours. Come on over to the hall when you've got your things sorted out. Lunch should be ready by then, and I'll let you know our programme."

The tent allotted to them turned out to be a fairly sizeable and relatively modern ridgepole style in militaristic olive drab. It was situated in the centre row at the end closest to the dormitory.

"Thank God it's got a sewn-in floor," said Philip, "otherwise it'd be hell when it rains."

"Thank goodness it's close to the shower and toilets," said Geraldine. "I don't think I could face a safari in the middle of the night."

"Especially if there's a wild Bob on the prowl," added Philip, with a mock snarl.

"Aren't I lucky I've got a big, strong man to protect me!" Geraldine clasped her hands to her breast and attempted to simper, but the effort was too much for her and she burst out laughing. "I really don't know what comes over me sometimes," she gasped at last.

"Whatever it is," Philip told her, "I like it. Come on, let's get our gear in before it rains. Did you bring a hot water bottle?"

"No. It never occurred to me. I'm not sure I even own one."

"Oh, well, if you're very, very good, I'll let you share mine." Philip strode off towards the van, so he didn't see the pink glow that suffused the tan of Geraldine's face, or the smile in her brown eyes.

* * * *

"...and a very warm welcome to all our newcomers, especially the couples who have come here to share in this bold, new spiritual and social experiment." Bob raised his head and gazed around the church. Twenty or so people, about half of them obviously couples, sat or lolled on cushions in a semi-circle in front of him. Their expectant faces were lit by the flickering light from the candles in their sconces around the walls. The clouds had made good their threat, and rain was now pouring down from the darkened sky, clattering on the slate roof and against the leadlight windows. Behind Bob, however, the sun still shone brightly over the snow-capped mountains, and the lambs, secure under the benign gaze of the Good Shepherd, still gambolled innocently among the spring flowers.

"That's some window!" Philip whispered to Geraldine, huddled beside him under a shared blanket.

"It looks like Rosicrucian symbolism," Geraldine murmured. "I must see if I can find out who made it."

Bob's voice rang out again across the flickering gloom. "I say 'experiment' because this is the beginning of a New Aeon, and although the Great Cycle of the ages is repeated endlessly, and will be until the end of Time itself, no two aeons are ever the same. The quality of an entire Aeon is dependant on the quality of its inauguration. And that," his voice sank dramatically, "is what this Centre is all about. The time is ripe to give birth the New Aeon, and to do that, we must create the right conditions. And how do we do that, you may ask.

"As with any birth, the first requirement is parents. Suitable parents must be trained so that when the Child of the Aeon is born, they will have the power and the wisdom to train him aright. You will realise, I am sure, that I am using analogy here, at least partially. What I am aiming to do here at the Circle of Light Centre, is to provide a supportive training ground for the attitudes and skills needed to give birth to the New Aeon. Then, when the time is right, we will

274

usher in that bright new dawn, and all the power of true magic will be ours!"

His voice had risen in a steady crescendo. On the final word, however, it cracked, rather spoiling the effect. Stepping back slightly, he accepted a glass of water held out to him by a rose-pink-clad Anita, and sipped it slowly, allowing time for his words to have their full impact on his audience before he went on.

"I want to talk for a moment about attitudes. I am sure all of you realise already the value of a positive attitude in any undertaking. How much more vital it is, then, in an undertaking of such huge importance. For what I am talking about is nothing less than the rebirth of the Universe. The old order changeth, giving place to new..."

"Yielding, actually," Geraldine murmured.

"What?" Philip looked at her, puzzled.

"He's misquoting Tennyson."

"I'll take your word for it."

"...and if we are to be the parents of the new order, we need to develop a positive attitude, not doubting ourselves or each other, or the process we are involved in, but knowing that we can accomplish anything, if we truly want to. For that is the power of true magic." He paused again, arms outstretched towards them like some fire-and-brimstone preacher.

Philip nudged Geraldine. "Where do you reckon he had his acting lessons?"

"Well, it wasn't The Royal Academy, that's for certain." She grinned. "Hang on, I think Act Two is about to begin."

Bob lowered his arms, and fixed his audience with an earnest gaze. "But first, we need the right skills. So what are these skills? Those of you who have been to the Centre before will have heard me speak of the importance of the universal law of polarity. For our newcomers, and especially all the couples who have responded to our call, let me expand on that principle.

"In essence, everything in nature works on the harmonious interaction of opposites. Whether we're talking about the ebb and flow of the tides, the alternation of light and darkness, the cycle of the seasons, the positive and negative of electricity, or the dynamic interaction of male and female, every sphere of activity throughout the Universe is based on polarity. This universal law has been known since ancient times. It was the basis of the wisdom teachings of cultures as diverse as the Druids, the Illuminati, and the Tantric Magic of the East.

"I have been privileged to receive teaching from masters of all these teachings and more and, as a result of years of study and practice, I have been able to synthesise them all into a basic, accessible system, involving body, mind, and spirit. Now, the time has come for these teachings to be shared more widely. The dawning of the New Aeon requires it—demands it, even.

"I have asked for couples to join us, because the harmonious alignment of the basic male-female polarity of the Universe can be best achieved through acts of imitative magic, which you will learn more about as you progress with your training. But those of you who as yet have no partner still have a vital part to play. The first step in the process is to develop inner harmony within the individual self. And that, my friends, is what we are about to begin."

Bob paused again for more fluid intake. His pudgy face

glistened with perspiration, and his eyes as they flicked around the room gleamed with a feverish intensity. "Some of you may feel that dancing is a trivial activity with which to pursue spiritual development. But reflect for a moment on the sacred dances of the East, or of the Native American tribes or, closer to home, of the Aboriginal tribes of Australia." Philip and Geraldine exchanged glances. "Dance is, in fact, a type of imitative magic in itself, through which we can develop that inner harmony which is the basis of everything I have been talking to you about today. So, enjoy the circle dancing, which will be held in the hall today because of the weather. This evening after dinner we'll meet here again for a group ritual and discussion."

Bob held out his arms in another gesture of benediction, then turned and glided out through the vestry door, looking, in his white kaftan, like a cross between a dissipated Christmas tree angel and a dalek. Anita leapt to her feet to follow him but, by the time she reached the door, he had closed it. She turned and wilted back onto her cushion, her pink draperies fluttering about her like a blossom shedding its petals.

As the others began to make their way out into the damp afternoon, Philip stood up and held out his hand to Geraldine. "Shall we go and practise a bit of polar harmony?"

"Well the temperature's about right. I'm freezing!" Shivering, she rubbed her hands together briskly. "I suppose at least the dancing will help warm me up, but what I really want is a nice hot coffee."

"Come on, then. If we play our cards right, we might be able to manage both."

****

"Thanks again for the reading." The little, plump woman turned at the door, patted her fair curls with one rounded hand, then held it out to be shaken.

"You're very welcome, Janine. I hope it's been helpful."

"Oh, it has. I feel much better already." As she smiled at Isabel, her pale blue eyes were almost hidden in folds of flesh as her mouth, a pink rosebud nestled in creamy marshmallow skin, curved up at the corners.

"That's great. Goodbye now."

As Isabel closed the front door, the phone began to ring. Picking up Bartholomew, who had been winding his way round her legs as she spoke, she carried him down the hallway, stroking his soft, shiny coat, and picked up the receiver.

"Hello."

"Ah, Georgina. How are you this afternoon?"

"I'm fine, thank you." Isabel was non-committal, playing for time as she scrabbled to turn on Luke's recorder, juggling Bartholomew and the receiver as she did so. Bartholomew decided playing second fiddle to a machine was just not good enough. Jumping out of her arms, he stalked off down the hallway and curled up in a patch of sunlight by the kitchen door, regarding her gravely out of full-moon eyes.

"You've been very busy this week, haven't you?" Bob's voice held a smug, knowing tone. As it happened, he was right. Presumably he had tried to call her while she was out, and was using this to imply he knew what she had been doing. Isabel was not fooled.

"Have I?" she said.

Bob refused the bait. "Not too busy, I hope, to think over what I said?"

"Since I'd already given you my answer, I didn't imagine there was anything to think over." Isabel tried to keep her voice calm and devoid of emotion.

"Oh, but there is. Surely you can see how important it is for the right people to be involved in the birth of the New Aeon. I need your energy to complement mine."

"Bob, you're being ridiculous. Whatever it is you're trying to do, I assure you I have no intention of being part of it."

There was a pause. At the other end of the line, Isabel heard Bob swallow. When he spoke again, his voice was a razor blade encased in honey. "Then I'll have to see what I can do to persuade you, won't I?"

"Are you threatening me?"

Again, Bob ignored her, saying softly, as though thinking aloud, "I suppose it's only to be expected that an intelligent woman like you, Georgina, would be unwilling to accept things at face value. I quite understand. If I demonstrate to you that my powers are genuine, I'm sure you'll be willing to think differently about joining me."

"I wouldn't hold your breath." But Bob had gone.

Thoughtfully, Isabel turned off the recorder. It was going to be fascinating to see how Bob intended to demonstrate his 'powers'. Bartholomew meowed at her from his spot by the kitchen door. Isabel blew him a kiss. His golden eyes closed in a contented smile. "Come on, Barty boy," she said, scooping him up in her arms, "let's see what we can find you for tea, shall we?"

* * * *

"Oh, my feet are frozen! Geraldine pulled off her boots and began to rub them with her gloved hands. The day's rain had now diminished to a fitful drizzle, blown about by a bad-tempered wind full of ice.

Philip set down the gas lantern with care, and pulled off his damp parka, draping it over his pack in one corner of the tent. The wind tugged at the tent's edges, sending the lantern light skipping across its walls. He squatted down beside Geraldine. "Don't tell me you're getting cold feet already?"

"Only literally." Two tiny lanterns gleamed gold in her eyes as she smiled back at him.

"Would you like me to give you a foot-rub?"

Geraldine's smile broadened. "Ooh, yes please! That's the best offer I've had all day." She pulled off one sock and stuck out her foot.

For the next twenty minutes, neither of them said much, as Philip instilled warmth into first one slim foot, then the other. As he finished, Geraldine gave a long, luxurious sigh of contentment. "Thank you. That was wonderful!" She pushed her feet into her sleeping bag and snuggled down into it.

Philip looked down into her eyes. They were warm and brown, and reminded him of velvet. He reached out and touched her long hair, smoothing it out as it lay in folds on her pillow. She smiled up at him without saying anything. Philip found he couldn't say anything either, so he leaned down and kissed her gently on the mouth. Her arms that wound tightly round his neck told him it was what she wanted, too. Momentarily extricating himself from her embrace, he leaned across and turned out the lantern.

Some time later, as they lay curled up in a nest of sleeping bags and blankets, no longer the slightest bit cold, Geraldine said drowsily, "So, what did you think of this evening?"

"Even better than I'd imagined," Philip murmured, adjusting his head slightly on her shoulder. Geraldine lifted her head from the pillow, a look of incredulity on her face. Philip's head, dislodged from its resting place, fell back with a thud. "What did I say?"

Laughing, Geraldine bent and kissed him. "You're very sweet, but I was talking about Bob."

"Oh, well, that's another matter altogether. I didn't think much of his so-called discussion. If you ask me, it was nothing more than a chance for him to push his own barrow a bit further. I wouldn't be at all surprised if he set up the questions beforehand. He certainly does seem fixated on this imitative magic business. I wonder what he means by it?"

"Roughly speaking, he's talking about what we've just been doing."

"In that case, I'm all for it—as long as I can do it with you." A look of comic dismay crossed his face. "Oh, God, we're not going to be expected to play musical chairs, are we?"

Geraldine laughed. "I shouldn't think so. And imitative magic isn't always about sex, anyway. Basically, it involves a ritual imitation of whatever it is that you want to happen."

"Oh, I see. It's because of this so-called birth of the New Aeon that Bob wants couples to—er—imitate its procreation."

"You've got it."

"Hmm. I wonder what part he sees in the process for those without partners? He seemed very concerned to reassure them this afternoon."

"Mid-wives, perhaps?"

Philip chuckled. "I wouldn't be surprised if he intends to help them out personally if necessary. He really is a total creep, isn't he?"

"In spades," Geraldine agreed, looking thoughtful. "Your mentioning this afternoon reminds me, Bob mentioned Australia during his talk. Only obliquely, granted, but maybe we can ask him more about it next time he has one of his 'discussions'. You never know, he might let something slip that will be helpful to Declan."

Her long hair flowed down on either side of her face, washing over Philip's chest as she looked down at him. He took hold of it and very gently pulled her close to him. "A brilliant idea," he murmured, running his fingers down her spine, "but I've got a better one. Would you like to hear it?"

"I'd much rather you showed me."

"Isn't that what the bishop said to the actress?" Philip's voice became somewhat muffled towards the end of this sentence, and for some considerable time thereafter, he said nothing intelligible at all.

CHAPTER TWENTY FOUR

Isabel listened intently. Her suspicions were confirmed. That was the phone she could hear above the whine of the vacuum cleaner. As soon as she switched it off, Dali crept out from his hiding place under the settee and scuttled ahead of her, making for the relative safety of the kitchen. She hurried to get the phone before the answering machine took over.

"Hello," she said, praying the voice that answered wouldn't be Bob's. For some reason she had slept badly, and she was in no mood to bandy innuendo with him.

"Isabel, hi. Sorry I haven't been in touch lately. My report hasn't been as easy to write as I'd hoped."

Isabel had been unaware of the weight on her heart until suddenly it took wings and flew away, and her heart began to beat faster. "Declan! How nice to hear from you."

"It's good to talk to you again." His words did not show the grin that made its irrepressible way across his face. "Look, can I take you for lunch somewhere today? I'm sick to death of being stuck at a desk, and there are one or two things I'd like to check out with you. Also," his voice sounded a little breathless all of a sudden, and his words came out in a rush, "also I could really use some good company."

"Thank you. I'd love to have lunch with you. Where shall I meet you?"

"I can pick you up if you like."

"Thanks, but I was going into town later, anyway, and

then on to Joss's place, so I'll need my car."

"Ah."

Was that a hint of disappointment in his voice? Isabel found herself hoping it was. Don't be ridiculous, she admonished herself. You're a full-grown woman, not a teenager.

Declan's voice interrupted her, "Where do you suggest we go, then?"

"There's a cafe in the Arts Centre. Do you know where that is? I'm told they make a wonderful quiche there."

"Yes, I know it. It's just down the road from where I'm working today. How about we meet there at half past twelve?"

"I'll look forward to it."

"Me, too."

Declan was already there when she arrived, sitting at a table by the massive stone fireplace that dominated one corner of the cafe. A welcome fire burned in its grate. The cafe was part of a Neo-Gothic, grey stone building that had once housed the city's original university, and was now home to numerous craft studios and art galleries, as well as this cafe. Declan's jacket lay discarded across the back of his chair. His hair was rumpled, either from the cold wind blowing outside, or his habit of running his hands through it. He looked tired, the planes of his face more sharply etched than usual, his eyes darker than Isabel remembered.

As she crossed the floor towards him, Declan looked up and saw her. His lopsided smile made her want to touch him, perhaps to smooth those crinkled curls, or the weary lines on his face. The feeling sent panic pulsing through her, so she contented herself with an answering smile, and sat down in the chair he pulled out for her.

"You look tired," she said.

"Yeah, I haven't been sleeping too well. I tend to get a bit wound up towards the end of a case."

"So you think you are near the end of it?"

Declan nodded. "It's certainly beginning to feel that way. Nothing I can put my finger on, but you get an instinct for it after a while."

"Mmm, I expect you do. I suppose that means you won't be here much longer?"

Declan said nothing. Isabel couldn't quite decipher the look in his eyes. Or maybe she didn't quite want to. The appearance of a waitress at their table might have been a blessing or a curse. Isabel couldn't be sure of that, either, and by the time they had ordered their food, the moment had passed.

After lunch, they wandered through the various studios, admiring leatherwork and weaving, candles and jewellery. Declan bought a pair of pale green glass earrings for his daughter. "They'll match her eyes," he said.

"I didn't know you had a daughter."

"Yeah, I had a wife, too, once. Seems a long time ago, now. Another life. Dana—my daughter—is nearly nineteen. I'm hoping to get back to Adelaide this Christmas to see her, and then on to Tasmania to visit my parents. I don't get to see them very often, what with being stuck up in Brisbane." He sighed heavily. "It's a shit of a job I've got. Sometimes I wonder why I do it."

Isabel said, "Have you ever thought of doing something else?"

He shook his head as though to clear it, and gave a rueful

grin. "Sorry, I didn't mean to lay all this on you. I really must be tired."

"That's okay. But I meant what I said. We all need a change of direction sometimes. Maybe that's what you need."

Declan looked at her sharply. "You're a very perceptive woman, you know that?"

"Well, that is my job, I suppose." They had reached a square stone building that had once been a gymnasium, but currently housed a picture theatre. Isabel stopped and pretended to read one of the posters in the glass-fronted display-case attached to the wall. Declan came to stand close beside her. She felt his hand on her shoulder as he turned her towards him and stood looking at her, his eyes drawing hers up to meet them.

"Look, I don't want to, but I have to go now," he said. "I'm expecting a call from Brisbane, from my boss. Can I see you tomorrow? I think maybe it's time you and I had a serious talk."

Isabel nodded. "Yes," she replied, her voice a whisper. It was all she could manage. Declan's hand moved to stroke her cheek gently. To her astonishment, Isabel felt tears pricking at her eyes. This wasn't like her at all. She blinked them back, feeling frightened, and happy, and, above all, confused. She cleared her throat and swallowed, though it didn't seem to help much. "Yes," she repeated, "I think we should. I have a client tomorrow morning, but I'll be free after eleven-thirty. Would you like to come for lunch?"

"I'd like that a lot. Come on, I'll walk you to your car." He kept his arm lightly around her shoulder as they walked. It felt very much at home.

At the library, Isabel slid her returned books through the

slot in the front of the desk, and went to scan the shelves for some more. But her mind would not stay on the task. It insisted, instead, on dwelling on Declan's sea-water eyes, the brown curls of his hair, his arm around her shoulder, his hand on her cheek. Disgusted with herself for behaving in a way that even someone of Dominic's age would disdain, she eventually abandoned her search. She'd just have to come back when she was feeling more herself, she thought, though she suspected she ought not to regard this as a short-term goal. Oh, well, no doubt Joss would manage to bring her down to earth again for a while.

Traffic, as usual on a Friday, was frustratingly slow, and it was a good fifteen minutes before she was clear of the worst of it and heading towards Joss's place, on the eastern side of the city. As she passed the avenue, she became aware that a small mauve car had been behind her for some time. Isabel was sure she recognised it. She peered into the rear-vision mirror. The woman behind the wheel was young, with a thin, pale face and long black hair. Beside her was a young man who might almost have been her brother, they were so alike. *Bloody hell*, she thought, *that's Jessica and Jeremy! What on earth are they doing back in town?* As the garish little Volkswagen passed her with a shrill roar, she saw Jeremy's face staring out of the window, and knew he had recognised her. A sudden chill ran down her spine. The feeling that accompanied it did little for her equanimity.

* * * *

"Do you know anyone who drives a mauve Volkswagen Beetle?" Declan asked, depositing a bottle of wine and a very exotic-looking box on Isabel's kitchen table.

"Well, yes, sort of. Why?"

"Because I'm practically certain they've been following me. They were behind me when I drove through the city centre, then a few blocks later they turned off in a different direction. Or so I thought. But they turned up again a few blocks from here and, as I was parking the car, they whizzed past me in a puff of blue smoke."

"Huh. Must need new rings," Isabel commented, peering at the box on the table.

"Yeah, but who are they?" Declan rubbed his forehead. He still looked tired, but the shadows under his eyes were less noticeable.

"Was the driver a young woman with long dark hair?" Declan nodded. "And was there a young chap with her who looked a lot like her?"

"Yep." Again, Declan nodded.

"I thought so. That was Jeremy and Jessica, two of Bob's most avid acolytes. You might have noticed them lurking out at the Circle of Light Centre the other weekend, twined round each like the rose and the briar."

"Ah, I thought they looked vaguely familiar. Anyway, someone should tell Jessica to drive more carefully. She nearly bowled one of your cats over—the black one with white paws and chest."

"Oh, that's Bartholomew. He's always in danger of one kind or another. He seems to believe he's been allotted twice the usual number of feline lives. It's funny you should mention Jeremy and Jessica, though. I saw them in town yesterday when I was on my way to Joss's. They could have been following me, too, now I think about it. I saw Jeremy looking at me as they passed, and it gave me a very peculiar feeling. I'm sure they're up to something. Anyway, what's in this fascinating-looking box?"

"It's baclava, for dessert. It's Turkish, and incredibly decadent." Isabel reached for the box, but Declan whisked it away and held it behind his back, grinning. "No you don't—you have to eat up all your vegetables first."

In the end, though, neither of them managed to do justice to the meal, and the baclava remained in its box, untouched. Afterwards, they took their coffee through to the lounge, and sat drinking it in awkward silence. All of a sudden, Isabel put her mug down, unable to drink any more.

Abruptly, Declan stood up. For a panic-stricken moment, Isabel thought he was going to leave. But he sat down again just as suddenly, and began to speak. "Isabel, I expect—that is, I hope—maybe you already know what I want to say." Isabel looked at him with grave eyes. The way the light from the candles shone on her hair reminded him of a Renaissance painting he had seen once. Stifling a desire to bury his face in its scented warmth, he went on, "I'm not usually this inarticulate, but this is bloody hard for me, because I've got so little time here, and I know you've been hurt before—I can tell—and so have I, and I'm sure neither of us wants to get hurt again. And I wouldn't hurt you for the world, so after what that bastard Forster did to you I couldn't—I mean I wanted...oh, Christ, I'm making a right bloody fool of myself, aren't I?" He broke off, covering his face with his hands. He looked as though he were about to cry.

All of a sudden, Isabel saw him as the Fool in the tarot, having taken the plunge, but suddenly realising he was free-falling to a totally unknown destination. She herself, she saw, was the High Priestess at this moment. Always, with Stephen, she had been made to feel like an emotional incompetent. Now she realised she held stored within her, and always had done, the wisdom and emotional resources to help Declan in the transition he so obviously needed and desired, from Fool to Magician. And she realised it was what she wanted, too.

"Declan." He looked up. Isabel took hold of his hands and looked into eyes dark with feeling. "No-one ever wants to get hurt. And because we've both been hurt before, I think you and I have been busy avoiding that for a long time now. But the reason Stephen was able to hurt me was that he lied to me. And I let it go on for far too long, because I believed I had no choice. At first, I felt honoured to have gained the favour of such a brilliant and wonderful man." She gave a brief, ironic laugh. "Stephen would have agreed with me, no doubt. Then I thought I owed it to Dominic to stay with his father, regardless of what it was doing to me, or to Dominic for that matter, if only I'd realised it. After I finally threw Stephen out, I suppose I used the fact that I had Dominic to care for to avoid the risk of getting hurt again. In other words, I was lying to myself. And I don't want to do that any more."

Declan's eyes remained fixed on hers. Isabel saw a slight movement in his throat as he swallowed, but he said nothing. She took a deep breath and went on, "I may be wrong, but I suspect you got hurt because you lied to yourself, too. But I don't think you want to do that any more either—that's why you came here today. And, because of that, I don't think either of us is going to lie to the other. So if we do get hurt, it won't be like before—it'll be because of something beyond our control, like you going back to Brisbane. It'll be, sort of, *clean* pain. Does that make sense?"

To her amazement, Declan fell back in his chair and began to roar with laughter. Eventually, he sat up again, wiping his streaming eyes on his sleeve. "Thank you!" he exclaimed. "You really are amazing! How did you know all that about me?"

Isabel shrugged. "Well, you are human after all. Now, what was it you wanted to tell me?"

Declan took her hands in his and kissed them. "I wanted to tell you," he said, "that the first time I saw you I felt like my heart had started beating again for the first time in years. And since then, it's been one long fight to stop myself from doing something we both might regret. I tell you, when I saw you here the other morning I almost lost it completely. The only thing that stopped me was the fact that I had a job to do—that and the thought of making such a complete fool of myself that you'd give me up as a bad job."

"Well, you're not working now," Isabel told him, her grey eyes melting like sea-mist in the morning sun, "and you know what William Blake said: 'If the fool would persist in his folly, he would become wise.'"

"Fuck William Blake!" Declan's voice was fierce with emotion and his grip on her hands tightened.

"He's been dead for over a hundred years."

"Oh, Mother of God, Isabel, so have I, as near as makes no difference! Come here and give me the kiss of life—please!" He pulled her onto his lap in order to facilitate this enterprise. They had just reached a particularly engrossing stage when the phone rang.

Declan removed his lips from hers just long enough to whisper a plea, "Don't answer it!"

Isabel kissed the tip if his nose. "I think I'd better. If it's who I think I think it is, I'll need to turn the recorder on. He seems to be making a habit of these late afternoon calls. Come with me. I could do with a bit of moral support."

Heaving a sigh, Declan reluctantly released her. "That bastard's got a lot to answer for," he growled.

As she had suspected, it was Bob. "Ah, Georgina, I do hope you enjoyed your lunch." Isabel gave Declan a puzzled grimace. She hadn't expected this particular opening gambit. "And your visitor."

"I'm sorry, I have no idea what you're talking about."

"I take it you and your visitor have both had a pleasant afternoon?" *You could say that*, thought Isabel, stifling a hoot of laughter. She was obliged to avoid looking at Declan, who was not helping matters at all. He had subsided onto the floor beside her, where he was making valiant, but not particularly successful, attempts to control himself. Bob was saying nothing, obviously waiting for a response.

"How do you know I've had a visitor?" It wasn't much of a response, she knew, but it was the best she could do under the circumstances.

"How do you think I know?" Bob's voice was infuriatingly smug and mysterious.

"You tell me."

Instead, Bob told her, "You like cats, don't you, Georgina?"

"*What?*" The abruptness of his change of tack took her by surprise. What on earth was he getting at?

"Black cats in particular, perhaps? Black cats with white

paws? I promised you proof of my powers, Georgina." His voice had changed, too, sounding suddenly bigger, more authoritative, almost peremptory. "I've just given it to you. You ask me how I know these things. I say to you again, Georgina, ask yourself how I *could* know them, if I were not, in some sense, with you. Think about it, Georgina. Think about it carefully. I'll be in touch again—soon." There was a click, as the phone went dead. Isabel switched off the recorder.

"Doesn't improve any, does he?" Declan observed. He had more or less recovered his composure, and was standing close beside Isabel, trying to resist the temptation to destroy hers.

Isabel shook her head with a puzzled sigh. "How on earth did he manage that little trick?"

"I reckon he's got spies."

"Spies?"

"Yes. Spies in a mauve Beetle, I'd say."

Of course! Jeremy and Jessica! "So that's what they're doing back in town! I said they were up to something, didn't I?"

"You did." Declan pulled her close and began to kiss her face and hair. His lips were warm, moving softly against her skin. The smell of his skin in her nostrils was so intoxicating she felt light-headed. "Why don't we give them something really interesting to put in their next report?" he murmured in her ear.

Suddenly, the mere thought of any space between them was intolerable. She did her best to close the infinitesimal gap. Obligingly, Declan hugged her tighter. "What do you think?"

Isabel's heart was beating like a jungle drum, and its message was very clear. She felt scarcely able to breathe, but somehow she managed something vaguely akin to a strangled gasp. "I think that's the best idea I've ever heard!"

CHAPTER TWENTY FIVE

"Thank goodness the weather's cleared up a bit. I was beginning to think it would never stop raining." Geraldine gazed out of the dusty window of the hall at ragged clouds tinged with pink by the fading sunlight. It was Saturday evening, and they were just finishing dinner.

Philip put down his empty coffee mug and kissed her lightly on the cheek. "Yes, I kept wanting to look on the noticeboard for details of the ark-building roster."

"That would have a certain inevitable logic I suppose—you know, 'the end of civilisation as we know it'. What's on this evening, anyway?"

"Oh, another ritual of some kind, followed by the usual alleged discussion. Of course, we could just slip away and do a bit more practise for the birth of the New Aeon. You know what they say, practice makes perfect."

Geraldine's expression was deceptively demure. "Much as I'd like to take you up on your extremely interesting offer, I do feel it would be remiss of us not to take advantage of the opportunity to draw Bob out on the subject of Australia."

"Oh, well," Philip attempted to look hurt, "if you're going to take that attitude…"

"Fool!" Geraldine slid her arm round his waist. "We're not here to enjoy ourselves, you know."

"Well, I must say good old Bob does his best to make sure of that. I can't even remotely imagine what a kid like Anita would see in him—over-inflated, pompous git!"

They walked in silence out into the chill evening air. A soft blue-green glow still hung above the black cut-outs of the mountains, but stars were beginning to wink in the darkening sky.

Geraldine said thoughtfully, "I saw Anita yesterday, coming out of the trees over there. She looked as if she'd been crying. I asked her if she was all right, but she didn't say anything—just nodded and ran into the dormitory building."

"Poor kid. I hope she's all right."

"Mmm. I haven't actually seen her today. Have you?"

"No, but then I never thought to look. Haven't you noticed—" Philip burst into song "—I only have eyes for you?"

"Shhh. You can make a spectacle of yourself if you want to, but don't involve me." But the light that shone in Geraldine's eyes told a different story.

"If you keep looking at me like that, I'm going to end up making an even bigger spectacle of both of us. Maybe Anita's been with Bob today. I notice he skulks away to his lair in the vestry most afternoons while we poor devotees are tripping the light fantastic. And, let's face it, it's not as if he couldn't do with the exercise."

"I doubt if she was with him. Look how he shut the door in her face the other night. Still, if she's not there tonight, I think we should investigate."

In the event, Anita was in her usual place near the front of the church when they arrived for the evening session. She looked composed, but deliberately so, her face remote as though distancing herself from whatever she might be feeling. Bob's arrival seemed to shake her composure. As he made his way past her, she looked quickly down, and clasped her hands more tightly in her lap. Geraldine thought she saw tears glinting on Anita's face, but she was too far away to be certain.

The ritual involved a great deal of incense, soft, amorphous background music featuring a particularly gushing string section, a dagger, and a chalice of wine. The latter was eventually passed around for each of them to take a sip. As they did so, they were supposed to consult their inner vision as to some personal symbol relating to the New Aeon. When, as the music drifted to a nebulous halt, Bob invited them to share their insights with the rest of the group, Geraldine realised that here was her chance to introduce the subject of Australia.

"Quick," she whispered to Philip, as the massive woman with the excessively young and handsome boyfriend began to talk about some symbolism that sounded to her ears remarkably like a description of the Ace of Cups in the tarot, "what can I tell him to make him talk about Australia?"

Philip looked startled, then a look of understanding dawned on his face and he grinned. Discarding several highly unsuitable possibilities with a mental note to regale Geraldine with them later, he whispered back to her, "What about the Dreamtime? That should get him going."

Geraldine nodded, and squeezed his hand. While several others related their visions, she concentrated on an idea that had begun to form in her mind. Eventually, there was a silence. Bob looked around, his gaze apparently unfocussed. Into the silence, Geraldine raised her hand. Immediately, his eyes were on her, and she had the uncomfortable sensation of being snapped with a hidden camera and filed away for future reference.

"I didn't actually see anything," Geraldine said, "But I heard a voice that sounded very old and wise, talking about 'the new Dreamtime'. I feel sure it was referring to the New Aeon, but I don't quite understand the Dreamtime reference."

"Ah, yes," said Bob, his voice laden with instant self-importance, "I can explain that. The Dreamtime comes from the creation mythology of the Australian Aborigines. When I was in Australia, I was privileged to study this mythology with one of their greatest teachers. Of course, there was a great deal he couldn't tell an outsider, but I did learn that the Dreamtime is their term for the time of the creation of all things, a sort of golden age, when everything was new and powerful. You have been given this as your symbol of the power and creativity available to you, and all of us, as the New Aeon comes into its own. Thank you for sharing it with us, er..."

"Geraldine."

"Yes, thank you, Geraldine." Once more, he looked around the group, but it seemed no more insights were forthcoming, so Bob thanked them all and began to perform his usual closing ritual, making a bigger than usual production of it as he swirled incense and closed the circle in a flurry of prayers and thanksgivings.

As they stepped from the church into the ice-clear night air, Philip slid his arm around her waist. "That was brilliant!" he enthused, hugging her close.

Geraldine smiled up at him warmly. How pleasant it was, she thought, to meet a man who looked tall, even to her. "It was your idea," she said. "I just filled in the details. Anyway, we got what we wanted. Did you see his face when he realised what he'd said? And the way he tried to cover up, flinging all that incense around."

"Mmm. Just as well he doesn't know why we're here."

"Do you think it's too late to phone Luke and tell him what we've found out, while it's still fresh in our minds?"

"I shouldn't think so. He's bound to be up still—probably swigging coffee and watching some tacky movie on TV, if I know Luke. You'd never pick him for a philosophy graduate, would you?"

Before Geraldine could reply, there was a loud wail from the direction of the vestry, followed by a man's voice, then more strangled sobbing. Philip took Geraldine's hand, and they hurried towards the sound, keeping close to the side of the church, which was in shadow. As they neared the vestry, they heard Bob's voice, low, but insistent. Thanks to the stillness of the night, they could hear it quite clearly.

"Anita, for goodness sake pull yourself together. I'm trying to create a positive atmosphere here in which we can all learn and grow, and I will *not* have you destroying it by such negative behaviour. If you're not able to control your negative thoughts and emotions, I'll have no option but to ask you to leave."

Anita's sobs subsided somewhat. She was standing in the pool of light created by the open vestry door, sniffing disconsolately and wiping her tears away on one pink, trailing sleeve. As they watched, tears welled in her eyes again, and her shoulders began to convulse. She looked as though she was about to say something when, from the direction of the dormitory block, a form appeared out of the dark enquiring, "Is everything all right?" It was Pat.

"Anita's just a little upset. It's nothing serious," Bob called back softly, his words holding a warning for the still sniffling girl, "is it, Anita? Could you look after her, please, Pat?"

"Of course," replied Pat. "Come along, Anita. I'll make us both a nice cup of tea, and you can tell me all about it." She placed a motherly arm around Anita's shoulder and led her towards the hall. There was a dull thud as the vestry door closed.

"She won't, of course," said Geraldine, as she and Philip made their way back to their tent.

"Not now that Bob's put the frighteners on her," Philip agreed. "It's a good job she's got Pat here to look after her. Let's go and surprise Luke, shall we?"

* * * *

It was barely light when the shrilling of the telephone wrenched Isabel from a deep, untroubled sleep. Beside her, Declan sat bolt upright, shaking himself awake. "Mother of God, who the hell can that be?"

"I'll give you three guesses." Isabel rolled her eyes upwards, then slid out of bed and cast around for her dressing gown.

Bob's voice, when she picked up the receiver, sounded as hard and taut as a wire. "I warned you not to mock me," he grated, with none of his usual ingratiating preamble.

"I have no idea what you're talking about." Isabel's voice was as cold as the early morning air.

"I think you do. I have been very, very patient with you, Georgina. Let me remind you, it was you who came to me in the first place. You came to me and asked for my help. I thought we had a bargain. And now you see fit to discard someone who can really help you, for a... for a... You won't get away with it, Georgina. We do not easily forgive such betrayal."

"Forgive!" She was furious now. "How dare you call me like this with your threats and insinuations. I'm warning you, if you ever contact me again—"

Bob's voice interrupted her, "No, no, Georgina. I'm warning you..."

Shaking, Isabel slammed the receiver down. Declan came and put his arms around her, holding her and stroking her hair until she was calm again. "I think," he said, "we can do without him now." He switched off the digital recorder, and turned the volume control on the answering machine to 'off'. "Come on, sweetheart, I'll make you some tea."

He sat Isabel at the kitchen table, where she rested her chin on her hands and sat watching him. "Well," she said at last, her voice still shaky, "we've obviously been mentioned in dispatches."

Declan turned to her with his lopsided grin. "He doesn't know the half of it!" He brought her a mug of tea and sat down beside her.

"He was pretty angry."

Declan kissed her and ruffled her hair. "Look, if you're worried, I can arrange to have this place watched."

Isabel shook her head. "I can't really see him trying anything that serious. He may be a bit weird, but I don't think that's his style. Besides, it wouldn't exactly enhance his 'love and light' image, would it, if he were to harm me physically?"

"He'd bloody well better not try!"

Eyes shining, Isabel told him, "You have no idea how good that makes me feel!"

"If you'd like to put that mug down," Declan murmured, "I reckon I might be able to make you feel even better."

Later, after they had well and truly tested and proved his hypothesis, Declan asked Isabel to take him sightseeing. Quite apart from the fact that he had had no time yet to explore the local scenery, he judged the best thing for Isabel's peace of mind, right now, was to be somewhere where there was no possibility of Bob contacting her. So they packed an impromptu picnic and spent the day happily meandering around Lyttelton and its nearby beaches. Declan was fascinated by the quaint hillside houses of Christchurch's port town. And the fresh air and soothing clamour of waves on sand and rocks did almost as much to restore Isabel's spirits as did the company of that unlikely combination of cynic and romantic she could now scarcely imagine not being part of her life.

Arriving back at Isabel's flat in the early evening, they were greeted by an unusually irate Dominic. "Where have you been?" he demanded. "People have been trying to get in touch with you all day!"

"Like who?" asked Isabel, instantly tense.

"Like Joss," he expostulated, "and Luke! Why didn't you leave a message? We've all been worried sick!"

Suppressing an urge to laugh at this improbable role reversal, Isabel said contritely, "I'm sorry, Dominic. I've been out with Declan. Oh, have you two met?"

They both attested that they had. Dominic said, "That's all right then. Oh, and that weirdo, Bob, called again this afternoon."

"Yes?" Isabel felt her chest tighten and her throat constrict. Declan squeezed her shoulder.

"Well," Dominic said, "I, um, listened earlier to what was on that recorder by the phone. When he called, I knew it was him because he asked to speak to Georgina. So I told him if he ever bothers you again, I'll undertake personally to realign his chakras for him. Then I hung up on him."

Isabel and Declan both burst out laughing. Isabel said, a trifle weakly, "Thank you, Dominic. I hadn't realised you'd taken up physical violence."

Dominic wrinkled his nose in distaste. "Don't be disgusting, Mother. I have no intention of inflicting unnecessary pain on myself. Still, he doesn't know that, does he?" Now he knew his mother was safe, he sauntered back to his room, where the love of his life—his saxophone—awaited him. In the doorway he turned and, with an expression that might almost have been mistaken for a grin attempting to break through, said, "By the way, that balaclava stuff was excellent. My compliments to the chef."

CHAPTER TWENTY SIX

Peering into the mirror in the soft lamplight, Declan put the finishing touches to his grooming. It was rather more perfunctory than he would have liked for a Monday morning, but he had originally intended to go back to the motel last night. Not that he'd wanted to, but he did need to get that damned report up to date, and Isabel had insisted she'd be all right.

They had cooked dinner together after their return from Lyttelton, (Dominic having disappeared again by then). Afterwards, Isabel had played Astral Weeks for him, then Beethoven's Moonlight Sonata (they had discovered a mutual love of Beethoven, as well), as they had relaxed in the candle-lit sitting-room.

At two in the morning when he had arrived home, Dominic had discovered them asleep in each other's arms on the couch. He had herded them solicitously off to bed with severe castigations about wasting electricity, then sauntered down the hall to his own room, softly whistling the opening bars of The Wild Colonial Boy as he went.

"Sarcastic little sod," Declan had muttered into Isabel's hair, then had promptly fallen asleep again.

He ran his hand through his hair, though as usual it took not a blind bit of notice. Isabel was sitting up in bed sipping the tea he had made her, her hair tumbling over her bare, creamy-pale shoulders and breasts with a blatant disregard for propriety. He picked up her dressing gown from the floor and threw it onto the bed beside her. "Cover yourself up, you scarlet woman," he admonished her, his eyes belying the puritanical tone of his voice. "Don't you realise you're leading me into mortal sin?"

"Only venial, surely?" Isabel replied, blowing him a kiss.

Declan sat down on the bed and kissed her, rubbing his cheek against her hair, breathing in the warm, sleepy smell of her. "I think you'll find," he murmured, "that lust is, in fact, a mortal sin. Ah, well, now I've made my confession, I guess I'd better go and see what's lined up for me today as a penance." Sighing, he stood up again. "I really do have to go. What's your programme for today?"

"I have a couple of clients this morning. Then I promised I'd help Joss this afternoon with some research she's doing."

"Ah. Well, I expect I'll be busy myself most of the day."

Isabel couldn't resist a fond chuckle at his attempt to disguise his disappointment. For a detective, he really was remarkably transparent sometimes. "I was rather hoping," she teased, "that you might want to come up and see me later—you know, after you've finished doing your penance. I don't think there's a lot I can do about the state of your immortal soul, but I can do you a very nice moussaka."

A grin of delight lit Declan's features. "That sounds like an offer I can't refuse," he said, kissing her again, "and I know exactly what we need to go with it—a nice bottle of red and some more of that balaclava stuff!"

* * * *

As Isabel stood on tiptoe to pull another book from the

topmost library shelf, her eye caught a glimpse of the clock on the wall at the end of the room. Almost four o'clock. Damn! Declan was due to arrive at the flat in a couple of hours, and she still had to buy the eggplants for the moussaka. After the events of the last few says, she had not expected to be able to concentrate on anything. But, as fate would have it, the first cult she had chosen to research was Scientology, and the life and times of its leader, L Ron Hubbard—an eccentric's eccentric if ever there was one—had engrossed her for three solid hours. And they certainly helped put Bob in perspective.

Half an hour later, she parked the Corolla in the driveway, and began to haul books and brown paper bags out of the passenger seat. Dali came running up to her, rubbing against her legs and making little mewing noises. Isabel bent to stroke his head. "Are you hungry, sweetie? Well, you'll have to wait till I get this lot inside."

Holding her pile of books precariously in place with her chin, she pushed the car door shut with her hip. Dali seemed unusually nervous, staying close to her as she made her way round the side of the house and along the slabs of ancient concrete that formed the curved front path. "Don't walk under my feet," she told him. "If you're not careful, you'll make me drop all these books."

As they approached the broad, steep steps that led up to the verandah, the little black and white cat gave a peculiar cry and rushed off round the far side of the house. Shrugging and shaking her head at him, as far as the books would allow, Isabel felt her way up the steps, fishing in her pocket for her keys as she went. As she tried to fumble the big key into the keyhole, she felt something hard on the doormat. Declan must have been round already, and left his contribution for the evening meal. Fancy leaving it there, though. He obviously wasn't used to living with household pets.

The key, awkward at the best of times, proved impossible to manoeuvre into the hole with her arms full of books and bags. Clicking her teeth impatiently, she bent to put her burden down. Her hand brushed the parcel on the doorstep. Only it couldn't be a parcel. It felt warm and thick and wet, like... Isabel looked down.

On the doormat lay Bartholomew, his soft fur matted with congealing blood. As if this weren't outrage enough, his head had been severed and placed neatly above his outstretched body, so that its pale, staring eyes looked up at her—still, horribly, with the trusting expression she had always found so endearing. Underneath the sodden, reddened doormat, a single word had been scrawled on the wooden verandah in Bartholomew's blood: 'TRAITOR'.

She desperately wanted to scream, but the sound that emerged was no more than a hoarse croak. Pressing her hand to her mouth, she tried to breathe deeply as she struggled to open the door. Against her will, her eyes were drawn once more to the poor, mangled body of Bartholomew. A fat blowfly was crawling along the obscene red patch where his head used to be. "Oh, God!" Isabel felt her stomach heave. Finally managing to wrench the door open, she rushed to the bathroom.

Twenty minutes later, Joss found her there, sitting on the edge of the bath, her head in her hands, exhausted from retching and sobbing. All afternoon, Joss had been aware of a sick feeling in the pit of her stomach. By half past three, she had been certain Isabel was in some kind of trouble, and that it had something to do with Bob. There had been no replies to her phone calls, and each time she rang, she was sure Isabel was not at home. So she had waited, feeling edgy and helpless, and still vaguely nauseated, until suddenly, just after four-thirty, the nausea had worsened, and she had had a strong sense that Isabel had arrived home. She had phoned again, then. Still no reply, just the polite, impersonal message of the answerphone. Then the sick feeling had washed over her again, worse than ever. Hurriedly scribbling a note to Martin and the twins, she had locked the house and driven straight over.

Her initial instinct on seeing Bartholomew was to remove his body so Isabel wouldn't have to see it again. But she also knew the police would have to be contacted, and they wouldn't thank her for disturbing what might prove to be important evidence against Bob. There was little doubt in her mind that he was the instigator, if not the actual perpetrator, of this sick little act. So much for love and bloody light!

Stepping carefully over the lifeless form, Joss shut the front door behind her and hurried down the hall to Isabel. "It's all right," she soothed. "Come on into the kitchen and I'll put the kettle on." Then she went to phone Declan.

He arrived accompanied by a young constable, who took photographs of Bartholomew's body, then carefully placed it, still on the doormat, into a large plastic bag and carried it out to his car. He made a thorough search of the front garden, but there was no sign of anything that might have been used in the killing. Shaking his head, and muttering disgustedly about the kind of 'sick pervert' who could have done such a thing, he thoughtfully washed away the bloody message before making his way to the kitchen.

He seemed rather startled by the sight of Declan with his arms around a quietly weeping Isabel but, with a warning glance from Declan, he soon regained his professional manner.

"Sir..." he began tentatively.

"It's okay, Constable," Declan said quietly, but in a voice that brooked no argument. "I can handle things at this end. I'd like you to deal with the...er..." He waved a free hand at the constable.

"Of course, sir. Shall I...?"

"I'll get back to you later, okay?"

"Yes, sir. Right, sir. I'll, um..."

Joss ushered him outside and thanked him, then she went back to the kitchen. "Are you going to be all right?" she asked Isabel gently.

"I'll make sure of it," Declan told her.

Isabel raised a pale face streaked with tears from the general region of Declan's lower thorax and echoed his assurance. "I'll be fine."

Joss looked at Declan. His face was set hard with anger, but his eyes were warm and gentle as he looked down at Isabel, and so were his hands as they stroked her tousled hair. Yes, she was going to be all right with Declan.

"I'll get off home, then," she said. "I'm working tonight. You can phone me there if you need me." Isabel and Declan nodded. "Talking of which, do you want me to call Luke, so he can get in touch with Rhoda about Wednesday?"

"Please," Declan's voice was harsh. "I reckon the sooner we nail that bastard Forster the better."

Isabel stood up and began to pace restlessly about the kitchen, her hands tightly clenched.

Declan said, "I don't think you should be here on your own any more. There's no knowing what Forster will do next. I reckon he's cracking up in a big way. And, don't forget, we still don't know for sure that he wasn't responsible for Claire Lomax's death."

Isabel stopped pacing, a worried frown creasing her brow. "I think you're right," she agreed. "Still, there's always Dominic, I suppose. Or perhaps that police guard you mentioned the other day." But she didn't sound convinced.

Declan reflected for a moment on what little—what extremely little—he had seen of Dominic. "I think," he said, keeping his voice carefully neutral, "it's too big a responsibility for Dominic. I'd like to stay with you myself, if that's okay." The expression on Isabel's face told him it was.

"Thank you, I'd like that. But won't it be considered unprofessional or something?"

Declan laughed, and took her hands in his. He pulled her close to him and brushed the remaining tears from her eyelashes. "I'll worry about that later," he said. "Anyway, as long as you're safe, who gives a damn?"

As they drove to the motel for him to pick up his things and check out, Isabel told him what had happened, and he explained to her as delicately as he could about the forensic tests that would be done to try and establish who had killed Bartholomew.

"It seems strange," she said, "to do blood tests on a cat."

"It can't be too common," Declan agreed, "but someone somewhere has got his blood on their clothing, or shoes, or whatever. And they might have left evidence on him—you know, traces of skin, or hair, or even clothing. Or vice versa. It's amazing what the forensics guys can find out." A thought occurred to him. "You can have his—him back afterwards, if you want."

Isabel shook her head. "No. Much as I love—loved—him, I'm not sentimental that way. Besides, the Bartholomew I loved won't be hanging around—not after what they did to him."

Declan reached across and squeezed her hand.

For a while, they drove in silence. Then Isabel asked, "Do you really think it was Bob that did it?"

Declan's eyes went as dark as a thundercloud. "After the way he described him to you the other day, I reckon it's got to be him."

Isabel looked thoughtful. "After we've picked up your things," she said at length, "can we go and see Luke? I meant to call him back yesterday. Dominic seemed to think he'd heard from Philip at the Centre, so he might have some idea of Bob's movements. And, with any luck, he'll have contacted Rhoda by now, too."

The look on Declan's face softened and the storm clouds drifted from his eyes. "Not only incredibly attractive," he declared admiringly, "but smart with it! How did I ever manage to get so lucky?"

* * * *

"Hi!" Luke's eyebrows lifted in surprise as he opened the door. "Come on in. I've just finished talking to Joss. Are you okay, Isabel?" He ushered them into the lounge as he spoke, patting Isabel's shoulder solicitously.

"Yes. I'm still a bit shell-shocked, but I'm basically all right."

"I'm glad to hear it. I was pretty worried, I can tell you, after what Joss told me. I must say I'm looking forward to finally putting an end to Bob's little game."

"Me, too," said Declan. "Are we on for Wednesday, then?"

"I still have to call Rhoda. I was just about to when you two arrived. I tell you what—I'll go and do it now, while you're here. How about a coffee while you're waiting?"

Declan grinned. "You must be clairvoyant."

While Luke made the phone call, Isabel and Declan made themselves comfortable on the couch and sipped mugs of Luke's excellent coffee. With a shock, Isabel realised she'd had nothing substantial to eat since breakfast. She was ravenous, and the delicious odours drifting from Luke's kitchen were torture. *Well*, she told herself resignedly, *it looks as though moussaka is definitely off the menu now.*

Luke reappeared, his face enveloped in a haze of cigarette smoke and a great grin of satisfaction. "It looks like it's all systems go," he announced. "Rhoda's going to confirm it either later tonight or first thing tomorrow. How are things your end, Declan? Have you got all the information you need?"

"Pretty much. Though I wouldn't want to wait any longer in any case, after his latest little stunt. The sooner Forster is out of circulation, the happier I'll be."

Luke couldn't fail to notice the hard determination in Declan's voice, nor the look he gave Isabel. "That reminds me," he said, "Philip and Geraldine called me the other night with a couple of items of information you may find useful." He reported to them how Philip and Geraldine had gained an admission from Bob of his having lived in Australia, and of the scene they had overheard between Bob and Anita. "I've been wondering if it might be a good idea to ask Bob about Australia while I've got him on air," he ended, "to throw him off guard."

"The element of surprise." Declan nodded. "Sounds good to me."

Luke pushed his hair off his face and leaned forward to refill his coffee mug. "I've thought of an even bigger surprise," he told them.

"What's that, then?"

Luke explained, "Well, obviously I can't have you and Isabel in the studio to begin with because he'll recognise you. So, what I've come up with, is to keep you both out of sight until I've extracted as much information as possible, then wheel you in to confront him. Hopefully, his reactions will give him away."

Declan nodded thoughtfully. "That does seem to be our best plan. Let's hope it works. I've got an idea or two of my own I'd like to run by you all. So, how about we all meet tomorrow afternoon to make any last-minute plans and have a final run-through, and we'll see what we can come up with in the way of refinements." He bestowed a solicitous smile on Isabel. "In the meantime, you must be starving—I know I am. I seem to remember noticing a passable-looking souvlaki bar in the Square today. How do you fancy Greek takeaways and a nice piece of balaclava to follow?"

They left Luke to puzzle over these cryptic words.

CHAPTER TWENTY SEVEN

Luke stubbed out his half-finished cigarette and immediately lit another. Joss bit back the rebuke that rose to her lips. After all, they were all on edge. Bob was due to arrive in an hour's time. The fateful phone call from Rhoda had occurred on schedule the previous morning, and they had met that afternoon for what Joss thought of as the dress rehearsal. Now, here they were waiting for the real thing.

Joss looked across at Isabel, nervously chewing a strand of her hair. "Where's Declan?" she asked. "I thought you and he would have come together?"

"He got a call just before we were due to leave. I gathered he was expecting a phone call from Brisbane. And he said something about tying up a few loose ends while he was there," Isabel said. "But he said he'll be here well before he's needed. What about James? I suppose he's going to be late, as usual." A brittle tone in her voice betrayed the state of her nerves.

With painstaking care, Luke rid himself of a lungful of smoke. It sailed upwards in a thin, wavering stream, fanning out frantically as it neared the ceiling. "He's not coming. He rang me this afternoon. Apparently there's some important faculty meeting on this evening, and he has to be there."

"I'll bet!" Joss's tone was scathing. "Trust James to back down at the slightest hint of trouble."

"Oh, well," said Luke, "I dare say we can do without him

panicking all over the studio. We're going to have enough on our hands with Bob, I expect. Philip called this morning, by the way. He'd just heard the sad news that Bob won't be with them this evening. As you can imagine, he was devastated." He laughed nervously and drew so deeply on his cigarette that he made himself cough. "Anyway," he spluttered at last, "I explained to him what's happening, and he's going to call again later on for an update. I must say, he and Geraldine seem to be having a ball out there."

"I don't suppose you'd care to rephrase that?" Joss enquired demurely.

"Not at all! I know what I meant," Luke riposted, making a show of turning his back on Joss and his attention on Isabel. "I've rigged up a sort of intercom for you. You and Declan can sit out here and listen to the interview, then when it's time to spring our little surprise, I'll introduce you—by your real name, of course, which he won't recognise. Then you and Declan will come into the studio."

"I can't wait to see his face when he sees you!" declared Joss, rubbing her hands in anticipation.

Luke showed Isabel how to use the intercom, then the three of them made desultory conversation until the doorbell rang, making them all jump.

"That must be Declan," said Isabel. "I was beginning to think he wasn't coming."

Luke went to answer the door. They heard voices, and then the studio door at the far end of the hallway opening and closing.

"It must be Bob!" Isabel whispered frantically. "He's early! Where the hell is Declan?"

Joss laid a soothing hand on her arm. "Don't worry," she

315

said. "We don't go on air till eight. There's still plenty of time."

"I suppose so," Isabel responded, trying to sound more certain than she felt.

Luke stuck his head round the door. "Sorry," he said to Isabel, "but I need Joss. I want to run over the general format with Bob before we start."

"Don't worry," Joss said again, and followed Bob to the studio, leaving Isabel alone with her nerves and the intercom.

* * * *

Luke looked at Bob across the control panel. Eschewing the white kaftan, which by all accounts had become his habitual (as in religious order) attire at the Circle of Light Centre, Bob was dressed today in fawn canvas trousers and a gold striped tunic that might well have begun its life as someone's spare-room curtains. Cuddled against the pallid skin revealed by its open neck, the ubiquitous citrine was just visible. His hair hung as lankly as ever, now down to his shoulders. Clearly he was going in for the long-haired prophet look—either that or he was finding it hard to get to a hairdresser. Still, at least he seemed to be at ease, which was more than Luke cared to say for himself.

He glanced across at Joss. As always, she appeared to have herself well in hand. The wall clock told him it was five minutes to eight. He wondered if Declan had arrived yet. The sound-proofing in the studio meant he had no way of knowing. Oh, well, better get on with it.

"When the red light on the wall behind me goes on," he

explained to Bob, "we'll be on air." Bob nodded, and took a sip of the water Luke had provided. Luke waited for the sound through his headphones of the station announcer introducing the programme, then flicked the 'On' switch.

As the show's theme music faded, Luke gave his usual smooth introduction, then, with one eye on Bob, said into his microphone, "And now, as promised last week, we have with us in the studio Bob Ferris. Some of you will know Bob as a tarot reader, but recently he opened the Circle of Light Centre, just out of Oxford, where he runs courses and seminars on aspects of the Western Spiritual Tradition. Welcome again to The Psychic Connection, Bob. Perhaps you'd like to start by telling us what led to your decision to open a centre for spiritual teachings?"

Smoothing his hair back with one chubby, be-ringed hand, Bob leaned into the microphone and began to speak.

* * * *

Isabel hunched forward on the couch and tried to concentrate on the intercom as Bob began to explain his unlikely presence in a disused country church. There was still no sign of Declan and, in spite of Joss's words, the sick feeling in the pit of her stomach left her anything but reassured.

"I feel very privileged," Bob was gushing, "to be a channel for the energy of the New Aeon..."

Out in the hall, the telephone shrilled. Isabel started to her feet, then subsided again, waiting for Luke to answer it. As the ringing continued, it dawned on her that Luke could hardly interrupt a live broadcast to answer the phone, and he probably couldn't hear it in the studio anyway. Leaving Bob's voice spilling out of the intercom like the scent of some particularly cloying essential oil, she went to answer it.

Declan sounded surprised to hear her voice instead of Luke's.

Despite the soundproofing of the studio through the wall, Isabel found herself speaking in an urgent stage-whisper. "Declan! Where are you? Why aren't you here?"

"Look, something's come up that could be important. I have to identify someone, but it won't take long. I'll be there soon, okay?"

"But..."

"I'm sorry, I can't talk now. I'll explain it all later. Tell Luke to keep Forster talking as long as possible."

"But they're already recording!"

"Oh, shit! I really am sorry." Declan's words betrayed both frustration and weariness.

Isabel took a deep breath, then another. Panic wasn't going to help either of them. "It's all right," she said, keeping her voice deliberately bland. "They've only just started, anyway. You get back to work, and I'll see you soon."

"Sure. I'll be as quick as I can, I promise."

With a sigh, Isabel replaced the receiver.

Back in the sitting room, Bob's voice was apprising the listening public of his credentials as a spiritual teacher. Isabel felt her heart thud as she heard Luke say, "Tell us some more about your experiences with the Australian Aborigines, Bob. I understand it's very unusual for a European to be admitted to their teachings."

There was an awkward silence, during which Isabel could sense Bob's discomfiture. If only she could see his face.

However, he recovered almost immediately. "You must be mistaken, Luke," he responded smoothly. "I'm afraid I've never had that privilege."

Luke's reply was equally smooth. "I could have sworn you mentioned that when we last spoke. I must have misread my notes. Still, that's an impressive variety of spiritual teachings you've managed to pack into your life so far. Perhaps you'd like to tell us how you intend to use them at the Circle of Light Centre."

Indeed, Bob would. The awkward moment was over. Isabel breathed a sigh of relief as Bob waxed eloquent on his plans for the Centre. The more he had to say for himself the better. In keeping with his nature, they were nothing if not grandiose. In horrid fascination, she listened as he outlined what sounded like a cross between a religious community and one of those awful Nazi stud farms designed to produce the Aryan Ubermensch. It didn't take much to see that Bob thought of himself as chief stud. Though even with the evidence of Anita and Julie Hazelwood, it was hard to picture him as begetter of the New Aeon, or of any other aeon, come to that.

Nevertheless, she had to concede there was a certain bizarre appeal in his dramatic depiction of the Circle of Light Centre of the future and the new era it would bring forth—or unleash, depending on one's viewpoint—into an unsuspecting world. If nothing else, Bob knew how to tell a story. Isabel was musing uneasily on some of the more unsavoury ramifications of that particular ability, when she was startled to hear Luke's voice again.

"Thank you, Bob, for giving us such a clear and fascinating picture of your plans for your new centre. Now

319

I'd like you to meet two colleagues of mine who have recently visited the Circle of Light Centre. I've invited them here today to give us their perspective. One is a regular member of our panel, tarot reader Isabel Sinclair, and the other, a visitor from Brisbane, Australia, is Declan Kelly. While they get themselves settled, let's listen to a piece of music from sixties cult icon, The Incredible String Band. Here they are then with The Half Remarkable Question from their album, Wee Tam."

Isabel leapt to her feet. Her heart seemed to be suffering a sudden attack of St Vitus Dance. Breathing deeply to still its wild cavortings, she hurried out to the hall. On an impulse, she went and opened the front door. A swift glance down the driveway revealed no sign of Declan or his fawn Barina. She left the door off the latch in the hope that Declan would, as he had said, be there before long. In the meantime, she'd just have to proceed as planned and hope she could carry it off on her own. She steeled herself and opened the studio door.

Closing the door quietly behind her, she stood looking at the others. Behind the control panel Luke sat puffing, as usual, on a cigarette. His eyes widened in surprise, immediately suppressed so that anyone who didn't know him well would imagine him to be perfectly calm and relaxed. Isabel knew better. So did Joss, perched on a stool by the window on the far side of the studio. Immediately taking in the situation, she raised one eyebrow then gave a slight shrug as though to say, "Don't panic, we'll manage." Bob was, for the moment, absorbed in the music. Briefly, she pondered whether Luke had chosen the song on purpose for its title. If so, the irony seemed lost on Bob.

Just as the atmosphere in the studio became almost

unbearably tense, Luke took a final puff at his cigarette and extinguished it. He leaned forward across the drifting curl of blue smoke and spoke through the final notes of the music, "It seems Declan has been delayed for the time being, but I'd like to introduce Isabel Sinclair. You and she should have a lot to talk about, Bob."

Bob's eyes opened. He looked first at the empty chair between him and Joss, then around the studio, as though surprised Isabel hadn't taken a seat with the rest of them. Finally, his gaze found her standing motionless by the door. His eyes flew wide, then narrowed in an expression of equal parts shock and fury. His mouth opened, silently framing the word, "Georgina!"

"No, not Georgina—Isabel, Bob. Or should I say Richard Forster?" To her amazement and relief, her voice sounded perfectly self-possessed.

"But... but... how...?" Bob spluttered. For the moment, shock was in the ascendant.

No-one seemed to know quite what to do at first. It was like some weird tableau, a moment in time frozen for all eternity, a snapshot taken for the akashic photograph album. Luke sat poised over his controls, ready to react, but not yet sure how. Joss waited to see what Bob and Isabel would do. They had been counting on Declan's presence, so they hadn't thought to formulate a contingency plan. Isabel stood stock-still in front of the studio door, frighteningly aware that she was all that stood between Bob and his escape, should he choose that option. Bob, his plump backside spilling over the edges of his stool, stared at Isabel in disbelief. One hand went to his throat, clutching at his citrine as though it were a talisman against disaster.

A myriad of fleeting expressions pursued one another across his startled face, finally resolving themselves into a single gasped question, "What are you doing here?"

Isabel's voice was almost abnormally calm. "As you heard, I'm a regular member of the panel. The real question is, what are you doing here? I'll tell you, shall I, *Bob*? You're here because we want to know why you think you have the right to harass innocent women—like Anne, and Liz, and—and me."

"How dare you make such a slanderous accusation!" Bob's voice squeezed through his tightly clenched teeth.

"Oh, so it's slander, is it?" Isabel unlocked her cold eyes from his furious ones and turned to Luke. Her voice was so soft as to be almost inaudible. "Perhaps you'd like to play the recording we gave you yesterday, Luke."

Luke nodded, moving his hand towards one of the buttons on the control deck, but holding it poised, waiting for Bob's reaction.

Bob said nothing. His eyes flicked wildly between Isabel and Luke as he struggled to make sense of what was happening.

Isabel felt her breath rasping in her throat as she waited, praying desperately that Declan would arrive.

"You...recorded...? How... dare you...!" The strangled phrases struggled to escape Bob's clenched teeth. His face convulsed, growing red with fury, then deathly pale as he finally began to comprehend his situation. He leapt from his stool and made a rush for the door. The stool went flying, and Joss hurriedly slid from her own stool, backing against the window to avoid it. Meanwhile Isabel stood her ground by the door, determined at all costs to prevent Bob's escape.

But she was unprepared for his strength as, in one move,

he shoved his elbow hard into her rib-cage, sending her reeling to one side against a heavy bookcase, and wrenched open the door. Gasping, she struggled to her feet and stumbled after him down the hallway with Joss in hot pursuit.

Unfortunately, Bob had the presence of mind to relatch the front door as he left, and the extra precious moments needed to open it again were all he needed to reach his borrowed car and drive off. As the car disappeared round a corner, Isabel leaned against the door-post, holding her side and gasping for breath.

"Are you all right?" Joss asked. "Did he hurt you?"

Isabel gritted her teeth and shook her head.

"What happened to Declan?"

"Search me!" Isabel was unable to conceal her anger. "He rang just after you'd gone into the studio. Said something had come up that might be important, but he didn't think it would take long. Now the whole plan's ruined!" She flinched again as her ribs began to throb in earnest.

Joss put a comforting arm around her. "Not necessarily," she said. "Bob's bound to be hotfooting it back to the Centre. I'll phone and see what's happened to Declan and, as soon as he arrives, we can follow Bob and beard him in his lair."

The sound of a car squealing to a halt outside sent Isabel flying down the driveway. Declan came running to meet her. Between Isabel's tears of relief and anger, and Joss's explanations, he managed somehow to grasp the situation.

"Shit! We'd better get after him then." Declan looked around him. "Where's Luke?"

"Oh, hell!" exclaimed Joss. "He's still in the studio finishing the programme! You two go on. I'll be with you in a minute."

Luke was busy pushing a CD into one of the decks, while simultaneously talking into the microphone and keeping one eye on the open studio door. He glanced at Joss, giving her a 'thumbs up' sign before saying, "And now, a couple of messages before we listen to this week's instalment of our regular series."

As a commercial for a local hypnotherapist began, Luke switched off his microphone and turned to Joss, rolling his eyes in mock despair.

"Declan's just arrived," she told him. "We're heading out to the Circle of Light Centre. We figure that's where Bob will have gone."

Luke pushed his hair off his forehead and reached distractedly for his cigarettes. "You go on, then. I'll follow you as soon as I've finished here. Mind you, anything else I say is bound to be an anti-climax now."

"Oh, I don't know. Who knows what will happen out at the Centre? And there's always next week for the next exciting instalment." The sound of Declan's car starting up came from outside. "I'd better go now—the others are waiting. Could you ring Martin for me before you leave?"

Luke nodded, and turned back to his control desk as the second commercial faded. As Joss left she heard him saying, "And now, before we end this week's programme with another in our series, Explaining Psychic Phenomena, I just want to remind you to keep listening for further developments in the exciting real-life drama unfolding on our doorstep at this very moment at the Circle of Light Centre. And remember, you heard it first on The Psychic Connection."

On our doorstep is right, Joss reflected as she hurried out to the waiting car. Trust Luke not to miss a trick.

Seconds later, they were on their way.

As they drove, Joss explained what had happened in the studio. Isabel didn't trust herself to say anything just yet. She was still furious with Declan for letting her down, and equally furious with herself for minding so much, when she knew it wasn't really his fault. Besides, the pain in her side hurt with even the slightest movement. So she hunched silently and sullenly beside him as they sped along the motorway and took the turnoff onto the long, straight Tram Road. In the dark of a starless night it lay before them like a black velvet ribbon stretching to infinity on a sea of gloom.

* * * *

Through the screen of poplars fronting the Circle of Light Centre they could see lights shining from both hall and church.

"What do we do now?" asked Joss.

Before Declan could answer, they heard a shout and a strangled cry, followed by a heavy thud from the direction of the church.

"Ask a silly question," Joss panted as they raced for the church.

The group of people clustered round the conspicuously closed main doors of the church included Philip and Geraldine, who ran to meet them.

Straight away, Declan took charge. This was partly out of habit, but he was uncomfortably aware that it was also due to the guilt he felt for having let Isabel and the others down.

325

Still, this was hardly the time to deal with that. "What's up?" he asked tersely.

"Bob's just locked himself in the church," Geraldine told him, "with Anita."

"I think she was already in there," Philip added, "sort of mooning around after the evening session, as she does a lot of the time. Bob turned up unexpectedly about a quarter of an hour ago, and raced into the church. He turfed out the few others who were there, but he must have grabbed Anita before she could leave."

Geraldine took up the account. "We heard her yell, and then the doors slammed shut, and by the time we got here, he'd barred the door."

"What about the vestry?" asked Declan, with a glance towards the back of the church.

Philip shook his head. "We tried that. It's barred, too. They both have those heavy iron bars on the inside, so I think breaking in is out of the question."

Declan scratched his temple thoughtfully for the moment it took to make up his mind. "Can you two get all the others over to the hall and keep them busy?" he said to Philip and Geraldine. "Make a brew of tea or something. I'll be over as soon as I can to explain the situation, but first I want to see if I can talk some sense into Forster."

"Good luck," said Philip. "I don't fancy your chances." But he went with Geraldine and began talking to the others, gesturing once or twice towards Declan and the church. With a gratifying degree of self-interest, the group began to move slowly towards the hall.

In the ensuing silence, Declan moved closer to the church, walking quietly along the wall, listening. Muffled sobbing could be heard from somewhere near the front of the church. Anita. Standing on tiptoe, he peered through the greenish diamond panes of the window nearest the vestry. He could see a large, pale shape that was probably the altar, but nothing else. He watched for a moment longer, but saw no sign of movement. The sobs had subsided, but he could still hear faint, indefinable sounds. With a sigh of frustration, he went back to the others.

"I can't see anything, but I think they're up the front somewhere."

"Probably by the altar," Isabel suggested.

Declan nodded. "Probably. I'm going to talk to him and try and get him to come out—or at least let Anita out." He walked back to the church window and called out, "Forster, can you hear me?" No answer. No sound. Declan tried again. "Forster, this is Detective Sergeant Kelly, Queensland Police. I know you're in there, and I know you've got Anita with you. I just want to talk to you, that's all. Come out, and bring the girl with you, and there won't be any trouble."

There was a rustling sound from within the church, then Bob's voice, sounding oddly disembodied. "I have no need to speak to you or anyone."

"I think it'll be easier all round if you do," Declan told him. "Whether you meant to or not, you've caused a lot of bother for a lot of people. Don't you think it's about time it all stopped?"

"I have no idea what you're talking about."

"There's Anita for a start. The poor kid must be terrified." Another faint whimper from inside seemed to confirm this. "Let her go, Forster. She's done nothing to you."

There was silence as Bob appeared to consider Declan's

theory. After what seemed an age, he spoke once more, his voice stiff and pompous. "Anita," he declared, "is carrying the Child of the Aeon. The Child must be protected."

Declan sighed, and rolled his eyes skyward. This was not going to be easy. In fact, he had a feeling it was not going to be anything so simple as just plain difficult. "Let's see what Anita wants, shall we? Anita, this is Sergeant Kelly. I'd like to talk to you. If you come over to the window I'll be able to hear you better."

There was the sound of movement, then Anita's voice, too low to be heard outside, obviously speaking to Bob. It was followed by Bob's voice, also undecipherable, but with a menacing edge to it. Then a sharp little cry, and more muffled movement.

Bob's voice floated out to them, stiff with affronted majesty. "Anita has no wish to speak with you, and neither of us will be leaving this sanctuary. I have nothing more to say to you."

Declan ran a frustrated hand over his forehead and pushed it through his hair. He went back to where Isabel and Joss were standing. "I don't think there's much chance of persuading Forster to let Anita go. He reckons he's protecting the Child of the Aeon."

"Would you like me to talk to him?" Isabel asked. It wasn't so much that she expected to succeed where Declan had failed, but it was better than standing around feeling useless.

Declan shrugged. "Why not? You can't possibly do any worse than me. And I really ought to let the people in the hall know what's going on. Will you be okay here for a minute?"

Isabel's eyes flashed angrily. "I'm not completely useless,

you know. After all, I managed to confront Bob earlier without your help."

Declan turned away to hide his grin. "I'll leave you to it then." He had a growing suspicion that learning to deal with a warrior queen was going to be extremely interesting. He was already looking forward to the peace negotiations later.

Isabel called out, "Bob."

"Who's that?" came the sharp response.

"It's me, Isabel—Georgina."

"What do you want?" The tone was wary. Not surprising, really.

"I just want to talk to you. Look, I'm sure you never really meant to hurt anyone, but you have, Bob. You've hurt and frightened people who've never done anything to hurt you."

"No?"

"No, of course not. Surely you'd agree that we all have free will, and the responsibility to use it to the best of our understanding?" No reply. Isabel ploughed on, "All they were doing was exercising their right to do what they wanted to do. That's all I was doing, too, and look how you've hurt me. Is that what you wanted, Bob?"

More silence, then, "You broke a promise to me. You had no right to do that. And in doing so, you mocked the very powers of the universe."

Isabel decided to ignore the latter charge. "I never promised you anything, Bob. That was just what you wanted to think. And, even if I had, surely there was no need to kill Bartholomew. What did he ever do to harm you?"

"Bartholomew?" Bob sounded genuinely puzzled.

"My cat," Isabel said, swallowing resolutely. "How do you think I felt when you did that?"

"I didn't kill your cat. I have no need to resort to such measures." Bob's reply was not only puzzled, but indignant as well.

Isabel tried to think. Confusion was clouding her mind. She decided to give Bob the benefit of the doubt. "Look," she said, "you must realise you've hurt a lot of people. Please stop now, and get some help before anything worse happens."

"I have no idea what you're talking about," Bob said stiffly. "And I know precisely what I'm doing, believe me. I've told you before, the force that works through me is very powerful indeed, and will not be mocked. You may choose not to be part of the Divine Plan. That is your misfortune. I, however, have pledged myself already to those almighty universal powers that gave birth to all that is and was and ever shall be."

Isabel was unaware of Declan's return until she heard him beside her muttering, "World without end, Amen," through gritted teeth. Luke had also arrived, and was standing near Declan, his pocket voice recorder at the ready.

Declan called out to Bob, "Look, Forster, you're only making it worse for yourself. I've already called for police reinforcements. They'll be here any minute now." Ignoring the surprised looks from the others he went on, "If you let Anita go and give yourself up now, you can save yourself a lot of trouble, believe me."

Whether Bob felt inclined to belief or disbelief they were not destined to discover. At that moment, there was a deep, thunderous roar in the distance. It grew steadily louder, culminating in a sudden, blinding glare of lights through the poplar trees. They spun towards the road to see a fearsome array of lights careering noisily at them out of the dark. It was a great monster of a truck. There was a screech of brakes as the leviathan skidded to a halt beside the hall. The lights dimmed as suddenly as they had blazed.

A drawling voice rumbled out of the dark, "Gidday! Is that you, Georgina? I just called in on my way back from Wellington to see Bob about picking up his things from town. I promised I'd bring them out here for him. I should have been here hours ago, but the bloody ferry was late as usual. I didn't even touch down in Picton till after four, and I've been driving like a madman ever since. Still, I guess I can always kip down here for the night and head into town first thing tomorrow. Is Bob around?"

CHAPTER TWENTY EIGHT

"Bloody hell, it's Doug!" cried Isabel, and dashed across to the truck. The others followed, exchanging puzzled glances as they panted behind her.

The cab door of Doug's truck opened, and his great, bearded form swung to the ground with the agility of long experience. A mass of faces peered curiously at them from the hall windows, but no-one came out. Isabel briefly introduced Joss, Luke and Declan, and explained what was happening. Doug listened, growing increasingly irate as the tale unfolded.

"You can't bloody trust anyone these days!" he exploded finally, thumping his fist against the side of his truck! "Let me see him! I'll soon sort the bastard out!"

Isabel laid a soothing hand on his army surplus-clad arm. "He's barred all the doors," she told him. "He won't listen to Declan or me. Declan's phoned through to the police in Christchurch, and I think we should wait for them. Anita's frightened, of course, but she seems to be safe enough so far. Still I don't think we should do anything to upset Bob, just to be on the safe side."

Doug rubbed at his beard with one gigantic paw. "I guess we should wait for them, then," he agreed. But he looked disappointed.

"Listen, all of you!" Their heads swivelled towards the church again as Bob's voice rang out.

"What is it, Forster?" Declan was on his way to the front of the church. Isabel, Luke and Joss hurried after him. Doug, apparently reluctant to leave his precious truck, hauled himself up onto the running board and swung there, watching them.

"Listen! I have something important to tell you." They waited. The silence was a black hole in the starless night. Then Bob's voice rang out again, "Since I now realise you are all determined to destroy me, I have decided to save you the trouble. It is of no concern to me what becomes of my earthly form. It is merely a temporary vessel in any case, and such are easily acquired." Isabel noted the bitterness in his voice and was not surprised. "But that which it contains is immortal. You *cannot* destroy *me*!" Bob's voice rose in a crescendo of volume and pitch as he continued, "You spoke to me of free will. I choose now to use that gift to pre-empt your blasphemous efforts to destroy me and all I stand for. My final magical act will be to make of myself a holy sacrifice to the sublime energy of the New Aeon!"

Declan ran his hand through his hair. "Holy Mother of God! Can someone translate that for me?"

"In a nutshell," said Isabel, "'You'll never take me alive.'"

"Oh, shit!" He raced back to the window. "Forster! Don't be an idiot! I told you, I only want to talk to you, so do yourself a favour and come on out of there!"

The silence was ineffable.

Then Joss whispered urgently, "What about Anita?"

"Shit!" Controlling his desperation with difficulty, Declan called out again to Bob, "Forster, listen! I won't argue with your right to do whatever you want with yourself. But if you have that right, so does Anita. She has the right to leave if

333

she wants to. Let's find out what Anita wants, shall we? Let me talk to her. Anita?"

From inside the church came a scuffling sound and a strangled gasp, then Bob spoke again. "I cannot allow that," he intoned. "Anita is a vehicle for the Child of the Aeon. I cannot allow the destructive forces of a degenerate era to pervert the Child and use him for their own evil ends. No, his spirit must be set free, to return once more when the world is truly ready for him." His voice was hard and fierce, and oddly devoid of expression. Isabel gasped as she recognised the tone from her first private session with him.

"I don't think there's much use trying to reason with him," she whispered urgently to Declan. "I've seen him like this before. He's gone into one of his trances." Declan stared at her. He looked so worn and so helpless, she wanted to hold him like a child and tell him everything would be all right. But her intuition gave her no such confidence.

The air was suddenly rent by a scream. "No! Leave me alone!" It was Anita. She must have realised what Bob had been talking about.

They heard footsteps and a furious scrabbling, then Bob's voice, shocked and angry, shouting, "No! You cannot go! I forbid you!" There was more scrabbling followed by a heavy thud.

"What's he doing to her? We've got to stop him!" cried Joss, starting forward. Luke was close on her heels.

There was a brief silence, then Anita could be heard sobbing convulsively.

Before anyone had time to respond to Joss, another sound ripped through the darkness as the engine of Doug's truck thundered to life. As they turned towards the sound, the lights glared and the great beast began to lumber towards the church, gathering speed alarmingly. The four of them leapt back from the church wall. Horrified, they watched as the truck roared forward, a snarling juggernaut urged on in its mission of mercy by a grim-faced Doug.

Declan sprinted towards the truck, but Doug was oblivious to his cries.

In seconds, the truck had reached the church, ploughing through the massive doors with the ease of a fist through tissue paper. There was a crack of splintering timber and the shriek of metal on metal as the bar on the door gave way, then the truck was crashing up the aisle, squealing loudly as Doug applied the brakes. Miraculously, he managed to bring it to a halt, in a rubble of splintered wood and mangled cushions, less than a metre away from the altar.

As Doug doused the truck's lights, the softer glow from the candelabra on the altar revealed a bizarre scene. Bob was standing before the altar holding Anita with one arm twisted tightly behind her back. They both seemed frozen by the spectacle of Doug swinging himself out of the cab like an angry orangutan.

"Let her go, you mad bastard!"

His voice seemed to release them from the spell of immobility. Bob turned away from Doug, reaching towards the altar with his free hand. He grasped some object that lay there and raised it slowly above his head, where it glinted menacingly in the flickering light. It was his ritual knife.

With a scream, Anita twisted herself free of Bob. She ducked beneath his upraised arm and ran towards the open vestry door, a trail of maroon tie-dyed muslin and lace floating behind her. Bob was thrown suddenly off balance.

His arms flailed furiously as he clutched at the altar in an attempt to remain upright.

Doug leapt to the ground and strode after Anita, but she was already through the door, pulling it shut behind her. He heard the scrape and thud as she pushed the heavy bar into place. Battering on the thick planks, he called to Anita that he was there to save her, begging her to open the door.

Light flared suddenly from the direction of the altar. With a gasp, Doug stopped thumping and turned. Flames from the altar cloth were leaping toward the vaulted beams of the church roof. But the cloth no longer lay on the altar. It covered a mound that writhed, screaming, on the floor. As he stood there immobilised by horror, the writhing gradually grew slower until, with a last, feeble convulsion, it ceased altogether. The screaming had stopped already.

Doug swallowed hard, and tore his eyes from the scorched and reeking heap. Carefully averting his gaze, he made his way to where Isabel and the others were standing on the far side of the truck. He shook his head slowly and tried to speak, but no sound emerged.

As they stood in shocked silence, Declan bent and picked up a spar of splintered timber from the floor. "Don't look if you don't want to," he said to the others. "This could be pretty grim." Gingerly he lifted the remains of the altar cloth to reveal Bob's face and torso, charred and blackened, with shreds of burnt cloth sticking obscenely to patches of glistening pink flesh. His eyes were mercifully closed, but both eyelashes and eyebrows had been scorched into tiny, blackened globules of ash, along with his hair. Beside his head lay the massive candelabra in a pool of the blood that still flowed sluggishly from a wound on his left temple.

Declan looked at the others. "Looks like he pulled the altar cloth on top of himself as he fell. The falling candlestick must have knocked him half unconscious as well as setting fire to it." Luke clasped his hand to his mouth suddenly, and rushed back down the aisle. From outside, they could hear his violent retching. Wearily, Declan lowered the burnt remnant of fabric.

Sobbing from the vestry reminded them Anita was still there. "I'll go round to the outside door," Doug volunteered, "then she won't have to see all this. Do you know where Pat is? I reckon she's the best person to take care of Anita."

"I'll go and find her," said Joss. "She'll be in the hall with the others."

"Thanks." Doug nodded gratefully and hurried off.

Declan turned his back on the desolate heap in front of the altar and surveyed the hulk of Doug's truck, squatting stolidly in its self-created sea of wreckage. He was appalled, not by what had happened, not by what he felt, but worse, far worse, by the fact that he felt nothing at all. He looked at Isabel, his eyes betraying both exhaustion and disillusionment. "There's nothing we can do for him now, poor bastard. Come on, let's get out of here."

* * * *

The scene outside looked so normal as to seem bizarre. Warm, friendly light spilled into the darkness from the open door of the hall, emphasising the bizarre shadows cast by a group of figures standing in the doorway. As his eyes adjusted Declan could make out Luke, apparently fully recovered, talking to a couple of uniformed officers (it hadn't taken them long to arrive, then). Another of them accompanied Anita, almost obscured by Doug's protective arm, as they slowly made their way towards the hall. Pat was hurrying towards them, an anxious expression on her face.

Vaguely, as through a wall of foam, Declan heard her say, "Come along, Anita dear, let's get you into the hall. It's nice and warm in there, and I've made some tea."

A tall, skinny figure came hurrying towards them. "Detective Sergeant Kelly?" it was saying with a brisk efficiency that seemed all wrong, somehow. It was one of the Christchurch police officers.

"Sergeant Mitchell." Declan dutifully shook the bony hand extended to him and forced himself to concentrate. "I've got a couple of men talking to the people in the hall. I'd appreciate your help over in the church."

"I'll be in the hall with the others," Isabel murmured at his elbow.

Declan nodded, giving the best imitation of a smile he could manage.

He turned back to Sergeant Mitchell and spoke briskly. "Right, let's get it over with."

* * * *

At the door of the hall, Isabel was stopped by a young constable who politely but firmly asked who she was and why she was there. She explained herself to him and he scribbled the details into his notepad.

Joss came hurrying towards her. "How are you feeling? Come and have a cup of tea. There's toast, too, if you feel up to it."

"Excuse me, ma'am, but we'll be needing to ask you a few questions..." the constable called after her.

Isabel nodded vaguely, and followed Joss to the back of the hall where Geraldine and Philip had commandeered one of the long wooden benches and a plate of buttered toast. As Isabel sank gratefully onto the bench beside Luke, Pat came towards her bearing a mug of tea.

"Here you are." She smiled. "I'm sure this will help."

"Thanks. I'm sure it will. How's Anita?"

Pat shook her head. "I'm afraid she's not very well at all. I suppose it must be the shock, but she's been complaining of pains and nausea."

"Pains? Where?"

"Lower abdomen, why?"

"Anita's pregnant," Isabel explained, "about three months, I should think. Where is she? We may need to get an ambulance."

"Oh, my goodness! I had no idea!" Pat's kindly face took on a look of alarm.

Joss stood up. "I'll go," she said firmly. "You finish your tea, Isabel."

"I've heard her talk to the twins like that." Luke grinned. "It's safer not to argue. Have a piece of toast."

Isabel took his advice. The pain in her ribs had settled to a dull, throbbing ache, and she was more than happy to sit still for a while.

A short while later, Joss returned with the news that Anita had been rushed back to Christchurch in one of the police cars, with Doug and Pat following in Pat's car.

"Is she...? Will she...?"

At that moment, Declan appeared. He looked dead on his

339

feet.

Joss sat down beside Isabel. "Well," she said quietly, "she'd started bleeding, so they thought it would be quicker than waiting for an ambulance. They've called one anyway, so she'll have proper medical help before she gets to the hospital. To be honest, though, I don't think there's much hope of saving her baby."

Isabel nodded numbly. She was beginning to feel that if her brain had to cope with one more piece of information, it would explode.

"Poor kid!" Declan exclaimed sympathetically. "Still, maybe it's for the best, really." The ghost of a wry smile tugged tentatively at the corner of his mouth. "In the cold light of day, I don't imagine she would have wanted Richard Forster's kid, Child of the Aeon or not."

Joss brought him a mug of tea. He gulped it down greedily, but shook his head at the offer of toast. Right now, he wasn't sure he could cope with food.

The constable who had been on door duty came across to tell Isabel that they needed a statement from her. Declan looked at Isabel's strained face and drooping eyes. "Can't it wait?" he asked irritably. "She's had a lot to deal with."

Isabel stood up. "I'm not the only one, and I'm still perfectly capable of answering a few questions, thank you," she told him stiffly, then marched off after the constable.

"What did I do?" Declan asked Joss.

Joss patted his arm. "Isabel's a Sagittarian. They're very independent."

"I'll bear that in mind." His expression indicated that, in his opinion, this hardly constituted an adequate excuse.

Joss grinned sympathetically. "They also don't know

when to give up. She's as exhausted as you are, Declan—she just doesn't want to admit it. Come to think of it, a good night's sleep won't do any of us any harm."

Declan sighed. He, of all people, ought to be able to understand that kind of stubbornness. "I guess I'd better find out if Sergeant Mitchell has finished yet. I'd like to think we might just get out of here sometime before the weekend."

* * * *

"I," declared Joss, holding her hand out to Declan in a manner that brooked no argument, "am going to drive. It is my considered opinion that neither you nor Isabel is in any fit state to be behind the wheel of a car."

It was Declan's considered opinion that he was in no fit state to argue. He handed over the keys.

As they sped back down the dark ribbon of road, Declan leaned back gratefully against the back seat and closed his eyes. But he was too strung-out to sleep. He opened them again and looked across at Isabel. She was staring straight ahead, her skin stretched over the contours of her face like paper on a mask.

He leaned across and put his arm round her.

"There's no need to fuss over me," she said irritably. "I'm all right!"

Declan left his arm exactly where it was. "I don't doubt it," he said, "but what about me?"

Isabel looked up at him. His face was haggard and pale, and grimy with smoke from the fire in the church. His sea-water eyes were like the aftermath of a storm. In a flash of insight it dawned on her that most of the anger she had been

341

conserving so carefully since her confrontation with Bob in the studio was not for Declan at all. The real objects of her fury were the ghosts of her memories of Stephen, suppressed for years, but brought back to haunt her by the similarity of Bob's self-centred, pretentious deceptions. All the anger flowed out of her on the breath of a deep sigh.

"Oh, Declan, I'm sorry! I'm such an idiot!" she declared, and kissed his smoke-streaked cheek.

Declan's arm tightened about her waist. He brought his head to rest on her shoulder. "Whatever you say, sweetheart. I'm too tired to argue."

Joss smiled complacently and turned on the car radio.

CHAPTER TWENTY NINE

"Luke, that's amazing—even for you!" Joss's eyes sparkled as Luke placed two cakes on the coffee table. One was a chocolate sponge cake, its fluffy layers oozing whipped cream, its dark chocolate icing encrusted with walnut halves. The other consisted of layers of flaky pastry, rich and sticky with fruit and nuts.

"Think nothing of it," Luke demurred with a shrug. "I thought we deserved something special after last night. Anyway, you've got Declan to thank for this." He indicated the pastry confection.

"It's baclava. Payment of a debt I owe Isabel." Declan placed a large slice on a plate and ceremoniously presented it to her.

"Talking of which," said Isabel, accepting his gift with a smile, "you also owe me an explanation. I haven't received that yet."

"Come on, Declan," urged Joss, "we're all dying to know—what happened to you yesterday afternoon?"

"Oh, that," said Declan with his crooked grin. "I reckon I owe you all an apology on that one. As Isabel has probably told you, I was expecting a phone call from my boss back in Brisbane, so I thought I'd clear up a bit of paperwork while I was waiting. By seven, even allowing for the time difference, I'd pretty much decided the Chief must have forgotten all about me. I was just leaving to come here, when who should

343

turn up but young Jeremy from the Circle of Light Centre and his twin soul, Jessica." He paused to acknowledge the exclamations of surprise. Luke took advantage of the break to hand him a mug of coffee.

"Thanks. Well, as they say, you could have knocked me down with a feather."

"I've never heard anyone say that," murmured Joss.

"You've led a tragically deprived life," countered Luke, patting her indulgently on the head. "I should arrange for therapy immediately if I were you."

"Shut up, you two," said Philip, raising his head briefly from a large slice of chocolate sponge.

Declan grinned at him. "He was there to make a confession, so of course I got roped in to do the honours. Apart from anything else, I was able to give a positive identification of both him and Jessica."

"Yes, but what was he confessing *to*?" Isabel demanded impatiently.

"It was Jeremy," Declan told her gently, "who killed Bartholomew."

"*Jeremy*?" exclaimed Joss. "But—why?" Isabel said nothing, but pressed her lips together tightly in an effort to hold back her tears.

Declan took her hand and held it as he said, "It seems he and Jessica had got into the habit of skulking around near Forster's quarters to try and find out what he was up to. I think they wanted to impress him with their understanding of the more esoteric bits of his teachings."

"Yes," said Isabel, "I saw them several times lurking in the general vicinity. I wondered what they were up to."

"Yeah, me too. They must have impressed him, all right.

After you and I had left the Centre, Bob asked them to go into town and keep an eye on you and your activities, and report back to him. He told them he suspected you of trying to mount some kind of magical attack on him, and he wanted to be prepared so he could fend it off."

"Oh, that would have impressed Jeremy, all right!" Isabel's laugh was sardonic. "But it explains why he and Jessica were following us around that weekend when you... when we... So what happened then?"

Declan's lips twitched slightly, but his voice was steady as he went on, "Jeremy and Jessica reported back as per instructions. Jeremy knew Bob was furious with you and, after they almost ran over Bartholomew, he thought he knew how to scare you into calling off your attack and to impress Bob even more, all in one go. But when he got round to telling Jessica what he'd done, she wasn't impressed at all. She drove him straight to the Station and told him if he didn't go in immediately and admit to it, she'd have nothing more to do with him."

"True love triumphs over ambition," Joss said. "Isn't that sweet?"

"Positively sickly," commented Luke. "I just hope he gets what's coming to him."

"Shall we say," said Declan, "that he's learnt from his experience. He looked pretty sorry by the time I'd finished with him, I can tell you. He'll be going to court before long. Magistrates don't look very kindly on cruelty to animals these days, not to mention causing pain and suffering to the owner. Oh, and you'll be getting a personal apology, Isabel. That was my—ah—suggestion, but he agreed to it readily enough, and Jessica offered herself as guarantor. But that isn't really why I was late, in the end. I was just leaving when my phone call finally came through."

Isabel squeezed his hand. "I suppose you could hardly refuse to talk to your boss."

"I did try and make a run for it, but I wasn't quick enough." The others laughed. "Well, you know the rest."

James, who apparently had no pressing engagements this evening, adjusted his tie anxiously. "I don't suppose any of you have heard how Anita is?"

"I called Pat this morning," Joss told him. "Anita lost her baby, but she's recovering now. She's agreed to have counselling once she's out of hospital, and Pat has asked her to live with her until she feels able to cope again."

James gave a sigh of relief. "That's wonderful news. I've been very concerned about her, you know."

"Well you needn't be any more," said Joss. "Pat sounded quite excited about having her there. Anita's going to be all right."

"Is that a prediction?" asked Luke. Before Joss could answer, the telephone rang.

When Luke returned, he looked like someone who had just seen a UFO land on his front lawn, complete with little green men. "You'll never guess who that was," he said, lowering himself into his chair as though not sure it was really there.

"Ooh, I do love a challenge!" exclaimed Joss, rubbing her hands together enthusiastically. She closed her eyes and clapped her hands dramatically to her forehead in the manner of an old-fashioned stage clairvoyant. "Silence, please. I must contact my spirit guides..."

"I think we've all had our fill of challenges for the time

being," Philip chuckled. "For goodness sake, Luke, put us out of our misery."

"Spoilsport," complained Joss, consoling herself with a slice of baclava.

Luke donned his saint and martyr expression and waited for the laughter to subside. Then, "It was Malcolm," he stated simply.

"Who's Malcolm?" James asked, baffled.

"Disgusted of Dingley Dell," Luke told him, by way of explanation.

"Ah."

"*Him*?" Geraldine exclaimed. "Since when has *he* taken to phoning you after hours?"

"How long has this been going on?" sang Joss in a sultry voice.

"If you lot would just like to shut up for a minute, all will be revealed," said Luke. "You know how Malcolm is always going on about having been a drug-crazed, devil-worshipping hippy?" They all nodded. "Well, guess where?"

"Oh, don't start all that again!" groaned Philip, with a glance at Joss. But, by now, Joss, like the others, was wholly engrossed Luke's words.

"The Tree of Life Community," Luke announced. "And what's more, he was there when Bob—or Richard—was there. He recognised Bob's voice from the interview, and he's been wrestling with his conscience ever since."

"Can I take it," Declan drawled, "that if I were to speak to him I might learn something to my advantage?"

"Indeed you can. It seems Malcolm was not only at the commune with Bob, he was involved with him in some drug deal that resulted in Claire Lomax inadvertently taking the overdose that killed her. Malcolm helped him dump her body in the creek that night, then drove him into Cairns next day and put him on the first bus to Brisbane." Luke sat back and lit a cigarette, gazing with a satisfied air at the stunned silence that followed this statement.

Declan was the first to recover. "Yeah, we already knew he flew back to New Zealand from Brisbane a couple of days after he left the Tree of Life place. I wonder why Miriam never mentioned him?" he pondered, running his fingers through his hair.

"She probably had no reason to connect him with Bob," said Joss. "I don't suppose they publicised their drug dealing activities. After all, there's a world of difference between smoking the odd joint and dealing heroin."

"True. Most likely they were at pains to cover up their connection, rather than advertise it. Who gave Claire the heroin, Bob or Malcolm?"

"According to Malcolm, neither of them did. Forster had his share hidden in his room, and Claire found it."

"That's interesting. Miriam told us Claire had been trying to give the stuff up because she was pregnant. Maybe it all got a bit too much for her. Miriam said she was in a pretty bad way from withdrawal, and Forster had been trying to help her through it. At the time, we assumed Forster had given in to her and got her a fix, then panicked when she died. But it's just as likely to have happened the way Malcolm told you."

"You were right about Bob panicking," said Luke. "From what Malcolm told me, Bob found her in his room lying on the floor unconscious. He tried to revive her, but she went into a coma and died a few hours later. By then, he was scared half to death himself. And Malcolm was afraid Bob would do something stupid and give them both away. So he helped him get rid of the body that night, and next day he drove him into Cairns. I got the impression he wanted Bob out of the way before he got them both into trouble."

"Why didn't Malcolm go straight to the police yesterday?" Joss asked. "Surely he must have heard about Claire's death on the news."

"I don't think Malcolm listens to ordinary radio a lot," said Luke, "much less television. Also, he wanted to be sure he was right about Bob's identity before telling the police. After all, he was involved, too. However, he had a little chat with God last night, and now he's quite prepared to face whatever punishment comes his way. He's going in tomorrow morning to make a statement."

Isabel looked at Declan. "I suppose that pretty much wraps up your business here, then," she said carefully.

Declan was not fooled. He smiled at her and squeezed her hand. "I reckon I can manage to wring a few more days out of it, whatever Voodoo thinks. I'll have to see if I can track down Claire Lomax's next of kin, if there are any. She was a New Zealander, remember. No-one's come forward so far, but I'll need to look into it. Malcolm's statement will have to be processed, and someone still has to contact Bob's next of kin."

"What next of kin?" Joss looked surprised. "Now Anita's lost her baby, there aren't any are there?"

"For all we know his mother might still be alive somewhere, and Julie Hazelwood's child certainly qualifies."

"Do you think she'll be interested in inheriting a half wrecked church and a couple of tatty outbuildings?" Isabel asked.

"I doubt it, though I dare say the money they'd raise would come in handy. Anyway, she'll need to be informed, and since I've already spoken to Julie and her mother, I reckon it'll be less upsetting for her if I do it, don't you?"

"I imagine that could easily take up an entire day," Joss said with a smile at Isabel. "And talking of inheriting, I suppose *someone* will have make a full inventory of all that stuff of Bob's that was found at Nancy's place."

"Too true. I can't make head nor tale of all those tarot and magic books." He winked at Isabel. "I reckon I'm going to have to call in an expert."

Isabel laughed. "What a fascinating insight into the workings of the forces of law and order!"

"Talking of insight," Philip said thoughtfully, "that reading I had from Bob—God, it seems ages ago now!—that wasn't entirely devoid of insight, either."

"Do explain," said Geraldine, making herself more comfortable on the couch next to him.

"Well, first of all, he told me about this business at the Centre, though he wasn't able to see it was himself he was talking about." He reminded them of the salient features of Bob's reading.

"That figures," said Isabel. "Even the best of readers can rarely read for themselves. You may have all the images there, but you just can't interpret them."

Philip continued, "He certainly didn't have any trouble interpreting either me or my future. The Queen of Wands, he told me—a woman with long hair who works with numbers. He said something about horses, too. Oh, and I think he said she might be a Libran."

"Geraldine's a Libran." Joss smiled.

"And," added Geraldine with a laugh, "I love horses. In fact, I've been thinking lately about having one again. Someone at work has offered me the use of a paddock out at West Melton."

Isabel released the strand of hair she had been twisting round her finger. "Whatever else Bob lacked," she said, "it wasn't psychic ability."

"I'm no judge of that," said Declan, "but I reckon if he hadn't been so screwed up about women and power, he could have put his talents to a damned sight better use. It seems to me his intentions weren't bad—it was just the twisted way he interpreted everything. If it hadn't been for that, maybe he wouldn't have messed up so many people's lives—including his own. And all for nothing, in the end. It's a bloody shame, really."

For several minutes, no-one said anything, reflecting on Declan's words.

When Luke finally spoke, it was almost to himself. "It'll need a bit of work," he said with a thoughtful frown, "but I think that's just the angle I've been looking for on this whole business with Bob—good intentions gone wrong. I shouldn't be surprised if I get a whole series of programmes out of it."

Joss looked up from her own reverie and said to Isabel, "Do you remember that reading we got from Terry a while ago?"

"Mmm." Isabel nodded thoughtfully. "He was pretty well right, too, wasn't he?"

Declan, who hadn't heard the recording, demanded an explanation. When they got to the part about 'Mr Plod', he roared with laughter. "I'm impressed," he chuckled, "though

I don't think I've ever been described quite like that before."

"Well," said Joss, "he did say you'd be no ordinary policeman."

"He was right there," said Isabel softly.

* * * *

There was something crawling on her face, inching its way slowly down her cheek and onto her neck. Isabel reached up to flick it away, and it took hold of her hand. Her eyes flew open in alarm. The room was in darkness, but she could make out Declan's face looking down at her. He was stroking her face with his fingers. A sigh of relief escaped her lips. "I must have been dreaming. I thought you were a spider."

"Just as well I'm not, otherwise you'd be making a meal of me about now." He bent to kiss her, then drew back, seeing her eyes suddenly brim with tears. "Isabel, sweetheart, what's wrong?'

Isabel shook her head dumbly, lowering her eyes. "It's—nothing. It doesn't matter."

"It does if it's making you cry. Besides—" His finger traced the outline of her lips "—no more lies, remember?"

Isabel let go the breath she had been holding. "I'm scared."

"Of me?" Declan sounded so incredulous that, in spite of herself, she smiled.

"No, of course not, it's just—I suppose you have a very busy life back in Brisbane." The words came out in a rush as her throat contracted suddenly.

Declan burst out laughing. Isabel closed her eyes, but it was a poor alternative to invisibility. "Isabel, look at me." She felt his lips soft and warm as he kissed her eyelids. She opened them again to find his eyes looking down into hers. They were very green. "Look, we both know I'm going to have to go back to Brisbane now my work here is done. But do you seriously think I could just walk out of your life now and forget you, even if I wanted to?"

"Well, I thought your work..." Her words were cut off by a derisive snort from Declan.

"Yeah, so did I—once. I lost my wife and all but lost my daughter because I was stupid enough to let my job take first place. I guess I must be a bit slow on the uptake—I didn't even realise it was happening till it was too late. But, believe me, sweetheart, I don't intend to let it happen again. Besides, I haven't forgotten what you said about a new direction. It's been on my mind a lot, and I reckon you're right. Whatever it turns out to be, I promise you, Isabel, I want you to be part of it. I've been hoping that's what you want, too. Please say you do."

In reply, Isabel flung her arms around him and burst into tears.

"Well, I'm glad we've got that settled," he said, and set about sealing their bargain in the time-honoured way.

* * * *

Isabel drew back the kitchen curtains. Outside, the street lamp still glowed dull orange although the sky was just light. There was something almost unbearably poignant about the fragile turquoise above the sleeping rooftops.

She didn't hear Declan until he came up behind her and put his arms around her. "I wish I could paint that," he said softly. "We don't get skies like that back home. It just goes straight from dark to light or light to dark."

Something about his voice made Isabel turn towards him. His eyes were bright with tears, and he was making no attempt to hide them. It was one of the things she loved about him—though it sometimes felt strange, it was still so new to her. She hugged him hard and pressed her face against his shoulder. "You should see it when we have a nor'wester," she said. "The whole sky is red and orange."

"I'll look forward to that when I come back. Meantime, I'll think of it every time I remember your hair." He lifted her hair in one hand and let the glowing tresses fall back against his face.

"When do you think you might—come back?" So far she had avoided specific questions on this point. She hadn't wanted to pressure Declan. Or maybe she just hadn't wanted to hear the answers. But now, with a matter of hours to go before his flight left...

"If I can get leave, I'll be back right after New Year. We can go on holiday—have a good look at all those places I only got a glimpse of in the line of duty."

"Oh goody! I've always wanted to go on a guided tour of K Road!" Isabel grinned up at him. "Seriously, though, is leave likely to be a problem?"

Declan shrugged. "They owe me enough of it. Because I don't have family—well, not living with me anyway—I've tended to work a lot of overtime. They give you leave in lieu of pay. I reckon it's about time I called in that particular debt. I'll phone you as soon as I know."

Isabel swallowed hard and smiled at him. He was going to miss that smile, he thought. He was going to miss her eyes with the soft sheen of pewter, her skin like spring blossoms, the voice that was so rich and deep, like that saxophone of Dominic's. Oh, Mother of God...

"I don't want to forget your voice," he told her, struggling with the feelings that threatened to steal his own voice away. "I'll call you as soon as I get back to Brisbane. And, after that, I'll call you every week until I can see you again."

Isabel had intended to thank him, but what emerged was rather different, though equally heartfelt. "You can't do that! It'll cost you a fortune!"

Declan gazed over her shoulder and addressed the lamp-post outside. "I've barely known the woman a month, and already she's trying to tell me what to do with my money!"

Isabel giggled into his shoulder. "Sorry."

Declan kissed her. "Sweetheart, I can't think of anything I'd rather spend my money on. Unless..." His eyes took on a dreamy, faraway look.

"Unless what?"

"Well, you never know. I might just come across a Chagall, or a Picasso..."

"Or a Miriam Golden?" Isabel grinned.

Declan felt his face redden. "That tea must be ready by now," he said.

* * *

The others had all said their goodbyes the previous night at Luke's place. That was Joss's idea, so that Isabel and Declan could have time to themselves during the hours before his flight. Now the two of them drove in silence along the road to the airport. They had been talking over their situation since first light and, for the time being, there was nothing more to say. In the gardens of the grand old houses that lined the road, massive English trees flaunted their fresh, green foliage in the early summer light. Declan thought about what he was going back to. Somehow, it wasn't going to seem the same any more. He glanced at Isabel, intent on negotiating traffic lights, her red hair ablaze with morning sunlight. Nothing was going to be the same any more. He was alive again!

Isabel arrived home from the airport to find a mass of roses, all red and gold like flames crowded into a basket, on the verandah by the front door. Sitting on the step with the two cats lazing nearby in the sun, she untied the card from the handle of the basket. On the front was a print of a painting by Millais—a woman with long red hair sitting at a table. Inside was written a line from a poem by W.B. Yeats:

'For my dreams of your image that blossoms a rose in the deeps of my heart.'

Taking one of the roses from the basket, Isabel breathed in the soft, sweet scent. She turned the card over. On the back, Declan had written:

'P.S. Say goodbye to Madame George.'

Other Books by Lila Richards

The Tarot Murders

When a series of bizarre murders based on major trumps of the Tarot rocks the usually staid city of Christchurch, the panel members of radio show The Psychic Connection are drawn into the case when it seems panel member James Myerson may be involved – or even the murderer. Detective Sergeant Declan Kelly (see: Vicious Circle) arrives in Christchurch, on sick leave after being wounded during a stakeout in Queensland, and adds his weight to the Psychic Connection panel's investigation of what the press is calling the Tarot Murders. The murderer's calling card, The Magician, left with each new victim, offers a sinister clue to the killer's identity – if only the panel can solve it in time to prevent the death of one of its own members.

A Different Hunger

In Victorian London, when an ill-advised love affair sees young Rufus de Hunte challenged to an illegal duel, his father, to avoid the scandal this would bring, banishes him to New Zealand to become a remittance man. During the voyage Rufus meets the captivating Serafina Radzinska, travelling with Anton Springer, who may or may not be her father. Despite his uncertainty, Rufus finds himself falling in love with her - even after he discovers both she and Springer are vampires. When Rufus is badly beaten by the vicious Toby Fox, and seems certain to die, Serafina, who returns his love and fears losing him, turns him into a vampire. Rufus's horror and resentment threaten their love, but when they reach New Zealand and Serafina is captured by Viviana Alexandreau, an ancient and powerful vampire seeking revenge on Springer, Rufus must acknowledge his true feelings and find a way to rescue her and to end Viviana's insane vendetta once and for all.

Restitutions of the Blood

In 1890, when Alex Randall returns from university to his ancestral home of Shillington Hall, he finds his father remarried, less than a year after his mother's death. Dismay turns to anger when a son, Oliver, is born. Convinced the new Lady Randall means to steal his inheritance, Alex flees to London, where he meets and befriends Henri de Saint Clair, a charming, but enigmatic Frenchman. When Alex's friend Charles becomes involved in an illegal duel, and both parties are killed, Alex finds himself on the run from the law, and obliged to leave England. In Paris, he renews his friendship with the still strangely elusive Henri. After a series of misadventures that lead him to the very depths of Parisian society, Henri rescues Alex and restores him to health by means of a mysterious 'restorative', but before long Alex's determination to discover the truth about his friend plunges him into a world darker - and more addictive - than anything he could have imagined.

About the Author

Lila Richards lives in one of the leafy suburbs of Christchurch, New Zealand, with two black cats. She works part-time as a sub-editor and proofreader for the New Zealand Meteorological Service. As well as writing, Lila reads eclectically, sews vintage clothes, and collects things, in particular old movies, owls, and art deco paraphernalia. From time to time she enters the Middle Ages via the Society for Creative Anachronism (an international mediaeval re-creation group), where she transmogrifies into a ninth-century small-holder's widow living in the west of Ireland, and has attained the rank of Baroness.